The star blazed, roiled, fumed. Equilibrium tee-tered as the balance of forces groaned toward the brink of catastrophe. Temperature and density shifted, slid as the last and hottest fusions took place. Jets and streamers of ionized gases exploded away from the star's surface like ribbons and banners fluttering in a cosmic breeze. The star was drifting inevitably toward death . . . faster than it knew.

There were invaders here in the star's midst.

Threads of warpspace had slipped invisibly down through the convective layers, slipped toward the core, toward the center of mass. Threads of warpspace had spun their tapestry of death—clenching and stran-gling, pouring heat and fuel into the flames.

A thousand values fluctuated, changed with inex-orable speed. The collapse was moments away, and it would rend the very fabric of space.

And Ruskin's hands were on the controls, guiding and channeling the explosion. . . .

"As audacious and imaginative as the best of John Varley, with characters as memorable as those of Stur-geon or Zelazny, and with one of the most powerful endings in science fiction, this book will both hold and reward your attention."

—Spider Robinson

From a Changeling Star

*

Jeffrey A. Carver

BANTAM BOOKS
TORONTO • NEW YORK • LONDON • SYDNEY • AUCKLAND

FROM A CHANGELING STAR
A Bantam Spectra Book / January 1989

ISBN 0-553-27639-5

Published simultaneously in the United States and Canada

Bantam Books are published by Bantam Books, a division of Bantam
Doubleday Dell Publishing Group, Inc. Its trademark, consisting of
the words "Bantam Books" and the portrayal of a rooster, is Reg-
istered in U.S. Patent and Trademark Office and in other countries.
Marca Registrada, Bantam Books, 666 Fifth Avenue, New York, New
York 10103.

PRINTED IN THE UNITED STATES OF AMERICA

O   0 9 8 7 6 5 4 3 2 1

For Allysen, of course

Acknowledgments

I could not have written this book without the help of numerous talented and knowledgeable people, all of whom were exceedingly generous with their time and knowledge.

The novel owes its genesis in part to the work of K. Eric Drexler, who provided me with considerable information about the field of nanotechnology, not only through personal conversation, but also through his own excellent book, *The Engines of Creation*. If you like this novel, I heartily recommend his nonfiction account of the emerging technologies of the very small.

For help with the astrophysics, I must give the greatest thanks to Larry Molnar, who provided long hours of thoughtful conversation on a subject that could quite easily have been classified as bizarre. I hope I haven't damaged his professional reputation. Nor those of the following of his colleagues at the Harvard-Smithsonian Center for Astrophysics, all of whom sat down with the curious science fiction writer who appeared on their respective doorsteps and willingly explained the stuff of their trade: Bob Scherrer, for the scoop on cosmic string, which is not quite the same thing as the hyperstring described here; Margarita Karovska and Peter Nisenson, who joyfully told me all about Betelgeuse and how I might blow it up; Bob Kirshner, who told me about supernovas, and how I might *not* blow it up. Also C.F.A. librarian Joyce Rey-Watson, who would probably lose her job if her boss knew how helpful she'd been to a curious science fiction writer when she was supposed to be doing other things; and a librarian whose name I do not know at the Arlington Robbins Library, who helped me with prefixes.

The following is obviously a work of fiction; nevertheless, I've aimed for scientific credibility throughout (subject to some important future developments, such as n-dimensional fields, FTL, and the seventh force). However, please don't blame any of these people for the ways in which I have fiddled with their technical input.

I received more than technical help, of course. Special thanks to Amy Stout and Lou Aronica of Bantam, for their warmth, perceptiveness, and enthusiasm—and yes, it did make a difference; and to art director Jamie Warren for caring about science fiction literature and science fiction art. Plus, of course, Richard Curtis, without whose eagle-eyed assistance this all might have gone very differently.

And what would I do without the Group? Thanks, Victoria and Richard and Mary and Craig—for helping me rid the book of hokes and awaks and dreadful idioms, for being so damnably hard to please.

Crystal, Dave and Cathy, Norm and Peggy, Larry (again) and Cindy, Mark and Misty, Ted and Robin. Doug Stuart, too. You guys know why.

Chuck. You know why, too.

Sam. Who else would have lain at my feet every day for the length of an entire book?

And finally of course Allysen Palmer, without whose loving encouragement I probably would have thrown it all in the brook long ago.

Arlington, Mass., 1987

PART ONE

✳

CHANGELING

"The time is close when you shall forget all things. . . ."
                                    —Marcus Aurelius

PROLOGUE

✳

The image of the swollen sun blazed like a deep crimson ocean in the wall-screen, the dark supergranulations in the sun's surface pulsing slowly, hypnotically. Thalia Sharaane gazed at the image for a long time before turning. "Where is he?" she murmured, repeating the question that had just been put to her. "Don't you think I'd like to know myself?"

The man standing on the far side of her desk stirred. "We're going to have to make some decision about what to do if he doesn't show, Thalia," Snyder said.

"It might not be necessary."

"Well, in my opinion—"

"I didn't ask," she snapped.

"I'm giving it anyway. We're too dependent on him. He at least ought to let us know if he's planning to delay arriving. What was the last update he sent you?"

Sharaane didn't bother answering, because they both knew the answer: it had been weeks since the last n-channel communication, and no final itinerary had been received, nor any reply to their messages. Either he would come or he wouldn't. She gazed again at that enormous body of roiling, fusing gases: a supergiant red sun, over a hundred million kilometers in diameter. A box in the upper corner of the screen showed the near companion star, Honey, orbiting so close it practically caressed its primary, Betelgeuse. The Starmuse space station was actually orbiting in

2

the very fringes of Betelgeuse, at the outer edge of its photosphere. This sun system, as they knew it, would not be here much longer. She wondered, could they really hope to survive the violent transformation that would change it into something beyond imagining?

Thalia turned. "I *trust* him. He'll be here. I'm sure of it." She pressed her lips together, feeling tension rise into the back of her neck. Yes, she trusted him—to a point. She'd loved him once, after all. And she respected him— and needed him. The entire project needed him. But Project Breakstar would go off, had to go off, whether he was here or not; forces were converging that could not be stopped. She was prepared for either eventuality; but without him to guide it all at the end . . . she simply did not care to dwell on those odds.

Snyder had moved to stand beside her. "Sorry," he said gently. "I know you're worried, too." He joined her in contemplating the image of the sun system, assembled on this screen from dozens of remote satellites. It was hard to imagine, to really *believe,* deep down in the core of one's being, that they were actually floating inside this star.

"It's too lulling," Snyder said, startling her.

She frowned. "*Lulling?* What do you mean?"

"Just that *it's* so large, and so . . . steady. Predictable."

"With all of the trouble we've had mapping the changes, you can say that?"

He shrugged. "I just mean it's easy to start thinking of *that* as our only problem. To forget the other problems." Snyder cleared his throat, suddenly uncomfortable. Thalia looked at him sharply, and he sighed. "I'm sorry—I just keep wondering if something's happened to him. There *are* people who wouldn't like what we're doing. If they knew."

"That's extremely unlikely, you know."

He nodded. "Unlikely. Yes." He seemed about to say something more, then frowned, having apparently decided to keep it to himself.

Sharaane scowled. "Well, if something's happened, it would be out of our hands, then, wouldn't it?" When he didn't reply, she added, "Just do your part, and let me worry about the rest. Make whatever preparations you feel you need."

Snyder nodded dubiously. He hesitated, then turned away and left Thalia staring at the relentless, glowing face of the sun.

CHAPTER 1

✴

The shot crackled through the forest air, a line of exploding leaves and twigs marking the passage of the sputterbeam. The man who stood in its path was unaware of his danger, for an instant that lasted forever: he observed the flicker of the beam, and wondered at its source, and even its target. He was just beginning to wonder if the target could be *him*, when, with no more awareness of the hole in his chest than a slight tingle, he collapsed.

And then he died, scarcely feeling the scream of pain that his shattered nerve endings sent toward his brain.

He never felt at all the second, and entirely unnecessary, shot through the base of his neck.

The forest was still, as though all of its walking and flying creatures had paused to listen to the death-sigh of the man's passing. Then the rustling, the buzzing began again, and life returned to normal—except for the fallen man. Three grebel-mice hunted on the needles and leaves that matted the forest floor. They scampered near the dead man's left arm, which had twisted and dislocated at the shoulder as he fell. His fingers twitched once, but that was a dying reflex, nothing more. His eyes were open, vacant.

Overhead, felker birds soared high against the golden sun, gliding in effortless circles on the updrafts over the mountain escarpment that jutted up out of the forest. Two of the birds sank toward the treetops, swooping, peering through the tree cover, investigating a possible late afternoon meal. The grebel-mice scurried for cover. A rust-fox trotted past the dead man, unafraid of the felker birds and uninterested in the corpse.

The felker birds were not quick to action, preferring caution. While they were watching, so too was something else a short distance away in the woods, peering at the dead man through high-powered optics. Hir watched as one of the felkers landed in a treetop, then hopped to a lower branch above the corpse. After a few minutes the felker was joined by one of its brethren, and a moment later by a third, then a fourth. The birds peered down at the body, as though puzzled.

The killer, watching through the expensive optics, was puzzled as well. There had been a movement, a twitch. That was extremely odd. The body had registered in the sensors as cooling, unmoving, lifeless. In fact, hir had stayed only because prudence demanded it, not because there was any reason to expect anything to happen.

There was another twitch.

The dead man's dislocated left arm jerked toward his side. It appeared to pop back into place. The dead man rolled slowly onto his back and gazed sightlessly at the sky.

The killer moved to the left, seeking a clearer view. Was it possible that the man was breathing? More powerful optics clicked into place.

Slowly the dead man raised his hand.

The awakening was accompanied by a rush of pain, but it was masked and separated from the inner consciousness as though by a sheet of glass, one room from another. The man looked at the pain, felt it in a tentative, testing way, and wondered where it had come from.

A moment later he became aware of another sensation: He saw the sky.

It was a deep blue ceiling visible through the treetops, a golden sun shining through one branch. It was an unexpected viewpoint, as though he were on his back under a tree. *Under a tree?* As though he were waking from a nap. There was a buzzing in his head and confusion in his mind. He shivered. His left shoulder ached dully. Overhead he saw several shapes silhouetted, like birds of prey: felker birds. Vague signals of danger rang in his mind, but they, like the signals of pain, were on the other side of his brain, isolated.

Felker birds. Carrion eaters. Why here; why now?

And simmering beneath the surface was a more urgent question:

Where am I?

The killer carefully raised the sputter-rifle and brought its sights to bear on the target, but desisted from firing. Instead hir waited, curiosity joined by astonishment—and by a slight but nagging sense of fear. *The man had been killed; the long-range biological scan had confirmed it.*

Then why had its arm moved? Why were its eyes blinking?

The assassin waited. It didn't make sense. But if the subject had to be killed twice, then it would be killed twice.

His head cleared slowly. He started to push himself up; but he was weaker than he could have believed possible, and his left shoulder was throbbing. He collapsed again and lay flat on his back, breathing with difficulty. His ears were ringing. He moved his right hand to scratch at a burning sensation on his chest, then froze. There was a hole in his jacket and shirt, near his sternum. Fearfully, he probed at it with his finger. He gasped, drew a sharp, ragged breath. The hole went into *him*, and it hurt like hell.

And yet. Even as he touched it, the hole seemed to be closing, seemed to hurt less. The skin was tightening; the hole was becoming a tender-bottomed depression. It itched.

For a moment, he lay motionless, breathing quietly. Then he struggled again to rise. He felt a little stronger this time, and with a great effort, pushed himself awkwardly up onto one elbow. He squinted, looking around. He was surrounded by a dense wood. There was no sign of human life. Overhead, the felker birds flapped their wings, squawking in annoyance. Not today! he thought at them.

He heard a branch snap and turned to look.

Rifle at ready, the assassin watched in amazement as the man pushed himself up from the ground. The angle of attack was not quite right; the assassin crept a little farther to the left—carefully, but not carefully enough. Hir felt the branch underfoot only an instant before it snapped.

The man's head turned in surprise.

Aiming at the center of the man's forehead, the assassin squeezed the trigger.

The awareness of it lasted only for an instant: fire blazing in his eyes. Then he died again. His last memory was of a single dazzling star in darkness.

The *hrisi* assassin rose from hir crouch and stepped out of concealment. This time, no chances were to be taken. Hir aimed again from half the distance and burned another hole through the man's head. Moving closer still, hir shot the man several times in the chest. Finally, crouched near the body, hir took sensor readings and determined that: body temperature was dropping, heart-action had ceased, blood was pooling in the abdomen, electrochemical brain-function was nil, and pupillary reflexes were absent. Hir prodded the body once with hir foot. There was no response.

The assassin was not satisfied. The job was done, really, but the subject had already come back to life once and might do so again. Out of curiosity as much as caution, hir re-treated to a protected position to observe again. As the minutes passed, hir opened a shoulder pouch and withdrew a small plastic bag. Opening the bag, hir took out a food bar, unwrapped it, and began to eat.

Overhead, the felker birds circled against the sun.

* * *

Consciousness returned like a predawn light, and with it a memory. The memory was without context, but he remembered raising his head—and dying. It was enough to trigger the thought: *Don't raise your head.*

Sensation returned slowly. His face was pressed to the ground, his nostrils filled with the scent of humus and fallen needles—and the smell of burned flesh. A thread of fear rippled through his mind. *Don't raise your head.* He was so frightened that he held his breath for nearly a minute.

He lay absolutely still, trying to think. *Where am I—and why?* He had no recollection; no data. *What happened to me?* There was no memory of that, either—but he felt a burning itch in the center of his forehead, and in his chest, and at the base of his neck. He started to move his hands, heard the inner voice warning him again; he drew a slow, deep breath instead. The itch was subsiding anyway. Lying motionless, face to the ground, he thought: *At least I know who I am.* There was a long inner hesitation. *I am—*

His thoughts stopped, blank.

He remembered the sound of a snapping branch; remembered a wound in his chest. There were no sounds now. Perhaps he had imagined it. Perhaps whatever had made it was gone now. He couldn't lie here forever.

Decision made, he drew a sharp breath—and got a mouthful of needles. Coughing involuntarily, he spat the needles out and pushed himself up. His muscles hurt, but there was strength in them. He rolled and sat up and looked around. Nothing here but trees and brush. His gaze dropped, and he raised a hand wonderingly to an array of holes in his jacket. Tugging open his jacket and shirt front, he examined his bare chest. There were four wounds healing between his sternum and his left nipple. Three were angry red, but closed. The fourth was already covered over with pink scar tissue. Warily, almost not wanting to know, he touched his forehead—and trembled, as his fingers found another wound.

He heard something, caught a movement to his left, turned his head. Something stepped through the brush. A tall figure, crouching. Bringing a rifle to bear. *No, God, not again!*

* * *

The *hrisi* was growing impatient with this charade. And angry: Why was this target so reluctant to die? It should not have been difficult to dispatch a single unarmed man and make it stick; and yet, here it was, coming back to life again. The assassin inspected the sputtergun and tuned it to maximum power. One shot at this setting would use up most of the gun's reserves, but one shot was all hir would need.

The man coughed and sat up, looking around. It seemed not to see the assassin, but began inspecting its wounds.

The *hrisi* rose out of hir hiding place. As a precaution, hir projected an illusion, altering hir own appearance. Hir stepped through the brush toward the man—and brought the gun to firing position. Allowing a heartbeat or two to pass (enough time for horror to appear in the eyes—hir was angry with this man), the *hrisi* aimed at a point between the man's eyes.

And fired.

The eruption sent a shock wave through hir own shoulder—and took half the subject's head off. The man couldn't have felt a thing.

The *hrisi* stepped forward and gazed at the smoking remains with distaste. Hir checked the sensor readings, but it seemed superfluous; the corpse was a shambles. The brutality of the shot was offensive; hir greatly preferred a clean kill. Behind the corpse, a bush was blackened and smoldering; small flames were licking at the underbrush. The assassin carefully stamped out the flames; a forest fire could cause considerable damage. That would be not just offensive, but unprofessional.

The man must have moved at the instant of firing. A fair portion of the left side of its head was gone, but less than hir had been aiming to remove. Still, this time it was dead, incontrovertibly so.

And if it wasn't, this *hrisi* did not want to be here to face it again. Slinging the rifle, hir turned and strode off through the forest.

* * *

The felker birds glided in descending, tightening orbits. Eventually they landed in the treetops. One by one they dropped to the lower branches. *Yawk*ing to one another, they sharpened their beaks on the tree bark. And they waited a few minutes longer, just to be sure.

CHAPTER 2

✳

He dreamed of flailing his arms, of thrashing against darting enemies, of being bound and captive. He dreamed in red, bright red, the red of blood. Silent voices cried and shouted at him, and he could not answer. He did not know who he was.

He dreamed that his head was the head of a gargoyle. His face was being remade, turned into that of a poor changeling child: the head of a serpent, the nose of a snapping frog, the eyes and the brow of a newborn baby.

He dreamed that he was being split apart and put back together again.

He awoke with a gruesome headache and a terrible thirst.

At first he could not move at all, or even open his eyes. He lay still, conscious only of the thudding of blood in his temples, each heartbeat sending a shock wave of pain through his skull. A time passed that could not have been more than a minute, and yet seemed an eternity; then his eyes were open.

Overhead was the empty chamber of the sky, framed by dancing treetops. The sunlight was angled, the sun itself out of view; but the sky was so bright it made his head hurt worse than before. He remembered thirst. Just the thought made him dizzy, made him almost lose consciousness again.

But he didn't pass out. And as he clung to consciousness, he began to remember. . . .

Images: a tall figure moving through the woods toward him; a bird gliding overhead for a long time before finally flapping its wings and departing; himself climbing a trail

12

along a rocky cliff, the sight of a river winding its way
through a forest far below. . . .

The images faded. He tried to turn his head. The effort
hurt. He struggled to focus on the nearest object. It was a
felker bird, crouched on the ground a meter from his face.
It peered back at him, eyes glittering, beak dripping. He
held its gaze. . . .

■

A strangely frozen moment of time came to an end, and
the bird shifted its head a centimeter. It looked annoyed.
What had it been doing, preying on small animals while
waiting for him to die? "Go on!" he hissed, straining to
heave himself up to a sitting position, and danger be
damned. He was surprised by the strength in his body.
"Get lost!" He batted his hand in the creature's direction.

His left arm throbbed. When he looked at it, he nearly
fainted again. His sleeve had been ripped away; and beneath the shredded fabric, his flesh was torn open nearly
the length of his arm. Or rather, it *had been* torn open; the
wound, though ragged (as though ripped, perhaps, by a
beak?) was already closed over with delicate pink skin.
There was dried blood on the remnants of his sleeve, but
little on his skin. He swallowed and glared up at the bird,
flexing his arm. It worked, but painfully.

"*Rawwk!*" the bird muttered.

"Get out of here!" he growled, trying to put menace into
his voice. He groped on the ground for something—anything—to use as a weapon.

The bird bent and plucked at something reddish brown
and stringy that lay at its feet. It looked like a bit of flesh.
Human flesh?

Sickened at the thought, he almost failed to notice the
dead branch beneath his hand. Then his fingers closed on
it, reflexively. He brought it around with all of his
strength—intending to throw it at the bird. His hand failed
to release it, and it whumped down onto the ground in front
of the bird.

"*Yawk!*" The bird hopped back.

"You little bastard!" he hissed furiously. He gasped,
clutching his shoulder. He rocked back and forth until the
pain of the sudden movement subsided. He hurt all over.

The bird warbled deep in its throat and lunged to peck at him. He swiped at it with the branch. It squawked away, then lunged again. This time he caught it with the branch and sent it reeling. That was enough for the felker. With a *scree*ing cry, it took to flight, flapping up a cloud of dust as it went.

Coughing, he watched it go. He put a hand to his aching forehead—and cried out involuntarily. His skin felt spongy and tender, and the *shape* of his head felt wrong—bulbous where it should have been slightly flattened and angular. *What the hell happened?* He lowered his hand; there was no blood on his fingers. Swallowing hard, he felt his entire skull. The right side felt normal; but the left side of his head felt hairless, soft, and fibrous. He felt no bone under the skin. *No bone . . . ?*

He stared at his fingertips. Surely they were lying. But that was impossible. At least he could *see* his fingers.

His mind refused to think further of it.

The sun was dropping low behind the treetops. Did that mean it was going to become cold soon? He wasn't sure; but he knew one thing, and that was that he didn't want to be out here after dark. Whatever his other problems, if he didn't find shelter, he could soon be in far worse trouble.

He staggered to his feet, gasping. With a tremendous effort, he managed to keep his balance and turn around. There was no sign of whatever had attacked him. But what he did see made him reel: a blackened patch of brush; a scorched tree trunk; and, spattered among the scorch marks, bits of white and pink flesh, and a few fragments of—bone. He choked on his own bile and forced himself to turn away. Whatever that was—

He didn't want to know.

But he did know. An image burned bright in his mind: a blazing beam of fire, and an explosion. And then darkness. The darkness of death.

And yet he had lived. Against something that had . . .

Never mind, he thought dizzily. Whatever had happened, he was alive and he could move. If he really knew the answers to these questions welling up in his mind . . . he would probably just have more questions, impossible questions, to answer.

Right now, he really just didn't want to know. Before anything else, he had to find shelter, and that meant walking.

It was difficult going, but less difficult than he might have thought. He was weak with hunger, but a stream nearby satisfied the thirst. He gulped greedily at the frigid water; he felt strength returning to his limbs even as he drank. A glance at his arm showed the skin thickening and tightening over the wound. As he rose again, he felt less pain. He took a deep breath and chose a path among the trees.

He was unsure where he was going; but he felt some inner sense of direction that guided his feet, kept them moving. He stayed parallel with the stream for a time, then turned away from it to follow a ridge, less thickly wooded. The ridge ascended toward an escarpment of rock, in the distance.

He felt that he was heading in the direction of home, though he had no idea where or what "home" was. He felt a powerful sense of uncertainty about something else, too; but he deliberately kept that at bay. He did not want to admit to the question.

You are confused. It will come back to you.

He ignored the voice in his head and kept walking.

Higher along the ridge, he found a trail climbing toward the escarpment. At points, it was little more than an occasional smudge on barren rock. Nevertheless, he managed to keep it in sight; and eventually it brought him, puffing for air, to a point near the top of the scarp, a flat table from which he could look out over the top of the woods. The sun was low on the horizon, blazing golden; in the distance, across many kilometers of forest, he saw a river gleaming as it threaded its way through a wooded vale. The forest was blushed with reds and purples and browns; the sweet tangy smell of autumn was in the air, the smell of ripe grasses and changing leaves. The smell struck a chord in his mind—almost, but not quite, summoning forth a memory. Perhaps he had been in this place before.

He inhaled deeply and turned around. The ledge he was standing on was an extreme outcropping of a long, low mountain that stretched away in the other direction. A hazy

line along the eastern horizon hinted that he was perhaps
in the foothills of a great range of mountains. (Eastern horizon? The sun was setting in the other direction. Did the
sun set in the west on this world?)

There were many uncertainties in his mind, but one tow-
ered over all of the others. Finally he faced it.

My name is . . .

■

Another frozen moment. But when it ended, no name
came to mind. No name nor face.

It wasn't just a question of knowing where he was, or
why. He didn't even know what he looked like. He had no
memory of who, or even what sort of person, he was.

It will come back to you. You're confused, tired, hungry.
Will it?

Of course. You're—
Who? Who am I?

He knelt, feeling the frustration well up inside him, a
tangible pressure in his throat and his forehead. He covered
his eyes with his hands. An instant later, he stiffened in
surprise. He probed his forehead with his fingertips. Then
his temples.

The new skin had toughened and grown firm on the left
side. The contours beneath it had flattened along the temple, contracted around the brow. He felt resistance when
he pressed against it. *Bone*.

Taking a deep breath, he rose. He had a good long way
yet to walk. He wasn't sure why he knew that. But he was
starting to remember the way. Once he made it around the
point of this outcropping, it would be mostly downhill.

It took him perhaps two hours to make his way along the
ridge and down the descending trail on the northwest side
of the outcropping. The sun disappeared in a blaze of
golden-blooded glory, and he continued on into the twilight
that followed. Evening came quickly on its heels, and with
it a sky spattered with stars and one tiny moon. That didn't
last long; a layer of clouds crowded across the sky, blocking
the starlight, leaving him in near-total darkness. He nearly
stopped, thinking that whatever meager shelter he might
find would be preferable to stumbling in the dark. The air

temperature was falling. He should probably camp and build a fire. It was stupid of him not to have stopped earlier, while there was still light for gathering wood.

What changed his mind was a realization, as he began groping about for dry branches, that the darkness was actually diminishing—or rather, that his eyes seemed to be adapting astonishingly well to the dark. The trees and their limbs were becoming visible to him, like apparitional figures in the night. When he gazed up into the treetops, he saw clouds still blanketing the sky; but they appeared mottled with an exquisitely faint light. It was as though the stars behind them had somehow brightened, so that they shone through, illuminating the shape and form of the clouds. The small moon could be discerned as a slightly brighter smudge; no other single source of illumination could be seen. His eyes seemed to have become inhumanly acute.

Nor was it just his vision. He felt a resurging warmth in his limbs, even as he was aware of the air growing colder against his skin. His skin felt as though it had thickened and numbed. His arms and legs felt stronger, and he felt little pain now.

Well, if he could see, and if he could withstand the cold, the path lay clear enough before him; so he took it. The trail wound farther back into the forest, and though the darkness deepened, his eyes continued to adapt. He moved among the trees like a ghost passing through a crowd of ghosts in the night.

After a time, the path intersected with a larger trail, this one marked and maintained. Without hesitation, though he did not know where he was going, he turned onto the larger trail and kept walking. Soon his steps took him to the banks of a wide, murmuring stream, and the scent of open-air grasses and flowers began to mingle with the deep forest smells. The path widened and became graveled, and in the distance a light shone.

He regarded the light, his pulse quickening. Was there any reason not to approach it? A memory flickered across his thoughts: a figure walking toward him, and a blaze of light that brought on pain and darkness. Someone had tried to kill him, and failed. But suppose the would-be killer, too, had come this way? He reflected for a moment on that possibility. Still, what else could he do—hide in the woods all night?

Cautiously he stalked forward, coming at last to a lighted clearing. He shaded his eyes as they readjusted to what seemed like dazzling illumination. He finally discerned a lodge building with an exterior floodlight.

Lodge.

He half smiled. He stepped out onto the edge of the clearing, onto mowed grass. *The lodge.* He remembered it now—almost. The image reverberated in his mind: this building—he could almost picture its interior. But the people? He couldn't quite capture the memory.

His stomach tightened with hunger. He recalled that he had been walking more than half a day and half a night without food. He sighed and set out across the grass without another thought, the smell of broiled callfish in his nostrils.

CHAPTER 3

✳

The front door, he recalled, was around to the left. He circled the other way, and spied a small door at the rear of the building. He strode across the floodlighted lawn toward the alcove where the door was half-concealed. As he passed out of the coverage of the floodlight, a spot-beam blinked on overhead, swiveling to follow his movement. He hesitated in midstride, caught for an instant in indecision, then shrugged and continued forward. The spot-beam tracked him until the overhanging eaves cut it off. Then another series of lights came on, within the alcove, illuminating the steps to the door.

Two glass doors slid aside, and he stepped into a warm but dimly lit room, plush-carpeted. He shivered as the doors whispered shut behind him. The room was a lounge, paneled in wood, and deserted—except for a silver-and-black robot that floated toward him through the air. "Mr. Ruskin, I'm pleased to see you," the robot said. Its voice was a melodic baritone, vaguely familiar. "We were concerned. Are you feeling better after your walk?"

He gazed at the robot in bewilderment.

"Not to pry," the robot added. "Is there anything I might get you?"

He stared, knowing that he knew this robot, and trying to remember its name. And what had it just called him? *Ruskin?*

"You seem to have torn your jacket and shirt. Have you injured yourself?" A slender arm telescoped out and nearly touched his own arm where the fabric was ripped away. "Shall I alert the medic-unit?"

"No—uh, that's not necessary. I—" His voice caught.

The robot waited.

He struggled to frame his thoughts. "What did you call me?" he asked finally. "What name?"

The robot gazed at him for a long moment, its eyes dark and gleaming. "Mr. Ruskin," it said at last.

"Oh. Yes." He cleared his throat harshly. "I . . . must have misheard you the first time."

Ruskin . . .

The robot made a chuckling sound. "I shouldn't worry about it, sir. I'm at your service. Shall I awaken the kitchen for a late supper?"

His mouth watered. "Yes—please."

"Very good, sir." The robot began to swing away.

"No, wait—don't go!"

The robot rotated in midair. "Sir?"

It was foolish, but he suddenly felt afraid of being left alone by the robot. What *was* this place, anyway? "Is anyone else up?"

"I don't believe so. It's rather late," the robot answered. "Mr. Broder and Mr. Gorminski retired some time ago."

Broder . . . Gorminski . . . ? He nodded uneasily. "I see. Well, then. Is—that is—do I still have a room?"

The robot's chuckle was soothing. "Of course, Mr. Ruskin."

He closed his eyes, nodding, trying to remember. "Yes—ha, ha—of course." He swayed.

He felt the robot gripping his shoulder, steadying him. He blinked his eyes open and had trouble focusing.

"Sir, perhaps I should escort you to your room."

"Yes. Please—"

The robot stood by the door as he fumbled at his pockets. "I seem to have—" *How the devil do I . . .*

"Press your hand to the doorplate," the robot suggested.

"Of course. How could I not—" With a shrug, he touched the cool metal. There was a click. He pushed on the hard-wood door and it swung inward. He turned. "Thank you."

"Will you be all right, sir?"

"Yes, I . . . feel better now."

"Very well. Call me if you need anything more."

"Yes, uh—thank you, Jeaves." He watched the robot float away down the hall, and then thought: *Jeaves?*

Yes. That was the robot's name, he was almost certain.

He took a deep breath and stepped into his room. It was an enormous suite, with a wide variable-grav bed, a stained-wood desk with matching table and nightstands, and a console for reading, music, and cogitation. None of it looked exactly familiar, and yet it all looked . . . right. He knew without thinking which way to turn to find the lavatory, and as he walked through the door, he knew which way to turn to find a gleaming, full-length mirror.

He did not know the man who faced him in the mirror.

The man was a ghastly sight, jacket torn and scorched, trousers stained. His face was a nightmare, darkened with grime on one side only; on the other side, his hair looked half-shorn. He was medium tall, with fair skin, green eyes, and uneven auburn-brown hair. He recalled the feel of his head after waking in the forest: the swollen skin, the softness of his skull. Now, squinting into the mirror, he pushed his hair back to examine the left side of his head. It looked normal enough, except for the fine, clean, short hair on that side.

Mr. Ruskin.

"You're a goddamn mess, Mr. Ruskin," he murmured. "Why the hell don't you get yourself cleaned up?" He shrugged out of his shredded jacket and shirt and stared at his body. Five pinkish spots on his chest and neck were all that remained of the gunshot wounds. He poked at the healed-over skin. It didn't hurt. Shaking his head in perplexity, he switched on the whirlmist shower, peeled off the rest of his clothes, and stepped into the warm, invigorating fog.

He emerged considerably refreshed and padded naked into the bedroom. From the wardrobe closet, he selected a pair of casual pants and a turtleneck pullover, noting with satisfaction that everything seemed to fit. Then he began to think about food. Should he call the robot, he wondered, or just go looking for the dining room?

The real question, of course, was how long he could walk around here pretending that nothing was wrong. He couldn't imagine that Jeaves hadn't noticed his condition, not if the robot had known him before. Should he take the robot into his confidence?

But someone had tried to kill him. Twice, at least. How often could he be killed and still come back to life? The old story went that a cat had nine lives. How many did that leave him? The assassin might well be right here in this lodge. Could he assume, simply because he had a dim, positive recollection of Jeaves, that the robot would be an ally?

He sighed and touched the call-set. "Jeaves?"

"Yes, Mr. Ruskin."

"Any word from the kitchen? I'm about ready to eat a tree."

"I'm sure we can find you something tastier than that," Jeaves answered. "Would you like to eat in the dining room? Or shall I come around with something?"

He hesitated. He might as well scout the lodge now while he was the only one up. "I'll come there," he said. "Can you rustle up some callfish?"

"I'll have it ready for you in ten minutes."

The lounge was still empty, the lights coming up only briefly as he paused to look around. Crossing the room, he walked through a set of doors into an interior courtyard. He remembered it at once: The pool, stocked with saucer-shaped floaterfish, with neither heads nor tails, but radially arrayed mouths and eyes. The spiral staircase to the solarium above. The murmuring fountain that cascaded down through a long series of planters into the pool. The lighting was muted, underwater lights suffusing the courtyard with an eerie, watery sheen.

The feeling of such luxury made him vaguely uncomfortable. This lodge was clearly no haven for the poor. What, then, was *he*?

He crossed the courtyard to another set of doors. The aroma of roasting callfish touched his nostrils. He pushed through the doors into the dining room. Jeaves floated out to greet him and showed him to a table in one corner of the room. The lighting over the table was subtly brighter than in the rest of the room. "Would you care for a glass of sherry while you wait?"

He nodded and sat. Jeaves disappeared into the kitchen and returned with a long-stemmed glass filled with a pale violet liquid. The robot lifted the glass from the small service tray, set it before him, and floated away again.

Ruskin gazed at the glass for a moment, twirling it by the stem, watching the sherry run down the sides in rivulets. He raised it to his lips and sipped. The sherry had a sweetness that caressed his tongue. As he swallowed, he felt the alcohol enter his blood almost immediately. How long had it been since he'd eaten? He sipped again, and there was a slightly different burst of flavor in his mouth, and he suddenly thought: *Tandesko wine.* An image flickered in his mind: drinking another Tandesko wine, in this room—and feeling a peculiar explosion of flavor, and a rush of dizziness, and the world spinning . . .

He set the glass down, his mouth aflame with the taste of Califan grapes and yeast. *Tandesko Califan wine.* Why did it trigger such an intense recollection? He closed his eyes and drew a hoarse breath. *Concentrate.* He was on . . . Kantano's World . . . where Tandesko products were almost never . . .

"Are you feeling unwell, Mr. Ruskin?" Jeaves was at his side, balancing a tray laden with steaming dishes. The aroma of roast callfish was intoxicating, dizzying.

"No," Ruskin whispered. "I feel just . . ."

The lights seemed to dim. He heard the sound of glass breaking, somewhere in the distance. Jeaves disappeared, along with the room, into a gray and woolly darkness.

When Stanley Broder entered the dining room for breakfast at 0730, he knew at once that something had changed. Nevertheless, it took him a moment to recognize what it was, and that disturbed him a little.

He nodded to his heavier colleague, Ilex Gorminski, who

was already seated at the side table. With a glance around, Broder said, "Ilex, what is it I'm not seeing?"

"Eh?" Gorminski paused, a spoonful of sugar hovering over his tea.

"There's something—" Broder sniffed the air. There was a rich cooking aroma coming from the kitchen. "Where's Jeaves? There's something cooking that—"

"Mullenberry pancakes," Gorminski said.

"Yes, but that's not it." Broder rose suddenly. "It's yeaston-bread."

Gorminski looked startled, then confused; then understanding grew on his round features. "Ruskin?" he whispered.

"Who else? We don't eat the stuff." Broder strode toward the kitchen. "Jeaves! Where are you?" There was no one in the kitchen except the autocooks, preparing coffee, pancakes—and bread. The smell of the yeaston permeated the kitchen. Possibly it was a programming error; he prayed that it was a programming error. Ruskin, after all, was dead.

At least, that was what Ganz had reported.

He strode back into the dining room. "Ilex, I think we'd better—" He cut himself off as he spotted the robot floating into the room. "Jeaves! What's going on?"

"You called, did you not?" said the robot.

"Don't toy with me, Jeaves. Is Ruskin here?" Broder had his left hand curled around a small sidearm in his pocket; but a lot of good that would do, if Ganz had failed to kill Ruskin.

"Your estimation is correct," the robot answered. "He returned late last night."

"Alive? Under his own power?"

"Somewhat the worse for wear—but alive, yes. And under his own power."

"Why the hell didn't you wake us?" Broder snapped. Gorminski was rising from the table, looking very nervous. "Did you call Ganz in? *Damn* it—I should have known better than to take Ganz at his word."

"Ganz may have been telling the truth, so far as hir was able," Jeaves said. "Remember, Ruskin is no longer so ordinary as you or I. Short of total annihilation, I don't know—"

"Annihilation! Is that what it's going to take?" Broder felt a chill shuddering down his back. This lodge, and all of their work . . .

"Perhaps not," Jeaves said. "Ruskin's behavior was quite subdued. He seemed to want only to refresh himself, and to sleep. I judged it safe to let him do so."

"You took a big risk. How could you be so sure?"

"I performed several scans—and I took the liberty of offering him some Califan private stock."

Broder scowled. Califan sherry had worked on Ruskin before. But that was in the past. "Did he take the sherry?"

"Indeed, willingly. He seemed to have no memory of recent events."

Broder narrowed his gaze at the robot.

"What was your baseline for judging him *safe*?" Gorminski wheezed.

"I scanned, I judged, I drew the conclusions that seemed most appropriate," the robot answered. "I did not assume that he was completely safe—however, I do suspect that he has stabilized. I knew that you would want to talk to him, and I was trying to allow you all to be as rested as possible. Is that a sufficient answer?"

"Maybe," Broder said. "Where is he now?"

"Sleeping. My scans indicated that he is recovering remarkably from severe injuries. There are subtle but dramatic changes in his bodily structure."

Broder considered that. "So Ganz may actually have reported accurately." He swallowed. "I suppose we should have explained more to Ganz. If you're wrong about his being stabilized, our only option will be—"

There seemed a trace of sadness in Jeaves's voice as he answered, "Of course, sir."

Broder let his breath out, nodding. "Serve us breakfast, then, and let's be on with it."

He felt an odd giddiness as he awoke, but it passed as his eyes focused on the ceiling. He felt a lightness in his limbs; it took a moment to realize that he was floating on a varigrav bed. His mind was filled with images: of the forest, of falling, of rising, of falling again. Of staggering through a wood on foot, of coming home to a place he barely remembered.

"Good morning," he heard, a melodic voice interrupting his thoughts. Turning his head, he saw a tall silver-and-black robot floating beside his bed.

Jeaves. He remembered the robot, and speaking with it last night. He remembered going in search of food; there had been the smell of fish roasting, and wine. . . .

"Are you feeling stronger?" Jeaves asked. "I'm afraid the sherry last night put you out. I should have realized that if you hadn't eaten all day, it would be unwise to—"

He waved the robot to silence. Of course. No wonder. "If I haven't learned to hold my liquor by now . . . anyway, I hardly remember a thing from last night." He sighed and rose to a sitting position and blinked, looking around the room. A name popped into his mind. *Ruskin*. His name.

The robot seemed to study him. "Are you hungry?" it asked. "I brought a breakfast cart."

"Why, yes—I guess I am," Ruskin said. He had memories of ravenous hunger, but just now, oddly, he felt only pleasurably hungry.

Jeaves disappeared, then returned, bearing a large tray. Ruskin climbed out of bed, rocking a little as full gravity caught him. He found a robe and shrugged it on as Jeaves laid plates and saucers on the table.

"I took the liberty," Jeaves said, "of providing you with a mild nutrient infusion after I brought you back here last night. You seemed to need it."

Ruskin nodded and idly rubbed at the red infusion mark on the inside of his wrist. He felt better than he had in— how long? The coffee smelled wonderful. He broke off a piece of yeasty, fresh-baked, whole-meal bread and sank his teeth into it with an appreciative nod.

"Enjoy your breakfast, sir," the robot said. "When you are finished, I believe Mr. Broder and Mr. Gorminski would be pleased to see you in the den."

Ruskin raised his eyebrows and took another bite. "Great." He ran his fingers through his hair; it had almost grown in on the left side. "Before we do that," he asked

Jeaves, as the robot was turning to leave, "can I trouble you for a quick trim?" He didn't know what he was about to face, but there was no point in *looking* as though he'd been ambushed.

The robot murmured, "Of course, sir. As you wish."

CHAPTER 4

✳

The den was a windowless but cozy room, paneled with Vegan teakwood. Two of the walls bore elongated holo-screens, both blank, but with a dim blue glow that gave one a vague sense of infinite depth. The rest of the room was taken up by glassed-in bookcases, a desk, and over-stuffed chairs. A man rose from one of the chairs and came toward him: tall, lanky, sandy-haired, with furrowed brow and intense blue eyes.

Dark figure coming toward him, looming . . .

"Ruskin! Excellent to see you!" The man reached out as he regarded Ruskin with an expression of—what? Surprise? Curiosity? "What happened out there?" the man exclaimed. "You had us worried!"

Ruskin shook hands cautiously. The grip was cool but firm. Did he remember this man? Gorminski? Broder? Those were the names that Jeaves had mentioned. If he knew them, *how* did he know them? "Thank you," he murmured. "It's good to be back."

Stanley Broder. The name clicked into place, but no memory to accompany it.

Broder had a thin mustache and wore a powder-blue ascot with a cream-colored jacket. His movements were precise and exaggerated, an actor's movements—thrust of hand, puckering of mouth, creasing of brow. "Ilex was ready to head out on a one-man search," he said. "Isn't that right, Ilex?"

Ruskin started, as another man stepped out of the corner behind him. He was shorter, stockier, with thinning black hair, and a limp. His voice was gravelly. "We didn't quite know *what* to do. We sent out a couple of remotes to skim the trails, but it's a big forest, Willard. If you'd been any longer, we would have had to call in a whole search operation." He shook Ruskin's hand. "Anyway, it's good to see you intact. What happened?" Ilex grinned, with a smile that seemed uneasy. "Or is it a secret?"

"Sit," Ruskin heard, before he could answer. Broder was gesturing to a chair. "Jeaves said you looked pretty banged up when you came in last night." Broder touched his arm, voice full of concern.

Ruskin laughed shakily, as the memory flashed: the dark figure, an explosion of light; coming out of the darkness and finding his wounds; and on the ground, bits of—

He shuddered, gripping the arms of the chair. He felt cold, very cold.

And yet. Here he sat, neat and clean. Intact.

Except for his memory.

For a frozen instant, he gazed at the two men: a tableau of three, each wondering at the others' thoughts. Gorminski had called him *Willard*. Did he dare trust them? Broder could have been the tall figure; but somehow he thought not. And yet . . .

"You don't have to tell us." Broder chuckled. "You look to be in pretty good shape now, anyway." He narrowed his gaze at Ruskin. "Did you feel better by the time you got back?"

Ruskin opened his mouth and closed it. That was exactly what Jeaves had asked him. He stared at Broder in confusion. "I can't . . . exactly say that I did. I guess." He forced a smile. "I was feeling pretty exhausted. It's hard to say."

Broder and Gorminski exchanged glances. "You really shouldn't have gone so far from the lodge by yourself," Gorminski admonished him. "At least not without a monitor. Just for safety's sake."

"Were you injured?" Broder asked. "We could give you a medical scan—we're fully equipped, you know." His voice was almost buoyant with concern.

Too much concern? Ruskin wondered. And why did Broder keep fingering that medallion on the front of his shirt? Trying to hide his uncertainty, Ruskin rubbed the back of his neck. "I did take a nasty fall, I think. But I'm okay now."

Broder gazed at him with a frightening intensity. "You *think* you took a fall? You don't *know*?"

"Well—" Ruskin forced a laugh. The lie had come forth easily, without his quite knowing why. "I was kind of dazed when I got back."

"You didn't—" Broder frowned and tapped his head—"give yourself a knock, did you?" He glanced at Gorminski with an expression that Ruskin couldn't read.

Ruskin let his breath out and nodded. "I did have a bit of a headache. To be honest, I—" He hesitated. *To be honest* . . . did he want to be honest with these men? Something held him back from telling what he knew. Did *they* know he'd been attacked?

"You what, Willard?" Broder leaned forward, his hand still clutching that medallion. His eyes held Ruskin's again, in a sharp stare.

Why is he probing so . . . ?

"I'm going to call Jeaves," Broder said suddenly, rocking back in his chair. "If you got a concussion, we should have him close by. That okay with you?"

Ruskin shrugged. "Why not?" He wondered what had made him lie—what had made him distrust these men. But he knew. *I didn't fall . . . someone tried to kill me.*

Broder closed his eyes for a moment, caressing the medallion. When he opened them, it was to gaze back at Ruskin. "Since you had a bit of a head bump, maybe I ought to ask you this: Do you recall the state you were in when you left here?"

"Huh?" Bewildered, Ruskin turned to Gorminski, who was sober-faced and silent. He tried to reach back in memory: but all he found was mist and confusion. "I was . . . in a bit of a hurry, wasn't I? That's why I forgot to put on a monitor."

Broder's smile cracked into a grin. "In a hurry? I would have put it a little more strongly. You were in quite a state, Willard!"

Gazing at the floor, Ruskin tried to think, to probe the cottony darkness of his memory. There was something there, stirring in the dark. A memory of *anger* surfaced, then disappeared. Anger? Yes, terrible anger. Rage. Betrayal. And bewilderment. "We had an argument. Didn't we?" Yes, he knew they had. But an argument terrible enough to warrant attempted murder?

Gorminski barked a laugh, then looked embarrassed. "You really don't remember, do you?" Broder asked.

"Ah—" Ruskin cleared his throat. "No. To be honest." The door opened and Jeaves floated in, bearing a tray with a teapot, cups, and a plate of crackers. "I must have—" He frowned and allowed the sentence to die, as he watched the robot set the tray down on the desk.

Broder crossed the room to the bookcase. Opening the center glass door, he ran his finger along the row of spines. He pulled out a volume, held it up. "Do you recall our talking about Holdeson's theories of political equilibrium?"

Ruskin turned his palms up wordlessly. Theories of political equilibrium? What was so inflammatory about that?

"Do you recall our discussion of the Triunal mechanism for absorbing the Emir worlds? Or our discussion of the preSpace examples: socialism and capitalism on Old Earth? Do you recall any of that?"

Ruskin struggled to reach backward in time. There was something: he remembered the anger, but not the focus. Unless . . .

The Tandesko Triune.

"Ilex was trying to convince you that Holdeson—" Broder tapped the volume in his hand—"was right when he said that the Triune system was inherently fairer—"

Yes. Tandesko Triune. *Anger.*

He remembered rage at an assertion, at the very notion that anything about the Tandesko Triune, a group of some seventeen tightly bound worlds with a social structure that he couldn't and didn't want to comprehend, was fair for anyone except the Triune itself. The Tandesko system was mad—a despotic regime of several sentient races interlocked and merged into one. It was not at all like the Auricle Alliance of worlds, where individualism was encouraged to flower and grow.

The discussion itself was lost in the mists, but he remembered the anger. If these people were Tandesko sympathizers . . .

Gorminski was grinning nervously as Broder continued, "And you became rather *upset*, as I recall."

"Did I?" Ruskin whispered.

"I never knew I was such an effective debater," Gorminski chuckled. "I didn't even *believe* half the stuff I was saying. But it sure lit you off. You stamped off into the woods, said you were going to go find some place to think where you weren't surrounded by a bunch of idiots—"

"Did I?" he repeated dizzily.

"Would you care for tea, Mr. Ruskin?" Jeaves interrupted.

"What? Yes." He fumbled with the cup and saucer.

"You didn't care for the Tandesko viewpoint," Broder said, snapping the book shut. He replaced it on the shelf.

"No," Ruskin said huskily. "No, I didn't. Don't."

"Are you still angry with me?" Gorminski asked apologetically.

"What? No, of course not." Ruskin started to sip, but his hand was trembling. The cup rattled on its saucer as he set it down again. Something in him wanted to hurl the tea instead of drinking it.

"Willard, you're *not* all right. You're shaking," Broder said, moving quickly to assist him. "Jeaves, would you take that cup, please?" The robot lifted the cup and saucer away. "Willard, I think we'd better get you checked out. Will you go with Jeaves for a med-scan?"

Ruskin flushed. "That's hardly necessary."

"Call it a precaution." Broder touched his arm. "Or a waste of time, if you want. But you can never be too sure, when you've had a knock on the head. *We'd* feel better if Jeaves checked you out."

"Well—"

"What do you think, Jeaves?"

The robot hummed. "I would recommend it, certainly, if there's any reason for doubt. It will be quite painless, Mr. Ruskin."

All three were staring at him expectantly. Ruskin finally sighed. "If you insist. But I want to know what you find." *I do want to know. I wish I could believe that you'll tell me.*

"Sure. It's the smart thing," Broder assured him.

"I'll awaken the medic-unit," Jeaves said.

Ruskin nodded and followed Jeaves toward the door. *And maybe it'll be one more chance to kill me.*

Broder squinted at the readouts arrayed three-dimensionally in the holoscreen. "You're the programmer, Ilex. Quit wringing your hands and just tell me what we're seeing."

Gorminski peered back and forth between the readouts in one wall of the den and the computer-enhanced image of Ruskin in the other, floating in the zero-grav field of the medical scanner. At the edge of the latter image, Jeaves could be seen moving about, tending the scanner controls and evaluating the data that were being relayed to the den screens. Gorminski limped down the length of the data-readout screen and studied a list of codings. He scratched his head. "As nearly as I can tell, he's in good shape. And it looks as though Ganz's report was accurate, too. There are subtle changes in the bone structure of the skull, and in the ribs. As though bone was removed, you know—and replaced. There are also remnants of scar tissue in his heart, lungs, interstitial tissues, and in the skin."

"What about the NAGs?" Broder asked.

Gorminski shrugged. "They're there."

"And that's all you can tell me?"

"Well, I'd say it looks like he's stabilized just the way Jeaves told us he was." Gorminski limped back and forth, studying the data-structures. He pressed a switch. "Jeaves, can you talk privately?"

The robot replied from the examination room. "Indeed. My assessment is that my earlier speculation was correct. He healed from his injuries with remarkable speed, and the earlier violent episode appears to have been a transitional phase. He seems to have repressed all memory of it, as well as of Ganz's attempt to terminate him. The amnesia is not entirely unexpected, and is consistent with his confused state when he came in last night. I would attribute it to the injury, or to the transitional episode, or both. It may disappear. But I predict that the NAG control will stabilize. I have no reason at this time to expect that he will not ultimately prove reliable. I recommend going ahead as originally planned."

Broder frowned. He fingered his neck medallion, then dropped it. "I wonder. Has he really repressed the memory? Or is he just hiding it well? We'll have to watch him carefully."

Gorminski peered at him a moment, then pressed another switch to mute the connection to the robot. "What's the matter? Don't you trust Jeaves, either?"

"I do, just not completely. I don't trust anyone completely. Not even you." Broder paced, ignoring Gorminski's startled expression. "Besides, that robot is right too often."

"What's bad about that?"

"One of these days, it's going to be wrong. And we won't be expecting it."

"That's not a very politic sentiment, Stanley." Gorminski returned to his scrutiny of the data. "I'd have thought you'd be happy that we don't have to blow the whole thing up."

"I would be, Ilex. I would be very happy—if I knew. If I only *knew*."

He was still blinking off the effects of the suspensor drugs when Broder came in and asked cheerfully, "How are you feeling?" He shrugged, straightening his shirt. "Well, you'll be happy to know that you checked out fine," Broder said. "Jeaves says that you had a mild concussion—so it looks as though you were right. You must have taken a fall and knocked yourself on the bean."

"Ah." Ruskin exhaled fully, his thoughts slowly coming back into focus. He nodded, in what he hoped was a sufficiently casual manner.

"Jeaves gave you an anticoncussive, which ought to fix you up pretty well, but you should still take it easy for a while. Anyway, we'll be flying back to the city today."

Ruskin drew another deep breath. "So . . . I check out okay, then?"

"Absolutely." Broder looked at him closely. "If you want to see your readouts—"

Ruskin waved off the suggestion. "Maybe later." One question was answered already. It was obvious that they wouldn't show him the actual readouts—not if they wanted him to believe that he'd suffered a simple concussion. There was not much point in pursuing that avenue.

"Sure. Fine." Broder seemed to accept his response. "Oh, you should probably talk to Jeaves about getting your things packed for you. We'll be leaving after lunch."

"Right."

Broder clapped him on the shoulder and left him alone. Ruskin nodded to himself and stared thoughtfully at his hands. He rubbed his thumb against the tip of his right index finger, wondering at a tiny bump that he'd just noticed there. Wondering why Broder had lied to him.

"Tell me something, Jeaves."

"Of course, sir. If I can." The robot drifted alongside him, humming.

Ruskin pointed out the window to the edge of the forest. Behind him, the fountain and pool were murmuring, whispering in the courtyard. "What's out there, Jeaves? Really."

"I'm afraid I don't quite understand your question, Mr. Ruskin. The forest preserve is out there. The sky. The mountains. You've seen them. You've walked among them. Did you want to know something more specific?"

Ruskin scratched his right sideburn. "Well, there's a lot that I haven't seen. Pretend I'm just a tourist here for the first time."

The robot rotated in midair to regard him. "But you are."

Ruskin opened his mouth, closed it.

Jeaves's eyes gleamed. "But you are having difficulty remembering. Is that correct?"

He hesitated. "Let's say there are gaps. Probably from my . . . fall." He glanced over his shoulder. They were apparently alone. "What would you tell me about this place? What forest is it? What are its charms? And its dangers?" Aside from attempted killings, of course.

"The forest," Jeaves said, "is the upper arm of the Kandanaro Protectorate. It is the largest wildlife preserve on Kantano's World, and one of the three largest in all of the Northeast Orion worlds. Do you recall overflying the Slyphus River valley and the Mukato Canyons on your way in a few days ago?"

Ruskin closed his eyes. Pictures flickered in his mind in response to those names; but were they from literal memory, or had he merely seen holos of the places?

The robot pointed out the window. "The trails, one of which you followed, go on for hundreds and thousands of kilometers through the wilds. Should you have gotten lost without a monitor, it could have been very difficult to find you. You might have traveled for days before encountering a trail maintainer or a shelter."

Ruskin cocked his head curiously. "Are there other lodges like this one?"

"Why, yes. Various governments and organizations own lodges throughout the Protectorate."

"But—" Ruskin paused, as Jeaves's eyes dimmed momentarily.

"Excuse me." The robot's voice suddenly became sharp. "Mr. Broder has requested that we complete preparations for departure. If you have not yet finished gathering your personal effects—"

"Of course. Could you assist?"

The deltacraft shuddered as it rose into the air. The lodge fell away from them, then was lost in tree cover. Jeaves was piloting, plugged into a socket where he sat facing Ruskin and the others, chatting as they climbed to a fast cruising altitude.

Ruskin only half listened; he quietly peered out at the shrinking landscape, trying to recall, if it was in his mind anywhere, the memory of flying in. The brown and gray outline of the mountain range caused a brief, dizzying flurry of memories, or hints of memories, none of which he could capture for more than an instant. When the flurry drained away, it seemed to take his energy with it. He blinked, trying to focus on his companions; but if anyone had spoken to him, he would not have heard. His thoughts were turned inward, spinning futilely.

Among his effects he had found a slim wallet containing

both personal and work identification chits. He'd slipped the wallet into his breast pocket, intending to examine its contents later. Now he chafed at the presence of the others, preventing him from poring over his own possessions. But at least now he had names and addresses for his places of residence and work.

A changing landscape reeled by, far below. The deltacraft was chasing the sun, leaving behind rivers and lakes and mountains—and more rivers, gleaming ribbons over the land. Their destination was apparently far across the continent. They were chasing the sun, but the sun was winning the race. It was growing enormous and red as it set toward the horizon ahead of them. The last thing he remembered was glancing into Jeaves's inscrutable gaze, then looking back with a shiver of fear at the crimson orb of the sun swelling behind bands of dusty clouds, swelling as though threatening to swallow them whole into its fiery, smoky furnace.

CHAPTER 5

✳

The star blazed, roiled, fumed. Equilibrium teetered as the balance of forces groaned toward the brink of catastrophe. Temperature and density shifted, slid as the last and hottest fusions took place. Jets and streamers of ionized gases exploded away from the star's surface like ribbons and banners fluttering in a cosmic breeze. The star was drifting inevitably toward death . . . faster than it knew.

There were invaders in the star's midst.

Threads of warpspace had slipped invisibly down through the convective layers, slipped toward the core, toward the center of mass. Threads of warpspace had spun their tapestry of death—clenching and strangling, pouring heat and fuel into the flames.

A thousand values fluctuated, changed with inexorable speed. The collapse was moments away, and it would rend the very fabric of space.

And Ruskin's hands were on the controls, guiding and channeling the explosion. . . .

◾

The landing sent a bump through the craft, and the vision evaporated. Ruskin realized with a start that Stanley Broder had said something to him. He was nodding in agreement, though he had no idea what Broder had said.

But where were Jeaves and Gorminski? This wasn't the deltacraft. . . .

His thoughts receded into a gray haze.

Through the haze, a red star burned bright: a complex image rotating, zooming, fast forwarding, filling a simulation-space with a vast matrix of data. The image had brought him out of the darkness, like a bolt of lightning, illuminating a memory.

What memory?

His workplace. Associative Frontiers Institute.

The image faded as his head cleared. He was on the ground now, riding in an autocab through the streets of a city. He squinted out the window, shivered, glanced at the time. What the devil? Hours had passed since they'd taken off from the lodge. What had happened during the flight? He couldn't remember a thing. He must have blacked out. And yet Broder was riding calmly beside him, as though nothing were wrong. Apparently he had been carrying on a conversation. At some point, they must have landed, transferred to this car, entered the city (what city?); and Jeaves and Gorminski had gone their own ways. He had no memory of any of that.

Broder turned to peer at him. "You okay, Willard?"

"Sure. Why?" Outside, government offices spun by in fading twilight.

"You looked a little funny there for a minute."

Ruskin stared out the window. It all looked vaguely familiar. "I'm fine," he said. "Tired, I guess."

Broder nodded. "We've been talking at you too much, I expect. Well, you'd better make it an early night. You'll want to be in shape for work tomorrow."

Ruskin nodded, wondering what exactly he did for work. "Thanks. I will." He closed his eyes to slits, as though lost in thought. Some landmark might trigger a recognition of this city. Architecture heavily populated by spires and obelisks: *Minora Cayla?* As blocks of buildings passed by, he drifted in and out of a reverie, only half-aware of Broder's presence beside him in the car. He imagined a man trudging across a plain, peering at occasional clusters of trees on silent knolls, wondering what land he was in and where all the people had gone. The sun was setting over the plain; only emptiness and loneliness awaited him in the night.

"Here, Willard—I'll help you with your bag."

Ruskin blinked. The car had stopped in front of a brownstone apartment building. He peered at the structure and nodded. His apartment building? "Don't bother," he said. "I can manage."

"Are you sure?" Broder's eyes bored into his.

Ruskin felt a little shiver. "Yes. Thanks for the lift."

Broder shook his hand. "Well—okay, then. Look, Willard, you take care. I'm going off-planet on business in a couple of days, so I don't know when I'll see you again. But it's been a pleasure. You *will* take it slow for a while?"

Ruskin nodded, pulled his bag out of the luggage compartment, waited while the hatch hissed closed. "Yes. Thanks for everything." He hesitated, but couldn't think of anything else to say. Broder nodded, and with a wave, drove off.

Taking a deep breath, Ruskin walked up to the front door of the brownstone. He felt a tingle of vague associations. He knew that the outer door was not automatic, even before he touched it; and yet he did not remember the building itself exactly. It seemed in some musty corner of his mind that he had been here before. But did he live here? Broder could have been testing him, he supposed, leaving him at the wrong address; but his intuition hinted otherwise.

He was baffled by Broder's motivation for lying to him at the lodge, or for dropping him off so casually here. But whatever else had happened during the flight, he must have been convincing in his portrayal of a sane man. He sighed. The act might not be over yet.

The address on the front-door plate, 92 Alpha Boulevard, matched the address on the identification chit that he had found in his wallet. He pressed his palm to the scanner beside the inner door, and the lock clicked open. He opened it with a tug and walked through.

The hallway was empty and silent. Beige walls, green-flecked carpeting. Which way? Drawing his wallet from his breast pocket, he examined the I.D. again. Apartment 404. He looked up, realized that he had already walked halfway to the stairs, past a lift. His legs seemed to know where he was going. He felt a familiar tug in his muscles as he began climbing.

The fourth-floor hallway was carpeted in russet. *Yes.* He passed two doors on the left before reaching 404. After a long hesitation, he pressed his palm to the lock-plate.

The door clicked and slowly swung inward.

The room was pitch dark. No light came on in response to his entering, even after he'd closed the door behind him. For a moment, he simply stood in total darkness, not breathing. He dropped his bag, and the thump it made hitting the carpet was just enough to make him release his breath.

"Hello, Willard."

He drew a sharp breath, then let it out in a gasp. He blinked in the darkness. "Max!" he cried, almost laughing out loud, as conscious recognition followed the reflex.

A sound of chuckling made him smile. "I am pleased that you have returned safely," the voice said.

Ruskin nodded in the darkness. *Max . . . Tokandro Ali'-Maksam*. His friend's name spelled itself across his mind like gleaming diamonds in space.

"The light will not hurt my eyes," Ali'Maksam said.

Ruskin frowned. "I'll leave it off," he said softly. "You should be comfortable when you visit me." His eyes were already beginning to adapt to the darkness, which was not total. The windows were tightly shuttered; but somewhere in the room, green diodes were emitting traces of light. Probably the music console. In the faint glow, he could almost make out the lithe form of his friend, crouched in lotus position in the corner of the living room.

"As you wish. Then I thank you."

"Have you been waiting long?"

For a moment, Max didn't answer. Ruskin pondered the silence and realized that the recognition of his friend was only partial; he recognized Max as one might notice a favorite old book by its cover, without quite being able to recall its contents. Max was his friend; he was a tele'e-Logoth, a serpent-man and scholar of Logos-Kwatrn. He was a nocturnal creature who, unprotected, could not tolerate much light. And at this moment, Ruskin could remember little else about him.

Hell of a thing. He felt almost certain that Max was his best friend.

"I have been productive while I waited," Max said, not quite answering his question. The Logothian enunciated his syllables cleanly and evenly.

"Good. Sorry I was away . . . so long. I—"

"Willard, do not apologize for time spent in renewal and reflection."

Reflection. Is that what I was doing? A smile crossed

Ruskin's face, as a memory of a long-ago conversation flickered through his mind. "You always were better at justifying time off than I was."

"And you, better at underestimating pursuits that did not satisfy your work-ethic values," Max answered, his voice barely inflected with Logothian humor.

Ruskin chuckled along with him. Their voices filled the darkness with a comfortable warmth, like an invisible, crackling fire. Max's ghostly, slender form swayed with his laughter, like a treetop barely visible in the night. Ruskin could turn on a red light to see Max better, but it hardly seemed worth the trouble. He stepped cautiously to the center of the room, then settled onto the carpet in a cross-legged sitting position, facing the dim visage of his friend at a distance of a couple of meters. "How long," he said slowly, "was I gone, anyway?"

"Have you lost track?" Max asked.

Ruskin shrugged. "Time flies when you're—" His voice faltered. "I'm feeling a bit . . . unsettled, Max. It was a strange trip."

"Ah."

As they faced one another in silence, Ruskin wondered why he didn't just blurt out the whole bewildering story. And then he realized: because someone had tried to kill him, that was why. And everyone else had lied to him. How could he possibly know whom to trust? He *thought* that Max was his friend. But. His eyes were slowly adjusting to the darkness, as they had in the forest last night. (Was it really only last night? It seemed ages ago.) The thin rays of emerald diode light seemed to grow stronger, and the outlines of the room gradually became more distinct. To the left of Max was a curious mechanical shape; he gazed at it for half a minute before realizing that it was a universal exercise machine. He wondered if he used it often.

"You were gone six days," Max murmured. "It was the most time you could take from your work."

Ah. Was there urgency in his work, then? Ruskin frowned into space, grateful for the darkness that hid his emotions. Or did it? Ali'Maksam was an empathic—

"Willard."

He blinked. "Yes?" Of course: the darkness hid nothing from Max. What was he thinking?

"You need time alone, don't you?"

"Well, I—"

"I quite understand. But before I leave, may I ask you one thing, for my own peace of mind?"

Ruskin drew a painful breath. "Of course." There was no question: he needed time alone to think, to dredge through the murky depths of his memories. And yet, Max was his one link. He hated to see the serpent-man go.

Max's gaze seemed almost to glow in the darkness. "I just wanted to ask—"

"Yes?"

Max's breath hissed out in a sigh. "Did they keep their assurances to you?"

"Did they—?" His jaw seemed to lock with tension and uncertainty. "Did *who* keep *what*—?"

Max's eyes blinked slowly. "As I feared," he whispered, his voice a dry leaf rustling.

"You feared—*what*?" Ruskin asked. "Max?"

The slim Logothian profile shifted in the near-darkness. "I am sorry. I should not have alarmed you. I must reflect on certain matters before I can speak with integrity or knowledge."

"What do you mean?"

The eyes blinked again. "Willard, I must ask you: Do you trust me?"

"Why, I—" His voice caught. "Yes. Of course I do."

"Then I will speak with you again, when I am full-bodied. When I know more. I dare not say the wrong thing now and alarm you unnecessarily. In the meantime—"

"Max, tell me what's going on!"

"As soon as I am able, Willard." The Logothian sounded anxious. "We must meet soon, in person. But until then, please take great care!" The serpentine shape bowed toward him and then dissolved in the darkness.

Ruskin's mouth opened. He blinked in the gloom, trying in vain to locate his friend's visage. Gone. He'd been talking to nothing but a virtual image. Max had never been here at all.

Virtual image . . .

Of course. How could he have forgotten? Max's ability to project virtual images of himself had been a subject of much banter in the early years of their friendship.

If he could forget that, then what hadn't he forgotten?

"Room," he said softly, shielding his eyes. "Bring up the lights. Very slowly, please."

Exploring his dwelling, he felt like an adult returning to an old childhood haunt. The apartment was full of discoveries and puzzles—bits of his past that brought back fragments of memory or, more often, frustration at his inability to put the fragments together. The place was small and tidy, walls adorned with holomurals and permanent photo-images that tended toward the astronomical and the abstract. There were no human faces or figures in any of the photographs. The living room was carpeted with a wine-red deep pile; the sofa was upholstered in a rough-textured charcoal-gray, and two chairs in a smooth, cream-colored fabric. The consoles and shelves were all wood with natural finish. The room seemed altogether comfortable, but not ostentatious. It appeared that he earned a respectable income.

He switched on the music console and told it to replay the last piece played. He recognized it at once, a brash and flowing synthesis of Josephson-mode orchestrations. He hummed the counterpoint as he inspected the books and storage slivers on the shelves. The books were mostly poetry and novels; the slivers were labeled with cryptic titles and numbers. Perhaps they had something to do with his work. He paused and closed his eyes. The music, or something else, was making it hard for him to concentrate. He turned away from the shelves and went into the kitchen and set the cook to work preparing dinner from a well-stocked cabinet of flash-preserved meals. He selected a cheese-and-fish dish, slid it into the cook, and went on with his exploration.

The bedroom had a varigrav bed, medium size. He poked through the closets and clothing leaves, recognizing little —except for one burgundy pullover that caught his eye so suddenly, it left him breathless. He drew it out. It looked unworn, and when he held it up to himself before the mirror, he realized that it was too small for him. Puzzled, he returned it to the leaves, then took a second look in the mirror, this time focusing on himself. There was no sign at all now of his head injury, and Jeaves had given his newly grown hair a perfect trim. He ran his fingers through it, feeling its fine, clean texture. He shook his head and walked back out through the kitchen. The aroma of cooking fish dizzied him, not with hunger so much as memories, or fragments of memories. *A park by a river; a picnic supper on a summer evening, with a woman . . .*

What woman? Reach back . . .

The memory disappeared.

Reluctantly, he returned to the living room. Perhaps it was time to do what he'd been avoiding. He eyed the think-tank consoles. It appeared he possessed considerable cogitative power in his home. For work? Perhaps; but it could be personal storage, as well: diaries, scrapbooks, photo albums. Sliding tentatively into the console seat, he switched on the cogitative system and called up "personal files." Or tried to.

The console informed him that those files were locked.

"Unlock them," he said.

The console answered, "Please bend forward for brain pattern identification."

Puzzled, he obeyed. What files did he have that were so sensitive?

The console said, "Incorrect identification. Please state your name."

"Willard Ruskin! You ought to know!"

"Your brain patterns do not match. Please desist from attempting to view those files. If you attempt again, the police will be notified."

What the hell? In frustration, he rose from the console. He began pacing the room. *Your brain patterns do not match.* Was this his home or wasn't it? His gaze came to rest on the exerciser. He sighed and climbed into it, closing the restraints around his feet and arms and gripping the hand grips. He started working out slowly, moving his legs in gentle presses, then gradually stretching out his back and arm muscles. Although he could not actually remember using this machine, his muscles seemed to. They took up the movements automatically, limbering first, then pushing harder until he was puffing from the exertion. He began sweating; fatigue came and went, and though he was breathing rapidly, he felt as though he could continue indefinitely.

Finally bringing the machine to a stop, he gave himself a few moments to catch his breath, then nudged the release control and climbed out. His mind was alive with déjà vu: feelings he couldn't place.

It was time for dinner, for more déjà vu. A dinner by a river, with a woman . . . He inhaled the cooking smells, hoping to recapture the memory, and failing. He sighed. Carrying his dinner into the living room, he sat staring at the thinktank unit. The door scanners had passed him; but the scanners on the console were undoubtedly more sophisticated, more sensitive.

The question had to be asked all over again: *Was* he Willard Ruskin?

As he ate his dinner, the console seemed to gaze back at him with a tireless, baleful eye.

Interlude

✳

Bright had been dreaming.

It did not know what dreaming was, exactly—in fact found the notion peculiar. Yet surely that was what it had been doing. Imagining. How could something live within a star? Except the star?

Bright had been dreaming.

It had dreamed that others had come to it, passed through it like things of the great darkness, things with perhaps thought but not soul. It had all happened so quickly, Bright could hardly judge, except that for a flicker of an instant, far less than the time for a flare to be cast into the dark, Bright had felt the presence of something other than itself.

In itself.

Something other than star.

There *were* others, to be sure. There was Near, and there was Small; but though they sang a little and comforted Bright against the dark, they did not think, as Bright thought. There were still others in the beyond, but they were

far
    and tiny
        and not so bright
    as Bright

Several times now it had happened, the awareness of something strange. There was a tightness and a heat that was not right. Bright was old, and not without wisdom. Bright had known lives and Bright had known deaths. Of others, many others. Bright's own

47

death was perhaps closer than wish, nearer than hope.
But still Bright sang, still it listened to the music from
the others, from the stars.

Bright lived and knew. Knew what was real.

Knew what was not.

This thing, this feeling that it had touched others
out of the night, touched them in the instant that they
had fled, was a conjuring of the imagination.

Bright had been dreaming.

CHAPTER 6

✳

It was the Thirty-Fourth InterOrion Congress for Astro-
physics, and an impossibly spindly-legged man from Ark-
ham's Lesser Belt was holding forth on certain aspects of
stellar evolution related to Type One Reinhart-sequence
supernovae. Ruskin was trying to hear what the man was
saying. His efforts were mainly futile, due to noise from a
nearby Triune splinter group—a bonded trio of Human-
female, Mandoran biped-phase female, and Thresko
worker-male, who were vocally complaining about a pro-
cedural ruling handed down in the previous day's session.
Ruskin tried to move through the crowd away from them,
far enough to hear some of what the speaker was saying,
because he was just reaching the point that . . .

▪

"Authorization withdrawn," said a voice, much nearer.

With a flicker, the photodiary files closed. The screen
darkened.

Ruskin blinked, breath catching. His voice rasped: "Wait!
Go back on! Reopen those last files!" What was happening?
What was he doing? Somehow he had gotten into his per-
sonal thinktank files.

But how? Was there a code-phrase? Had he blacked out
again?

The console answered: "You are unauthorized to open
those files. Do not try again."

He closed his eyes tightly and took a deep breath. Not
authorized. And yet he had just been *in* the files.

What is happening to me? He expelled his breath and
reached for his glass of wine. His hand groped and found
only air. He blinked, looking down. He was sitting naked
on the carpet, his dinner nowhere to be seen, not even an

49

empty glass. Had he cleaned up already? *Of course. And you went to bed.*

He stared dumbly down at himself, shocked to realize why he was naked. He'd undressed for bed. *Then how long have I been—?* He glanced at the time and was stunned to see that it was past five in the morning. *Did I get any sleep at all?*

He would have to be leaving soon if he was going to go to work—or to the address shown on his work I.D. The thought sent a shiver down his spine. This couldn't go on forever. Sooner or later, he had to try to get help. But how, and from whom? *Someone tried to kill me. Who do I trust?* Would he know anyone at his work address? Would the memories return? If not—what then? Max had promised to see him when he knew more. He hoped that would be soon; hoped desperately.

There was no point in trying to sleep again; indeed, he was a little afraid to try, afraid of letting go of consciousness. *But who was the person who was able to open these files?* He sighed, rising. He might as well get dressed and go in early.

He noticed the bump again as he was dressing, but he ignored it until he'd left the apartment, walked to the nearest tube platform, and boarded the first car that felt right. Since he was early, he didn't worry that he might get sidetracked by going the wrong way; he had the address, and he had plenty of time to try again. But he had an intuition that his body remembered the way to his office.

While riding the tube through the city sky he found himself picking with his thumbnail at the little bump on his index finger. It had not grown since he'd first noticed it at the lodge—it was the size of a small insect bite—but it felt harder, as though a bit of buckshot had become embedded in the skin. He wondered if it was a growth that he ought to have checked, but he remembered the med-scan at the lodge. If it was anything dangerous, Jeaves surely would have excised it, or at least informed him.

Unless there was some reason why they hadn't wanted him to know.

He sighed and gazed out the window at the city skyline, flashing past as the tube passed among the spires. The view seemed familiar, and yet he felt as though he were being propelled along on a dream. Presumably, he would feel an urge to get off at the right time. The city was striking from this vantage, with a golden-red sun glowing over the eastern skyline, glinting off the spires and towers. He shivered, yesterday's vision coming alive again in his mind:

A sun caught in the moment before its death-collapse: an explosion that would spew starstuff across the light-years . . .

The vision was etched so clearly in his memory that in the moment it took him to blink it away, his mind had transformed the landscape outside to a city of glass, on the verge of conflagration. He rubbed his eyes until shots of color against his eyelids replaced the image. The tube-car was slowing as it glided into a midair station. A few people got up to leave. Ruskin glanced at the platform in uncertainty, then leaped for the door just as it began to close.

A glassed-in causeway conveyed him silently into the nearest building, at the fiftieth floor. The lobby was nearly deserted. It was still a good hour before the morning rush. A directory glimmering in the air showed him the name he was looking for, on the sixty-fourth floor. He took the nearest lift.

Associative Frontiers Institute. The door winked open in response to his handprint, and the smell of herbal tea filled his nostrils. He almost closed his eyes as he walked into the reception area, so starkly did the room suddenly appear in his mind: smoked-glass desk to the left, dark-eyed woman named Fariel at the desk, holopainting of the galactic center filling the right-hand side of the room.

His eyes had trouble focusing for a moment. The room was empty, the holopainting turned off. But in the alcove just beyond the desk, a flask of aromatic herbal tea was steaming. He poured himself a mug and walked into the back offices, trying to think of who might be here early; whom he might know. No names came to mind.

The offices were arrayed in a starburst pattern. He found his own office at the end of the leftmost hallway. The name *Willard J. Ruskin* was etched on a small carbon-and-chrome nameplate. He touched the nameplate with a frown, then tried the handprint lock. The partition winked open.

His office was half eggshell, half cockpit. The curved white wall was unadorned, and the desk was really just a ledge following the curvature of the wall. The chair, however, was a swiveling command seat festooned with keyboard pads and interface controls and holographic projection lenses. He set his mug down on the ledge and ran his hand along its smooth, clean surface. Several patches lighted as his hand passed over them, and one section silently rotated upward, revealing a rack of storage slivers and bound books and notepads.

He started to pull out a random selection of materials, then hesitated, touching the spines of several books. He felt a tingle of familiarity in his hand, like a glow of static electricity that went up his arm, and as his breath caught, seemed to fill him. *What is it?* He ran his fingers along the labels of the storage slivers, and his breath tightened further.

Something in him wanted to be let out; and the key could be here. But where?

He closed his eyes and pulled out half a dozen slivers, plus the notebooks he had already touched. He laid them out and scanned their titles. They ranged from a tattered volume labeled *Project Notes—Political,* to a sliver called *HYperSpace/HYperProfits,* to another entitled *Gravimetric Factors in Large K-space Interactions.* Frowning, he flipped open the notebook. It was filled with scribbled handwritten notes and scraps of hard copy. Nothing looked familiar about it; he could not say whether the handwriting was his. But as he paged through some notations on political conflict between the Auricle Alliance and the Tandesko Triune, he felt a sudden flush, remembering feelings of anger.

Someone had been trying to defend the indefensible: the supposition that the Tandesko worlds somehow held a moral high position because of their interracial linkages . . . the supposition that the "enhanced free trade" policies of the Auricle Alliance somehow led to greater involuntary leverage over weaker colony-world economies. . . .

Closing the notebook, he climbed into the chair and

placed the storage slivers into their slots. He rested his arms on the armrests, closed his eyes, took a deep breath. If his body remembered; if the system would allow it . . .

His hands found their control-nudgers. The headrest self-adjusted, cradling his skull. Squeezing two of the fingertip nudgers, he counted to three and opened his eyes. The office was darkening, the holoprojectors coming to life. The walls vanished; he was surrounded by reddish-orange space. A finely traced spherical grid enclosed him, giving dimension to the space, extending outward to infinity. A blank cogitative workspace. His fingers nudged again, and one of the slivers—he didn't look at the title—was drawn into memory.

A title drew itself across the bottom of the grid: *Expansion and Deformation of K-space through Ultralong Warp-thread Connections: A Reference Design Study / Classification: Secret.* He read the title three times. He wasn't sure what it meant. But bells were ringing: Was this something he should know?

"Open file for scanning," he murmured. He prayed for luck. If his system at home had rejected his identity, what would this one do?

"Present ident-chit and handprint," said a low, synthesized voice. He complied. "Opening file," the system said a moment later. "Welcome back, Willard."

"Thank you," he grunted, surprised. Was his home security more rigorous than his office system, then? Or more fallible?

There was little time to think about it. The space around him was filling with diagrams and figures, and another voice, a teaching voice, was providing narration. He used the nudgers to highlight, to slow and speed the motion, to direct the narrator to points of interest. The material was all dimly familiar, like a subject once studied and now nearly forgotten. Soon he had lost track of time, forgotten everything except the grid and the bewildering array of facts, and the voice:

"*. . . The reference design calls for a folding K-space warp-thread process to be extended over a distance of five light-years in a testing configuration. No effort will be made to transmit material objects through the connection; how-*

ever, in-situ measurements of the spatial deformation will be made by preset monitoring beacons. Application to more ambitious schemes must await analysis of test results, under the methodology outlined by Rumley and Thompson in Appendix C to this proposal. . . ."

A graphic display unwrapped around him, both fascinating and bewildering. He skipped ahead.

". . . Update Five, on testing of reference design at sixty light-years. Following are results determined through a compressed time-line test, under additional constraints imposed by the Budgetary Committee of the Alliance Scientific Council. . . ."

He squeezed the nudgers to jump ahead again . . .

■

. . . and the two people facing him across the table started. He blinked, hiding his astonishment.

"Well come on, do it, Willard," a blond-haired young man said.

"Do what?" Ruskin whispered. *Not again. Another blackout.*

The young man laughed and pointed to a holographic display that was flickering with static bars. "Just when you're getting to the interesting part, you scramble the picture! Is that your way of showing us what you got done on your vacation?"

Ruskin frowned at the disabled image and realized that his hands were on the controls of the conference room projectors. "Oh."

The other person, a tall, wispy-haired woman with enormous eyes, was shaking her head. "We didn't really expect you to have it done yet, Willard. Why didn't you just tell us, instead of making us go through all this? I know you're feeling the time pressure, but really!"

Ruskin swallowed, trying to still his trembling hands. "I—I *had* something here. But I don't seem to be able—" He fiddled futilely with the controls. "I must have done something wrong in transferring it over," he mumbled. And was that an out-and-out lie, or had he really had something to show? What the devil had he been doing while his conscious mind was locked up in a closet somewhere? And who were these people? Flushing, he turned the projection off and took a chance. "Nelly, how soon do you need to see it?" The name had just popped into his mind; he wasn't sure which of them it belonged to, but he was sure it was one of them. And as soon as he'd said it, he sensed he'd done something wrong.

There was a long silence, while the young man blushed crimson. It was the woman who answered, and her voice was reproving. "He doesn't need it—I do. As you well know." Her eyes flashed from the young man to Ruskin. "You should have it within the week, at the very latest."

Ruskin's face burned as he tried to think what he'd done wrong. This was a nightmare; it was absurd; he should confide—

No. He didn't dare.

The young man spoke softly, angrily. "What you just called me, Willard—you have no right to use that name. I'm—surprised at you. Judith—" He cleared his throat and rose. "I'll speak with you on the other matter later."

Ruskin stared helplessly after him, and when he was gone, turned to Judith. She was scowling in puzzlement. "Why did you do that, Willard?" she asked finally.

His voice was hoarse. "I didn't mean . . . I don't remember . . ."

Her eyebrows went up. "Don't remember? That he nearly quit when Ankas called him that? That we all agreed his private life was his own? That just because he said some things at a party once—"

"No, I don't remember," Ruskin said, his voice tightening with shame, which stopped her in midsentence. "I'm sorry. Please tell him I'm sorry. I . . . forgot."

Judith gazed at him in incomprehension. "Jesus," she said finally. "What did that vacation do to you?"

He closed his eyes and shook his head.

"Well . . ." Her voice trailed off, and she sighed. "I'll tell Galen you're sorry. But you might tell him yourself."

Ruskin nodded as she left. "Thanks." Thanks for telling him Galen's name. What was the name he had used? *Nelly.* Some sort of pet-name, maybe—or love-name. Who or what did Galen love? he wondered. He sighed and looked around at the empty conference room. White walls, translucent amberine table, handy projector controls. Apparently they didn't go in much for decoration here, except in the reception room. Holo thinktanks everywhere, and white walls for projection. The place looked neat, and uninformative as a blank page.

Damn it, when would he come back to reality?

He fiddled with the control-nudgers, bringing the static-filled projection back to life. He tried adjusting it, but the most he could do was turn the static bars into hash. Back-tracking, he found a series of unfamiliar figures and graphs. He was about to switch it off when a stocky man stuck his head into the room. "Hey, Willard—how was the trip?"

He looked up, trying not to appear startled. "Great," he said. "Just great."

"Wonderful. Look forward to seeing your presentation," the man said and continued on his way.

Ruskin rubbed his forehead wearily. He switched off the projector, extracted the sliver that contained his presentation, and tossed it in his hand. Whatever it was he was supposed to be doing, it must be in here. He closed his hand around it and hurried back to his office.

CHAPTER 7

✳

Ilex Gorminski took a bite from a large, sugared cookie and looked up with that smug, self-satisfied expression that so irritated Broder. "If I didn't know better," Gorminski said, "I'd say Ganz was slipping a gear. Hearing that Ruskin has gone right back to work seems to have been the last straw." Gorminski chuckled. "Ganz wants to—"

Broder cut him off. "Forget Ganz. Hir can wait for the next chance. Hir'll be waiting forever, I hope. What about Ruskin? Does Jeaves have anything more on his amnesia? We can't have him stumbling around, without risking the whole operation." And was I too quick to believe he was recovering? Broder thought. Because I wanted to believe it? Because the tests looked good? Because on the flight back he was lucid—introspecting about his work, and about politics? What did I miss? There must be a more reliable way to gauge this man.

But they had to take risks. Especially since they'd failed once to remove him when they'd tried, when they'd thought he'd gone out of control. Broder was prepared to repeat that attempt, if necessary, though it would be trickier here in the city; and they knew now how hard the man would be to kill. *Credit Ilex for that. He did at least part of his job well.* And anyway, he hoped it would be unnecessary The operation still had a chance of succeeding; and the smell of success was a strong attractant—for them, and for the family of worlds. But there was so little precedent for what they were trying to do. It was hard to know what to expect, what risks were reasonable.

"Well," Gorminski said, brushing cookie crumbs away, "we can only guess at the extent of the amnesia. It's one thing to watch him look worried on his way to work, and another to conclude that—"

"You saw the report from April, didn't you?" Broder snapped. "He doesn't know what he's doing!" *But he did know—yesterday! What's happening to him?*

Gorminski gazed back evenly. "Don't shout at me, Stanley. Yes, I saw the report. I'm telling you, it could just be a case of scattered, isolated lapses—"

"*Lapses?*"

"—due to integrational problems with the new matrix. April's in a position to notice changes that others might not, including trivial changes. That's why we risked the multiple infiltrations, why we set up the whole agency thing, to get that kind of coverage. But take the reports with a grain of salt."

Broder groaned. "Spare me the Auricle Review Agency speech. I didn't trust that setup then and I don't trust it now. Even if they're the best we've got. What's Jeaves say, anyway?"

Gorminski's breath escaped in a snort. He looked away, scowling.

"Ilex—don't take it personally. Just because we're living among them doesn't mean we have to start thinking like them. I just want to know if our metal friend has any new data that might bear on the subject."

"I haven't been able to ask it," Gorminski muttered. "It's been out following Ruskin."

"So?"

"So—I haven't gotten through on a secure channel yet."

"Have you *tried?*"

Gorminski looked annoyed.

"Okay, okay. When is it going to check back in with us?"

"I assume, when he's learned something useful. Stanley, quit *worrying.*"

"I'm supposed to worry. This isn't a game we're playing."

"Just for once, why don't you try trusting my judgment?" Gorminski snapped open another packet of cookies. "I'm supposed to make accurate judgments on these things. You play the tough guy and I play the clever programmer. Isn't that how this is supposed to work?" He popped a whole cookie into his mouth and turned back to his console, cheeks puffed like a squirrel's, chewing.

Broder glared at the back of Gorminski's head—and admitted that Ilex was probably right. He worried too much. He ought to learn to relax.

But relaxing at the wrong time could mean failure and a loss of everything they'd worked for. Everything they'd risked. No, he would never relax—not until it was over.

He was, perhaps, finally onto something. It had been a long day, one that had brought less enlightenment than he'd hoped. But since the fiasco of his meeting with Judith and Galen, he hadn't blacked out again, nor had he left his office. He was hungry—but for answers more than for food.

Coaxing the holoprojection to fast forward, he studied the progression of an analytical problem from one side of the workspace to the other, an economic projection proceeding along five diverging lines. He'd worked his way through the material in the storage sliver that he'd used in his "presentation," and some of it was at least becoming comprehensible. It seemed to be an analysis of projected expansion by the Auricle Alliance, comparing the predicted costs and benefits of colonizing various large populations of stars outside the known Habitat of Humanity. It was a vast juggernaut of an analysis, entirely hypothetical as far as he could tell, based upon magical new transportation methods to the regions of the galaxy in question.

It involved data from deep-space sky surveys, and modeling of certain colonization and trade routes, primarily into the Sagittarian arm in the direction of the galactic center. Was this his area of expertise? It didn't feel like it. He hadn't figured out yet just what the relevance of the thing was, since the star groupings in question lay far beyond the reach of current exploratory capability. Apparently it was a long-view policy study for the Auricle Science Council; at best it was a guessing game, since there was no way to know what worlds and civilizations might be found in the various star groups. In the sixty-some worlds of the known

Habitat, only five nonHuman technological civilizations had been found. Who knew what might be discovered in other parts of the galaxy?

It was a fascinating read for a leisurely afternoon. But did it have anything to do with someone trying to kill him?

He had nothing but a memory of a dark figure in the woods, which wasn't much to go on. The physical scars from that encounter had faded now. But someone had tried to kill him. And that someone might be a coworker, or might have a confederate here. Until he knew more, whom could he trust? Judith? Maybe. Galen? Probably not now.

He knew of no reason why anyone should want him dead. And so he would keep to himself, until he learned more. And that meant fumbling on, searching through files like this one that he was fast-scanning right now.

So fast in fact that it was blurring, becoming hard to follow . . .

•

> **to complete the connection with desired results, timing must be accurate to 15 milliseconds, necessitating appropriate monitoring equipment . . .**

•

He blinked away a moment of dizziness. His fingers pressed the nudgers, slowing the images. There were voices in his head. But no: it must have just been the sound of the narration:

"*. . . the density of the hyperstring structure is such that the gravitational refraction is . . .*"

Blurring . . .

•

He blinked again hard, and stopped the movement. *Gravitational refraction?* The images surrounding him were of no economic analysis—but a discussion of extragalactic astrophysics. He scanned quickly. Cosmic hyperstring. The effect of hyperstring on K- and n-warpspace and vice versa. What the hell? There was a curved diagram showing bewildering gravitational interplays and strains in spatial structure.

Jesus. He didn't know anything about stuff like that— did he? A shiver went through him as he reached back in

his memory, struggling to find those words and images in
a deeper memory. There was a moment of recognition . . .

■

**The dimensions of the connection are related
to the density of the string by the Lankmann-
Tei equation . . .**

■

And it was gone, leaving dizziness in its wake.
What is happening to me?
He'd been studying an economic analysis.
Blackout . . .
Cursing, he rotated his seat to check the chronograph.
It was late afternoon: p535. He hadn't noticed the time
earlier, but he'd been here searching and studying most of
the day. Probably he hadn't been unconscious long. But
what had he been doing during that time?
There has to be a way to find out.
A way to gain control of my mind.
Ali'Maksam.
He sat blinking. He had nearly forgotten the encounter
with his Logothian friend last night. Max seemed to have
known something. Max could probe his thoughts and feel-
ings, perhaps find out what had happened, learn the reason
for the blackouts, learn the key to the puzzle. At least he
could try.
But what if Max—
No. Don't think it.
What if Max is one of the enemy?
He had no reason to distrust Max. But he had no reason
to distrust anyone else, either—except that someone had
tried to kill him. He had to distrust everyone. But
Ali'Maksam?
You have to trust someone . . . sometime.
Tonight he would go to him, ask his help. *Beg* his help.
Tonight—as soon as he'd learned as much here as he
could.
But what to do with these pieces of the puzzle? Cosmic
hyperstring: large filamentary structures in n-space, remnants of a transitional phase in the primordial universe—
and that was about all he knew about it. Diagrams and
artifact-images wrapped themselves around him like a ki-

netic expressionistic art form, shapes evolving and colors
representing waves and towers and human figures and who
knew what else. The bottom of the grid flowed with equations. He had no idea how they might interlock, but he
sensed that they pointed to the meaning of the entire display. If only he could understand it . . .

∎

He removed his dinner from the cook and ate in
front of the console, images spinning before him.
And afterward, he lay in bed, remembering . . .
ignoring the sound of a call coming in on the console . . .

∎

If only he could understand it. But it was all blurring . . .

∎

**synonymous: the conferring of wealth and
power . . . according to Beiser, the control
of the destinies of worlds is linked inexorably
to . . .**

∎

He blinked until his eyes smarted. Voices: taking over
his mind. He massaged his aching temples and began fast-
forwarding again, skimming. If he could drench his mind
in the material, if his subconscious would serve as filter and
interpreter . . .
There was a fresh cup of tea steaming on the ledge of his
office. He felt as though he had recently eaten.
He shook off the observation. Who cares?
His fingers worked at the nudgers, speeding and slowing.

∎

**penetration of sun will require full-array n-
space screens for protection . . .**

∎

His mind, blurring . . .

∎

**Querayn studies of Kônô-type consciousness
suggest a much-disputed possibility that sentience could occur in large cosmic structures—including stars, maser clouds, galaxies . . .**

•

Damn. DAMN.

He squeezed the nudgers, refocusing . . .

•

**growth can be expected to take one to two
weeks including stardrive . . .**

•

What the hell was all this? Charts of specifications. Prices.
Authorization codes.

Prices? For what?

He slowed the scan and drew a ragged breath. He'd just
lost another piece of his day. *Wait—what day is this?* He
checked: it was Tuesday. *Tuesday!* Back at work for the
second day. *Did I go home last night?* The memory, if there
was one, was lost in shadows.

What was he doing now? Studying an array of prices and
options on—apparently—

—starships.

It appeared from these data, in fact, that he was not
just exploring starship costs, which might make sense in
the context of a study; no, he was actually *purchasing* a
starship. And he was specifying some extraordinary special
equipment.

Most likely this was a hypothetical purchasing exercise.

"System," he murmured, his voice cracking from disuse.

"Speaking."

"Explain the purpose of this exercise."

There was a moment's pause. "If by exercise, you mean
the purchasing operation currently under way, it is for the
purchase of a long-range singleton starship."

"Yes, I can see that. But, I mean—*no.*"

"Excuse me, Willard. In what sense do you mean, 'No'?"

Ruskin felt faint. "You aren't telling me that this is *real.*"

"It is a real purchase, yes."

"But—it *can't* be. I mean, how?"

"Willard, if there's a mistake, it's not too late to cancel
the commission. You have not signed off on it yet. But it
was our understanding that you had been planning this
action for some six months now—"

"*Wait.* Just wait. Do you mean to say that I've been
planning for six months to buy a starship?"

"That was our understanding." The system's voice became audibly concerned. "If we have been mistaken, then a total system and project diagnostic reexamination may be in order. We should not have misunderstood a matter of this magnitude; therefore, other understandings may be in doubt. Perhaps you should—"

"Wait," Ruskin said. "Wait. Don't do anything yet. And don't sign off on any order until I've clarified matters."

"Understood."

"Don't sign off on *anything*." He struggled to think. Could he ask for a reexamination to find out what was happening, without alerting anyone else here to his uncertainty? "System—"

"Speaking."

"Let me scan and see what this is all about. Can you show me the purpose for buying this ship?" His fingers worked at the nudgers.

"Do you wish to scan before I answer?"

"No, explain while I look."

"What level of explanation? Shall I reference specific project files?"

"Yes. But give me an overview first." He squeezed the nudgers for a wide-scan. He tried to follow the logical thread, to find the connection that would tell him how this purchase was to be used. The system's voice droned in his head. A project heading flew past; he squeezed the nudgers to go back and see what it was; but now he couldn't find it again.

Blurring . . .

■

arrangement completed. Thank you. Growth modification will commence at once . . .

■

Blurring . . .
What was that? "Wait!"
He squeezed . . .

■

. . . and the weapon fired with a soft sputtering sound. The target in front of the wall exploded in a puff of white.

He dived, rolling on his shoulder, and came up again, firing a second time as the retort echoed from the first shot.

A second ceramic target was blown to powder. He crouched and peered one way, then the other. He heard an appreciative whistle and turned.

"I can see you know what you're doing."

He rose and was met by a wide-eyed stare in the eyes of a thin-faced, olive-skinned man. Ruskin gaped at him, then looked down at the compact weapon in the palm of his hand. His breath went out in a shudder that hurt his chest. He felt as though he had swallowed something cold, pasty, and sickening. *Dear God*. Who was this man?

It's happening again.

They were standing at the end of a long, walled-in yard littered with shot-up targets.

"What do you think of it?"

Ruskin stared at the weapon in his hand, trying to conceal his shock. And fear. He swallowed and looked up at the salesman, whose smile said it all. He looked down at the tiny, but obviously deadly, sidearm.

"It's a very handy piece," the salesman said. "Polite but convincing. And you can see its accuracy." Ruskin raised the object for closer examination. "That's the best shooting I've seen around here in a while," the salesman added.

Ruskin nodded. The weapon was a small ovoid, about as large as an avocado seed, but nearly flat. It was silvery gray and lightweight, made of a ceramic composite. It didn't look nearly as deadly as the demonstration had just proved it to be. It was designed for concealment and convenience. For killing quietly.

For killing? Or defending?

A shudder ran through him, and his vision blurred until he blinked his eyes clear. He murmured, "Yes. Yes it looks very good."

Why am I buying a weapon? Self-defense . . . against another assassination attempt?

"Shall I write it up, then?"

He started. "What? Oh—" He closed his eyes and drew a deep lungful of air. He produced a tight smile. "Yes, why don't you do that? And give me a full charge on it." He handed the weapon back to the salesman and followed him out of the yard into a small, dimly lit shop crammed with locked cases of personal weaponry. *Discreet Personals*, the shop was called. He shook his head and gave the shopkeeper his handprint in exchange for the neatly boxed, fully charged palm gun.

It was on his way out that he passed a small mirror. He glanced into it, and froze.

The face looking back at him was heavy, rugged, dark, with eyes that were deep and brown and quick. It was not his face—not as he remembered it. It was not the face of anyone he knew.

CHAPTER 8

✳

"Max—help me!"

"Willard, is that you? Your voice sounds so different—"

The sun streaming through the silence-screen of the public booth blinded him. *Max, can I trust you? I have to!* Voices surrounding him:

> **A good knock on the head, that's all; be up and back to normal in no time at all . . .**

•

Running down a street lined with grimy cafés and stim-stores, the Gray Mountains looming to the left. He was running hard, but not breathing hard. But he didn't know what he was running toward, or from. His head was full of sounds, voices. Tucked under his arm, a small, square box wrapped in brown spun-paper.

> **Tandesko sympathizers! What am I doing here with them? If I had a gun, I'd . . .**

•

Max, I need your help; I need it now.

"I don't recognize your voice. Is this Willard?"

"YES! Damn it to hell, Max!"

"Why did you leave the line before? I was trying to—"

"Never mind! Max, I—"

"Where are you, Willard? What's wrong?"

"I'm at a public booth, and—"

And I have voices in my head and a face I don't recognize! Max, I need you! What's happening to me?

Look out the window of the booth, through the screen. There's a tube-train up there. You can get away, home; you can get to Max or to anyone else.

"Max, help me! Where are you? Tell me how to get to you!"

"Calm down, Willard! Where are *you*? I can get to you faster than you can—"

Blurring again, out of focus: the street scene outside, the sound of Max's voice. But another:

Love? What does it mean, anyway? Who are my friends? I need them, I need them now. . . .

Max's voice penetrated the babble in his mind. "Where are you, Willard? Tell me where you are right now."

He gasped, "Not sure . . . don't know . . ."

Max's voice was a cold draft dispelling the haze. "Can you see no signs, Willard? Look and find a sign. I'll be right here, Willard. Go and look."

Talking to me like a child. But isn't that what I am now? I don't know how to find my way home. I don't know what's wrong with me, and I need help. What's happening? What's this thing I'm carrying? A weapon. But why?

"Willard." The voice was dry and calm in his ear. Tokandro Ali'Maksam, Logothian, scholar of teleology and consciousness. Calm. Calming. "If you can hear me, Willard—go and look for a street sign, or a storefront, anything that will identify your location."

"Sign." Of course! "Hold the line."

There was a trace of amusement in the voice. "I'll be here."

•

I'll be here, to love and comfort you, if you let me. Know that you can come back . . .

•

Blurring . . .

•

Sensation of speed, tube-express shooting him across the city, mountains looming large and close as the train rose, streaking up toward the foothills. Fingering the tiny nub on the end of his index finger. Someone to love him?

Or to kill him?

Blurring terribly, now . . .

•

Remembered in crystal clarity: Ali'Maksam, sinuous in the gloom of the near-total darkness, stretching close, reaching to join that exquisitely delicate contact that would unite their minds, not in thought so much as feeling: the contact that would let the Logothian explore the topography of his soul, the emotional and spiritual being that made him the Human he was.

If indeed he was still Human at all.

■

The weapon, cool and smooth like a slim seed in his hand. Seed of destruction for his enemies, if they tried again to kill him. But he was no longer alone. He was working with his friends, and together they would abolish the enemy from the planet, from this life.

He no longer knew who he was.

He fought like a tiger.

It was not just for his life, and not just to kill his enemy. He fought to *know* his enemy: to know what she was, how she thought, what she wanted. There could be others of her kind.

She'd met him at the door: a dark figure, against the glow of the light—attacking instantly.

He'd parried the attack easily; but his reflexes were off, his hand-chops flying wide, the lance of fire from his fingertip somehow missing its mark. He seemed to be working against himself. The enemy dodged and darted, a fleeting shadow across the room. He ducked, evading a heavy glass object that shattered behind him. He lifted his finger, fired, missed again. He had to hurry; he had to prevail; his friends were depending on him.

He dived across the room and tackled his foe and rolled and came up on top, hands closing around her throat.

■

The woman's scream surfaced somewhere in the inner recesses of the mind where human and reptilian consciousness merged, where the bedeviling clamor of·voices was stilled. It was a shocking scream of terror, and the intensity of it snapped him to full fighting alertness.

He drew his hands back, ready to strike out, to defend. "Release that woman!" he demanded. He spun, rising to a crouch, taking in the surroundings at a glance: living room of an apartment—not his, but familiar. On the floor beneath him was a woman. Familiar.

Her foot flew up and caught the side of his head. He reeled and fell across the floor. "Wait!" he shouted, clambering back to his feet. "Someone's in trouble!"

A heavy object thudded off his shoulder. The woman was on her feet, running. "*Fucking bastard!*" she screamed.

"Wait!" he croaked, bewildered. His hands tingled. He remembered the feeling of something soft under his fingers: yielding flesh. He staggered drunkenly to his feet. What had he been doing? Why was he here?

"*I'll KILL you, fucker!*" she screamed, diving across the room on the far side of a polished-wood table. She was groping for something.

He blinked, rasping in a breath. Who was this woman? Where was he? She was familiar; this place was familiar; but he had to hurry and finish . . .

Finish what?

The woman rose, holding something in her hand. She fumbled with it, pointed it at him. Her hands were shaking.

"No, wait! I can expl—" he cried.

The object flickered in her hand, and pain seared his right ear and temple. He fell to the floor—

—and remembered—

—why his hands had tingled. Remembered them closing around the woman's neck, squeezing . . .

I know this woman.

Fiery pain blazed in his shoulder, and he rolled, trying to get away. Got to explain! He knew this woman from—
Where?

■

Willard, I care for you no matter what you think. I do love you, Rus'lem. . . .

■

(Candlelight reflected in the glasses, flickering, as they talked deep into the hours of the night when only mystics and lovers were meant to stir. . . .)

■

And I love you, Twig. . . .

•

Dear God—
I loved her—
And I just tried to kill her—

"I have to talk to you!" he shouted, pushing himself up despite the searing agony in his shoulder.

"I'll show you talk, shithead! You think you can—"

"Don't shoot! It's Willard!" He rose, hands in the air. If he could just explain . . .

It was the clear shot the woman needed. She aimed, and fire erupted in his chest. Numbness exploded through him like a ball of smoke. His vision darkened as he fell.

Sound of a gasp.

He groaned and pushed himself up to a near-sitting position, heedless of the pain. *"No!"* he heard, from a voice so frightened as to be pitiable.

"W-wait . . ." he whispered, wishing he could claw away the darkness that blotted out his vision.

"DON'T MOVE!"

He tensed. "Wait. Please."

"Wait—shit! Who are you? What are you?"

He blinked and focused, discovering light in his eyes—and saw her pointing the gun at him. Her eyes were filled with fear and fury. "Please!" he gasped. "I won't . . . hurt you!"

She circled sideways, used both hands to steady the gun. "You were *dead*, damn it! You were dead! Why aren't you still dead? Why—?" She choked off her words, glaring, maybe waiting to see if he would do something aggressive. She was a slim but athletic-looking woman, with thick dark hair and blazing golden eyes. She was clearly struggling not to panic. "Who—or what—are you?" she demanded.

Ruskin felt his reflexes beginning to return. *Tall, dark figure . . . but not her. . . .* His gaze was trapped by hers; he remembered those eyes, slitted like a cat's. He remembered, he had loved her.

"Answer my question," she said with contained fury. "Or

you'll die again. And this time I'll do more than burn a hole
in you!" Her voice caught on the threat, but she was so
angry, so frightened that he didn't doubt she would try to
do as she'd threatened. But he knew what she didn't. He
dropped his gaze to his chest—and saw what on any human
would have been a mortal wound, closing before his eyes.
She saw it, too, and her eyes widened at the sight. "Who
are you?" she demanded again, but her voice was weaker
this time.

Tamika. Tamika Jones.

The name materialized in his mind. Of course; yes . . .

"Tamika," he croaked. "Don't . . ."

She stepped sideways again, circling behind him. He
tried to turn to follow her movement. "Freeze!" He swallowed and obeyed. "So you know my name. You can tell
me later *how* you know it. Right now, just tell me who the
hell *you* are."

His breath escaped and he spoke almost too softly to be
heard. "Willard Ruskin."

She circled quickly in front of him. "What did you say?"

He raised his voice, which was husky, almost gravelly
from fluid in his lungs. "Willard Ruskin." He sank back
onto his elbows. "I think."

"And I'm the queen's consort," she growled. "Try again."

He closed his eyes, thinking. His face: his face had
changed. He didn't know why, or how. But of course she
wouldn't recognize him. *Reach back . . .* "You know me as
Rus'lem," he whispered. "Rus'lem Ruskin."

"I . . . *what?*" She let her own breath out in a hiss, and
her eyes narrowed.

"And I love you . . . I think."

Her head rocked back in shock. She backed away from
him, blinking. Her hands were shaking again as she struggled to keep the gun trained on him. As she struggled to
keep tears out of her eyes. "How do you know that name?"

"It's . . . from my middle name." *Which is? J.—Jerusalem.* An image flashed in his mind of a plumpish, kindly
woman—his mother, Sari Ruskin. His middle name, her
maiden name. "Jerusalem. Willard Jerusalem Ruskin."

Her anger seemed only to increase.

"I love you," he repeated in a whisper. "I don't know

what was happening. I don't know why I was—" *Trying to kill you*, he meant to say; but the words would not leave his lips.

"Damn you," Tamika said, her voice trembling. "*Damn* you. I'll ask you one more time. *Who are you?*"

"Willard Rusk—"

She strode forward and slapped him hard. "*How dare you take the name of a man I love!*" Swallowing, remembering her danger, she backed away.

His own eyes filled with tears. For several heartbeats they stared at one another in silence. "I love you," he whispered. When she didn't answer, he hissed, "Say something, damn it, Twig."

She gazed at him, her whole body shaking. "I don't know . . . who you are . . . or why you . . ." Her voice caught and she shook her head. "Why you . . . tried to *kill* me, but—"

"Twig—"

"*But* so help me—" The gun started to slip from her grasp, and she quickly caught it.

He had been pushing himself toward an upright sitting position. He froze at her movement, then straightened up slowly. He was still on the floor; she stood at a safe distance. "I won't hurt you," he repeated. And as he said it, he prayed that it was true.

"But you—you're not Willard. You're not—" She struggled to force the word out. "*Rus'lem.*"

He stared down at his hands. Rough, unfamiliar hands. Hands that had tried to kill the woman he loved. On his right index finger, there was a bump. A bit of burnt flesh was healing over a bit of something shiny. He had a dim memory of fire erupting from that fingertip.

"You're not Rus'lem," she repeated, more defiantly.

He looked up. "Twig, I am." He closed his eyes, trying to think of how . . .

He opened his eyes. "Can you call Max? Can you reach him?"

"*Max?*" There was astonishment in her voice. And disapproval?

He remembered. "I know you don't much like him. You don't approve of him. But—"

Her head jerked. "How do you know that?" she whispered.

A trace of a smile came to his lips. "You never wanted me to know. You pretended, for my sake, to like him. But Max told me that you seemed to have an instinctive dislike of him, because he was a Logothian. Part serpent." He didn't know why he had just remembered that.

She lowered the gun, her face heavy with shock. Perhaps shame. "I never told that to anyone."

"Max could tell. You couldn't hide your feelings from him." As she struggled to decide whether to believe him or not, he said, "Just as he will be able to tell whether or not I am Willard Ruskin. Will you call him, please?"

Tamika stared at him. "If you are—who you say you are—then how can I reach him?"

"He's at—" Ruskin hesitated. He could not remember Max's phone code. But he had called him; he remembered, through the blur of blackouts and frantic fear. "He's listed in the call directory. Tokandro Ali'Maksam. Please? To prove to you who I am?"

Tamika gazed at him for a long time, before finally nodding. She crossed to the phone, keeping the gun trained on him. As she began to make the call, her brow suddenly furrowed in horror. "What's happening to your face?" she whispered.

Before he could answer, the phone lighted, and she cried, "Ali'Maksam? This is Tamika Jones. . . ."

"The room will have to be darkened when he gets here," Ruskin said. "You'll have to tie me up somehow. For your own protection."

She looked at him without answering. She was seated in a straight-backed chair with the gun in her lap. He was sitting cross-legged on the floor. "I should call the police and have them here," she said finally.

He said nothing.

"You did try to kill me, you know."

"I know. I'm very sorry. I . . ."

She scowled, shaking her head. "Why is your face changing like that?"

His face felt as though it were crawling with insects. He massaged his brows, his cheekbones, trying to make the sensation stop. His face seemed to be growing thinner. "I don't know. I don't know why any of this is happening. I don't know why I tried to kill you." He looked up sharply. "*You must not trust me.*"

"I thought you wanted me to trust you."

He shook his head. "I want you to believe me. But—" his voice became hard—"do not trust me. No. Not at all. Not until you're sure. Until we know that I can be trusted."

She stared at him, and he looked away.

Please, Max! Hurry!

CHAPTER 9

✳

She was tightening the cords around his wrists when the door chime sounded. "Will that hold?" she asked, yanking on the knot. She circled around and stared at his face, with an expression caught somewhere between fascination and terror. He could hardly blame her.

He shrugged. "Maybe you should let him in."

As they waited for Max to come up from the lobby, he tried to remember what he could of Tamika Jones; but in this area, as in so many others, he could find only shadows of memories. He was adrift in darkness; and he dared not question her, for fear of confirming her worst suspicions. He could only guess at Tamika's feelings as she'd watched a monster who claimed to love her change, like a human chameleon, into the man she herself had known and loved.

"Willard," she said, interrupting his thoughts. "If you *are* Willard—"

He raised his eyes questioningly.

"What the hell did they do to you?" she whispered—and there was more than just fear in her voice.

Before he could answer, the inner door chimed. Tamika checked the monitor before opening the lock. "Ali-'Maksam," she murmured in relief.

Max entered, wearing what looked like a white spacesuit, with a fabric hood enclosing his head and a dark visor across his eyes. The Logothian moved with a sinuous, rippling gait, which was only partially concealed by the suit. He paused and gazed at Ruskin, who was still sitting cross-legged, and now bound, on the floor. Max's expression was concealed by the hood; but when his voice hissed out, the dismay was plain to hear. "What is the meaning of this?"

Ruskin was silent while Tamika locked the door again.

She stood, glancing between the two of them, the weapon still in her hand. "It was necessary," Ruskin said, tugging instinctively on the cords that bound his wrists. "You tell him," he said to Tamika.

"Where the hell do I start?"

"At the beginning. Don't try to make sense of it. Just say what happened, from the beginning."

She nodded, eyes half closing. When she spoke, it was in a different voice—harsh, angry, afraid. "You tried to— you came to the door, and you tried to kill me. But it wasn't you. You were different. I don't—"

"Please," Max whispered, crossing the room. "I do not understand."

They looked at one another in silence. "None of us understands," Ruskin said. "Why don't you sit, Max? But don't get too close." He tugged experimentally on the cords binding his wrists. "I don't know if this would really hold. I might do something that I can't control."

Max nodded and settled into a position on the floor that seemed more coiled than cross-legged. The Logothian, Ruskin knew, could move fast at need. "Tamika, might I ask you to dim the lights, please?" Max asked.

"But leave them bright enough to keep a watch on me," Ruskin cautioned.

"Yes. That would be satisfactory, for now," Max said.

Tamika complied and drew up a chair, so that the three of them formed a small circle in the gloom. Ali'Maksam adjusted the visor on his hood to a more nearly transparent setting and blinked at them with eyes that were large and dark, with glittering diamonds at their centers. Tamika cradled the weapon in her hand. She began explaining.

A man had come to her door and identified himself as Willard Ruskin. Having no reason to fear or doubt that it was Willard, she'd not checked the monitor before opening the door. Instead of her friend, however, she'd come face-to-face with a brawny, thick-browed man—with large hands and eyes full of hatred. She'd had no time at all to react before he'd forced his way in, pinned her against a wall, and begun choking her.

Ruskin tensed as he listened. Had *he* done that?

Max asked, "But you were able to defend yourself?"

Tamika shrugged. "I'm not defenseless. But he took me by surprise. I managed to break free, and when I saw him with this weapon, I was able to knock it out of his hand. But he caught me—and began strangling me again—" Her hand went to her throat, rubbing the spot where Ruskin's fingers had closed over her windpipe.

"But he didn't succeed," Max said.

Tamika shook her head in the near-darkness. "Something distracted him. He began acting crazy—in a different way, I mean, talking to himself or something—and I got free again. I grabbed the gun and I . . . I shot him." Her voice came near to breaking. "I shot him dead. Do you hear me, Max? *Dead*. I blew a goddamn hole in his chest—I swear it!"

For a moment, no one spoke, and Ruskin was conscious only of the slow hiss of Max's breath. The Logothian was peering with interest at Ruskin's chest—which bore a scar, but no hole, though the front of his shirt was burned open.

Tamika finally regained her voice. "I was about to call the police—wondering what the hell to tell them—when, when he . . . when he woke up. He sat up and talked to me! *Just sat right up*. And said he was Willard. But he *wasn't* Willard. He wasn't Rus'lem."

"But," Max said softly, "he appears to be Willard now."

Tamika struggled. "His—face changed. From the time I called you, until . . ." She shrugged helplessly, like a tree shaking in the gloom.

"What she says is true," Ruskin said.

"About your face?" Max asked.

"Yes. And the other—the attack."

Max gazed at him with glittering Logothian eyes. "You attacked her without warning?"

"Yes."

"Without reason? Do *you* know why you attacked her?"

Ruskin took a slow, deep breath. He shook his head; his mind was spinning. "I don't know. I have no idea. I can't *conceive* of an idea. But everything she said is true, that I can remember."

"And are you . . . Willard Ruskin?"

Ruskin barked a laugh. "As far as I know."

"And were you, when you attacked her?"

His laugh died. "That's what I want you to tell us."

Max seemed to contemplate that statement. "When did you last speak with me, Willard?" he asked. His head swayed from side to side. "When did you last see me?"

"I called you today—twice—three times—I don't know how many times. And I—I saw you—last night. Virtual. In my apartment." He closed his eyes, thinking. "Night before last, I guess it was. I've . . . lost track of time, you see."

Max gazed at him without answering.

"But why? Why, damn it?" Tamika's voice was a strained whisper. "What's happened to you? *What did they do to you?*"

He returned her agonized stare. "They?"

"You went on a trip. With some men."

"Men. Yes. I don't know." As the two stared at him, he began to explain what little he remembered.

"You wish my help in trying to understand the changes to your psyche?" Ali'Maksam asked at last.

"Yes. Everything. Tell me if I am still Willard Ruskin, if you can. If not, who am I? Or what?"

Max nodded slowly. He turned to Tamika. "If it is satisfactory with you, this will require a deep meditative state—and more complete darkness, so that I might remove my suit. I should like to invite you to join in the meditation, but the difficulty, and the danger—"

"Never mind. Just please find out what's happened to him." Tamika rose to dim the lights.

Ruskin's next words made her pause. "I'm concerned about your safety," he said slowly. "If it happens again in the dark. If I—" He cleared his throat. "Will you be able to protect yourselves?"

"I still have the gun," Tamika pointed out.

"If you kill me, I will just rise up again."

She answered as though she hadn't heard him. "I don't want to kill you," she whispered.

Max studied the two of them. "I might have some warning and be able to do something." Ruskin knew dimly what Max was going to say, before he said it. "If you threaten to become violent, I might be able to stop you . . . with inward pain. By using a technique I would greatly prefer to avoid."

Tamika scowled, but Ruskin had no hesitation. "Use it if you need to."

"It could be fatal."

"To me? I'll just come back."

"I hope so. But you may come back in pain. Severe and lasting pain."

"What I have now is worse. Do it, if you have to."

Tamika turned off the lights.

In darkness, the Logothian's voice was a dry whisper, the sound of a night wind rustling needles in a bone-dry wood.

> —*Listen to the whisper, Willard; let your feelings spin free like the winds on the plain*—

(Yes.)

It was the voice of wind, sighing across a nighttime prairie, rustling in the chimeweed that clinked softly beneath the cottony darkness of the clouds.

Ali'Maksam's voice carried him backward; took him deep into realms of solitude and memory, to a place of peacefulness where the voice of the speaker and the voices of memories stirred free and floated up and away from the confusion of feelings.

(He remembered his first sight of the plains of Kantano Aries: plume of smoke curling in the moonlight from the chimney of a solitary dwelling. It made his heart ache with a lonely thrill as he tried to remember . . . who was with him that long-ago night?)

The wind curled its way back into the forest, searching out the secret places of the heart. It became the sound of

tiny flames licking and crackling as they grew, leaping up
through a kindling of parched needles.

   —Listen to the whisper of the flame; unlock
   the inner worlds, flow deep and through and
   release them into the night—

(Memories: a night of magic and chances and love,
the first time he'd allowed himself to love again,
the night he drifted on a breeze of desire, intox-
icated . . . and slipped headlong into love with a
woman with golden eyes, a mouth that only rarely
smiled, and oddly but exquisitely angled breasts.
He remembered a smell of hazelwood and incense . . .

There were secret places too many to count; but the wind
searched where mere thought could not go. Ali'Maksam's
voice wrapped itself around his thoughts like webbing from
a magical spider of Erian, drops of dew melting into the
traps at the apexes of the webbing, releasing an aroma of
hazelwood.

   —Release, Willard; spin backward; share
   and find truth—

Whirling, rotating, it was not like any invasion he had
known; it was a mingling of thought and feeling, and his
were not the only secrets to be given up to the night.

(Of course—he had known Max as well: the wonder of discovering the soul of an alien being, the
topography of spirit so unlike, and yet so like his
own; the fascination and fear of the Kwatroni Rotation, the empathic union; the joy of discovering
a friend in the unseen places of the mind and
soul. . . .)

The wind caught him up and carried him away from that
memory. This was a time for another kind of discovering,

a search for the feelings that had twisted and distorted and carried him to a place he'd never wanted to go.

> —*Spin free*—
>   —*spin and let it free*—
>   —*spin back*—
>   —*Willard*—
>   —*release it to the flame*—

Now it hurt, the wind did; but it was a kind of hurt that made him want to find its center, to find the focus of the pain and let it out. The flame, the fire.

But it was an elemental fire in the cold and dark of space.

(He felt its heat, a terrible conflagration that would consume everything. But out of destruction, a promise of something new, something wondrous that would take his breath away . . .)

(But something was wrong. There was anger, anger that was a jet of fire—erupting from a facade of civility, making him want to strike out and destroy . . .)

The wind was trying to tell him something, but its whispering was so soft he could hear almost nothing but the pulse of blood in his ears.

(Stirring in his blood—something stirring in his blood, something he couldn't control . . .)

The whispering came now from his own blood, from the power of the thoughts that rippled up and down inside him. But were they driven by his own mind, or by Ali'Maksam, or by . . .

> —*Spin free*—
>   —*spin free*—
>   —*spin free*—

. . . by something else altogether?

Memory had slipped away, but behind it was a vacuum in which emotions could expand and take on structure.

(....frustration...
.............anger.........(against what?).............
....
....bewilderment...
....terror.............
..............longing.............................
....
.......a desperate need to know................)

(He'd been pierced; and flowing in his lifestream was a power he did not understand, did not know how to name, a power that stole his memories and desires and left behind a changeling body that could climb back from the abyss of death and assume shape at will. . . .)

(But where had it come from . . . ?)

Thundering now, the sound of the blood in his ears, in his thoughts; and whispering at the center of it, Ali'Maksam's voice, calling him deeper still into his memories; but there was only emptiness there, an echoing maze that wound forever inward.

(And enemies: dark, tall figures that brought death; but *he too could kill*, if the enemies persisted . . .)

No!

There was a voice at the center of the thunder, a voice controlling him. If only he could kill that voice . . .

No!

(It was the source of the evil.)

Willard!

(He could not be stopped.)

No!

(Yes!)

And pain shot through him like a needle, driving straight to the center of his brain, pain such as he'd never felt before. . . .

His eyes jerked open at the sound of a hoarse, rasping cry in the darkness. It was his own voice. And in front of him, scarcely visible in the light of a single red-glowing diode from the console, was the weaving form of his friend Max, gasping for breath.

The incredible hot-poker pain . . . he remembered it now. And before it, the bubbling desire—the urge to kill. *God, no!* Had he been about to try again . . . ?

"Max!" he shouted.

The Logothian's head jerked back, hissing. "Willard?" The voice was agonized.

A small white light blinked on, and there was a sudden movement, and then Tamika was crouched nearby, holding the gun near Ruskin's head in a wavering grip. "*What's going on?*" she demanded in a shrill voice.

"It's . . . all right," Max hissed. He had drawn back away from the light, covering his reptilian face with his hands. "It was not his doing. He stopped in time."

Tamika lowered the gun cautiously. "Is it safe, then? Is he . . . *is this man Willard, damn it?*"

"Yes," Max whispered. "The light—off, please!" Tamika looked from one to the other, before reluctantly dimming the lamp. Ali'Maksam quickly readjusted his garb, then said, "You may turn it on again." The light came back on. Max was in his suit again, head and body enclosed. Ruskin could just make out the diamonds of Max's eyes through the visor.

He realized now the source of the Logothian's pain. Max had stopped his incipient attack with a blast of pain, had jolted him free of the change that was coming over him. But Max had borne the pain, too, felt it as keenly as Ruskin. *The empathic connection.* Ruskin blinked, gazing at his friend. "Max—are you all right? What did you find?" He was rubbing the bridge of his nose—then realized what he was doing. He stared at the broken cords dangling from his wrists.

Ali'Maksam peered at him before answering. "You are indeed still my friend Willard. But there is a change in you."

"I know that." Ruskin tossed off the broken cords, which brought a gasp from Tamika.

Max nodded. "But why? That is the question."

"Yes."

"I suspect the answer. But I cannot be sure."

Tamika swore. "What does that mean, Max?"

Ruskin waited patiently. When Max spoke this way, answers were usually forthcoming. Eventually. He remembered that now.

"I know people who might be able to help us find out," Max answered. He looked at Ruskin, at Tamika, at Ruskin. "Do you trust me to try?"

Ruskin answered slowly, but without hesitation. "Is there anyone else we can trust?"

Tamika looked in dismay from one to the other, but Max's only answer was a chuckling whisper, a serpentine hiss.

CHAPTER 10

✴

Ruskin's living room looked as though it had been ran-sacked. The deep scarlet glow of the lights he kept for Max's visits did nothing to dispel the feeling of frightening dis-order, of strangeness. Items from his personal wardrobe lay draped across chairs. Books and albums were jumbled open on the floor. A thin streamer of smoke curled from a stick of incense. Plates and glasses littered the room. A jug of wine was barely touched, but two cartons of take-out San-yooko were nearly empty. On top of the music console was a pile of music cubes; a folk-jazz cantata, which Ruskin did not recognize, was playing.

Ruskin sat on the floor, leaning back against the sofa, gazing silently at the ceiling. Blood-red, the light. Shadow-spirits seemed to swim across the ceiling in the glow: wispy shadows cast by the tracers of incense smoke. Ever so cau-tiously, he had sipped at the wine—a little afraid of what intoxication might do to him, but desperately wanting the comfort, the relaxation of sipping good wine with friends. He hadn't felt a thing.

Tamika had drunk a small glass, to steady her nerves. She was sitting cross-legged on the overstuffed chair; she was crying now, and had been for some time. It had not been easy for her, watching him try to recap-ture lost memories, sorting in vain through piles of me-mentos in hopes of triggering a recollection, seeing him look at secrets they had shared and seeing him shrug blankly. She could have told him much of what he couldn't remember, perhaps—and did so, when he asked—but really what he wanted was to summon the recollections himself.

Max had finally advised them to stop; it was only bringing on frustration and emotional exhaustion.

How right he'd been about that. . . .

■

"What's the matter, Tamika?"

"What the hell do you think?"

"Well, I know. But I'm the one who has the problem. You look like you're taking it harder than I am."

Nod. Downturned eyes.

"So—why?"

Her gaze came up to meet his, her voice unflinching. "Because it's my fault—at least partly."

His mouth opened in astonishment. He began to laugh. In fear. "Your fault?" He looked up at Max, whose expression was inscrutable—and back at Tamika, whose gaze had not left his. "Why your fault?"

She answered with obvious difficulty. "Do you remember . . . what happened just before you went on your trip?" Even as he shook his head, she continued. "Do you remember our discussions? About the Auricle Alliance, and its expansionism in the galaxy?"

He could only gape in bewilderment.

"And you agreed with me eventually—that Kantano's World was just one more example of a world that could have gone another way, if it had been allowed to. And eventually you even said that your own work was contributing to the problem, not to its solution?"

She didn't even pause to notice his bewilderment. What could interstellar politics have to do with what happened in a forest in the wilderness? And how could he have agreed with any of that? He was as loyal an Auricle citizen as there was. . . .

He missed the next thing she said, but now she was talking about an organization she was involved in. "And you told me you were interested in Omega's plan to get people involved at the places where they worked, to try to change things from within. So I—" her voice was quavering now—"so I put you in touch with these people, and they invited you to a week-long retreat. A Mr. Broder talked to you?"

Broder!

"So you took time off." She laughed, half crying. "I wanted to go along, but they said, no, it was better if new people came alone to this kind of thing. And so instead of our taking a trip together, you see, you went off alone. And what could I say, because after all, it was my idea?" She took a rasping breath. "And the next time I saw you was in my apartment, and you were trying to kill me. . . ."

Yes. But why?

Why?

Why?

■

Ruskin gazed at the ceiling shadows, writhing and wrestling with one another, and thought of how tired he was and wondered if any of them would dare to sleep. Even his fevered alter ego must have to sleep. Surely. How long could they keep going?

At the cogitative console, Ali'Maksam sat joined to the neural interface. He'd been working there for over an hour, first trying to adjust the thinktank security system so that it would recognize its owner. Max had designed the system in the first place and had left himself coded for entry. Now he was trying to make some other arrangements about which he was being tight-lipped, something about contacting a researcher he knew.

Ruskin's gaze drifted down from the ceiling to study Max's profile, moving ever so slowly in the blood-red light, the constant motion Max displayed when he was working. To Ruskin, it was a reassuring sight: the tall, slim form of his friend, shadowy against the gloom of night . . .

. . . shadowy as it leaned toward him, figure of darkness against light . . .

■

The blurring of his consciousness ended in agony. The room wavered around him, swam in a mist-fine sea of blood. He gasped, blinking. He was crouched beside Ali'Maksam at the console. Ali'Maksam's eyes glinted as he stared at Ruskin. His scaly forehead was glistening.

"Are you two all right?" Tamika asked, looking from one to the other in puzzlement.

Ruskin took a deep breath, trying to clear his head. The

pain was gone, but he felt as though a huge bell had just rung inside his skull. "Yeah," he murmured finally. He shook his head, returning to sit on the floor. "Not all right, no." He squinted at Tamika, in a concerted effort to look— to feel—as though he were in control. "What's wrong with me?" he whispered. "Max, when are you going to tell me? Are *you* all right, Max?"

The Logothian's head bobbed, and his voice was raspy with pain. "He is safe—for the moment—Tamika. But it was again a near thing." His breath whistled in and out as his eyes slowly blinked. "Yes, I am all right. But I am an academic—not trained for this," he sighed. "Let us be grateful that it works."

Tamika frowned at the Logothian. "That really *hurts*, doesn't it?" And she shook her head as though to say, Of course it hurts, and it must be done.

Three times now Max had caught Ruskin at the brink of a blackout, and each time he had borne at least as much pain as Ruskin. When he spoke again, it was in a carefully controlled whisper. "Willard, I am assuming that the agency responsible for your physical changes is also interfering with your memory-recall—though some memory loss may have resulted from your head wound."

"I suppose losing half my head could account for some of it, yes," Ruskin grunted.

Max fingered his ridged eyebrow and spoke more energetically. "Perhaps less than you think. Your memory is hologramic, to a degree. That is, it is distributed throughout the brain, not point for point, memory for memory. The loss of some neural structure would likely cause the loss of faculties and a general degradation of memory—but not necessarily the loss of specific memories. This seems consistent with your slow, intermittent recall."

"Is that good or bad?"

"Difficult to say. Something seems to be interfering with the recall process itself. It could be psychological trauma, or something else. Whatever, it is particularly noticeable in your processing of emotion-laden memories." The Logothian smiled oddly. "That, of course, is the most interesting area to study anyway. But we must discover the agency involved."

Ruskin turned his palms up. "Maybe I should just check into a psychalign clinic."

"I suggest not. Unless I fail in my efforts here."

"Which are—?"

Max shook his head with a twitch. "I do not wish to create false hopes. I am awaiting guidance from one of my colleagues."

"And meanwhile we just sit here and wonder?"

Max chuckled, hissing. "Your console should now recognize you. Perhaps you could spend some time on your personal files. Your work files, I expect, are classified—" the Logothian glanced at Tamika—"meaning, we shouldn't see them."

Ruskin raised his eyebrows. But of course: he would not necessarily have shared all of his work knowledge with his friends.

"Personal files, then," Tamika said softly. "Rus'lem—are you ready for it?"

"Am I ready to discover who I am? I think so. Since you guys have been keeping it secret from me for so long."

Tamika tried to smile at his attempted joke. At least she'd stopped crying, for which he was thankful. He felt guilty when she cried. He rose to approach the console. Ali'Maksam bowed, making room. "I must take partial leave of you while you do this," the Logothian said. "I must try to contact another of my colleagues." He settled onto the floor. "If you please," he added softly, "keep the lights low."

Ruskin nodded and turned the hood of the holodisplay away from him. "Join me, Tamika?"

The photo files were the most tantalizing, and frustrating. It was like looking at someone else's family album—faces of people he didn't know. Often enough, the person he didn't know was himself. Willard Ruskin at home, posing by the bookcase. (Who had taken that? Tamika? From her little intake of breath, he guessed so.) A group of strangers, at a lakeside picnic. There was Willard Ruskin, among them; and there was Tamika. "Office party?" he guessed. He didn't recognize anyone else there. Maybe it was Tamika's office party. (He panicked suddenly: he couldn't remember what she did for a living. Would he have to ask, or would it come to him?) "Your office, right?" he murmured, changing the image.

She gazed at him unhappily. "Yours," she said. "Last summer. You don't remember John, or Judith? Come on, you used to have a crush on Judith."

He flipped back and studied it again. Yes, way at the back—Judith, the woman he'd talked to yesterday . . . or the day before. Had he had a crush on her once? He didn't remember. A tall, skinny man looked vaguely familiar. "John?" he asked, pointing.

"That's Todd. He was with Judith, I think." Tamika pointed to a heavyset man. "That's John."

"And what's he do?"

"He's your boss."

Ruskin stared at the image for a few seconds longer, then shook his head and flipped forward.

The next scene was a sunset, Willard Ruskin and Tamika Jones arm in arm beneath the outstretched branch of a tree, watching the sun blaze in its final glory over a mountain valley. "You and me," he said, a lump growing in his throat—not because of the memory, but because there was no memory.

He could sense Tamika's tension. She could tell that he didn't remember. She was getting ready to cry again. He could stand to cry himself, maybe, but he didn't think he knew how. Maybe that was something else he had forgotten.

The next sequence was of some astronomical images: several gorgeous star clusters, nebulas, brightly glowing filamentary structures. They almost looked alive. There was no information accompanying them; he must have filed them here because he liked them. He still liked them.

Next: a moving image of several children playing in someone's living room. He stared at them for a time, until a woman walked into the field of view. The woman looked like Tamika, but a little older, a little stockier. She mugged self-consciously at the camera. Ruskin turned to query Tamika.

"My sister Sharon and her kids," Tamika whispered. "Don't you remember *them*, even? They left for Graemonholde last year, and we gave them a big send-off."

He winced at the pleading in her voice, and had no answer. He started to flip.

Her hand stopped him. "Please—she begged, her whisper becoming a cry. She shook her head and turned away, blowing her nose. When she looked back, her eyes were glistening. "Could we stop for a while?"

He stared at the image for a moment longer, before murmuring, "Screen dark." He rose, his eyes not quite focusing in the dim red illumination. Tamika returned to her chair, rubbing her eyes. Max was gazing in Ruskin's direction, but his inner eyes were directed elsewhere. Ruskin turned and walked through the kitchen into the bathroom.

Closing the door, he turned the light up slowly, to about half-normal. He gazed impassively into the mirror. His face was familiar enough to him now. Fair skin, brown hair, green eyes with a shade of gray—now, at least. It was familiar enough to despise, to fear.

Damn you—you were beginning to remember things before. It was coming back. You remembered Max . . . Tamika . . . so why not now? Finally you've got pictures here to see—and your brain's nothing but a lump.

First you try to kill the woman you love. Now you're killing her slowly, breaking her heart. What next?

He closed his eyes and breathed deeply. He had bought a weapon, unaware; he had tried to kill a woman, unaware. Had he tried to kill anyone else? *Had* he killed anyone else?

He examined his fingertip, the tiny bump there. He remembered fire blazing from that fingertip—from what was apparently an implanted, or biologically grown, weapon.

Slowly he raised his finger to eye level and placed its tip directly between his eyes. What if he fired it right now? It would be a terrible, perhaps a cowardly, thing to do—but if he didn't stop himself, who would? He remembered, dimly, the blast that had taken half his head off—years ago, it seemed. He remembered himself rising, like the phoenix, from the dead.

But suppose you hit the one point in the brain that contains the vital structure that enables everything else to work. The central processor of the soul. The one point that, if you vaporize it, cannot be restored. Surely there is such a point.

He closed his eyes, willing the finger to fire.

He opened his eyes and looked cross-eyed down his finger. With a bitter laugh, he dropped his hand to his side. How could he kill himself if he didn't know how to fire his finger?

Probably it wouldn't have worked anyway.

He relieved himself, snapped off the light, and returned to the hearth-red sanctum of the living room. Tamika looked up at him. "You okay?"

"Okay is a relative word." He let his gaze drift around the room without seeing. "Yeah. I guess I'm okay."

With a sigh, he returned to the console. Maybe what he hadn't learned from his photo files, he would find in his financial records, bills, receipts, and appointments past and future. Somewhere there had to be a key that would release his past.

As he adjusted the display-screen hood, Max stirred where he sat on the floor. His voice whispered, echoing in the stillness and the gloom: "I have arranged an appointment, Willard."

Ruskin looked up. "Should I hope?"

Max's head tilted, his eyes glinted. "Hope, yes. But do not expect."

PART TWO

✳

WORLDS WITHIN

"Being invisible to every mortal nature, he is seen through his works themselves."
—Aristotle, on God

PROLOGUE

✳

Starmuse Station
Auricle Alliance Science Council
in close orbit, Alpha Orionis A (Betelgeuse)
Date: 5/9/178

The memo glowed irritatingly on the screen, until Thalia Sharaane cleared the workspace with an angry flick of her hand. As if she didn't have enough to worry about, with convergence fast approaching, now she had to start getting complaints from the guest observers. Their complaints—and questions—were becoming increasingly difficult to answer.

"We request explanation for your refusal to abide by the joint worlds exploration agreement. . . ."

Request, indeed. The joint worlds agreement had made no guarantees. It was a carefully crafted diplomatic deception to appease the observer-status worlds, a pretext to give the Alliance expedition freedom from interference for the critical time period needed to complete the project.

Requests from the Querayn Academies she could usually deal with, at least in principle. The robed scholars were actually here for purported scientific studies, even if their subject was nonexistent, in her opinion. They were attempting to observe the so-called Kônô consciousness of the sun, an alleged primitive sentience for which they had never produced any actual evidence. Still, it was a harmless endeavor, and it added a layer of scientific legitimacy to the whole "Starmuse" side of the project. Unfortunately, the Querayn were becoming increasingly demanding, in their polite scholarly fashion, about their need for better data—and, by extension, their dissatisfaction over their restricted movements about the station. There was little she could do about it; they wouldn't be here at all but for politics beyond her control. As for the data they wanted: if they were given access to much more, they might begin to suspect how they were being misled.

Frowning, Thalia shook her head. She hated this; she was supposed to be a scientist, not a diplomat—or professional liar. But she had to draw the line somewhere.

And as for the Tandeskoes, her patience had long since given out. She scarcely understood why they'd even been allowed status here. Relations between the Auricle Alliance and the Tandesko Triune were deteriorating, almost to the point of outright hostility. The culmination of this project would hardly improve matters in that regard—which, in truth, she regretted. Certainly, she had no love for the Triune worlds, which were competing for the same regions of space as the free-marketing Auricle Alliance—nor for Triune citizens, who willingly submitted to the authoritarianism of their regime. It was a strange interspecies union, the Triune. In addition to its political insufferability, it was marred by deviant social mores: many of the Tandeskoes gave themselves over to a psychosexual bonding system that repelled her, that she couldn't and didn't want to understand. They claimed that their way offered a "deep-soul" spiritual experience that the "bonding-free," as they referred to Auricle citizens, would never comprehend. Sharaane doubted the claim, and found the whole system morally questionable. In any case, she was proud of Alliance leadership in galactic exploration and had no intention of seeing it eroded by a group of political and social fanatics. On the other hand, she had no desire to be the cause of an interstellar incident.

The memo. You can't just ignore the memo.

She sighed and punched the call-code for the chief Tandesko representative. There was a short delay before the narrow-faced, bony countenance of the man appeared in her screen. He was wearing a high-collared shirt bearing a three-pointed starburst emblem on his shoulder. His gaze was sharp, his eyebrows perpetually arched. He was a Tandesko *talisan*, a so-called "wielder of communication and understanding"—and among his own people, he actually appeared to carry out that role. How, was beyond her. Granted that they were in adversarial roles, she could still scarcely ever see eye to eye with him. "Greetings, Talis," she said wearily.

"Dr. Sharaane. Madame Director—you have received my request?" the Tandesko asked.

"I have. I'm afraid I must deny it," Thalia said. "I want you to know that there is no personal animus toward your team."

The Tandesko's gaze did not soften. "May I ask for an explanation, in view of the joint worlds agreement that both of our governments are committed to . . ."

She let him run on for a few moments. Explanation? What did he think? The Tandeskoes were demanding access to primary instrumentation in the station's control room—a ridiculous demand, in view of the directive to visiting observers: that this close-range study of Alpha Orionis was funded by the Auricle Science Council, and that while the council was pleased to share scientific data, it was unwilling to reveal proprietary technologies used in the gathering of the data. To do so in the present interstellar marketplace could jeopardize Auricle leadership in certain competitive disciplines. And that was perhaps true . . . as far as it went. "You know the directive as well as I do," she said finally, when the Tandesko had run out of words.

"As you know, we consider that directive to fall short of the agreement, Dr. Sharaane."

"I am aware of your feelings, Talis. Perhaps in a time of better political rapport, the directive could be loosened. But I have my responsibilities laid out for me by those who—"

"Really, Madame Director—" the talisan protested.

"And now, I must deny your request. I have urgent work before me. Good day, Talis," she said sharply. And with a jerk of her finger, she broke the connection.

She glared at the screen until her temper subsided. *I'm a scientist. Why am I dealing with this crap?* She couldn't help wondering if the Tandeskoes might in fact suspect the real purpose of "Starmuse." Well, she could only guess how they would react when they learned the full truth. But that was supposed to be for Auricle policymakers to worry about, not her.

However, one thing she *was* worried about, in the absence of word from their missing team member, was that he might somehow have been waylaid—or turned from his intention to rejoin the project. Was it possible that Tandesko mischief was to blame? Or interference from one of the dozens of other splinter groups that might have learned of the project? She doubted it; the man had only barely agreed to be present at all, to come out of his self-imposed exile. She had not given up hope; but in the meantime, she had to be ready with alternative plans.

Turning, she punched up station security and spoke to the console. "Memo from the Director to Security Chief: It may become necessary to isolate all guest-observers until the culmination of Breakstar. I would prefer to avoid this, for obvious political considerations. However, I want special attention paid to any breaches or attempted breaches of visitor restrictions. Please report to me soonest on your current appraisal of secrecy. End memo."

At last, she turned back to the science that was awaiting her. She was coordinating one of the most difficult and ambitious projects in human history. Decisions had to be made, whether she had everyone here to help her or not.

As she summoned the latest remote-sat readings to her console, she was deeply conscious of the gigantic crimson sun swimming in the big wall-screen—the star Betelgeuse, in which she and her station floated like a speck of plankton in a vast ocean of fire. And more than ever, she was keenly aware of the swift passage of time, and of the approaching convergence that no human agency could stop now.

CHAPTER 11

✳

"Do come in."

The voice came from a mural on the wall of what looked like a reception room—except that there was no one visible to greet them. Tamika looked as puzzled as Ruskin, and Max's expression was hidden behind his visor. They had entered a low, brick-fronted building at the edge of the city—having followed a tortuously evasive route here at the request of the man they were scheduled to see. Ruskin had thought the request odd, until they'd passed through a commercial security screen, which had informed him of the presence of a tiny locator-transponder in his wallet. They'd gotten rid of that, and taken extra care the rest of the way here.

Ruskin studied the mural. It filled the wall: a winter forest scene, trees capped and frosted with snow. "Where do we go in?" he asked, looking for an inner door. As he spoke, a mound of snow fell from a tree in the mural. It puffed into the air, sparkling, and drifted out of the wall. He felt a tingle of bracing cold on his cheeks.

"Follow the trail," answered the voice. A line of footsteps appeared in the mural, leading away through the trees. Ruskin's gaze narrowed. They were supposed to walk into a hologram, then?

Exchanging glances with the others, he stepped forward through the wall. He shivered, blinded momentarily by a swirl of snow. When he blinked his eyes clear, he looked down and saw a path at his feet, through real snow that scrunched underfoot. The path behind them led across a whitened meadow; there was no sign of a wall or of the reception room they had just left.

"What the hell?" Tamika said. "I thought this was supposed to be a laboratory."

Ruskin glanced at Ali'Maksam, who was staring straight ahead, showing no reaction. Ruskin thought that Max looked worn. They all did; they had not left one another's company in twenty-four hours, and in that period, Max had five times kept Ruskin from blacking out—each time at great cost to himself. "You okay, Max?" Ruskin asked.

The Logothian turned first one way, then the other, his eyes blinking one at a time behind his visor. "It's not precisely what I expected. But I understand that E'rik Daxter is . . . unusual. He's nearly three hundred years old as a nonincarnate, and I suppose one's tastes might . . . evolve, in that time."

"Nonincarnate? You mean, cyber-consciousness?"

"One of the very first. He died, physically, several centuries ago."

Ruskin was impressed. One of the first? There weren't many, even now, who chose—or could afford—that form of immortality. Ruskin looked up into the treetops. The leaves and needles seemed to glimmer in the fading "daylight." He thought he'd seen something move overhead. Shading his eyes, he searched the high branches. He *had* seen something, and there it was again—a dark shape jumping from one tree to the next. A small animal? Perhaps just the image of one.

Was this whole scene an illusion? No—when he reached out to brush snow from a branch, his fingers touched icy grains and prickly-soft needles. There was a chill in the air, but he didn't feel cold.

"Please come!" said a voice deeper in the woods.

Ruskin moved on, followed by his friends.

The path led through a dense thicket of trees, into a small clearing. The light was fading rapidly, but over their heads appeared a number of softly luminous globes, drifting among the branches. As Ruskin turned, Max's eyes looked like two points of light floating in blackness, behind his visor. The Logothian spoke before Ruskin could ask. "I believe we are in the right place."

A cloud of what looked like fireflies floated over their

heads and alighted among the branches. The cloud coalesced into a glowing man-shaped form, sitting in the tree. "Welcome," it said. "How may I help you?"

Ruskin took a deep breath. "Well—"

And Tamika finished, "We were told that there was a laboratory here, and that a Dr. Daxter could examine Willard and find out what's wrong with him. Are you E'rik Daxter, or can you tell us where he is?" Impatience was plain upon her face.

The shape answered without expression. "I am E'rik Daxter. Whether or not I can help remains to be seen."

"Then—excuse me, but what's all *this*?" Tamika gestured around them.

The glowing shape seemed to solidify further, until an identifiable face appeared, narrow and bony, with real-looking eyes. Daxter chuckled, the first sign he had shown of human emotion. "If you had three hundred seventy years behind you, you might be more relaxed about the urgencies of the moment, too. Please excuse my foibles."

He was interrupted by a hiss from Max. The Logothian had drawn away from the tree nearest him. "Max?" Ruskin asked, and at once saw the answer. A small creature in the tree, about the size of a large squirrel, was peering at Max with great interest. It had glistening black fur, two eyes on each side of its head, and a tapered snout that gaped open, displaying long rows of gleaming teeth. It was panting slowly.

"What the hell?" Ruskin said, allowing Max to edge past him. The creature seemed to have eyes only for the Logothian.

Daxter's eyes followed the movement. "Oh dear—"

He was interrupted by another hiss. Now Ali'Maksam was backing away from another tree. Peering out of this one was a red, oblong thing that looked as though it were made of gelatin. It was full of eyes, and it was oozing forward toward Max. "Terrakells!" the Logothian whispered, drawing into a crouch.

"What *are* they?" Tamika asked. "They're creepy."

Ruskin realized that his own hands were clenched—a reaction to the others' fear. Or was it just that? He felt a

strange tingling at the back of his neck. What *were* these
things?

"They are terrakells—quite harmless, really." Daxter
muttered something that was a mix of squeaks and guttural
hiccups. "But they are curious. I'm afraid they have a tendency to fixate on those who are most wary of them."

One after another, the creatures twittered and drew back
into the trees. Ruskin could have sworn he saw the flutter
of a silvery wing on the first. The second extended a rubbery
pod backward, then recoiled out of sight.

Max slowly rose from his crouch. "I . . . apologize."

"Quite all right. My fault," Daxter said.

Ruskin felt an almost physical sense of relief where the
uneasy tingling had been.

"My fear is quite irrational," Ali'Maksam explained quietly. "It is their empathic faculties. I cannot, for some reason—they do not mesh with my own, without—" The
Logothian was uncharacteristically at a loss for words.
"Well, I find them upsetting; that is all I can say."

"Terribly sorry," Daxter said. "They are excellent company to me. But I will try to keep them out of your way."

Max bowed slightly.

"Would someone explain to *me*?" Tamika demanded.

"The terrakells are empathic shapechangers. Marvelous
companions, if one has a rapport with them," Daxter said.
"But they can be rather alarming otherwise, I suppose."
He turned his glowing head. "Ali'Maksam, I did not realize
that Logothians were shy of terrakells."

"They are not, generally," Max said. "It is my own . . .
foible."

Ruskin recognized the embarrassment in Max's voice.
Defensively, he interrupted: "Perhaps now you could let
us in on the meaning of all this, Dr. Daxter."

"My forest? Why, that's simple enough . . ."

Daxter's voice suddenly became indistinct, as did the
woods.

Blurring . . .

∎

An iron-hot poker brought him back to reality with a
gasp. He struggled to catch his breath. Ali'Maksam, beside

him, was in worse distress, his breath hissing in and out rapidly. But Daxter was speaking, and his voice was full of urgency. ". . . can wait. I did not realize the immediacy of your danger. We must begin the examination immediately."

Ruskin heard Tamika say, "That's what we're here for. Where's your laboratory?" Then he felt himself growing light, as though his feet were leaving the ground.

As though he were floating.

A warm radiance from somewhere seemed to envelop him. A relaxing glow filled his thoughts and his consciousness. He blinked drowsily and saw a moonbeam breaking through the treetops, illuminating him. He drifted among the trees, bathed in a surreal moonglow; and he was aware of his friends on the ground, peering up at him.

A creature with gossamer wings fluttered out of the darkness and flew around him, circling; its breath, glittering like a cloud of tiny swarming sprites, enveloped him in a haze of light. He wondered sleepily what the creature was doing. . . .

A voice reached him through a luminous, cottony ether. It was a familiar voice, though it took some time to recognize it as the voice of E'rik Daxter—dead to human form for three hundred years, but alive and well in an organocrystalline cogitative system. It was the voice of the man whose expertise Ali'Maksam had sought out, in hopes of solving the mystery that was destroying Ruskin's life. It sounded like the tinkling of a hundred chimes, all lost in the haze of mist and light that surrounded him.

It was difficult to remember where, exactly, he was. He had the feeling that he had blacked out more than once recently—that personalities that were not his own had rampaged through his soul.

(Can you hear me . . . ?)

Hear? Yes, of course he could hear. What was he supposed to do? Where was the flying creature? He remembered a flying creature.

(If you can hear me, I want you to know what I am doing.)
Doing . . .

Chimes in the middle of a pleasant, drifting doze . . .

(You are being examined. If you feel unusual sensations, do not be alarmed and do not resist; however, please report them to me as they occur. Can you hear me, and can you reply?)

Ruskin opened his mouth, but couldn't quite make a sound. What was wrong?

(You won't be able to move until we're done. But if you can formulate the words in your mind, I should be able to pick them out of the noise without too much trouble.)

Out of the noise?

(That's right. You're hooked into the cogitative thinktank, which should speed things up a bit.)

What are you doing to me?

(Medical scan, including molecular-scale sampling. I think, frankly, that someone's been tampering with your molecules.)

Is that a joke?

(Yes and no. Can you feel what I am doing now?)

Prickling sensation. You're poking me with needles.

(Yes. And you are healing almost instantly from the wounds. I am investigating the process on a microscopic and molecular level. I would like to try a slightly greater injury, if you don't mind—)

The hell you—ow!

(Remarkable. The incision is closing already. Well, my basic hypothesis is confirmed. But I must refine my understanding.)

Damn it, tell me what's happening!

(I would almost like to try something more drastic—say, the amputation of a limb—to observe healing in a more extreme instance—)

WHAT?

(—but in fairness, you came for help, not to be used as a guinea pig—so I will refrain.) There was a chuckling sound.

Jesus, Max, who is this guy . . . ?

The cottony feeling closed in around him again, and he felt himself drifting off into a nether realm of not-quite-sleep. He was aware of Daxter muttering in the background; he was aware of changes in the light-field that surrounded

him; he was aware of a prickling electrical presence. He
was aware of impulses to move, to run, to hide, to strike
and kill—and of the impulses evaporating even as they
arose. He was aware of voices, some of them his own:

Buy a starship and prepare for . . .

■

Enemies . . . must be willing to destroy . . .

■

The one who tried to kill you will return . . .

And some of them the voices of his friends, indistinct at
first and then becoming clearer:

Max: *(. . . as I suspected, but there was no way to be
certain without scanning completely.)*

And Tamika: *(Are you sure? How could they have done
this without his being aware?)*

And Daxter again: *(A simple injection would suffice; the
NAGs are self-replicating and could populate his body in a
matter of hours. It's the programming and design that's
hard. But even if he had known and agreed, his knowledge
might have been altered after the fact. It is clear that his
cognitive processes are being manipulated. . . .)*

He struggled to bring himself to full consciousness, to
form the thoughts clearly in his mind:

What are you talking about?

The others stirred in the nonphysical realm around him,
and Daxter answered, *(Sorry. We have confirmed that you
are infected with NAGs.)*

I beg your pardon?

*(Molecular-sized, invasive agents. Nano-agents. NAGs. A
bit smaller than viruses, but not actually living. Machines.
Intelligent cell-repair machines. Except that—)*

Wait a minute. Cell-repair machines don't—

*(As I say, these are not conventional medical cell-repair
machines. Their programming is . . .)*

That's what I mean, they—

*(. . . quite illegal, actually. And that's what makes this
so interesting.)*

Interesting? Ruskin simply blanked for an instant and
floated in a dreamy space of wind and light. There were
the chimes again, speaking to him. They rang with a clear,

melodic sound; and Daxter's voice was present in the center of his mind, speaking with urgency:

(It is vital that you understand this. You are familiar with the uses of cell-repair NAGs in medicine?)

The answer floated into his thoughts from some packet of information learned long ago:

Healing, at the cellular level: molecule by molecule, controlled by intelligence units far smaller than the organelles within cells. They were self replicating—

—and incredibly fast by human standards.

(Exactly. Your healing is faster than anything I've ever seen. But medical units are designed to heal and then to self-destruct harmlessly in the bloodstream. The legal regulations are quite strict, because of the potential for abuse. They could be programmed wrong, or used to create genetic monsters, or to deliberately manipulate . . .)

Manipulate!

(Yes. And now, are you beginning to understand?)

I am being controlled by these—

(Not only controlled. Altered. The changes in your facial appearance were caused by a deliberate disassembling and reassembling of your bone and tissue structure.)

But that fast?

(The time scale of molecular-repair operations is utterly beyond your experience. Consider the difference between manual arithmetic and organocrystalcore operations. The difference is similar.)

But WHY?

(Ah. That is the question. Why. I do not know. But we can assume that the manipulation of your consciousness is the primary tool—for whatever objective. The changing of your physical appearance probably is a secondary tool.)

But . . . who would want me to go crazy like this? Who would want me to . . . kill Tamika?

(I cannot say. But someone went to a great deal of trouble to do this to you. It would be staggeringly difficult to program NAGs for reliable manipulation of thought or behavior. I am astonished—and impressed. To repair a billion strands of DNA causing a genetic defect is simple, compared to the difficulty of altering the chemical and neurological

structure of the brain in order to manipulate a man's thoughts, emotions, actions. I cannot even say what degree of control is possible. It may in fact be that this effort, whatever its purpose, has gone awry.)

Then that is why I am blacking . . .

(Your blackouts may indicate a struggle between your own mind and the nano-agents.)

Dear God. Can't you help me? Max!

(Ruskin, we are trying. But Ali'Maksam cannot continue saving you from the blackouts. It is killing him. Therefore we must find another countermeasure.)

What can you possibly do?

(If we cannot beat them, perhaps we can join them.)

Funny.

(Not meant to be. If the replicating agents in your system were designed for longevity, and to deliberately control you for someone else's purposes, then we probably have no hope of removing them from your body. But we can design new NAGS, *programmed to act defensively, which you could communicate with through their direct interaction with your brain chemistry.)*

That sounds—

(Frightening? Perhaps, but—)

How can I control things I can't even understand? How can I defend myself when I can't see what the enemy is doing?

(I am going to try to make it possible for you to see. And to understand. And to take appropriate action. But you are going to have to trust me.)

Trust? Why do I have the feeling that I was told that once before? And that is why I am here now.

(Indeed—you trusted Max. And you came here.)

That's not what I meant.

(I know it's not.)

I meant the people who did this to me. Was it Broder? Or Jeaves?

(I cannot tell you whom to trust. That you must decide for yourself.)

Max. Tamika.

(Would you like to confer with your friends?)

Yes. Please . . .

* * *

Perhaps he lost consciousness, or perhaps he simply blinked, but without knowing how, he found himself back in communication with Ali'Maksam and Tamika. The first thing he realized was that Max was trying to reassure him: Max trusted E'rik Daxter.

That meant a lot. But it wasn't enough.

Where am I, Max? What has happened to me?

(You are being held suspended in a medical scanning field which looks like a cloud of forest sprites in a moonbeam. Your link with E'rik in the thinktank is protecting you against lapses or violent blackouts. You could not move or harm anyone even if you wanted to.)

Should I want to?

(Rus'lem, what do you mean?) That was Tamika.

Well, I tried to kill you, and I don't know why. Who is this man, really—and why should I trust him?

Max answered carefully: *(He was one of the original experts in the field of artificially intelligent nano-agents. You don't know him because he's out of the public eye now. He does his own eccentric brand of research, and you can see the results of some of it in his lab. The forest is part holo, part forcefield manipulation, part artificial substance created by—)*

Nano-agents?

(Yes.)

He is very clever, then. But that doesn't tell me: Is he honest? Is he wise?

Max's reply came as a mixture of thought and feeling, and echoes of images they had shared over the years: trust and caring shaped by knowledge of one another and by faith, and sometimes by fear, as well. He felt echoes of Max's own fear, minutes ago, of the creatures that Daxter kept as companions or pets. *(He keeps beings that frighten me, yes. But my reaction to his creatures is not his fault. Just as Tamika's fear and distrust of me are not my fault. Or so you judged in the past. You have trusted Tamika and me both.)*

Tamika's voice: *(Max, I don't—)*

(Yes, you do, Tamika—though your fears are lessening. And yes, Willard—I trust this E'rik Daxter. And he is trusted by people whom I trust.)

Then I, perhaps, should trust him, too.

(Have you decided?) Daxter queried.

Yes.

(You wish me to try to help you in this way?)

Yes.

(Then I am going to have to ask you to sleep for a time. When you awaken, you will have a great deal to learn. A very great deal. . . .)

CHAPTER 12

✴

He woke just long enough to realize that he was in bed in a bright and airy place. As his eyes swam into focus, he was aware of Tamika and Max seated on either side of him, and he heard their voices and Daxter's; a moment later, it all slipped away. He went to sleep again thinking that it was odd that they seemed not to have been talking to him, or paying any attention to him at all.

But to whom, he wondered, were they talking?

When he returned to a kind of consciousness, it was with a feeling that he had been hearing voices for a long, long time—as though he were seated at the center of an enormous classroom, and all around him voices were declaiming on the intricacies of molecular biology, brain physiology, memory-trace chemistry—one subject after another—and sometimes several simultaneously. It was not like other times, when the voices he'd heard were his own; these were voices talking *at* him, lecturing him.

He was not fully awake to wonder about it. But neither was he dreaming, exactly. He had no sensation of body, only of thought. And his thoughts were being *led*.

But by whom? Whose were these voices?

(*The correct balance can be achieved only through your watchfulness, together with the monitoring of the new units. Clear feedback of information is crucial. . . .*)

(*Discrepancies must be analyzed so that countermeasures can be programmed and executed. . . .*)

There was a familiar quality to the voice, but he was distracted from trying to identify it by a sudden feeling of

111

urgency, a feeling that he needed to understand its message:

(The population of replicating units has now reached two thirds of optimal; saturation will be achieved within the hour. Expect a period of disorientation. There will be a learning interval, in which the units will map and determine parameters for action, and communications procedures will evolve. During this period, you may be subject to invader actions which you will be unable to counter. Expect this. It is why you are being kept immobile. . . .)

He listened in puzzlement, with only the haziest idea of what was being talked about. After a while, thankfully, the voices went away.

He slept in a land of green rolling clouds. . . .

The next time he heard the voices, he was feeling more awake. He was in a *place* now, or at least was surrounded by the image of one: a vast cavern of some sort. His first thought was that he had blacked out again. What mischief was he into now?

"Come along," he heard and was startled to realize that a huge, floating snowflake had just addressed him in a voice very much like E'rik Daxter's. He himself was (apparently) standing at one end of an enormous underground cavern half-obscured by geologic growths from walls and ceiling and floor—stalactites and stalagmites and heaven knew what else. The air was crisscrossed by strands of something that looked like threads of melted translucent plastic. Some of them were lighting up intermittently, flickering.

"What did you say?" he murmured.

The snowflake's voice was stronger this time. "I *said*, there's a great deal you have to see. Come and let me show you." The snowflake pulsed with its own inner light and floated away from him.

"*Okay.*" Ruskin hurried to keep up. "But would you mind telling me where we are?"

"Your brain, idiot."

Ruskin blinked and followed. "Of course. My brain. How stupid of me." The snowflake glided up and over a craggy ridge, then floated out into space over a startling drop-off.

Ruskin followed. "What do you mean we're in my brain?" he asked finally.

The snowflake paused and rotated. Several of its crystal facets sparkled. He had the feeling that they were eyes, watching him. "Haven't you been listening?"

Ruskin gestured helplessly.

"Okay, never mind." The snowflake rotated again, and rays of light flashed out from its facets, glimmering off distant points in the cavern. "Look around. You're getting a conceptual tour of your brain."

"I beg your pardon?"

The snowflake sighed. "Forget it. You'll pick it up as we go along."

"Wait a minute. Are you *really* inside my head?"

"Of course. I'm stimulating arrays of nerve endings to communicate my thoughts and convey the appropriate visual sensations. You're not seeing a *literal* view of your brain, obviously. I mean, I don't have cameras, or—"

"But you're—are you E'rik Daxter? You sound like him. Or are you . . . a NAG?"

"Nag, nag, nag—here a nag, there a nag—yes, that's me."

"Be serious, damn it!"

"Yes, I am a NAG, imprinted with certain personality aspects of E'rik Daxter. You can call me Dax, if you like."

"Huh? Where are you, exactly?"

"All through your body. I'm not really *a* NAG. I'm more like a colony consciousness."

Ruskin blinked, or felt that he did.

"Now then, what do you know about the molecular physiology of thought and memory?"

"Not too much."

The snowflake bobbed slowly in the air. "Just as well, I suppose. Half of it's a mystery, and the other half wouldn't help you much. But there are certain things you ought to know." Ruskin waited while Dax paused, as though in thought. "A lot of your memory is distributed throughout the brain," Dax said suddenly. "That is, it's not all lined up point by point, a memory here, a memory there. It's more like—"

"A hologram," Ruskin said. Ali'Maksam had talked about that.

"Well, yes, although the hologramic model doesn't entirely hold up. However, holograms and the brain have this in common: both have even the simplest information stored in a distributed fashion. You can cut out a piece of a hologram or the brain and still have intact information, though you lose some detail."

"Right. Everyone knows that."

"Terrific. Proud of you. Nevertheless, the memory is still fixed in the neurological structure of the brain. But on the molecular level, which is where the NAGs are interfering with you, your memory does not for the most part exist in discrete nerve cells. It's spread out and cleverly interlaced, so that you can't fool with one memory without messing up others, as well. That makes it tougher to implant fictional memories, for example. Millions of nerve cells would have to be altered to implant a single memory."

"Yes, but I—"

"Shut up and let me finish. The point is that memories are modulated by the entire brain chemistry. Specific memories are addressed by association with other memories, and memory-recall is affected by emotional state, which is tied up with the limbic system—the so-called primitive brain, though actually it's not primitive at all. The limbic system is complex, delicate, and absolutely essential to the functioning of human consciousness. What you need to know about the limbic system is that it's a key point at which thoughts, especially emotion-laden thoughts, can be altered or subtly deflected."

"By the NAGs. They're screwing around with my emotions."

"Among other things. In so doing, they're exerting influence on your behavior, because you are an emotional being. They're also, indirectly, changing your memories—in effect, if not in fact—by distorting the ways in which they are recalled. It's easier to block recall, or to change its emotional coloration, than it is to alter its content. For example, your apparent hatred of the Tandesko Triune and everything connected with it . . ."

That caught him by surprise. *Apparent* hatred? Just hearing the name of that group of worlds made his vision darken.

"See what I mean?" Dax said softly.

"No. I don't." But he felt an unnerving sense of dread, an uncertainty as to whether he could trust even such a basic emotion.

The snowflake rotated sideways, and a structure off to one side of the cavern lit up in blue light. It looked like a melting ice sculpture on a pedestal, with a single large structure arching out to the cavern wall. Within it, cells were flickering. "Here's a portion of your limbic system. Now look closely."

Ruskin looked. He hadn't noticed it before, but a thin haze was enveloping the structure—a cloud of swarming dust-motes. As he watched, the icelike structure shimmered: tiny cracks forming, then healing instantly, leaving behind almost invisible changes.

"Those are unfriendly NAGs. I can't tell you yet exactly what they're doing, but it's definitely having an effect. Some of your strong emotional reactions may be a result of what's happening there right now."

"Can't you stop them?"

"I hope to be able to. But I can't overcome them by numbers alone; that would turn your body into a battlefield, and probably harm you more than it would help. We must take more subtle action, and that means observing and trying to discern patterns, and from the patterns, purpose. Then we can try to devise action. In the meantime, our action will have to be limited to emergency—"

"Hold it!"

The highlighted structure darkened, and the snowflake waited patiently.

"You're saying that you don't *know* what they're doing, even though you're right in there, in *me*, watching them work?"

Dax sparkled. "I can observe structural changes, but I cannot describe all of their consequences. I cannot yet predict, for example, the emotional change that will come of what we just observed."

"Then how am I supposed to know what I'm really feeling? *Me*. What *I'm* feeling."

"Precisely. That is the problem. I cannot know the intelligence behind the unfriendlies. I can only watch, infer tactics and purpose, and attempt to build a base of knowledge. And my conclusions will only be hunches."

"But can't you *read* their knowledge base? Or find whatever is controlling them and destroy it? I thought it was all contained in the NAGS."

"Of course, but there is no single agent in control. Remember, this image of *me* is only a representation for convenience. Like me, they are a dispersed collection of molecular-sized processors, all working in concert. And their knowledge and purpose is dispersed through millions of agents, each carrying some part of the information, with lots of redundancy. If I were to begin destroying individual agents in hopes of destroying their intelligence, they could begin replicating faster than I could destroy them, and so perpetuate their command structure. It might force an evolutionary adaptation, but that would probably just work against us. But as I said, we can watch it unfold. Observe—"

Everything went dark for a moment, and then a new image came to life around him: tumbling molecules colliding, glinting with energy changes, twisting and contorting following the collisions. A tremendously complex molecule appeared, with bonds that rotated and stretched, chains of atoms all bound together, but folding and twisting like a fantastic puzzle. "You see," said Dax's voice, "this molecule carries information in the positions of the atoms, in the bumps and depressions in the chains, in the bonding levels. The processors that read it know the language, the form of the coding; they know the kind of information to expect. I know none of that; but even if I did, I could not read all of the secrets in this molecule, because the programming resides not just in the structures, but in the ways that they come together as the chains fold and join, or as other molecules collide, leaving segments or taking them away."

"Then how the hell am I supposed to *know* anything? What's the *point*?"

"I merely state the problem. The solution is to watch the patterns unfold, and to be quick to comprehend and respond. In short—to be smarter than they are."

Ruskin was silent for a long time. He felt as though he

were panting, as though he could not catch his breath. He was afraid. "How can we hope to beat it," he whispered finally, "if I don't know what is me . . . what are my thoughts, my feelings, my memories? How can we possibly beat it?"

Dax reappeared, twinkling. "We cannot—immediately. That is why we must uncover the hidden purpose. Willard, this problem does not concern you alone. We are all of us involved. It is conceivable that entire worlds are involved."

He was stunned. "*Worlds?* What do you mean?"

"What has been done to you has not been accomplished by a minor technology, nor at any small expense. Someone wielding considerable resources is attempting to control you. Consider your body's capabilities: it can heal itself from terrifying wounds, it can change shape at will, it can control your thoughts and actions. And in your finger is a laser grown by NAGS, controlled by your nervous system, and powerful enough to kill. Does this suggest anything to you?"

It suggested only one thing to Ruskin, and he did not want to voice it.

"I was thinking, myself, that a special agent for any one of a dozen organizations would be happy to have those attributes," Dax said.

"Sounds good to me," Ruskin whispered. It did not sound good to him at all.

"You could make a formidable enemy."

Ruskin felt dizzy. "Enemy to whom?"

"We'll never know if we don't let it act itself out."

Too many things were hitting him; he could scarcely think. Too many thoughts wanted to get out at once. Finally he said, "There is another way."

"Yes?"

He hesitated. "You could kill me now. While I'm immobile. Destroy me. Annihilate me."

The snowflake pulsed with light. "Kill to prevent killing?"

"I'd give you permission," he said, struggling to get the words out. The words resisted; he did not want to die yet.

"Would you?"

"I'd . . . try."

"And so you might," Dax said. "So you might. But that wouldn't solve the whole problem—as I was trying to explain. Willard, someone has done a terrible thing to you. We need to discover who has done it, and why."

"Oh."

"So it might let *you* off if we kill you. But what about everyone else?"

"Everyone else, who?"

"Whole worlds, possibly, as I said."

"Oh, yes. You said that. Right."

Dax was silent for a moment. "Ruskin, we need you to act as a detective. Against yourself. It's unlikely that you were intended to kill Tamika Jones. In light of everything you've told me, I'd guess that that was a malfunction in the programming. But we need you to find out what crime you *were* created to commit."

The silence this time was prolonged. Ruskin saw no way out of the argument. At last he sighed. "What about the authorities. Shouldn't we go to them?"

Dax seemed to hesitate. "You may, of course, if you believe it the right thing to do. But frankly—well, there are many different authorities. Which ones would you trust? And consider who might have done this to you."

"Broder." And at once he realized: he didn't know whom Broder really worked for. And he didn't know how to find the man. Broder had said he was going off-planet; he could be anywhere now.

"My list of suspects starts with the government," Dax said.

Ruskin considered that. "*Which* government?"

"*Any* government. That's the trouble. My list is a long one."

"What about someone like you? You could do this."

"Someone like Daxter, you mean? Maybe. But there aren't many like him around—which most people would probably consider a blessing."

"Why? What's wrong with him?"

Dax chuckled. "Well, *I* approve of him, obviously. But he's stubborn and eccentric. And he doesn't like governments."

Somehow that made Ruskin feel better. "Okay, we keep it to ourselves, for now. What about Max and Tamika? Do they know all this?"

"They are being filled in, yes. Not every detail, of course."

"Dax—" Ruskin suddenly found himself struggling, but he had to ask. "Did Tamika . . . she sent me to that lodge with Broder. Did she know what was going to happen?"

"She says she did not, Willard. And Ali'Maksam says that he believes her."

Ruskin nodded. "Good," he whispered.

"You will need the help of your friends, Willard."

"Yes. What do you want me to do?"

"You should try to return to life as usual. Observe all that you can. It will be my job to help you learn and to control your blackout periods, to prevent harm to you and to others. But your life must *appear* normal to an outside observer."

"You think I'm being watched?"

"Of course you are. That's why your directions for coming here were so circuitous. Remember the transponder?"

Ruskin remembered; he was grateful they'd gotten rid of it. He wondered if the NAGs in his body were capable of communicating information to the outside.

"I doubt it," Dax answered, reading his thoughts. "I, at least, will be unable to communicate with E'rik Daxter once you leave this laboratory."

"So they'll be watching me to see if I'm living up to their expectations."

"Presumably, and I further presume the following: that your erratic behavior is the result of incomplete control by the unfriendlies—that your own will and theirs have been in conflict, that they are in the midst of their own learning curve—and that our enemy knows or guesses this as well. It seems likely that it is their intention that your behavior appear normal—until the time. If you follow me."

Ruskin thought he did. "It all seems a little risky."

"So it does. So it does."

"What gives us such hope that we can overcome them when the time comes?"

"Their control," the snowflake said slowly, "is imperfect. It can only be so. Their programming must derive from a certain amount of guesswork, just as ours does. Even if the programming were perfect, its control would still be imperfect. Willard, the memory structures of the brain are essential to the functioning of the mind; but they are not themselves the mind."

Ruskin remained silent.

"What I am telling you is that there are other factors involved. There is the extended nervous system. There are hormonal and other chemical factors. And there is, well, the *spirit*. You are *you*."

Ruskin said nothing.

"And that, Willard, is the wild card. Are you ready to keep learning?"

Ruskin stared at the snowflake.

Dax took his silence as assent. The snowflake dissolved into a molten drop of light and streaked toward the ceiling of the cavern. Its voice echoed behind it: "Follow me."

There was no time for understanding, barely enough time for surprise. He had never imagined that his brain, on the inside, would look anything like this:

A subterranean forest, cloaked with snow and icicles, gleaming with interior illuminations. Dax led him swooping and diving through the landscape. The place was infused with an eerie light, and with confusing sounds, like the strains of a steel band. This was the heart of the amygdala, where emotions sprang up from underground streams—where trees of memory and icicles of thought were transformed by the blink of an eye.

No time to ask about it. They soared into a star-filled night and watched the passage of winking spirits across the sky. Stars blossomed, stars died, new stars appeared in constellations strange and frightening.

They landed, and the ground trembled and split into rivers of fiery lava. On a ridge, figures of light and shadow contested with one another, striving for control over the eruption. They sank into the molten flow, blazing with heat and light; and through a blur he saw a vast translucent wall, with dim shapes moving and bumping on the other side. No time to understand. They plunged through the wall, and as his thoughts blurred again, he realized that he was inside one of his own cells.

Interlude

✳

If in dream there was a hint of death, then in Bright the True there was more than a hint, there was a promise. So it felt and so Bright believed.

The dreams never came for long. Always brief, too brief for any real chance to know them, to feel their expression in the rhythm of the fire, in the ringing of the layers. Brief and superficial, they never touched the belly of the fire where the hurt was, but only that which faced the dark, which stood against the cold and the empty, which listened to those afar.

Do you know   ?
   Have you heard   ?
      If the dark is great and the cold endless and the far without limit, can there be such a thing as something that cannot be in all of the dark   ?
         Have you heard   ?
            Have you sung   ?
   Never heard
      Never sung

In all of afar, neither word nor hint of any such thing. Life within the life of a star.

Long indeed Bright had thought on the spirit and the will, and though Bright believed itself True, it doubted that it was Special.

But was not dreaming special?

Dreaming with neither understanding nor hope?

Could dreaming be the special messenger of Death, come to challenge the spirit of Life? Had that ever been sung?

121

Never sung
  Never heard

Not in Bright's memory, and that memory was long. Perhaps it was a thing that could never be sung, a Secret of the ages, kept from each until the time of Ending—the time of Need.

Or perhaps it was simply a madness come upon this True One, too soon before its end.

Or perhaps, in the rhythms of the fire, there was another answer. An answer that Bright would find.

Sing to me
  And I will sing

CHAPTER 13

✳

"You don't know where he went, then?" the voice of the Querayn Senior asked.

The robot's eyes winked in the darkness. "Unfortunately, no."

"But you were following."

"I was outfitted as a corporate messenger. They had already noticed me twice, and when they changed tube-trains quickly I had no choice but to abandon the direct surveillance. It was too late for the backup to arrive."

"And the microtransponder?"

The robot was silent for a time. "My backup traced it into the city sewer system," it answered finally. "It entered the sewer somewhere in the vicinity of the downtown crossing. I regret that I can provide no further detail on their whereabouts." The robot paused. "We know, however, that his friend made a number of contacts while they were at Ruskin's apartment. Perhaps you can discreetly trace those contacts."

"Indeed," said the voice of the person known to the robot as Karel. "We have already tried to do so. Ruskin's security system is excellent; however, we believe that Ali'Maksam called several of his nonQuerayn colleagues—unfortunately. We might have wished that he had trusted us more; but he was quite angry when he spoke to us last. We can only speculate on whom the others might have referred him to, if he was seeking help for Ruskin. Several possibilities concern us—individuals who are not necessarily our adversaries, but who might interfere unwittingly with their facilities and expertise. There is Councilor Sussinsky, of great influence in the research community. There is Martha Shariff, the academician. Either of them might be able to command an intervention. And there is E'rik Daxter."

"The nonincarnate?" the robot asked.

"Yes. He was a brilliant researcher in the field while alive. As a cybernetic consciousness, however, he is quite reclusive. We do not know his present capabilities or location, but we know that he is on Kantano's World, and that he maintains contacts with certain members of the Logothian academic community. We dare not underestimate the danger if any of these people are involved—but especially Daxter. We judge him the most likely to be secretive in meeting with Ruskin. And perhaps the most capable of decoding the programming."

The robot hummed in thought. "Could he undo the plan, then?"

"Perhaps. We doubt that he could disable one set of instructions without disabling all. If so, there would go our best hope. Still, it would be no easy matter, even for him. They may be content with trying to restore Ruskin's behavior to normal, which is what we hoped for anyway."

"Do you wish me to undertake any action?"

There was a moment of silence in the gloom before the Querayn Senior answered. "Continue your observations. We are deeply concerned about the premature change, and the apparent violence at Tamika Jones's residence—notwithstanding your belief that it was a temporary instability in the Tandesko programming, rather than ours. We must be cautious. We may ask you to try to obtain further information, perhaps a small tissue sample, after he returns— *if* he returns—to help us determine whether or not we have lost him. And keep in mind that we must know, as well: Can we trust Ali'Maksam?"

The robot blinked. "He appears to be a loyal friend. But yes. I understand."

"Thank you, Querobo Jeaves."

The robot rose. "And now I must change form, and go and make my other report. I will do my best to assure my other employer that Ruskin is behaving normally. We don't want them intervening again, if we can avoid it."

"Of course."

The robot turned with a whir and passed back out through the dim passageways by which it had come in. Eventually it made its way to the exit lock and out into the afternoon sun.

Stanley Broder eyed his coworkers balefully. He hadn't slept worth a damn last night, and he'd figured there was some reason why. Now he knew. It had been a premonition.

He asked incredulously, "Are you telling me that you've *lost* him?"

Ilex Gorminski stood between the two of them, looking perplexed. But Jeaves answered the question calmly. "I shouldn't worry too much about it, sir. The man's work allows him to come and go as he pleases, and no one at his office is seriously concerned. He's always done much of his work at home; he's known for not coming in for several days at a time."

"But he's not *at* his home, is he?"

"No, but he was last seen in the company of two of his friends." The robot lowered itself to a resting position. It was dressed in a new body, that of an appliance repair mech—which did nothing to enhance Broder's instinctive suspicions. He wished he'd been more suspicious of the robot from the beginning. Well, it wasn't too late to start. "Don't forget, sir," Jeaves added, "he was recently reunited with his girlfriend, Ms. Jones. Is it not reasonable to expect that a romantic encounter may have ensued? Perhaps a getaway, of sorts?"

"Jeaves, what do you know about romance?" Broder asked with a sneer.

"Only enough to infer that a resumption of relations with Ms. Jones could be a sign that he is stabilizing into a normal mode of behavior."

Broder snorted. "By running away? It could also be a sign that he's *not* recovering, that the masking programs aren't working worth a damn, and that he's gone looking for outside help!"

Ilex really looked uncomfortable now. And Broder knew that his outburst wasn't strictly fair. What he was really angry about was that he himself had relied too much upon the robot for monitoring Ruskin; he hadn't been insistent enough on the need for a human backup. And that was his own fault. Now, for all he knew, the robot was absolutely right, and Ruskin and his girl were simply holed up somewhere humping their brains out, with that alien friend of theirs standing lookout, or maybe taking part. But he couldn't afford to take that chance.

"Stanley," Gorminski said, "aren't you overreacting? All the signs have been positive, after all."

"What? The fact that Jeaves heard him have an argument with Jones first thing after seeing her? That's positive?"

"Well, some dislocation seems inevitable. Consider the adjustments. Anyway, Jeaves says it wasn't a long argument—and they did make up afterward."

"As nearly as I could tell," Jeaves interjected. "I was, after all, monitoring from outside the woman's apartment, so I am really only drawing inferences."

Broder grudgingly acknowledged the robot's admission. "And then they team up with this Logoth and disappear," he said. "How *did* you lose them, anyway, Jeaves?"

The robot seemed to consider the question carefully before answering. What, did it need to think about it? Broder wondered. Or was this part of its pseudo-personality programming?

"A simple miscalculation on my part," the metal being said finally. "I'm afraid I was being overcautious in following them—perhaps being too cognizant of my cover role. They might have seen me, or not. In any case, they left a tube-train too quickly for me to follow without betraying myself. I observed the policy that losing the quarry was preferable to letting him know that he was being followed."

"Yes, but I thought you had a damn *transponder* on him. It was supposed to back you up if you lost him."

"Indeed I did," Jeaves said regretfully. "I'm afraid it seems to have failed."

"Failed—?"

Jeaves shifted position slightly. "Cheap imported components, perhaps."

Broder glared at him.

"Joke," the robot said hastily. "It was a joke. But based on a genuine possibility."

Broder shot a glance at Gorminski, whose eyes seemed

to protest, *I didn't program his personality!* Broder turned
back to the robot. "When I want jokes, I'll hire a comedian.
Are you telling me that it was a defective unit?"

Jeaves clicked. "I cannot be certain, but it seems the
most likely explanation. The unit normally stayed in passive
mode, of course, to avoid needless detection of its signal.
After I lost Ruskin, I was unable to activate it; but it might
have failed at any time during that day, and I wouldn't have
known." The robot gazed back at Broder.

"But it might have been removed."

"That, of course, is possible also."

Broder turned away, unsatisfied. Still, there was nothing
he could do except put Jeaves back on the job and hope
that the man returned. Well, perhaps he could do one other
thing.

"All right," he said to Gorminski. "Unless you have anything else, I suppose we should get our metal friend here
back on the job."

"Absolutely. I agree," Gorminski said.

"And Jeaves—don't take this personally, but I intend to
get a backup agent on the job with you. A *living* backup
agent."

"I look forward to it," Jeaves said. "Shall I return to my
station now?"

Broder stared at the robot thoughtfully. Its mech body
was smaller than its butler body, and more ordinary—a
standard commercial model, to all appearances—but still
not entirely unobtrusive. "Jeaves, do you really think a
repair mech can hang around an apartment building
unnoticed?"

"For a time, perhaps. Waiting for a customer to return.
Plus, I was hoping to visit his office—on a repair call."

"Leave that to April. You watch his home."

"Very well. But do you think that this cover role is
inappropriate?"

"I don't know, Jeaves. Jesus. If he doesn't show up after
a while, change into something else. Ask the surveillance
team for that sort of help, not me."

"Of course. If that's all, sir, I'll be going. He could be
returning anytime."

Broder made a gesture of dismissal. The robot turned

with a whisper and a click and rolled out of the room. Broder sighed and poured himself a cup of coffee. He grimaced as he took a sip and peered at Gorminski, who was studying him worriedly. "What's the matter?"

Gorminski shrugged. He unwrapped a hard chocolate and popped it into his mouth. "Just that you were pretty hard on old Jeaves, there. Do you think it's that serious?"

"For chrissakes, Ilex, Jeaves is a machine! We don't have to be careful about hurting its feelings!" Broder shook his head. "Yeah, it's serious. Ruskin will be leaving soon, and we have to *know*. But it may not be fatal. I'm just going to watch—very carefully. And that means getting in a call right now for another agent."

"Okay." Gorminski dropped into his seat and switched on his terminal, ignoring Broder. After a moment, he turned. "You're going to take care of that, right?"

"Yeah," Broder said, "I'll take care of it." And now, he thought, I've not only insulted the robot, I've insulted the robot's best friend. Am I supposed to care? Ilex cares more about whether we think he did the programming right than whether we succeed. Jesus Christ, we should get him off this planet. He *is* turning into one of these people. So am I, probably.

"I'll be back," he muttered, walking out of the room. He'd make these calls in private, until he was ready to let Ilex know what he was thinking. Ilex would have to be in on it eventually, of course, but only after the necessary preparations were done.

Closing the door to his private office, he switched on the security screen and the console. He was going to have to have it out with the surveillance office about getting him more help. But first he had another call to make.

He punched in the code. The holo glowed to life, and the familiar pattern swirled before him. "Ganz?" he said.

"Ah," the pattern answered. "I was wondering if you'd give me the chance to try again."

"Don't be bloodthirsty."

"I am not. I am merely troubled by a job unfinished. What are the details?"

"I just want you ready, if it has to be done."

"I am always ready."

"The method will be different this time. *If* it happens."
He sighed, hoping desperately that this eventuality would
not come to pass. If Ruskin died, the entire operation could
go to the enemy. But if they lost *control* of Ruskin and he
lived, the political costs could go even higher. No, he had
to be ready.

"It will require preparation, Ganz. And possibly a spacecraft. You might be doing some traveling."

"Ah—"

CHAPTER 14

✳

"How are you?" he heard.

Ruskin blinked. Tamika's face slowly came into focus. Over her shoulder, he saw Max. He turned his head and realized that he was in a varigrav bed.

"I just met my own mitochondria," he murmured. He gazed at the ceiling for a moment, then laughed out loud. Tamika looked puzzled. But he couldn't explain yet; the memory was still too dizzying.

"Are you okay?" Tamika asked.

He tapped his temple, sighing. "I've still got a small army running around inside me. But I feel better now that it's two armies instead of just one."

Tamika peered at him intently. "E'rik told us that the implants were adapting successfully. How does it feel? You look healthy."

He closed his eyes and tried to analyze how it felt. Everything had been so disjointed. What was it really like, knowing that he was not alone in his own skull? "I've had some enlightening conversations. And I've been given a tour of myself that not many people have had." He told them what he'd experienced, as nearly as he could put it into words.

"The strangest thing was going into my own cells—actually seeing the inner structures, as a visitor. Not quite a literal view—but not totally symbolic, either." He paused, reflecting. "I saw the nuclear matter. DNA. RNA. Ribosomes."

"And mitochondria," Max said.

Ruskin opened his eyes. "And mitochondria, yeah. I felt a special affinity for them—on behalf of Dax, maybe, I don't know. Fellow benevolent interlopers, I guess." In each cell he had seen myriads of mitochondria—the strange little

organelles that shared none of the human genetic component, but nevertheless reproduced along with the cells.
They not only resided permanently in the human body,
they played a crucial symbiotic role in the cells' metabolism.
And now here were the NAGs, smaller and more alien, and
yet seemingly as necessary to his survival as the
mitochondria.

With an effort, Ruskin sat up. He shook his head—and
drew a sudden sharp breath as he felt something open in
his mind: like a gate to a windswept mountain pass, and
through the pass came a whisper of wind, and in the wind
were voices. *(What's happening?)*

> *((I'm simply releasing some of your anxieties,
> freeing up a few memories.))*

That last voice was Dax's, he realized dizzily; but the
others were the voices of his own memories. He struggled
to catch his breath as a torrent of images poured through
his mind. "Dear God," he croaked.

"Rus'lem?" Tamika gripped his arm. "Are you blacking
out again? Max! Can you tell if—"

"No—no—" Ruskin gasped. He started to laugh again.
"I'm just—*remembering!*" It was coming in a torrent: memories of work, of days and nights with Tamika, of friendship
with Ali'Maksam, of the years before Kantano's World when
he worked for the Auricle Science Council . . . the images
were coming with cinematic speed, flickering so fast he
could barely absorb them. "Dax—thank you!" he cried
joyfully.

He heard another laugh; but this one came from a hologram beside his bed, a hologram of a man. "Wonderful!"
the hologram said, in E'rik Daxter's voice.

Ruskin blinked rapidly, trying to separate the internal
torrent from the information his eyes were giving him. The
memories faded. "Dax? Is that you? I thought you were—"

"No, no—I'm Daxter," the hologram said. "Don't confuse
me with my offspring. The NAGs you call Dax are just an
AI device with some of my personality traits."

"Um—right. I guess I didn't expect to see you here.
Looking so human."

Daxter chuckled. "I try to keep my hand in it. And I
wanted to say good-bye in person."

Ruskin started. *"Good-bye?"* He looked at his friends. "Do you really think it's safe to let me out of here?"

"We don't have much choice," Daxter said. "You need to show your face at your job. And you probably need to show some results from your time off. I gather that there is some sense of urgency to your work."

Ruskin nodded. "I wish I could remember what that work was," he murmured, feeling a cold pang of fear.

((I may be able to help you some with that.))

Dax. Well, that's what he's there for, Ruskin thought, swallowing. "I hope your confidence is warranted," he said with a sigh. He hooked a thumb toward his friends. "I'd hate for these two to have to deal with me if I go over the deep—" He flinched at a sharp pain in his forehead. It vanished instantly. "Ow. Who did that? Was that you, Max?"

The Logothian stirred. "Was what me?"

E'rik Daxter was chuckling; but when Ruskin glanced at him, Daxter turned his palms upward, denying responsibility.

((That was just to let you know that I can protect you the same way Max did—until I find a better way.))

(Oh.) Ruskin took a deep breath. "Okay," he said to Daxter. "I get the idea." Tamika was looking at him in puzzlement, and he explained, tapping his head, "I've been given my own little safety device. I've been told not to worry."

((I didn't quite say that. I said I can handle emergencies.))

(Okay—)

((But be warned: we need to allow the invaders room to work, if we're going to learn what they're up to. So there may be difficult times ahead.))

"I stand corrected," he murmured. Raising his voice, he added, "The voice of my conscience says . . ."

((Not your conscience.))

(Figure of speech.) ". . . that he can keep me from maiming and murdering, but the confusion has only just begun." *(Close enough?)*

((It'll do.))

Max and Tamika exchanged glances. As Ruskin stood, Tamika extended a helping hand. He turned back to the hologram. "Thank you, sir. Shall we be in touch?"

Daxter nodded. "Ali'Maksam knows how. And Dax. In the meantime, I will do some checking to see if I can trace this fellow Broder. I suggest that you leave the outside detective work to me and focus on your own affairs. Good luck, Ruskin. It's been a pleasure and a privilege."

"To use me as a guinea pig?"

"Correct. Take care." The holofigure saluted jauntily, then vanished.

Ruskin turned back to his friends—and raised his eyebrows. The far wall of the room had disappeared. In its place stood a pleasant stand of trees. Beginning at Ruskin's feet, spiraling once and winding into the woods, was a narrow path of carefully laid bricks. Yellow bricks.

Ruskin stepped carefully across the spiral, then shrugged and followed the path out, flanked by his friends. He felt a momentary shiver as he glanced up and saw two small pairs of eyes peering out of the treetops, watching them depart.

The trip home took on an air of dreamy restfulness, at least for Ruskin. Tamika looked as though she was bursting with questions, none of which she could ask in public; and even Max had a look of anxious impatience about him. Ruskin watched the scenery and left the navigating to Max, who again took care to follow an evasive route.

The city seemed at once a fantastic landscape, filled with towers and spires and illuminated by a sun sinking through a smoky haze of clouds—and a place of astonishing solidity. Ruskin felt like a man who had stepped from the rolling deck of a ship onto dry land: the *feeling* of movement persisted long after the movement itself had stopped. So preoccupied had he been with his own inner landscapes that it was disconcerting to make the shift back into what they were all pleased to call reality. If this be reality . . . he mused, and left the thought unfinished.

They were coming into the city from the hills on the east, though Daxter's laboratory was located somewhere much farther to the north. The tube-train brought them into the downtown crossing, and after a quick change they headed at last for Ruskin's home. He asked Max if they were going to try to sneak into his building.

The Logothian's eyes were concealed behind his visor, but his voice conveyed a note of warning. "No, Willard—we have nothing to hide, do we?" He turned his head slightly, as though scanning the tube-car.

Ruskin took the hint. If they were being watched, they must convey an impression of normality and well-being. He reached for Tamika's hand and gave it a squeeze. She peered back at him uneasily, and he forced a smile. If he had relaxed during the ride, Tamika had grown more anxious. He wondered whose state of mind was more appropriate to the situation they were facing.

They found his apartment apparently as they'd left it. If it had been searched, the job had been a professionally unobtrusive one. Still, they looked the place over, taking care not to appear as though they were searching for bugs. Max was in charge of locating any spying devices; not only did he know more about that sort of thing, he could walk around looking somber and mysterious and nobody would think it odd if they saw it on camera. He found none, however, and finally said, "Willard, I think this apartment is as clean as your housekeeping habits allow." Tamika chuckled, causing Ruskin to raise his eyebrows.

"Shall I kill the lights all the way so you can get out of that suit and relax?"

Ali'Maksam's head swayed. "Thank you, no, Willard. I need to relax, but it has been too long since I have properly rested in my own home. And perhaps you and Tamika have . . . talking . . . to do." The Logothian gazed in Tamika's direction. She looked away in embarrassment. Ali'Maksam nodded almost imperceptibly. "I'll leave a ready-connection between your console and mine. And I'll check in by virtual." He hissed laughter at Ruskin's worried expression. "Fear not, Willard. You are well protected by Daxter's little friends. Probably better than I could protect you."

((He is right, you know.))

Ruskin started, then shrugged. "Right. I guess I've just gotten used to having you around." He frowned. "Max, I don't know if *you* might be in danger, by association. Be careful. And—thanks." He extended an open palm.

The Logothian's palm opened toward Ruskin, then closed. "Yes. You are most welcome. You both be careful also." With a gesture of farewell to Tamika, he closed the door behind him.

Tamika perched in a corner of the sofa with a sigh of relief. Ruskin gazed at her without a word until she lifted her eyes to meet his. "Are you glad to see him gone?"

"Max?" She shook her head. "We had some time together, you know—while Daxter was working on you. He's . . . a gentle individual, Willard. I hadn't quite realized that. And he sacrificed a lot, keeping us safe from your blackouts." She gave a little shiver, then chuckled. "Besides, he was more afraid of those little creatures—the terrakells—than I was. It's the first time I've ever seen him not in control."

"But you still don't exactly feel comfortable with him."

One corner of her mouth curled up in a smile. "We're making progress. I don't know if we'll ever be best of friends—or as close as each of us is to you." She dimpled a cheek with one finger and gazed with those golden eyes, her catlike pupils taking his breath away. And she asked slowly, as though considering each word with great care, "Are *we* still close that way, Rus'lem—you and I?"

He had trouble getting his breath back. He looked away, nodding. "Sure. I mean—I hope so. I—" He cleared his throat and looked back at her. "So what did you two talk about, while I was unconscious?"

She gestured noncommittally. "Oh—you. Politics. Religion. Science. The usual things one talks about with strangers." A nervous grin came over her face.

"Well—as long as you can joke about it, I guess it must have been okay." He ran a finger along the spines of the books and data slivers on his shelves, and closed his eyes, wondering, Will I remember what any of this is? Will I remember about Tamika and me?

And from within he felt, not exactly an answer—but an encouraging nudge.

"And what should *we* talk about?" Tamika asked softly, close behind him.

He scanned the titles for an instant longer before turning. "Oh—" he said. "Politics. Religion. Maybe a touch of science to round things off." He met her eyes finally, acknowledging the need there. "And maybe, you. And me."

CHAPTER 15

✶

The console flickered, murmured, as he paged through his work files—reading, listening, questioning. There was a lot here to assimilate, much that challenged him. Many of the files seemed fragmentary, or carelessly organized. Nevertheless, it was obvious that he had worked in advanced astrophysics; one of his specialties seemed to be gravitational interactions through the n-dimensional folds of space-time used for interstellar travel. Another subject that kept coming up was the behavior of large superconducting hyperstrings—interspatial structures thousands of light-years long and billions of years old, infrequently observed remnants of a critical phase-change in the expanding primitive universe. The subject jangled at his memory— he recalled it as an important part of cosmological theory— but the practical applications, if any, eluded him. He recalled seeing references to it in his searches at the office. But what exactly had he learned there?

It seemed that *everything* was hard to remember—not just details from the past, but details from two minutes ago.

He shifted to another file:

"... *the Tandesko Triune, which grew out of a period of exploration dominated by the NewAge Socialist Coalition—which itself had originated half a century earlier on Old Earth in the turbulent days of the first interstellar colonizations. At the time of the boldest NewAge explorations, the capitalistic colonizing ventures were mired in a period of retrenchment and consolidation. The latter had passed through a long period of rivalry marked by costly interstellar war; and the uneasy union that had emerged from the Ceti Peace Conference—later to become the forerunner of the Auricle Alliance—was then passing through a time of testing and adjustment. The NewAgers took advantage of the post-Ceti hiatus to open new exploration lanes into southern Orion space. Shortly afterward, the Descan cultures were discovered, and the NewAge Coalition was changed forever. . . .*

"The tight interlinkage that grew out of the synthesis of the NewAge and Descan cultures was, almost from the start, anathema to the alliance of 'free marketers' that was emerging from the Ceti agreement. There existed among the free marketers a potent distaste for the sacrifice of individuality that the people of the new Triune chose for themselves. . . ."

Information shimmered into focus in his mind and shimmered away again, out of his grasp. It was like trying to reconstruct a dream even as the details slipped away in a fog of forgetfulness.

((*An accurate analogy.*))

(*What?*) He glanced at Tamika as Dax spoke to him. Her hand was touching his shoulder, squeezing gently. He caught her hand and pressed it to his cheek.

((*You may or may not be losing the knowledge. It's a question of processing and storage, and it actually is much like the forgetfulness of dreams. Sometimes dreams return unbidden.*))

"So what's causing it?" he growled in frustration.

"What?" Tamika cocked her head in puzzlement. "What's causing what?"

"What?" He blinked. "No, sorry—I was talking to Dax."

"Oh." She hitched her chair closer, looking worried.

((*I'm guessing. Partly interference from the unfriendlies, though maybe not intentional. Probably conflict between them and your subconscious mind. Possibly trauma from your head wound.*))

(*Well, for godsake, can't you do anything about it?*) As the litany of obstacles grew, so did the temptation to despair.

((*I'm trying, Willard. But it's not easy; there are problems of both short-term and long-term memory. It's a process of discovery. I*

can help to trigger your recall when the as-
sociations occur, but it's—))

Ruskin was aware of Tamika's hand stroking the line of his cheekbone. She was bending to peer up into his face. "Rus'lem, what's happening?"

For a heartbeat, he was conscious only of her fingers touching his skin; then his heart *skipped* a beat, and with a start, he let his attention return to Dax. (*What was that for?*)

((Please listen! I need your attention. The
point is, you must not try too hard. That only
inhibits the process. Sometimes you have to
let them control you, so that I can study
them.))

(*Let them control me . . .*) And do *what* with my body, with my mind?

((Your memories may seem to come and go.
You have to accept that.))

"Can't you tell me what's wrong?" Tamika was stroking his hair now, running her fingers along his temples.

"Wrong? What do you mean?"

And then he realized—tears were streaming down his face. He hadn't even known he was crying. He caught Tamika's hand again and held it, unable to speak, unable to move. The fear washed through him in waves, the anger, the self-pity. "I'm sorry," he whispered finally and drew away to blow his nose.

"Rus'lem?" She reached out to him again.

He shook his head, willing the tears to stop. He had to get through this, had to keep control.

((Willard, you have to let go.))

(*Shut up.*) He cleared his throat and wiped the tears out of his eyes until he could focus on the display again. He forced himself to read. *Supernovae . . .*

All kinds of detailed information. Probably it was important. But he didn't know why, or what it meant. "Do you—" he cleared his throat again—"do you know anything about this supernova stuff—about what I was doing with it?"

"Rus'lem, maybe you should stop for a while." He

looked at her uncomprehendingly, and finally she sighed and peered at the screen. "You were studying supernovas, yes. I don't know much beyond that, except that you were involved in some expedition that you couldn't tell me about—"

"Expedition!" He swiveled in his chair and stared at her.

"Yes—and you were to be leaving fairly soon. But I can't tell you about it. I just don't know. I think you wanted to tell me, but it was classified."

His gaze intensified. "Would I have been planning to buy a spaceship?" he demanded.

"Maybe. I—I don't know, really."

"*Damn!*" He glared at the console display, then rubbed his forehead until the intensity subsided. "Twig," he whispered, a note of fear creeping into his voice again. "I have to ask you something."

"Yes?"

He took a breath. "Do you trust me?"

"*What?*"

"I mean, can I count on you to stick with me through this?"

"What the hell kind of question is that? What do you think I'm doing here now?"

He nodded stupidly. "Yes—of course. But if there comes a time when . . . when I start acting strangely . . ."

She reached toward him. "Rus'lem, don't—isn't Dax supposed to stop that sort of thing?"

He shook his head in agitation. "I don't mean violent, or psychotic—I just mean strange. Dax is working on this memory problem. But he says I have to . . . give him freedom. So if I start doing things that you, and I, might not understand—"

"Willard, please—"

"I just want to know that you'll forgive me. Please." He looked up to meet her gaze, pleading. "Please, Tamika. I just want to know that you'll forgive me."

She gazed at him for a moment with her golden cat eyes, then bent forward and kissed him lightly on the cheek. "I forgive you," she murmured.

* * *

He sighted through the slender-stemmed, wine-filled crystal, ruby against the light. After a moment, he lowered the glass. "So—there was this big astrophysical project for the Alliance." Tamika was facing him on the sofa. They were sitting cross-legged, their knees inches apart. "Only, I gather, it wasn't strictly what you would call pure research."

"And that," she answered, "was what got us into all those talks about politics. And political morality."

"I remember, a little." He sipped the tart wine and peered through the glass again. The ruby glow seemed to help him focus his thoughts. "It distracted me from my work, didn't it?"

"A little." Tamika smiled faintly and swirled her own glass. "I guess I didn't mind that—since I had some reservations about what you were doing, anyway. What I knew about it."

"Did you?" he whispered. "And did you tell me about it?" He was starting to feel a little lightheaded.

"Well—I tried to be subtle. But you were working for the Auricle Science Council, and you knew how much I trusted *them*." She shrugged. "You were very sincere about what you were doing. I just thought you were misguided in where you put your trust." Her eyes seemed to change focus, gazing off into space. Her lips pursed, shaped a frown.

Thinking of where she had put *her* trust? he wondered. There were enough mistakes to keep them both feeling guilty for a long time. She had trusted her Omega group, and especially Stanley Broder. Look where that trust had gotten them.

"Chasing demons, Twig?" he said softly.

She looked startled, and a smile flickered across her lips, followed by a look of remorse.

"Don't. You didn't know."

"Yes, but—"

"Tell me why you had reservations about my work." And he wondered: Had he been engaged in crime, or torture, or exploitation of the wretched and the poor? No. No—he was engaged in scientific research. Cosmic hyperstring. Supernovae. Evaluating areas for exploration. But all for the Auricle Science Council. Was that it? Did she think the Science Council's business *was* the exploitation of the wretched and the poor?

((Listen to her, will you?))

". . . because of the Auricle policies," she was saying. "I'm not saying that they were all bad—I never said that— just that there should be more to choose from than unre- strained economic expansion on one hand, or forced polit- ical structure on the other. There are alternatives that just never get an equal opportunity to survive and prosper."

"You always were an idealist, weren't you?" he said, al- lowing himself a quizzical smile.

She looked away from him, embarrassed.

Something stirred in his heart, and he found himself saying something that he only in that instant knew to be true: "It's one of the things I liked about you, isn't it?" *(Right, Dax?)*

((You remember well.))

"That's what you always said," she murmured. She turned back to him, raised a hand, touched his cheek again.

When I remember, anyway. Like a dream, evaporat- ing . . .

She seemed to read his thoughts. "Rus'lem, don't try too hard. Give it time. All right?"

He nodded, feeling her fingertips walk against his bristly skin. Beard hair coming back in? His beard growth had been turned off years ago, by—medical agents. NAGs, per- haps. Was this another sign of skirmishes raging inside him? He sighed. "I need to know these things, Twig."

((And many other things. There was urgency;
time was short . . .))

(Yes. I was buying a spaceship. . . .)

"It will come," Tamika said softly. "It will come."

He met her gaze, and felt his smile return with a flutter. Reaching for the decanter, he poured for both of them.

"Rus'lem, how do they do it?"

"Mm?" He shifted position slightly; her head was now

resting on his shoulder. They hadn't been talking much. "Do what?"

"The NAGs. How do they know what they're doing inside you? How can they be that fast *and* smart?"

"Well," he murmured, "remember the scale. Think of molecular vibrations, and think of beads sliding on an abacus. The one is a billion times faster than the other. And the memory storage is . . . well, a NAG that looks like a speck next to a human cell probably has a larger data base than my system here. Think of the information packed into a DNA strand."

She nodded, her head still on his shoulder. Maybe, he realized, she wasn't really all that interested in the NAGs. He set down his glass and began stroking her hair. "Twig—"

"Mm."

"Tell me something."

"Mm-hm?"

"About yourself."

She didn't move. "What should I tell you?"

"Anything. Tell me about—I don't know—you and your sister."

"Sharon?" She sighed, thinking. "Okay, Sharon. You remember the picture of her, right? Do you remember how she used to invite us over for dinner?"

He shook his head.

"Well, she did—and you liked her cooking. You always said her bean-curd parmesan was the best."

"Hm." He tried to remember, and couldn't. "What was she like? *Is* she like, I mean."

"Oh, she's very gracious—makes me look like a mule, by comparison. She always used to look at us like, so what's with you two, are you ever going to settle down? But she never *said* it. For which I was even more grateful than you."

Ruskin nodded silently. Tamika rocked her head back against his shoulder to look up at him. "She was my best friend, Rus'lem. We came here to Kantano's World after our parents died, and she was the one who convinced me I could make it on my own. She never had any doubts about me, which was more than I could say about myself. Of course, after she had a family, it was different; then she couldn't wait for me to follow her example. You used to tease me that I'd turn out just like her, if I gave up my independence."

"Ho-ho. Did I like her?"

"Uh-huh. You teased each other a lot. You called her the Happy Homemaker; she called you the Sorcerer's Apprentice."

He chuckled. "Was she political, too?"

"Sharon? Nope. But she knew I was always needling you about the Science Council."

Ruskin nodded, picked up his wine, swirled it. "So, you said she went off-planet. To Graemonholde?"

Tamika sat up straight. Her voice dropped in pitch. "She and her husband got all excited about moving with the kids to the new colony. I couldn't believe it. She tried to—she wanted me, or us, to come along. But I—wasn't ready. And you had your work here, and all."

He felt a lump growing in his throat. "Why weren't you ready?"

She didn't answer until she'd rested her head back on his shoulder, and when she spoke, her voice was muffled in his shirt. "I *might* have. Except you were here . . ."

After a time, he began stroking her hair again, and then he pressed his cheek against her hair; and she put her arms around his chest and hugged him hard.

For a long time neither of them moved, and in the near-silence, he realized just how much he had missed her, how terribly much he had missed *knowing* her—how deeply he had once drunk of her tenderness and her understanding and beauty, and how much he now desired her. A tension grew in his shoulders as he tried to modulate his breathing, thinking how much he desired her. His heart beat faster. Was he crazy? But Dax had told him to let go, let go. . . .

After an eternity, Tamika looked up at him. He cradled her head in his hands and studied her face, haloed by her disarrayed hair; he studied her angular brow and her narrow mouth with her lips parted as if she wanted to say something. He studied her honey-colored eyes and struggled to think what to say.

"Rus'lem," she whispered, and her gaze dropped to look at his sinewy arms, and she stroked his biceps; and for a moment, perhaps, both of them thought of another time, not long ago, when his hands had cradled her neck but not so lovingly.

"Twig," he murmured, and her eyes came back up to meet his. Her slitted pupils were nearly oval in the gloom, oval with desire, and perhaps with fear. "Twig, I—"

(Dax!) he thought, with a sudden twinge of desperation. *(I need to know.)*

((Yes?))

(Is it safe?)

((Do you mean—))

(If anything happens, can you keep me from harming her?)

For a moment, there was no answer. He swallowed, holding Tamika's gaze, wondering if he was crazy for not getting up and walking away right now. Then Dax answered:

((It's safe, yes. As safe as I know how to make it.))

"Thank you," he whispered in reply, and he closed his eyes, wondering if Tamika would be as confident as Dax was.

"You're welcome," he heard. When he opened his eyes again, she was studying him with a trace of amusement. "Willard Jerusalem Ruskin," she murmured, placing a finger to his lips. "Were you talking to Dax?"

He tried to nod, found he was so overcome with desire that he could scarcely move the muscles. Her face was so beautiful, framed by the shadow of her hair, that it nearly stopped his heart to look at her. At last he whispered, "It's me. Just you and me." And before she could answer, he touched his lips to hers, feeling her breath on his mouth. They both began to sigh at once, and he kissed her again. This time she returned it, her lips softening, then growing firm, pressing hard against his.

They broke and hugged tightly. Tears were leaking from his eyes again. When they pulled back from each other, her face seemed to glow from the shadows. He had never wanted her so much. "Yes?" he asked.

"Oh yes. . . ."

* * *

In the near-darkness, in the cradling embrace of the var-igrav bed, their bodies were like fluid objects in space, slowly and rhythmically moving. Naked, they explored the wondrous newness of their bodies, as though they had never made love before; and they reveled in the familiarities, the joy of remembered movements. Her eyes, and the hair that drifted across them, so enchanted him that he could scarcely look away except to admire the rest of her body: her slim torso, ribs just showing; the angular shape of her small but sharp breasts, nipples skewed slightly outward; the sharply defined lines of her hips, and the tuft of shadow at their center; her movements, legs entwining with his, hands running through his hair.

And awakening in his mind, the memories . . .

So well they had once known each other, so well they had loved. He remembered the touch and the smell and the sound and the movement . . . the memory of joining, two becoming one, the pressure that would build and the desire, and the shuddering release that would follow. . . .

And awakening in his mind was a new fear. *(Dax!)*

He could not help pulling back a little with the sudden-ness of the thought, the fear. She peered at him in the dark, tugging him toward her again. He resisted. He had to know—

(Dax, damn it!)
    ((I'm here.))
(Is it safe, Dax? Tell me!)
    ((Yes. I told you. I won't let you hurt her . . .))
(Not that, damn it! Is she safe from—)

"Rus'lem," she whispered, closing her legs around him, pulling him in. He was as hard now as he could possibly be, and he wanted her so badly, but . . .

(Am I going to infect her, damn it? Am I going to pass on your NAGs to her? Dax, I can't risk that!) Jesus, he wanted her, and her hands were cradling him now, guiding him. . . . *(Dax!)*

((It's safe, Willard. The NAGS *have been cleared from that part of your—))*

(That's all I want to know.)

In the darkness they drew apart, then drew together. In the darkness, the two bodies moved together, one body now moving.

CHAPTER 16

✳

He faced her, cross-legged in the darkness. "Do you mind if we talk politics some more?" She groaned, letting her head fall back onto the pillow. "Well, I just thought, as long as neither of us can sleep . . ."

Her eyes surveyed his face in the gloom; her fingers ran down his bare left arm, pausing in the crook of his elbow. "We could talk about us," she said. Her hand moved to his chest, fingering his hair.

He nodded. "Yeah." He caught her hand and kissed it. "But there are some things—" He shrugged. "Can you tell me about the Omega group? I hardly remember it at all."

"Good God, Rus'lem! So soon after making love?" He shrugged, looked down as her hand lingered over his stomach, then moved lower. He exhaled slowly as she cupped him. "You sure?" she murmured. He hesitated, closing his eyes, focusing for a moment on the sensation of her touch. Finally he nodded.

She withdrew her hand. He caught and held it between his own. "Forget the Omegas. Tell me about how I was politically naive."

"Hell," she said, and drew the thin coverlet up to her neck. She rolled away from him, laughing bitterly. "*You* were naive? How about me?"

He shook his head. "Let's just talk about my mistakes. Not yours. Tell me what I believed. What did I say?"

She sighed and rolled back. "You didn't really have formulated opinions. You just wanted to do your science and let other people worry about the rest, and you were content to defend the system you'd lived in all your life."

"What else?"

"You said it only made sense that the worlds that had the

148

power to expand and encompass others *should* do that."

He blinked. Yes; that seemed to make sense. At least it sounded like something he might have thought. He remembered that his political views had been unsophisticated. He'd seen no need for sophistication when simplicity served.

"Well, I tried to convince you otherwise. And after a while you agreed. Maybe because I showed you enough examples of planets that had either been raped or swallowed whole by the Alliance, all in the name of stable economic growth." She rolled her head on the pillow, then smiled. "Or maybe it was because you thought I was good in bed."

He closed his eyes as an eruption of memories filled his mind. Memories of Tamika, of making love. "Have I hit upon the answer?" she asked wryly. "I never did really know."

He grinned and shook his head. "Why did you hang around with me, if you thought I was so dumb?"

"At first?" She grinned back at him. "Because I thought you were sexy. And I always did like dumb brilliant men."

He nodded, not quite able to laugh.

"And after that? Well, I always liked a challenge. And I liked making love with you." She kissed the back of his hand.

He smiled in answer, but his thoughts drifted. He still believed in the Auricle Alliance, didn't he? What else was there? The Tandesko Triune: a collection of worlds that was more like an interstellar beehive, and far less democratic than the Auricle worlds—a culture dedicated to an interlinkage of three races where individuality was as highly valued as the dirt on the floor. Was that a better alternative?

"Hey!" She nudged him. "Come back. Where'd you go?"

"Sorry. Just thinking. Remembering."

"Remembering *us*, I hope?" Her hand crept up his leg.

He didn't move to stop it, but said, "Tell me what you were offering as an alternative."

"To what?"

"To the Auricle Alliance."

She sat up, trying in vain to hide her exasperation.

"You didn't side with the Tandeskoes, did you?" He peered at her in puzzlement—not wanting to make her angry, but he had to know. His memory was a confused swirl. Fragmentary images rose up in his mind and darted away. Images of arguments, of beliefs, of hopes.

"Ruskin, you're about as romantic as a stone, you know that?" She sighed and looked away. "*No, I didn't side with the goddamn Tandeskoes.* All right?"

"I'm sorry," he said, and meant it. "But I have to ask. What did you *want* me to believe in? Who were the Omegas? I mean—who did you *think* they were?"

She snapped, "I was an idiot about the Omegas, okay? I've admitted that."

"I'm not trying to blame you, Twig." He reached out and gently entwined her hair in his fingers. "But it could be important."

Finally she nodded and faced him, knees drawn up to her chin. She spoke mutedly. "The Omegas are dedicated to nonexploitive progress. To the idea that worlds can be opened without their having to be *owned*. Or so it was presented. But apparently I was deceived." She rested her chin on her forearms, frowning. "I don't know whether the whole thing is a fraud, or I just got taken by some—"

"Infiltrator."

"Yes."

"How'd you first get started in it? Where'd you hear of it?"

She looked away again. "You really don't remember?"

"No."

"I wish we didn't have to dredge this all up again."

"Dredge—?"

"Yeah." She chewed her lip for a moment. "Well. You and I had been seeing each other for, I don't know, a few months. And I . . . had a brief flirtation—" her voice weakened—"I had an affair with a guy who quickly turned out to be a *shit*, which was exactly what I deserved, and I wish I didn't have to repeat all this. It wasn't exactly the highlight of yours and my relationship." She paused, and he gazed at her without speaking. Hints of a remembered pain danced at the back of his mind.

"Anyway, the one good thing that came of it—at least I thought it was a good thing at the time—was that through him I heard of the Omega group. Mind you, he was totally insincere—he only talked about it to get me into bed with him—and he dropped out right away after I dropped him. But I kept going to their meetings."

"And you got me interested in going, too?"

"Right. Well, sort of—after a while. You were no easy convert, let me tell you." She scratched her head and grinned sheepishly.

Ruskin nodded, studying her face. Would he have been attracted to a group like that, if their views seemed reasonable? He wasn't sure; it would require thought—and memory. He wondered how Dax and his army of NAGs were doing, back there inside his skull.

((We're working on it, but it's going to take time. It'd be best if you let things come naturally.))

He twitched. *(Ah.)*

Tamika was still staring at him in the dark. He smiled and rubbed the back of his hand against the back of hers. "Do you have to be at work or . . . anything, tomorrow? I mean, today?" It was, he suddenly realized, hours past midnight. He was still wide awake.

Tamika shook her head. Her eyes seemed luminous in the night, flecks of gold catching stray light from the clock, from the tiny LED night-lights that marked off the edge of the floor. "I don't have any work lined up for this week. I've been taking time off."

He felt a moment of confusion, then clarity. Of course. The memory had crystallized so suddenly, it was almost as if he'd known it all along: Tamika worked as a free-lance editor on the internet, out of her home. She edited all sorts of political and scientific material, and in fact—"That's how we met, isn't it?" he said suddenly. "You edited a paper of mine, on—" He rubbed his forehead, trying to recall.

" 'Patterns of Growth in the Habitat of Humanity.' Do you remember how I called you after I'd worked on it— and asked to meet you, because I liked what you'd written? And you said okay—but it took months to convince you that I didn't just call up every man whose work came across my screen?" She nudged him.

He grinned and put his hand over hers. She squeezed back. For a few heartbeats, he gazed at her, aroused all over again by the sight of her wide eyes, her shadowed face and hair. The coverlet had slipped down, exposing her right breast. She made no move to cover herself.

As his hand rose to cup her breast, she leaned forward to meet him, to kiss him. They floated just off the surface of the bed as their lips touched. It was a long kiss, and did not end there.

"Twig." Ruskin stood in front of his closet, flipping through the racks of clothes. He pulled out a burgundy-colored pullover. "Do you remember this?"

She padded in from the whirlmist, wearing his bathrobe. "*That?*" She took it out of his hand and held it up, chuckling. It was far too small for him. "You don't remember?"

He shook his head.

"It was the first present I ever gave you." She handed it back. "I got the size wrong, but you insisted on keeping it because you said it was precious to you—wrong size and all. You said it symbolized your current stature in the world, and you wanted to make sure that we both remembered it years later."

"I did not."

"Yes, you did. But see now who remembered?" Her expression softened and she blew him a kiss as she walked into the kitchen.

Ruskin stared after her, stared down at the maroon pullover. Something in her words resonated.

Stature in the world. Was I worried about that? What was I doing that I might have cared?

Images were crowding into his mind, more dreamlike sensations that he couldn't quite retain long enough to make sense of. He seemed to glimpse in his mind people, crowds of them in large meeting rooms, and research holos, laboratories, and telescopes. He swayed dizzily. Where was this memory from? There was a sense of fear, of deep anxiety. . . .

"Rus'lem, how does broiled waffle-cheese sound?" Tamika was standing in the doorway.

He trembled, startled. "What? Yes. Fine." She disappeared. What had he been remembering? *Anxiety and disillusionment . . .* he couldn't quite recapture it. *(Dax?)*

((*Yes.*))

(There's something in that memory. I don't know what. . . .) His stomach fluttered as a greater wave of dizziness came over him. He felt beads of sweat on his forehead.

((*Something in you is fighting it, Willard. I'm trying to trace it, but you've got to let go. Trust me to protect you.*))

(Easy to say. I'm trying—)

((*Don't try. Just relax.*))

He breathed deeply and paced the room. The images and the dizziness receded. Give it up to Dax, he thought. Give it up to Dax.

"Rus'lem, someone's at the door!" Tamika called.

Suddenly alert, he strode out through the kitchen. "Who is it?"

Tamika was at the front-door monitor. "It's a robot."

"What the hell?" He went to the door. In the monitor he saw a short, gray mech waiting patiently in the hallway. He thumbed the intercom. "What do you want?"

"Repair unit Forty-six Fred, under contract to the apartment management," the mech answered. "You were notified last week of scheduled service calls to check on kitchen utilities."

"Like hell I was."

"Yessir, all tenants were memoed," the mech said smoothly. "In any case, it's a routine service and won't take more than a few minutes of your time."

"Not a chance. You'll have to come back another time."

"Sir, I have a schedule to keep. If I make exceptions for one tenant, it will inconvenience others."

"Nevertheless, you'll have to come back. Next time, confirm the appointment before you come," Ruskin said.

The robot stood silent in the hallway. Ruskin watched it in the monitor, wondering suddenly if it was a bomb. But something in him felt unafraid. No effort had been made to kill him since his return. Why would anyone try now?

The mech turned. "As you wish, sir. But please—could you double-check, sir, to see if our notice to you arrived?"

Ruskin shrugged. "I told you, I didn't get a notice."

"Could you please just double-check your console, sir? If our memo didn't reach you—"

"I'll check," Ruskin promised. "All right? Now, good-bye."

"Thank you, sir, and good day." The mech swiveled and trundled down the hallway.

Ruskin watched until it disappeared from the monitor. With an exasperated look at Tamika, he strode to his console and checked incoming memos from the past week. He grunted. "Son of a bitch, there *is* a memo here from the service company. And they say I acknowledged." He flipped off the console. "Well, I don't remember it."

Tamika rubbed the nape of his neck. "What difference does it make? We don't need it interrupting our morning." She kissed his neck. "Come on, help me get breakfast ready."

"You mean lunch?"

"Just come, okay?"

CHAPTER 17

✳

"Are you sure you're ready for it, Rus'lem?"

"What choice do I have? If I don't show up soon, they'll put me on the missing persons list." He felt a growing need to get back to his office, a feeling that the unraveling process that he both desired and feared was about to start happening.

"But aren't they going to ask—"

"What I've been doing? I'll tell them it's all on my home system and I'll show it to them the minute it's finished." He reached for his jacket. *(Sound okay, Dax?)*

((You do what you have to do. Just stay cool.))

He blinked.

((Don't lose your composure when we get in there.))

(I like that: We.) Ruskin kissed Tamika on the forehead. "You sure you don't mind staying here?"

Her tone was resigned. "I can't argue with your logic. I'm safer here with your security system if they try anything."

"I hope to God you're *not* in danger, but they've used you as a pawn once already. Call Max if you need help and can't reach me."

"I can stand it," Tamika said. "It's you I'm worried about. How do you know it's safe out there?"

"I don't. But what they did to me, they did for a reason. And I only know one way to find out."

"All right, just go, will you?" She pushed him toward the door. "Before I lose my nerve and tie you up here."

He went, before he lost his own nerve. Outside the building, he crossed the street to avoid several construction

155

mechs working on the front sidewalk and hurried straight
to the nearest tube-train.

At least he was regaining his bearings around the city.
For all of the volatile memories he'd recovered—and lost
again—in the last few days, others seemed to be returning
to stay. He trusted that Dax would know how to develop
that latter tendency. Still, there was only so much that Dax
could do. The NAGs could poke around and map, but they
couldn't reconstruct his memory wholesale. A lot was up
to him, including acceptance of the situation. If Dax was
right, that the greatest obstacle was his own stubborn resistance to the NAGs, then as he learned to accept them,
his faculties should gradually return.

Except, of course, for those places where the unfriendlies
did not *want* him to recall. And there he could only put
his trust in Dax.

Any hopes of slipping unobtrusively into his office evaporated when he walked straight into three people in the
front foyer. He had a fraction of an instant to gather his
thoughts.

(Dax!)

((You must remain calm.))

(Calm!)

((I can help—if you give me permission.))

(Yes. Yes!) He blinked, trying to take in all of the faces:
A stocky, bald-headed man in a navy-blue blazer. A tall,
wispy-haired woman in a long plaid skirt, with enormous
brown eyes and a serious expression. Behind the desk, a
dark-haired slip of a woman, strikingly attired in a purple
dress, very attractive. On the right, floating in what appeared to be a deep, empty space, was a holopainting of
the galactic center. At the corner of the painting, a tiny
image of two spindly-looking humanoid offworlders gazed
at the star clusters. He took a breath and felt a moment of
dizziness.

And a vapor rose up into his brain, carrying with it a
feeling of intense well-being. It was so powerful that he
almost erupted in laughter. After a moment the intensity
ebbed, leaving him breathless and confident.

*((See what a little shot of endorphins can
    do?))*

The people in the lobby had all turned to him with vary-
ing expressions of surprise.

"Well!" said the wispy-haired woman. "Speak of the
devil."

"Hi, Judith," he replied, flashing suddenly on the aborted
meeting with her and the other fellow (Galen?). Yes. Judith
was his coworker and cross-checker. They handled different
projects, but helped each other with input and review. "Hi,
Fariel," he said to the dazzling receptionist and got a wave
in return.

"So where have you been, old man?" the stocky fellow
was saying. He clapped Ruskin on the back, rather forcefully.

"I told you, he's been at home hooked up day and night
to his console," Judith said. "Isn't that right?" She winked,
but her eyes were questioning.

"Almost," Ruskin answered. "It's pretty close to the
truth."

"Now that you're here, does that mean that you have
some results to show us?" the stocky man asked.

Ruskin gazed at him, waiting contentedly for the memory
of this man to surface. . . .

John Ankas, of course, the director of the institute. Ruskin was his employee—though of course Ruskin answered
more directly to the client than to Ankas. Of course.

They were both smiling now, but Ankas's smile was the
less expansive of the two. He was awaiting a reply.

"Soon," Ruskin said. "Very soon."

"Well, I hope so. There's a bill on my desk for a rather
expensive spaceship, and I hope your client is ready to pay
for it." Ankas's tone was superficially jocular. It was time
to produce, Ruskin heard.

"Yup. I hope so, too."

Ankas hooked a thumb at the galactic holo. "Those two
guys have been trying to reach you."

Ruskin frowned. The images of the two humanoids had
looked familiar. Now he knew why: they were the representatives of the Yonupian Crafts Guild from whom he was

buying his spaceship. "Thanks," he murmured, and gestured to Fariel to delete the two figures from the corner of the holo. He started down the hallway.

"Hey, is that all you have to say?" Ankas called.

"Sorry, I have a ton to do! I'll get back to you later!" He hurried into his office and closed the door. He wasted no time in powering up the thinktank projectors, and he sat in his workseat surrounded by a gridded orange glow.

Scanning the rows of storage slivers, he selected everything that looked useful. He had no clear memory of what he was about, but certain slivers felt right, while others did not. He felt as though he were walking down a twisting path at night, with vague impressions dancing before his eyes and only his intuition for guidance. He racked the slivers and called them to life.

His mail sprang up, and he sorted through it. Some of it provided backfill to what went on here at Associative Frontiers; it seemed that AFI consulted to a variety of corporations and governments. The references ranged from agricultural bioengineering to interstellar transportation systems to (surprise!) structural nanoengineering. He paged through endless bulletins and notices; some of them rang bells in his mind. He dared not spend too much time digressing, but it helped to remind him of what his colleagues did. Judith was a transportation engineer; Galen was a mathematical economist. There was a memo from Judith, advising him on features he might want to custom-order on his singleton starship; he clipped it off to the side of his workspace to study later. There were several notices from the Starmuse Project office at the Auricle Science Council, requesting an update on his travel plans; the last one urged him to move up his departure date, if possible. He clipped them with Judith's memo.

Finally he found a message from the Yonupian Crafts Guild, confirming his order of one singleton starship, scheduled for completion by . . . four days from today! He called up everything he could find on the starship order. What appeared, in addition, was a complete itinerary:

STARMUSE EXPEDITION
SCHEDULED DEPARTURE KW: 25/9/178

LPO Shtl #3 Aries / Hanswell Prt: Dp. 0944
Kantano Skybase: Ar. 1107
HPO Shtl #134 Aries / KS: Dp. 1400
Grissondon Orb. Cty: Ar. 0130 (26/9/178)
Call Yonup. reps for insp/factory
Final flt trials: cmplt by (29/9/178)
Final loading (30/9/178)
Dp. system (30/9/178)
Ar. Betelgeuse system (5/10/178)
Ar. Starmuse station (6/10/178)
Rtrn.: (?)

He gazed at the listing in astonishment. He felt bits of
memory surfacing and accreting together with the details
on the list, lending a sense of familiarity, if not genuine
recall. Something seemed very important about these travel
plans. Had he composed the itinerary himself? He scanned
further and discovered a note appended:

"Willard: In your absence, I set up these travel arrangements, based on your most recent memo. All
subject to change, of course. Hope your vacation was
a good one. —Fariel"

The arrangements were made, then. He wondered if he
should be relieved or worried. There was that note from
the Science Council, urging him to come quickly. What
was that all about? His mind was a fog-shrouded stage across
which players danced and cavorted, the sets changing without warning, the fog parting only occasionally to allow
glimpses of the action. And yet another inward sense of
movement told him that Dax was active inside him, and so
were the others. . . .

A momentary dizziness came over him. . . .

■

He blinked and looked at the clock. He hadn't lost any
time. Had Dax just protected him from a blackout?

((You're welcome.))

"Thank you," he murmured.

He touched the control nudgers and resumed work, re-
viewing everything he could find related to the Starmuse

expedition: a project for the close-up study of Betelgeuse, a supergiant red sun which was apparently on the brink of becoming a supernova. There was material here that he understood at once; much of it, though, left him bewildered. What the devil were these references to tracking updates on a piece of cosmic hyperstring? He felt a growing pressure in his forehead as he tried to put the pieces together. *(Dax?)*

    ((Don't know, Willard. It's clearly important, but I don't see the pattern yet.))

He sighed and continued scanning. An hour later he dimmed the display, switched on the safecom board, and called Tokandro Ali'Maksam. "Max, I need help."

"If I can, Willard. What do you need?"

He pinched the bridge of his nose, trying to decide just what he did want, and just how to say it. "I need help in understanding some of my work. Do you have time right now?"

"I have to deliver a seminar shortly over at the Querayn Academies. But I have a few minutes. Can you tell me over the phone?"

"Well—" He sighed.

"Shall I come over in virtual?"

"No, no, somebody might walk in. Actually, some of it is classified. But screw that. I need the help."

"Are you sure?" The Logothian sounded worried. "I don't want you getting into trouble over it."

"That's the least of my problems, Max. Here's the thing." He hesitated, afraid to say what he really wanted to say. Oh, to hell with it, just ask: "Max, how would you like to come on a trip with me?" *A trip I must take, though I don't know why.*

There was a short silence at the other end. Then the Logothian's startled, and perhaps amused, voice: "I suppose that depends. How far are you going?"

"To Betelgeuse."

"Um—" Silence again. "Betelgeuse, the star?"

"Right. To watch it maybe become a supernova."

"I see. Not a day trip, then." Max chuckled. When Ruskin didn't answer, he added in a somber tone, "I assume you wouldn't ask if you didn't think it important."

Dizzily: "Max, I know it sounds crazy. I know you have seminars and obligations at the university—"

"Yes."

"But—" And his voice caught, and he had to force it to work again. "I know I'm asking a lot. But what happened to me is all tied up with this trip. I'm sure of it. And if it's not just me—if this thing goes half as far as E'rik Daxter thinks, well—" He took a breath. "I sure would like to have you along. If there's any way you can arrange to do it."

Max didn't answer right away.

"I *know* it's a lot to ask."

"It would be difficult. But perhaps not impossible."

Ruskin held his breath. He was fighting the dizziness, but also a kind of euphoria. If Ali'Maksam said yes . . .

"If you really feel that I could help you."

"Max, I wouldn't ask—"

"Well—Willard, you always did know how to throw a good party. I'll see if I can make some arrangements at the department."

Ruskin closed his eyes, nodding. *Thanks, Max.*

"When are you planning to leave?"

He swallowed. "In about three days, if possible."

Another long silence. "Willard—I don't know. Maybe I can justify it on the grounds of investigating Kônô consciousness. Or personal emergency. I'll do my best. What about transportation? Do you have a ship?"

Ruskin felt faint as he answered, "I'm having one built." Kônô consciousness . . . why did that ring a bell? Why did it make him uneasy?

"Ah." Max made a rumbling noise, laughter.

"Anyway, there's apparently a big research station there, all ready to watch the star explode," Ruskin hastened to add. "That ought to pique your Logothian curiosity."

"Indeed it does, Willard. Will I be allowed onto this station?"

"I'll arrange it somehow, when we get there. Even if I'm not sure what *I'm* supposed to be doing there."

"Perhaps it will come to you. Will anyone else be traveling with you?"

Ruskin hesitated. That was the other difficult question.

"I'm wondering whether to ask Tamika along. What do you think?"

Ali'Maksam took a long time to answer. "She's a good friend to you, Willard. She could be a help. But . . . as I recall, there was evidence that someone wanted to kill you."

Ruskin nodded. It was precisely what he'd been worrying about.

"Do you want to expose her to that danger?"

"Of course not. I don't want to expose *you* to it, either. But where would be safer? Here, where *they* are? Or with me, light-years away? Maybe they'll follow—I don't know. But at least together, we can watch out for one another."

"I do not know the answer, Willard."

Ruskin sighed. "Neither do I."

"Perhaps you should ask her."

"I know what her answer will be."

"Do you? Yes. Perhaps you do."

"I'll call you later, Max. Thanks."

He called Tamika to see that she was all right, but did not raise the subject of the trip. Afterward he threw himself into his work with a renewed sense of urgency, trying to reconcile what he found here with what he'd seen on his home system. He copied numerous storage slivers to take home. He was determined that he would have all the information possible—even if some of these files, like those at home, seemed fragmentary. Perhaps his own knowledge would emerge from beneath the sheer onslaught of data.

After studying his itinerary, he placed a call to the Yonupian Crafts Guild factory at Grissondon, outermost orbiting city of Kantano's World. The call was brief, confirming his intention to take delivery on the new spacecraft. Then, hesitantly, he asked the cogitative system to authorize the payment from his Science Council account; and he held his breath until the thinktank acknowledged the transfer. He was relieved to see that his account remained solvent.

Back to his studies. Surrounded by the holographic workspace, he was startled when a soft buzzer cut through his concentration. He nudged the intercom. "Yes?"

"It's Judith. Do you have a moment?"

Reluctantly he dimmed the holo and opened the door. "Hi."

Judith stepped into his office, and the door winked closed behind her. She leaned back against his desk-ledge and gazed at him. "So. How are you doing?"

He frowned. Was this it, then? Time to face the music? Nowhere to run and hide.

"That well?" Judith asked, squinting at him. When he didn't reply, she fumbled in her skirt pocket and extracted a resin smokestick. Before he could protest, she flicked it alight and inhaled a long stream of smoke.

"What the—?" Ruskin stuttered. His coworker smiled and allowed the smoke to waft out of her mouth in a curling cloud. He coughed and waved it away. "For chrissake, Judith, do you have to do that in here?" He punched the ventilator control, cursing the thing's ineffectiveness.

"I'm sorry—is this bothering you?" she asked, with mock wide-eyed innocence.

He glared at her. "Put that damn thing out, will you?"

Judith chuckled and snapped off the end of the stick with her fingernail. "Finally got your attention, did I?"

"What the hell's that supposed to mean?"

She laid the smokestick carefully on his desk and sighed heavily. "I think you know."

His throat tightened. "Do I?"

She looked determined. "Christ, Willard, there had to be *some* way to get through to you. Since you're not talking—and you're locking yourself up like a monk in a cell. And—"

"What?"

"Willard, you've been acting weird. And I want to know why." Her eyebrows arched high over her enormous eyes. "So tell me."

"I've been very busy," he said defensively. "I'm leaving on a field trip soon and—"

"We know that."

His breath caught. "Yeah. Right. Well, I have a lot to do

before I go." He cleared his throat. "So I've been working at home. Nothing new about that. Right?" Judith's gaze bored into him. "I've been preoccupied."

"Jesus, Willard—listen to yourself! What are you trying to hide?"

He fought down a surge of panic. "I'm not—"

"You're a crummy liar. You know that?" She shook her head. "Remember me, Willard? It's Judith—your friend. Remember?" Her hands fidgeted, poked at the air in annoyance. "Why are you bullshitting me? Don't bullshit me, Willard."

Ruskin tried to swallow, found it impossible; his throat was dry. He turned his head to the dim, almost invisible hologrid. How could he answer? He wanted to trust her, desperately. His friend? He wanted to believe, to confide in her, but . . .

He didn't dare. He was afraid. Perhaps if he could just allay her fears . . .

((Calming your own fears will probably do a lot to calm hers.))

Maybe. But she was speaking again.

"Do you remember when you almost lost the Koppel contract because you'd hit a snag on the projections, and you were afraid to tell anyone about it? Except you finally came to me and said you were in a mess, and I was able to help you get it untangled; and we didn't even have to let the client know how close they came to getting nothing? Willard, are you listening to me?"

"I'm listening."

"Well, do you remember that?"

The nod was automatic, and the frown. Memories jangling in the back of his mind. He remembered, sort of . . . Judith's helping him out of a jam. It *had* happened that way, hadn't it?

"Does that mean anything to you, Willard?"

He was aware of himself nodding again. He looked up into her eyes, looked away again.

"Remember when you helped me on the Patterson proposal? When *I* was in a jam?"

"Yah." All rattling around in his head. It sounded familiar.

"Or when you wanted advice on your love life, and it

took you weeks to ask?" Her voice suddenly deepened, softened. "Is that it, Willard? Is there something that—I don't mean to pry. But—damn it, you can tell me. Can't you?"

He took a deep breath. "No," he sighed. "It's not that." He met her eyes finally. Fear trembled, jangled with trust. Wanted to trust . . . but he couldn't just tell her this insane story. How could he explain it? *Someone tried to kill me, and I don't know who*.

He was afraid. And the fewer people who knew, the better.

"Well, what? For chrissake, Willard, you can't just—"

"I know," he barked abruptly. She fell silent, listening. "I know I've been acting strangely."

"Well?" Her eyes didn't let him go.

"It's not that hard to explain. Look, I'm just having trouble getting all of this work done before I leave. I feel guilty as *hell*, because I didn't get anything done on my week off."

"Jesus, Willard—you're not *supposed* to work on your vacation. That's what vacations are for."

"I know. But now I'm afraid of blowing the whole job, and maybe screwing up the entire project. So I'm just working full bore. My concentration had been way off, but now I'm getting on track." He took a breath. "Anyway, that's why I've been keeping to myself. I've got to lick this thing."

She just stared at him.

"What?" he protested. He felt as though he were under a microscope.

"Willard, that's just about the dumbest confession I've ever heard. *Christ!* You keep something like that bottled up inside you and you're just going to explode! *Shit!* Why didn't you come to me? I could have helped you." She looked angry. Angrier than he'd probably ever seen her.

"I don't know." He looked away in genuine shame.

"If you don't trust me, at least trust yourself, for godsake! Afraid of screwing up the project? How far would that project have gotten without you? You *know* that."

Numbly, he nodded. *(Do I?)* he asked Dax. But there was no answer.

Judith sighed with disgust, crossing her arms. "All right.

Do it your way. But will you at least take some advice?" He looked up, scowled. "One—take a night off and *take your mind off it*. I don't know, make love to Tamika. Are you still talking to *her*?" He felt his face flush; he said nothing. "Two—before you have to present this to John and me for vetting, bring it to me first. All right? If I see problems, I'll help you iron them out. And three—" She took a deep breath and stared straight at him. "Believe in yourself, Willard. If you screw it up, it will only be because you didn't believe in yourself. I mean that. You haven't lost it. I work with you—I *know*. If you can believe in yourself, you've got it beaten. Okay?"

Nod.

"*Okay?*"

Crooked smile. "Okay."

She straightened and rested a hand on his shoulder. "If you need to talk, will you call me?"

"Absolutely."

That seemed to satisfy her. "By the way—in case it's been bothering you—I told Galen you felt bad about what happened the other day. He said, forget it. He said, we all have a little racism lurking in us, so he understands."

"Thank you," he murmured. Racism? An image crowded into his mind, making it clear: Galen was involved in an unusual love arrangement with nonHumans, and though he denied it, there were those who thought he was a likely candidate for Tandesko conversion. Ruskin's subconscious, knowing this, must have gone straight for the offending nickname.

"You're welcome. See you tomorrow," Judith said.

"Right."

Long after Judith was gone, the door closed behind her, he was still motionless, lost in glum contemplation. Finally he shook the cobwebs out of his head and quickly finished gathering up his files.

CHAPTER 18

✳

Incredible. The service robot was back in the hallway outside his apartment. Ruskin cursed as he approached the door.

The mech turned at the sound of his footsteps. "Good evening, Mr. Ruswick. I'd hoped you might be along. I'd hoped I might complete the job we spoke of earlier."

Ruskin stared at it in disbelief. Are you an exceptionally stupid mech, he wondered, or a surveillance device trying to *look* like a stupid mech? Either way, he didn't want it around. "My name's Ruskin—not Ruswick," he said finally.

"I'm sorry, but that's the name I was given," the mech said. "One of us must have the wrong information."

"One of us must," Ruskin agreed. "Well, you're not coming in now. I'm tired. I told you—call and make an appointment. All right? Now, get out of here, please."

The mech whirred. "But sir, if you would just consider—"

He exhaled noisily. Anger was starting to boil up inside him. He would love to thrash this machine. *I wonder if I could just . . . ?*

Rubbing his index finger with his thumb, he felt the tiny nub of the implanted laser. It was tempting. Could he still make it fire? he wondered. It wouldn't exactly be legal; but if the thing wouldn't listen to him, surely he had the right to protect his privacy. He pointed his finger. "I'll give you three seconds to leave before I—"

"Excuse me?" the robot said. "What?"

He almost lost his nerve. "Before I inflict serious damage on you," he growled finally. (*Dax, can we make this thing fire?*) "One . . ."

((*I've disabled the laser, Willard.*))

167

(Now you tell me.) "Two . . ."

The mech lurched away from the apartment door. In satisfaction, he walked toward the door himself; but the mech lurched again and altered course, back into his path. He hopped out of the way, stunned. The robot seemed confused; now it was bouncing off the wall. "Stop that!" Ruskin yelled. The mech rolled in his direction, shuddering, as though it were fighting itself. He fended it off with both hands, but not before it nearly rammed him into the wall. "HEY! *Are you crazy? Get the hell out of here!*" He heaved it away.

The robot turned with a loud clicking sound and edged in the other direction. "Sorry . . . apparently some difficulty . . . very sorry!"

He gave it an angry shove toward the exit. "*That* way!" To his relief, it rolled away down the hall. He sucked the back of his hand where he'd scraped himself; he was still breathing hard as the mech disappeared into the lift. Only then did he utter a sigh and finally unlock his apartment.

"Rus'lem!" Tamika came out of the bedroom to greet him. "Is that mech still out there?"

"I just chased it off." He tossed his jacket over a chair, unbuckled the belt pack that held his data slivers, and dropped it onto his console. "Has it been out there all day?"

"It came and went a few times. I kept telling it to go away, but finally it just camped out there." Tamika looked annoyed. "It insisted that only the legal resident could order it to leave. Do you think it actually belongs to the service company?"

"Easy enough to check." Ruskin stepped back over to the console. "System, please retrieve the identification of the service mech that just left. Contact the company and ask if it was theirs." He turned his head. "Anything else happen while I was gone?"

Tamika grimaced. "I got bored and did some editorial work. But eventually our little friend showed up and we played cat and mouse." She glanced at the door again; the robot had indeed unnerved her. And no wonder, sitting here just waiting for some word from him.

"It didn't try to force its way in, did it?"

"No, it wasn't violent, just obnoxious."

He sighed. And how would she feel, sitting here while he flew off to watch a supernova? He decided to postpone bringing the subject up.

Tamika slipped an arm around him. "How'd it go?"

His answer was interrupted by the console's voice: "I have the information you requested. There *was* a service mech dispatched, marked as a special order, origin unlisted. I was informed that the order must have come from your console; but I put in no such order, Willard."

"Thank you." He glanced at Tamika. "So we can't tell whether our little friend was legitimate or not. But I know what I think. How about you?"

"I think it makes me damn nervous."

"Yes, but as long as they're only watching us . . ."

"Uh-huh. What now?"

He let out a long sigh. "Dinner?"

Tamika shoved her plate away. "Like hell you're going without me! Not in your condition!"

He tried not to smile at her anger. "Easy, Twig. I had a feeling you might say that."

She glared. "*Well?*"

"I'm open-minded. You might be able to convince me."

"Yeah, well, you are in no position to turn away help. *Any* help. That means me. And I suppose it means Max, and those guys in your head." Her frown deepened. "Is Max going?"

"If he can get away. Twig, it's the *danger* I'm thinking of." She rolled her eyes. "Well—" He gestured helplessly. He honestly didn't know whether she'd be in greater danger staying here, or going with him; but the truth was, he was grateful that she wouldn't take *no* for an answer.

But something else had just occurred to him, something troubling: "*No position to turn away help . . .*" He recalled Judith's invitation to bring his work to her before it went to Ankas—surely a well-intentioned offer. But did he dare betray how incomplete his knowledge was? It could take him many days to piece together the total picture; almost certainly he would have to work on it all the way out to the site. But if he presented his knowledge to either Judith or Ankas in such a state, they might not let him leave at all. And the one thing his intuition told him with absolute certainty was that he had to go on this expedition; and time was short.

He might have to leave even sooner than he'd thought—without clearing it with them at all. They didn't *have* to see his work beforehand, did they?

"Willard! Hello—are you there?"

He forced a smile. "Sorry, just thinking."

"Well? Have you come to your senses? Will you take me along?" He took a breath and nodded. "Good," she said. "When are we leaving?"

His eyelids closed; his brain filled with flashes of light. "In a day or two, I think." He found her gazing at him in wordless astonishment. "Still want to come?"

She nodded, her lips moving silently. At last he tuned in and heard, ". . . you're crazy. But yes, I'm with you. I'll have to cancel some jobs—but what the hell, I guess you're worth it."

"Thanks," he murmured.

"And what about tonight? More of the same?"

He shook his head, eyes closed. He'd been intending to ask Ali'Maksam's help in sorting through the information in his files—and in his own brain—looking for something that would provide illumination. But perhaps that wasn't what he needed tonight. Lights were strobing up and down his optic nerves. He remembered Judith's advice to take a night off. Perhaps she was right. (*Dax, what's happening to me?*)

((*You're a battlefield, Willard.*))

(*Big help.*) He opened his eyes. "What do you say we just relax. What's on the channel tonight?"

Her eyes widened. "Are you kidding? You *hate* watching the channels."

"Do I?" He smiled. "Well, tonight I don't."

*   *   *

They settled on an interactive light/dance concert. It actually caused him to forget his worries, at least for a little while. He scarcely felt the two featherweight probes that rested atop his head. His living room was submerged in the spectacular light effects of the holographics; his mind was enfolded by a crazy quilt of sensual feedback. He felt a soaring exhilaration as he stood atop a craggy peak on a world of mountains and watched a flight of new-eagles soar dizzyingly about his head. The wind moaned in his ears. The music soared and danced.

High off to his left, Tamika was floating against an exploding star. No, it wasn't a star; it was a kaleidoscopic light effect, now turning to molten rivulets of color.

Change—

Where were they now? The mountain was gone, but the music was thrumming in his head and people were dancing on all sides, whirling by like great diaphanous wind-figures; and farther away, more solid to the eye, were rows of dancers, rising and rippling in waves. Overhead, clouds swirled and scooted. Bass rhythms broke the air; glass strings melded it back together again. The sensation was intoxicating. Euphoric.

He found himself astride a cloud, borne by the power of song. As he strode, soaking in the rhythms, and the sadness and sensuality of the music, he began to feel changes in himself, a free association like that which often followed upon lovemaking: memories and ideas floating free across his mind, a haze of emotions expanding after a great explosion of feeling. Images raced across the sky—a spaceship, a forest, an assassin, Tamika's naked body, a research file. One after another, they vanished or burst into flowers of light or changed into other images altogether. For a fleeting moment he wondered if they meant anything, but he didn't care; it was not a time to think.

A beacon of light blazed across his vision, and the holographed dancers spun by again, and he was caught up by another change in rhythm. The performance was turning into a provocateur for the subconscious; the music trembled and melted around him—

—and a series of images rose up like flat photographs,

turning to show their faces before rotating away and disappearing into the mist of the music and the lights. He felt silent astonishment as he glimpsed memory or imagination—he couldn't tell which—glimpses like reflections on a glass:

A dark fortress floating in an amber sea-mist, and a glow emanating from deep in the heart of the mist; and almost lost in the glow a tiny living thing huddled, waiting . . .

And at the very edge of the reflection, a figure in black cracked a whip, sending an invisible shock wave through the amber mist, which could free the fortress or destroy it. . . .

He blinked and the images were gone, and a feeling of total helplessness caught him in the pit of the stomach, lifted him like a wave on an ocean. He was swimming in a blue-green sea, a distant bell buoy clanging; and he was drowning . . .

▪

A jolt of electricity jarred him awake. Stunned, he knocked the probes away from his head; he blinked his eyes open. He was on the sofa, Tamika beside him.

> *((That was a tricky one, Willard.))*

He took a sharp breath. *(What happened?)*

> *((Something was coming up out of your memory, something you didn't want to look at. You've got some conflicts inside you, fellow.))*

(Great . . .)

> *((And I've got to tell you: I can't resolve all of this for you. I'm just a working stiff; I'm not a psychiatrist.))*

(I stand reassured. All right if I talk to Tamika?)

> *((Go ahead. I'll be right here.))*

A deep feeling of weariness had come over him; he could barely focus his eyes. He forced his breath out and turned his head. Tamika was still lost in the holographic concert. The lights and images danced in silence around his living room; with the effects-probes pushed away, they were pale and ineffectual. He watched as Tamika's eyelids fluttered, as her hands twitched in her lap. Finally he lifted the probes from her head; as he did so, the holographics faded to darkness.

Tamika stirred in confusion. "What happened? Why'd you stop it?"

He gazed at her, remembering the jolt with which Dax had brought him out of the blackout. It seemed impossible that she hadn't noticed. "I—" he began, then shook his head. The associations were still stirring in the back of his mind. "I couldn't watch anymore."

Her brow creased, her eyes suddenly alert. "Are you okay?"

"Yes. And I—" His breath caught, as the images flashed again through his memory. (*Dax, are you doing that?*) A feeling of peace welled up within him. With a sudden clarity he remembered something else, something triggered by those images, by his memories of work. *Star-mapping across the galactic spiral arm / cosmic hyperstring / supernova . . .* Something was coming to him in a rush. . . .

Interstellar gateway.

"Tamika," he whispered. And stopped, because his mind was suddenly so full of details and fragments of pictures that he couldn't hold it all together, couldn't contain it in one place in his mind. Interstellar gateway . . . There had been talk of such a thing: yes, a gateway so vast and powerful that it could put enormous tracts of the galaxy within reach. But what did the talk amount to? Was that why they were studying a supernova, to find clues to how such a thing could be created?

"What is it, Rus'lem?" Fingers touching his temples.

"I—" He swallowed. He blinked, focusing on her. It had seemed so clear in his mind at that instant. And yet so much remained hidden. "Tamika—" And his voice, little more than a husky whisper to begin with, cracked.

"Yes?" She kissed him gently on the cheek.

He was startled by the touch of her lips. Whatever it was he'd been trying to grasp, it was gone now. Lost to the wind; lost to the kiss. "I don't know anymore," he whispered. He met her eyes, eyes of startling gold. She kissed him again, this time on the lips—a dry, brushing kiss. He drew a breath and let it out in a long hiss. "Yes," he said. He was having trouble breathing. She nodded, murmuring. Their lips met again and this time lingered.

Whatever it was, it would come back. It would have to. Perhaps in the night. Or in the morning.

CHAPTER 19

✳

He had a sense that Ali'Maksam appeared once, perhaps twice, in the bedroom while they were making love. If it happened, it was only an eyeblink of an appearance. Ruskin was aware of his friend's virtual presence without quite seeing it; he was aware of many things in addition to the sensations of lovemaking. He was aware of lights passing by outside the window; of the rhythm of music they'd listened to hours before still echoing in his mind; of the nagging presence of the thing he had almost remembered, hovering like a mysterious agent at the edges of his mind. He was aware of the warmth of Tamika's body, of her breath rushing past his ear, of the pleasurable tension crowding together in her body and releasing.

He was aware of time passing, as she slept. He could not sleep; he lay contemplating the darkness, remembering or trying to. He talked a little with Dax, but that wasn't the conversation he needed. Dax wasn't quite alive, and he wanted to talk with the living. He began to wish that Ali'Maksam would return.

His friend did reappear late during the night, shimmering into the darkest corner of the room and almost disappearing again before Ruskin called out—softly, so as not to awaken Tamika.

"I did not mean to intrude," Ali'Maksam whispered, reappearing. "I was concerned, however. I wanted to make certain that—well, that you were—"

"I'm glad you came," Ruskin whispered back, slipping out of bed and reaching for his robe. "Can we talk in the living room?"

The Logothian's image was waiting for him when he got there. Ruskin sat and studied his friend's face. He noticed lines of strain in the half-reptilian countenance; Max was carrying a greater burden on Ruskin's behalf than he let on. The fact that he had appeared in the middle of the night was evidence enough; Max would not have done so without need. He clearly wanted to know what was happening in his friend's mind.

"I'm remembering bits and pieces," Ruskin said, nudging the overstuffed rocker into creaking motion. "But every time I feel close to an understanding, it comes apart in my hands. There's something at the center of it all that I just can't . . . *grasp.* And the worst part is, my files just don't seem to add up." He felt the frustration well up inside him. "Is it me? That's what I want to know. Or is it the files themselves?"

Ali'Maksam stretched and bent his neck to gaze at Ruskin. "Do you suspect that your files have been tampered with?"

Ruskin shrugged. "How can I tell? I'm depending on *them* to remind *me.* But I don't know if the information I need is there at all—or if it's been altered, or what." A horrifying thought struck him. "Max, what if *I* tampered with the files?"

Max's eyes gleamed a fraction brighter. Ruskin gazed back at him, terrified.

"Perhaps we should talk about what I know of your work," Max said softly. "Perhaps I can help you jog together associations."

Ruskin's mouth felt dry. Something in him hesitated to do that. Why? he wondered. Am I afraid to look within myself, afraid of what I might find?

"I have been reluctant to tell you too much directly," Max continued, "because it seemed important that you find your own path to understanding, that you reconstruct your own memory, your own comprehension. But it seems that time grows short."

Ruskin nodded, feeling again that sudden weariness, the weariness of not wanting to face a daunting task. (*Dax? I need help.*) A moment later, he felt the blood vessels opening in his brain, a renewed clarity coming to his thoughts. "All right," he said. "Let's start with this. Have I ever spoken to you about the possibility of an interstellar gateway? A gateway that could increase the volume of habitable space by a factor of a thousand or more . . . ?"

Max's eyes burned bright with interest.

When he awoke, the first thing he thought of was Ali'Maksam's visit; but already his memory of it had taken on a dreamlike quality. What he remembered most was a feeling of hope, a feeling that—however slowly—details were returning to him, even if at the moment they seemed shrouded again in smoke. He rolled toward Tamika. She was already up on one elbow, watching him, her hair falling away at an angle. He remembered their lovemaking and smiled. She kissed her own fingertip, touched it to his lips, then slipped out of bed and disappeared, wearing his robe.

Breakfast was a disjointed affair, their talk ranging from what they should take with them on a trip to a distant, unstable star, to the interstellar politics that kept the Auricle Alliance and the Tandesko Triune locked in a struggle for domination over interstellar commerce and culture.

"Max thinks he can arrange to break free of the university to come with us," he said, changing the subject one more time. He poured more syrup over the buckwheat cakes he had cooked for them.

"Max? When did you talk with him?" She took the syrup jug from his hand.

"Last night. While you were asleep. He came over in virtual."

Tamika looked startled. "I *thought* I heard you talking. I barely woke up." She chewed on a mouthful of griddle cake, then made a sudden growling sound and slapped the table. She swallowed. "*Damn* it, Ruskin—was Max in the room when we were making love last night?"

"Huh?" His face flushed. "I don't think so. Well, he might have flashed in for half a second or so, and out right away when he realized—"

"Shit, Willard! I mean, Jesus!"

"Tamika, he didn't mean—"

"Yeah, yeah, I know. I *know*. It's just that—" She shook her head, grumbling.

Ruskin was silent for a moment. Then he said, "We talked about something that might—" He paused and framed his words. "We talked about the notion of opening a gateway across the galaxy." He squinted at Tamika. "Did you and I ever discuss that?"

She shrugged. "Yes, sure we talked about it. It was one of your pet ideas. You said in a hundred years or so it might be feasible. And my reaction was, Great, then we'll be able to exploit a thousand more native races. And you would say, 'What?' And off we'd go again." She chuckled and tapped her fingernails on the table. "That was early on. Eventually, you started to agree with me. At least I think so. Didn't you?"

Ruskin stared past her, scarcely hearing her question. "You *knew* I was working on that?" he whispered.

"The gateway thing? It was no big secret." Her mouth silently framed an *Oh*. "You mean, you only just remembered it?"

He nodded.

"But that was one of the reasons for studying supernovas, wasn't it? I'm sure I've heard you mention it—I mean, since all this happened."

He stared at her in amazement. "Tamika, I don't remember talking about any such thing!" Could it have happened during a blackout? Possibly. "Tell me about it."

"Well, I never meant to hide it from you. But you worked on a lot of things and this was one of them."

"Okay, but tell me about it!"

She thought for a moment, brow furrowed. "Well, let me see if I can get this right. As I remember, you told me that before a gateway could be possible, you needed to understand better the process of black-hole formation. And that was one of the reasons for studying supernovas—because one causes the other, right?" He nodded silently. "And that would be why you were going to Betelgeuse, because it's relatively close, and it might be on the verge of going supernova." She peered at him uncertainly. "Does that sound right?"

He stared at her, not answering.

"But none of this was secret, Willard! You talked about it as everyday scientific research. What could that have to do with—" she gestured helplessly—"all this? And with someone trying to kill you?"

For the space of several breaths, he could say nothing. There was a tightness in his chest that hadn't been there a minute ago. (*Dax, what is it?*) And there was something . . . that didn't ring quite true in what Tamika had just said. But what? (*Dax?*)

((*I don't know yet. . . .*))

He gazed back at Tamika and found himself blinking back tears of frustration. *That's what it's all about, though. The supernova.*

"Rus'lem, if I'd known, I would have said something earlier."

"I know." Sighing, he rose. "Twig, I'm sure of it now: the sooner we're on our way, the better. I'm going to book tickets." He could not explain his urgency, but the feeling was stronger than ever. He would just have to explain to his office colleagues when he got back. If he got back. "And I need to talk to Max right away."

((*And E'rik Daxter, please . . .*))

"And E'rik Daxter, before we leave. Right." He took a deep breath. He felt better now that he'd made some kind of decision. "We have a lot to do."

Tamika disappeared to tie up the loose ends of her own work obligations, while Ruskin checked in with Ali'Maksam. To his joy, he learned that Max had succeeded in obtaining an emergency leave of absence from the university—though not, apparently, without calling in some favors. With that confirmation, he made flight reservations for three, then set to work copying most of the contents of his home think-tank onto slivers that he could take with him. Halfway through, he remembered a crucial detail and placed a call to the Yonupian Crafts Guild. The starship he'd ordered had living quarters for just one person. It would have to be altered; fortunately, he was told, the changes could be made before he arrived to take delivery. He accepted the increased cost without hesitation; he could worry about his expense account when he returned.

Max and Tamika rejoined him late in the afternoon, and together they made their way back to E'rik Daxter's laboratory. They found it subtly changed from the first visit: springtime had come to Daxter's forest, never mind that it was still autumn on the outside. The ice and snow drooped, and buds were poking out on many of the branches. Rivulets of water ran everywhere. The terrakells were nowhere in sight. Daxter dispensed with the fantastic imagery for himself, appearing instead as a ghostly but sober image of his original corporeal self.

"I'm glad you came," he said. "I understand you're on a tight schedule, so I'll try not to delay you. Willard, it would be helpful if you would allow me to communicate with your inner servants. Would you mind stepping over here?"

Ruskin stood beside Daxter's image. An aura of golden light fell around him and he felt himself rising, turning . . . and, so quickly he was scarcely aware of it, falling into a peaceful dream-state.

He was aware of voices, talking back and forth. Sometimes they spoke to him, and he answered; but the reality of it always seemed distant, like a dream glimpsed from afar.

Eventually he was awake again, lying on a bed of soft moss. His friends and Daxter were sitting beside him; the sun shone warmly. He sat up and stretched; he yawned. "Well, what did you learn?"

"That you're healthy," Daxter answered, with a firm nod.

"That's nice."

"And that your faithful servant, Dax, has made some progress in deciphering the coding of your less friendly inhabitants."

"Good, good."

"That you've regained some of your memory, and that Dax has succeeded in protecting you from blackouts."

Ruskin cocked his head. "I could have told you all that myself."

Daxter smiled. "Here's the important thing. Dax required some additional programming tools to help him carry out his job. We put our heads together and came up with something that I hope will do the trick." Ruskin frowned uncertainly. Daxter's smile disappeared. "I'm sorry to say, we've learned nothing concrete about your enemy, or its plan. I've tried to trace your friends Broder and Gorminski, but they seem to have disappeared—and yet there is no evidence of their having left Kantano's World, at least not under those names."

Ruskin glanced at Tamika. "I guess that's not a surprise."

"I've used some connections of my own," Daxter continued, "as well as the names Tamika gave me from the Omega group, and I haven't found anyone who admits to knowing them. People whom I have reason to trust, however, tell me that the Omega group is quite loosely organized and that infiltration by agents of one or another government would not be difficult. The question then is which government."

"That's where we started, isn't it?" Ruskin said.

A sardonic smile flashed across Daxter's face. "So sue me. I've been trying to evaluate the possible motives of either the Auricle Alliance or the Tandesko Triune, and I find them equally probable, and equally impenetrable. Neither would be averse to using questionable methods in pursuit of gain; but I cannot for the life of me guess at a specific motive for this. The planetary government seems less likely. Nongovernmental groups are also lesser suspects. For example, the Querayn Academies have the technical capability, but—"

"The Querayn?" Ruskin interrupted, with a sharp glance at Ali'Maksam. "They're a scholarly society, aren't they? Philosophers and—forgive me, Max—ivory tower researchers? Aren't they pretty isolationist?"

"Quite so—though perhaps not quite so much as they once appeared. They do have the capability, I judge. But Ali'Maksam here has academic connections with them, and it seems unlikely that he would not have gotten wind of some such extremist movement. Ali'Maksam?"

The Logothian tilted his head, studying the two before answering. His eyes were barely visible behind his visor. "It is true, I share certain interests in consciousness research with the Querayn. But whether I would have heard? Who can say? Still, I think it unlikely that they would have initiated such a thing."

"So where does that leave us?" Ruskin asked impatiently.

The Daxter image scratched its head. "Well, this super-nova business certainly puts everything in a new light. That suggests either the Triune or the Alliance, since they could muster the resources to do something with a supernova. But—" and he spread his palms—"I cannot guess what. I still surmise that the only way to find out is to let it all unfold and hope for the best." He shrugged. "Trust to Dax, and hope that among you, you can handle whatever you find."

Ruskin sensed that there was more. "And—?"

For a moment, Daxter seemed to gaze past him. "And . . . well, there is one other thing. Willard, it seems that your problem is not *entirely* connected with the NAGs."

Ruskin narrowed his gaze. "What do you mean?"

Daxter's eyes shifted to meet his. "Something in you doesn't *want* to reach certain memories. That's Dax's opinion. And mine. You may be unconsciously sabotaging your own recovery. You mentioned it yourself: you wondered whether you might have damaged your own data files, during a blackout period."

Tamika moved closer to him, frowning. Ruskin said nothing.

"Dax thinks that that is a possibility. Something in you is resisting. But as he told you, he is no psychiatrist. For that matter, neither am I."

"Yeah."

"Well—" Daxter's image stroked his chin. His eyes twinkled. "I have provided you with some assistance along those lines. I hope they will be helpful."

"What's that supposed to mean?"

Daxter smiled. His image was beginning to grow transparent. "If I tell you *too* much, the expectation might subvert the process. I think it'll be better if you learn about it as it happens. But I'll say this: Look for friends in unlikely places. You might be surprised what you find. And now, since you've expressed urgency about leaving—" His image became pale. His eyes were closing.

"Wait a minute, you can't just—"

Daxter's eyes fluttered open. "What? Oh, sorry. Terribly rude of me." He grinned. "Good-bye, then." And his image faded altogether.

Ruskin stared after him, disbelieving. Indignant. Angry. "What the hell?" he murmured. He looked at his friends. Nobody spoke. Finally he raised his eyebrows and pointed. "Let's go."

A way out had just appeared: another brick road, curling away into the distance—but this time rising up into the infinite starry darkness of outer space. The path was outlined by two rows of tiny white lights that seemed to extend forever.

As they trooped together into Daxter's universe, a voice boomed around them: "YOU ALL BE CAREFUL, NOW!"

Ruskin cracked only the faintest hint of a smile.

They gathered one last time at his apartment. Ali'Maksam took a final crack at Ruskin's cogitative system to see if he could find any data files lurking behind abstruse security routines. He couldn't. Ruskin paced while Max worked, hunched over the console, looking like a saurian wizard trying to extract some alien alchemy from the system. Tamika went through Ruskin's bags, checking on details of packing that he never would have gotten right in his present state of mind.

Ruskin was a nervous wreck. What, he wondered, or *who* had been added to the inside of his brain? *(Dax?)* he asked.

((We'll talk later.))

He sighed. Even Dax was too busy to talk to him.

When Ali'Maksam had finished, Ruskin prepared a memo to be transmitted to his office the following morning, explaining that circumstance had mandated his immediate departure and apologizing for his failure to clear his work first with Judith and Ankas. He knew that this would in no way satisfy them, but he hoped it might at least temper their outrage. He also dispatched a second memo, this one via interstellar n-channel communication to his destination at Betelgeuse, giving his expected arrival time.

At last they were ready to leave. The console was secured, with an active line to E'rik Daxter. They locked the apartment, carried their bags out front. The construction mechs—if that was what they really were—were still working on the sidewalk, though they seemed to be doing more standing around than working. Ruskin tossed them a salute as he walked by, but they showed no reaction. Eventually the autocab arrived, and the three piled in. "Hanswell Spaceport," Ruskin said. "Aries Line."

The cab lifted and accelerated into a highway lane two hundred meters above the rooftops. Soon the city had dwindled in the growing twilight, and the southern mountains loomed, lines of navigational markers winking. The twilight had deepened to night by the time they made it through the mountain pass, and before them the great plain seemed to roll up to them like the edge of a vast ocean; and floating silent and still on its surface was a glowing necklace: the spaceport, bright and full and crowded with evening business. The cab, gliding with the flow of traffic, descended to ground level and entered the spaceport access lanes.

They emerged at the east terminal and made their way to the Aries counter. Inside of two hours, they were settled aboard the low-orbit space shuttle, awaiting departure.

An hour later, they were peering out the shuttle windows at the curvature of Kantano's World, watching their second sunset of the day as the sky darkened to black and filled with stars. Ahead of them was the station called Kantano Skybase, jump-off point for the high-orbiting space cities— jump-off point for the stars themselves.

PART THREE

✴

PROJECT BREAKSTAR

"For a man can lose neither the past nor the future. . . ."
—Marcus Aurelius

PROLOGUE

✳

She was in the control room when the message arrived. "Thalia, a priority on your screen," said one of the tech-aides, passing behind her as she leaned over the gensat programming board.

"Mm?" She glanced up, then walked over to her own screen and tapped in her security code. A message appeared, under the screenhead of the Station Communications office: *"Memo just received, as follows: 'Departing Kantano's World. Expect to arrive Starmuse Station by 24/9/178. —Willard Ruskin.' No other information provided. Hope this cheers you. Com-Chief."*

Thalia drew a slow breath. The twenty-fourth. That would give them practically no time at all to bring him up to speed. Damn it—hadn't he gotten their update? Well, never mind; at least he was coming. She could forget her nightmares that he had been kidnapped by enemy agents. Now, just don't give him a hard time when he gets here, she thought. He's going to feel strange seeing you, and there's no telling what he'll be feeling about the project. So go easy; don't make a fuss.

She chuckled silently. But not so easy he doesn't know it's you.

Realizing that she had a silly grin on her face, Thalia carefully replaced it with a frown, then blanked the screen. She looked up and caught Snyder's eye back at the gensat programming console. She gave him a brief thumbs-up gesture, then let her smile out again, just for an instant. Snyder's eyebrows went up; then he, too, grinned and returned to his work.

Thalia gazed up at the enormous image of the billowing sun on the front screen. And for the first time in weeks, her heart lifted with genuine hope.

CHAPTER 20

✳

Kantano Skybase seemed like little more than a gigantic spaceport, wheeling through the sky a few hundred kilometers over the clouds and oceans of Kantano's World. Tamika, Max, and Ruskin made their way across the lobbies like all the other tourists, rubbernecking out the windows at the sight of the world they had just left, pulling their baggage along behind. Ruskin didn't trust automatic baggage handling, especially with his data slivers. It meant they had to pass through inspection the slow way. Once they'd cleared customs, they made their way across the spaceport to the gate for the high-planetary-orbit shuttle.

Max hardly looked out of place at all here, even in his visored exposure suit. The station was full of non-Humans, including the occasional Logothian. Ali'Maksam's kin tended to wear disconcertingly similar garb, and at one point Ruskin almost called out to a Logothian he thought was Max, wandering away from him—only to realize that Max was at his side, just a step or two behind him. Tamika chuckled at his double take and latched onto his opposite arm.

They passed through a tropical garden in the restaurant district, where it was a little less crowded—possibly because the humidity hit them like a wall of moisture as they passed into the display of aromatic bay rum bushes, white-and-purple-blossomed frangipani, Seven Sisters orchids, and Barnard's elephant ears. As they paused to admire the blossoms and inhale the sweet fragrances, Ruskin noticed a small knot of Querayn academicians seated beneath a stand of bamboo-ferns. There was nothing terribly unusual about the sight of Querayn scholars; but for some reason, his gaze was drawn to them: two Humans and several noliHumans, all wearing the distinctive mauve-bordered robes of their disciplines.

He felt a curious urge to engage them in conversation— a totally involuntary urge, which was extremely odd. He had no particular interest in the Querayn; Ali'Maksam had far more in common with them than he. As a class, the tele'eLogoth and Querayn shared overlapping interests in some of the more abstract disciplines—logic and ethics, universal consciousness psychology, mathematics, and certain abstruse branches of epistemology and teleological exegesis. Ali'Maksam was in fact exceptional among tele'eLogoth for his practical skills; the majority of his fellows kept to the more arcane branches of knowledge, pursued in part through empathic meditation. The Querayn, however, were even more extreme in their devotion to the esoteric disciplines. They were best known for their studies, generally dismissed by mainstream science, of such notions as supposed consciousness in quantum and cosmological systems. Though some of their work had earned them high regard, many scientists (including Ruskin, so far as he could remember) considered the majority of their studies unempirical at best, more fringe-element religious philosophy than science.

"Willard?"

He turned, startled.

Ali'Maksam angled his head. "Are you planning to join in their conversation?"

"What?" And then he realized that he had not merely been staring at the Querayn, but walking toward them. "No—no—of course not." In response to a quizzical look from Tamika, he shrugged, his cheeks flushed. "Let's get going. It's hot in here."

Ali'Maksam pointed the way out of the garden. Ruskin followed, but his mind was in a haze, wondering why those people had caught his eye. He looked around dreamily, noticed several noliHumans of other varieties: their pale, hairless, almost featureless faces setting them off from their genetically different Human cousins. Most noliHumans were not Querayn. Why did that matter? Now they were passing a pair of dark, lean Tandesko talisans, carrying food from a nearby lunch counter. Ruskin stared after them, suppressing a feeling of anger—which the two Tandeskoes had done nothing to provoke.

((Willard, your emotions are a cauldron here. I wonder why.))

He walked a little farther before replying. *(I don't know.)* It shamed him to see the prejudice in his own heart. *(Is that really me?)*

((We're working on a test to find out.))

(Great. Let me know.) Dax and his new programming. He recalled napping on the shuttle ride up; in the midst of it he'd had a feeling that somehow his dreams were being altered, manipulated. What kind of strange capabilities had Daxter given his little synthetic offspring, anyway?

((Tsk, tsk . . . resistance and hostility. That's no way to treat someone who's only trying to make you better.))

Ruskin growled inwardly. *(Nobody ever told me I had to enjoy being headshrunk by someone a millionth my size.)*

((Actually, Willard, I'm more like a billionth your size—))

Ruskin sighed, walking with Max and Tamika into a passenger waiting area.

((—but I understand your feelings.))

(Dax—can't you take an insult?) He ignored the NAGS's rejoinder. "Is this the place, Max?"

"Aries Grissondon City shuttle number one-three-four," Ali'Maksam said, pointing to the sign. Passengers were already clotting the waiting area. Max led the way across to the far side, where they stacked their bags and perched for the wait on a short bench. "And here," Max said whimsically, "we await our destiny to the stars." He rested his head against the wall and went instantly to sleep.

Tamika curled her legs up on the bench, laid her head on Ruskin's lap, and followed Max's example.

Ruskin stared at the crowd of passengers and unconsciously started counting aliens as they walked by, making a list of the ones he instinctively trusted, and those he didn't.

*   *   *

The offices of the Associative Frontiers Institute were unusually silent this morning. That was fine with Judith; she didn't want to have to speak with anyone right now. She sat at her desk, scowling at a memo that had come up on her work-display. It was from Willard Ruskin. It said that he was terribly sorry, but he'd had to advance his departure time and therefore hadn't been able to clear his research results first with Judith and Ankas. By the time she read this, it said, he would be on his way off Kantano's World.

Judith's left eyebrow twitched as she reread the memo for the fourth time. What bothered her was not so much the breach of company policy about internal review—which was serious, but not unforgivable—as the confirmation in her own mind that Ruskin's behavior had become dangerously erratic. If she'd needed proof of his instability, then this was it. The day before yesterday, he'd been confused and unable even to summarize the state of his research results. Today, he was on his way off-planet, because time was too short for him to submit to review. Highly unlikely: far more probably, he was *afraid* to submit to the review.

Judith felt a terrible pang of dismay. She genuinely cared for Ruskin and didn't want to hurt him. Nevertheless, she seemed to have no choice. With a sigh, she flicked a smoke-stick alight and turned to open a com-channel. It took only a moment to make the connection.

Broder took a chance and left the office on automatic for a few minutes while he went to grab some lunch. He had a terrific headache from lack of sleep and food, and Gorminski hadn't come in yet. He'd been up all night tracking reports of Ruskin's departure from Kantano's World. It was a delicate time, because soon he would no longer have any direct control over the operation. It would be up to Ganz and Jeaves; and he didn't want to turn them loose without maximum information and instructions. One thing that worried him was that Ruskin had taken his two friends, the Jones woman and the Logoth, with him. That hadn't been in the original itinerary. Did it mean that the man suspected something—that Gorminski's NAGS were failing? The thought was enough to give Broder a sour stomach. He wondered, not for the first time, if it had been a mistake for them to drop out of sight as they had; perhaps they should have taken the risk of continuing contact with Ruskin, continuing the charade.

Another thing: why the hell hadn't April checked in? Or any of her colleagues?

His favorite diner was just down the block. He hurried, and bought a salad sandwich crammed with greens and cheddar cheese, and a large coffee. Fretting over the time even as he did so, he tore open the end of the sandwich wrapper and took a huge bite, growling with satisfaction. Gulping a mouthful of coffee, he hurried out of the diner.

It was a gorgeous, sunny day—yet another day, lost to worry and fear. *It's for the good of the worlds. Remember that. For the good of the worlds.*

Gorminski was in the office when he got back. "Sorry I'm late," he wheezed. "Staying up last night did me in. I've got a touch of nuflu, I think." He blew his nose. He looked awful.

Broder shook his head silently. That was just what he needed, was Ilex passing some goddamn bug on to him. "You don't have to stay if you're sick," he said, none too diplomatically.

"I'm okay," Gorminski said, snuffling. "We got a message from April. Priority."

"Shit," Broder said. "I knew I shouldn't have gone out." He punched up the message on the com. "Did you read it?"

"I just got here. No."

"Well, take a good look." Broder rapped the screen where the message was framed. He stepped back to let Gorminski peer at it.

Gorminski's face sagged as he read. "Unstable . . . com-

promised reliability . . . recommends removal." He looked
up. "Stanley, this isn't good."

"You don't say. And April's prejudiced in the guy's favor.
If *she* thinks he's far enough gone to turn in a report like
that . . ."

Gorminski rubbed his eyes wearily. "Ganz?"

"What the hell else?"

Gorminski looked unhappy. "You don't want to check
with Jeaves first?"

Broder sat down at the com, sandwich and coffee forgotten. "Sure, we'll ask. But I don't see what Jeaves could
say that would change what we've got in front of us right
now."

"No." Gorminski's voice was full of regret. "No, I guess
not."

"Bad breaks. They're part of the game, Ilex. I know you
worked hard on those NAGs. But it's just part of the damned
game."

"So if Ruskin's out of it, what do we do then?"

"Well, we'll just have to leave it to Ganz, won't we?"
Broder shrugged unhappily. "It might be better to sacrifice
the whole thing than to let it stay in the wrong hands."

Gorminski shuddered, but did not disagree.

Jeaves was in the darkness of his other employers' briefing
room when the call came in from Broder. The robot answered without breaking the stride of its conversation with
the Seniors. *(Yes, Stanley, I understand. Can I check back
with you in a few minutes? I am in the midst of preparing
a transmission to Grissondon Space City, quite important.
Yes, as soon as I can. . . .)*

To the Seniors, the robot continued, "My analysis of the
tissue sample confirms the presence of a third set of NAGs
in Ruskin's body. His visit to E'rik Daxter two days ago
clearly suggests their source; however, so far I have been
unable to decode the new programming. If Daxter deliberately disguised his design—"

One of the voices interrupted. Jeaves recognized the
voice as that of Senior Karel. "We understand that, Quer-

obo. We wish you to continue your analysis, of course. But just now we feel that more might be gained from an evaluation of Ali'Maksam's intentions."

"His intentions with respect to what?" Jeaves asked.

"With respect to his choice of E'rik Daxter. If he felt he needed further help, he could have sought it from us. He did not." Senior Karel sounded puzzled and perhaps a little hurt.

"I know of no way to determine Ali'Maksam's intentions," Jeaves said.

"Perhaps you can do so in the field," another voice said. "It is possible that you will solve the programming code, as well. We will work on it here, of course; but it is uncertain whether we will be able to convey our findings to you once you have left the system."

"Will you notify your representatives at Starmuse of the situation?" Jeaves asked.

"If I am able to travel there myself, I will," said Senior Karel. "Otherwise, no. Even if communications were secure, those at Starmuse are of a more conservative persuasion. Academic purists, really. Willing to study, but reluctant to act. To be safe, we must supply you with all of the tools and data that we can, before you leave."

"That must be in the next day or two," the robot cautioned. "I cannot predict exactly when my last updating transmission will occur. Once I am out of range—"

"Of course. We understand. Do Broder and Gorminski know of the tissue samples?"

"No. Not unless their intelligence sources exceed my estimation."

"Very well. Querobo, you have done well. We pray that you will succeed."

Jeaves withdrew its codelink. "Thank you. And now I must depart. My soulware transmission is scheduled for this evening, and there is much to be done."

"Much indeed. We will speak soon."

Judith was still thinking of her message to the Auricle Review Agency long after she had transmitted it, even after the acknowledgment had come back. More than ever, she felt the weight of the responsibility that the agency had laid upon her, to observe and report on security-sensitive activities at AFI. When they'd recruited her, six months ago, she had been shocked at the idea; later, reconsidering, she'd concluded that it was both a compliment to her and possibly a genuine service to the worlds-nation she loved. Not without pride—and not without misgivings—she had accepted the code-name "April" and agreed to keep her eyes open at the institute. This was the first time, however, that she'd actually blown the whistle on a colleague; and she didn't like the taste of it. Why did it have to be her friend Willard, of all people?

Never mind that she'd had little choice, that the success of important Alliance projects depended upon people's willingness to put their ideals ahead of even personal relationships. She flipped her memo back onto the screen, to read it one last time before erasing it: ". . . *Ruskin has become unstable to a degree that may compromise his reliability in so sensitive a position. With regret, I must recommend his removal from the Breakstar project.*" She exhaled slowly.

"Judith?" said a voice directly behind her.

"What?" Startled, she sat upright and turned. It was Galen. She stared at him dazedly for an instant, then hastily reached out and blanked the message. "What is it, Galen? I didn't hear you. You should knock." She was angry but tried not to show it.

"I'm sorry. I did knock. May I come in?" Galen said.

"Yes, of course." She tried to soften the rasping sound of her breath, deep in her throat. She felt as though she had just been caught in some shameful act. Maybe she had.

Galen nodded solemnly. His eyes went to the screen, now empty. "I was coming to talk to you about this ag report." He tapped a printout in his hand, but his eyes were still focused on her screen. He blinked and looked away. "Maybe I should come back later." He backed out of the doorway.

"Galen, wait!" But he was gone. *Jesus Christ—how stupid!* He'd obviously seen the message, or at least part of it. How could she have been so careless? Lost in her own thoughts . . . *But you did what you had to do. There was no other choice. Not with Willard acting that way.*

Guiltily, she erased the memo from her console's memory. Then she rose and strode down the hall to Galen's cubicle. The door was closed. She hesitated, then buzzed. The door winked open, but Galen remained seated with his back to the door, studying his printout. She recognized that posture. He was hunched forward, his shoulders tensed. He was upset. Deeply upset.

Because of what he'd seen on her screen?

Judith triggered the door closed and cleared her throat.

Galen turned suddenly, raising his eyes to meet hers. His expression took her by surprise. Uncertainty, and . . . *joy*, it looked like. *Joy?* But why? When he spoke, his voice was contrite. "Judith, I didn't mean to look at your screen—really! But I couldn't help seeing—"

"What was on that screen was none of your business," she said sternly.

"Of course not," he whispered. "I know. It's just that—I never knew that you and I were both—" His head jerked away. "I shouldn't even be saying it."

Startled, she tilted her head, studying him. "You shouldn't be saying *what?*"

He brought his gaze back nervously. "That we're both—I mean, I didn't know that you were working for the Group, too. That's all. I saw the header on your memo. I didn't see anything that you wrote—really—just that you were reporting to the Group." He pronounced *group* as though it were a proper name.

"The—" she hesitated, before saying cautiously—"*agency*, you mean?"

He smiled. "Right. The agency." He barked a short laugh. "The Auricle Review Agency. Right."

A knot of tension took hold in her throat. "Is there something funny about that?" she murmured.

He looked puzzled. "Well, I mean it's just—what better cover? I mean, than the name of the opposition." He rubbed his forehead with the back of his hand for a moment. "Right?"

Judith bit her lip. "Right," she whispered.

Galen nodded in apparent relief. He lowered his voice,

but it still cracked with emotion. *"God, Judith, I'm just so happy that I'm not the only one here. And you, of all people! I was afraid you were still strong on all that Auricle stuff!"*

Judith kept her mouth shut as her mind raced. Was she going mad? What was Galen saying? The Auricle Review Agency was a watchdog bureau for Alliance security. At least, that was what she had thought. What she had been told. Could he possibly be saying . . . *oh Jesus.*

Galen had admitted to a brief flirtation once with Tandesko-style sex, but that was all over. Wasn't it? And anyway, he'd never been political, certainly not with . . . them. Had he?

Jesus!

She struggled to take a deep breath. All this . . . was it possible that she had been deceived from the start? Auricle Review Agency. How could she have known?

"Judith?" Galen murmured. "I'm sorry, I guess I shouldn't have said—but I thought since we both—oh, shit, Judith, I'm sorry!"

For a moment longer, she could not speak. Straighten shoulders . . . take breath . . . get control. The idea that she had been . . . *deceived* by a political group (who? Tandesko?) had never even entered her mind. It had all seemed so real, so legitimate.

She focused her gaze narrowly on Galen. Her head was buzzing and she felt as though she were a million miles away. "Galen," she said, her voice far sterner than her heart, "I want you to tell me exactly what your connection is with the Auricle . . . Review Agency. You've just breached security, and I must know precisely how serious that breach is."

Galen's eyes looked wounded. Her gaze burned into his. Finally he nodded, took a breath. And began, in a trembling voice, to tell her what she wanted to know.

And as he spoke, a chill grew down her spine as she realized the enormity of her error.

CHAPTER 21

✳

The trip out from Kantano Skybase took just over nine hours. They spent most of that time trying to nap in the cramped flight seats. Ali'Maksam was motionless, lost in a meditative trance behind his visor. As the high-orbit shuttle approached the Port Grissondon Orbital City, Ruskin silently sipped juice and coffee, trying to revive himself, trying to take stock of the curious streams of thought that had been running through his sleep, and wondering what the devil Dax was doing to his head. Finally, crowding his face next to Tamika's, he peered out the window at the sprawl of the space settlement.

Out here a few hundred thousand kilometers from Kantano's World, Port Grissondon floated in a Lagrangian orbit trailing Kantano's primary moon; it was a center for manufacturing as well as an interplanetary and interstellar transportation hub. A smog of dissipating gases surrounded the city, blotting out all but the brightest stars. The settlement was full of lights, like any city. Many of them were moving: it was astonishing how many spaceships there were around Port Grissondon. Hundreds were clustered around the trailing edge of the settlement; that was probably the spaceship factory. Traffic moved silently through the haze like ferryboats through a misty harbor.

Across the aisle, Max stirred to wakefulness and joined them in peering out.

The shuttle closed on the leading edge of the city and, as soon as a gate became available, moved in to dock. They began hauling their gear out of the storage bins again; but Ruskin went through it all with rising good cheer—even through customs. The real voyage was about to begin, and that thought was enough to give him hope.

* * *

Following the luxury of a good night's sleep in a hotel
room, they made their way first thing in the morning, station time, to the offices of the Yonupian Crafts Guild. There
they were met by a fragile-looking humanoid named Farsil,
who was the Yonupian sales representative handling Ruskin's order. "Good-owner Ruskin." Farsil extended a hand,
palm up, and flicked it side to side between Ruskin and
himself in a gesture of greeting.

"My companions," Ruskin explained, introducing Max
and Tamika. "You received the message that my ship must
accommodate them, as well?"

"Indeed," Farsil answered. "These late changes always
are somewhat problematic, but I'm certain that our design
will satisfy your needs." The Yonupian gazed at them with
large eyes that drooped at the outer corners, conveying a
sense of inconsolable sadness. That was a fine irony, Ruskin
thought. The Yonupians were the premier makers of starships throughout the Habitat of Humanity—and for all Ruskin knew, beyond. If they felt sadness it certainly wasn't
for lack of business.

"I hope it wasn't too much trouble."

Farsil dismissed his concern with a flick of his fingers.

"I don't see how you could make a last-minute change
like that at all," Tamika confessed.

"If you would care to view our production line, perhaps
that would help you understand," Farsil said.

The Yonupian led them to a bubble-windowed lift-car.
He touched a control, and the car began to rise through a
wide shaft, passing other cars moving the opposite direction. Half a minute later, they glided out of the shaft into
a vast enclosed factory space, studded with lights. Tamika
gasped; Ruskin felt his blood stir with awe; even Max's
breath hissed out audibly. There were easily a hundred
partially grown starships arrayed in the factory space; some
were open to the air, with robots and workers swarming
around them, but the majority were enclosed in huge, clear
growth tanks.

Farsil noted their expressions with evident satisfaction.

"Our growth tanks are the most sophisticated in the Habitat," he said, pointing as he spoke. "Some you will see in hard vacuum and zero gravity, for assembly of certain critical components. Others contain liquid or vapors, and it is in those tanks that most of the actual structures are grown." The tiny car accelerated, high above the factory floor. As his three visitors stared, Farsil pointed out spacecraft in various stages of production: small skeletons of packet couriers arrayed like seeds in pods; a large passenger liner emerging newborn from a tank, glistening; freighters whole and in pieces; shrouded military vessels; and several strangely contoured ships—only half formed—that Farsil identified as scientific vessels under construction for the Querayn Academies.

Ruskin was surprised. "Why would they need all of those research ships? I thought their work was theoretical."

Farsil only smiled. It was not his place to comment on the activities of Yonupian clients, his expression suggested.

"Theory can only carry one so far before practical investigation is required," Ali'Maksam remarked. "Even in such areas as the Querayn study."

Ruskin raised his eyebrows. He felt a tingle somewhere in his forebrain. Were the Querayn moving out of the philosophical sciences, then? He shrugged finally and moved his gaze farther along.

"There you see the basic structural growth tanks," Farsil said, pointing.

Ruskin glanced at Tamika, who was squinting in puzzlement at the tanks. "Nanoconstructors, naturally," he said.

"Of course," Farsil said. "All components, including hulls, are assembled from raw elements, atom by atom, by molecule-sized assembly units—trillions of them—at speeds that to us would be blinding if we could see them at all." He turned his sad eyes toward Tamika. "This is why we were able to make your structural alterations on short notice. It required reprogramming and one reimmersion, but the request came in time to avoid serious complications." He nodded. "The total growth time for a ship can be as short as four days. The cost, of course, is a consideration for most clients."

Farsil appeared to ignore Tamika's piercing gaze at Ruskin, who was thinking, as the Yonupian talked, *Yes, the same things that are in me; isn't it wonderful?* Farsil continued, ". . . which accounts for atomic-scale precision, combined with low cost." Ruskin cleared his throat at that last assertion—"low cost" was definitely a relative term— but Farsil paid no attention. "The diamond-foam structures give our ships high strength with low mass. . . ."

Ruskin shook his head at the thought that he was being remanufactured from the inside out by machines just like those being manipulated by the Yonupians to build spaceships. And who, he wondered, was controlling *his* machines? He shivered, recalling for the first time in a long while the terror and bewilderment he'd felt when he'd first seen his body changing, when he'd realized that someone seemed to want very badly to kill him.

Was all that over now? He thought of how exposed he was, touring the factory, moving about in a strange city. If they were going to try again, they could easily do it here.

Or they could sabotage his spaceship. He made a mental note to speak to Farsil about a final security check before he took delivery on his ship.

"Up here," Farsil said, "is a bare skeleton emerging from its growth bath." They were approaching a huge tank in the process of being drained of a milky fluid. Remaining in the tank was a long, iridescent structure that looked more like an enormous fish skeleton than a spaceship. "What you see there is composed entirely of our own porous diamond material, doped with certain proprietary materials. Of course, it's the precise crystalline structure that makes our materials superior in quality."

"Of course," Ruskin murmured.

"The fluid carries both raw materials and the nanoassemblers themselves, including the intelligence units. Rather like blood . . ."

Ruskin closed his eyes, wishing Farsil would change the subject.

They were moving into a more confined area now. "This is our engine plant, where stardrives are grown separately— for sale to other manufacturers. Our own ships have their engines grown integrally with the hulls."

Ruskin nodded dutifully. Despite the sales talk, he was

fascinated by the tanks. Some were filled with milky fluids, some with clear fluids with intriguing shapes half-visible, some with swirling vapors. Several were being flushed clear, offering glimpses of the gleaming curved surfaces on the stardrive generators that would distort space-time itself, allowing ships to slip quickly between the stars. Nearby stars, anyway. Though Ruskin well understood the principles of stardrive, he could only wonder at the machinery that actually made it possible.

Farsil turned the car around and sent it speeding back the way they had come. "That is all that we can show you, for reasons of security."

"You mean the security of your trade secrets?"

"That, and the security of our clients, whose activities are their business and no one else's." Farsil gazed at Ruskin intently. "Be assured, Good-owner Ruskin, the security of your ship is guaranteed. That is a matter of strictest guild policy." Farsil stood ramrod straight then and seemed to give all his attention to the steering of the car.

Had Farsil been reading his mind, or were many of his customers concerned about the same thing? Ruskin wondered. He asked Farsil where his ship was now.

"In space, on its final inspection and shakedown, Good-owner. By tomorrow, it will be ready for you to take delivery." The Yonupian's sad eyes were strangely reassuring. "If you like, we can arrange for fueling and provisioning during the night."

Ruskin felt Tamika reaching to take his hand. He squeezed back, glanced at her and Ali'Maksam both. "That would be excellent. We'd like to be under way tomorrow, if possible."

Farsil nodded. "Then under way you shall be."

With departure time so close, he might well have begun to think that the danger was past, and that once they were in flight, he could put some of his fears behind him. He *might* have thought that way, if it hadn't been for a chance encounter that night while he and Tamika were downtown shopping for additional supplies. It was a momentary

thing—just a meeting of eyes across a crowded concourse—
and then the other person was gone. Ruskin had scarcely
seen the other's face; nevertheless, he was left with an
unsettled feeling in the pit of his stomach. *Who was
that . . . ? Not quite Human . . .*

Tamika caught his arm. "What's wrong, Rus'lem? You
look like you just saw a ghost."

"What? Oh, nothing really. I mean—I don't know, maybe
I did."

Her eyes sharpened. "Try that again, Willard."

"For a second there, I thought I saw someone I knew."
A tall figure, looming over him. He blinked dizzily. That
memory, welling up from—

((Don't you remember, Willard?))

A cold ripple went up his spine. *(The one who attacked
me?)*

*((Let's just say, that was my first thought,
too.))*

Ruskin twisted around to peer across the concourse, but
whoever it was had long since vanished into the mass of
people. *A tall figure . . .* a noliHuman? Perhaps; he couldn't
be sure. He'd caught the gaze, all right, but not the whole
person. But the silhouette . . . *(Dax, are you saying that
was the person who attacked me?)*

*((I wasn't in the game at the time, if you re-
call. But let's say that the* association *was
striking.))*

Ruskin realized that Tamika was staring at him. "Someone you knew," she asked. "Who? Someone good or someone bad?"

He shook his head. "I wish I could be sure."

Tamika scowled, her golden cat eyes narrowing to thin
slits. "I'm not *asking* you to be sure, you stubborn oaf. Who
did you *think* it was?"

He reflected before answering. Was it better for her to
know? Or would it just worry her needlessly? He sighed.
"I *thought* . . . that it might have been the person who
tried to kill me."

Tamika looked unsurprised. "All right," she said in a
sensible tone of voice. "Let's finish and get the hell back
to the hotel. We'll alert the security there."

Ruskin scratched his head. "I'm not sure, Twig. I just caught the eyes, really, and that's—" he shook his head— "well, anyway, it wasn't a proper Human. Maybe a noli-Human. I'm not sure."

Tamika was in no mood for discussion. She towed him by the arm down the concourse. Left to himself, he probably would have wandered around in a daze. As it was, his mind spun in circles, thinking: NoliHuman? A connection to the Querayn? Surely not. But who else?

By the time they were back at the hotel, the memory of the encounter had subsided to the intensity of mere curiosity, like a powerful dream half-remembered. But like some other dreams lately, he knew that it had not gone away; it had merely sunk into the abyss of subconscious consideration, a disturbance deep in his mind. A disturbance deep and silent.

Silent and slow.

The night passed with no further ripples.

Before taking them to the ship the next morning, Farsil handed Ruskin a small wafer. "This is a sealed transmission from Kantano's, Good-owner Ruskin. It was received by our office for forwarding to you." Ruskin looked at the wafer in puzzlement, as Farsil explained, "It will play back on your ship's control console, with proper identity verification."

Ruskin shrugged. "Thank you."

"Also, we received a software transmission from your home office, coded for loading into your ship's console." As Ruskin raised a startled eyebrow, Farsil added, "Since the identifications were in order and the ship's title is held by Associative Frontiers Institute, we followed the required legal procedure and loaded the transmission as instructed."

"I see. Can you tell me the nature of the software?"

Farsil leveled his hand in a palm-up gesture, flicking it side to side from the wrist. "We are not privy to content, Good-owner. We merely follow the letter of the law."

"Of course," Ruskin murmured with a scowl. He was far

from satisfied. But it must have been from Judith or Ankas. If so, what the dickens were they up to? Of course, he had left the planet rather abruptly. Maybe they thought he'd forgotten some essential piece of business; maybe he *had* forgotten something. In any case, he would check once they were aboard. He pocketed the wafer and bowed slightly.

Farsil turned and led the way to the ship.

From the viewing area, it looked like a sort of melted, mutated peanut, shimmering pearl in color. It was a small ship by interstellar standards, smaller than the shuttle that had brought them here from Kantano Skybase. Most of the vessel was power plant and fuel storage; the living quarters and flight deck occupied a nodule near its nose. It looked sturdy; it didn't necessarily look as though it could cross a hundred light-years in a matter of days or weeks.

"Can we board?" Ruskin asked.

Farsil took them down a snaking tube to the main space-lock and on into the ship, demonstrating various controls along the way. The tour of the bridge, living quarters, and power section took no more than an hour, including a briefing on the ship's main operational systems. "All of the information you might need is in the ship's console, with duplicates in your cabin and on the power-deck," Farsil said as they paused back on the bridge. "In the event of emergency, it's all there where you can reach it. Normally, you can just ask the ship to do what you want it to do." He gazed at them with drooping eyes and a sad smile. "Do you have any questions?"

"I'm sure we will have—" Tamika remarked—"when we're ten light-years out."

Farsil bowed, acknowledging the humor. "Then you can ask your ship," he replied. "It knows far more about itself than I do. Is there anything else?"

Ruskin shook his head. "As soon as we're loaded, we'll be ready to go." He stepped to the control console, running his fingers lightly across its new face. He turned to Farsil with a grin, and felt Dax putting a puzzling question at the tip of his tongue. "Does this thing come with road maps?" he asked.

The others looked startled. "Sir?" Farsil asked.

Ruskin felt Dax laughing inside him.

((Forget it. I'll explain later.))

"Never mind," Ruskin said with a sigh. "How soon can we launch?"

Farsil relaxed. "Whenever you like, sir. She's ready, and she's yours."

CHAPTER 22

✳

Ganz studied the layout of the Tandesko vessel for a long time before making a move. All the crew members were now off the ship making last-minute preparations for departure. They suspected nothing. Why should they? Their ship was a scientific courier. Now was the time for Ganz to act.

The hatch opened easily on the first try. The identification codes that Broder had sent hir were good then, and a lucky thing. Ganz could have broken in anyway, doubtless; but it would have been risky to be seen fiddling with the hatch programming. This way, who—other than the owners, and they weren't here—would be suspicious of Ganz boarding a Tandesko ship? Hir was projecting only a slightly altered appearance: Tandesko talisan, rather than *hrisi*. Port security had accepted hir identification without question.

The hatch rematerialized with Ganz on the inside. A quick look confirmed that the passageways were laid out exactly as the library readout had indicated. Ganz moved quickly to the forward power-decks. Hir had no way of knowing when the crew would return, but this job would take only a few minutes. The power-deck hatches opened and Ganz stepped through, treading the narrow service passageway.

The K-space generators looped around the passageway like a helical array of translucent jewels. At present they were dark; but when the ship made its long jump between the stars—when these generators were brought to life to distort the fabric of space—they would blaze with power and with the light of a sun. With the modifications Ganz was about to make, they would blaze even brighter. But they wouldn't blaze long.

The beauty of neutralizing a ship in this way was that the explosion would occur within the confined dimensional rift of K-space; and while there might be some flash-through along the K-space distortion lines, any radiation that might emerge in the normal-space continuum would do so light-years from the nearest observers. Even if, years later, a flash were observed, it would be virtually impossible to trace its source.

Ganz found the relay module hir was looking for, nestled among the generators. Hir opened a small tool pack and plugged a test unit into the module to verify the existing programming. Grunting in satisfaction, Ganz broke the module open with a molecular-bonding probe and examined its interior. Hir removed a thin quasicrys wafer and re-placed it with a similar wafer from hir tool pack; then hir retested, rebonded, and again retested the module. Done. Ganz rose and concealed the tool pack in the folds of hir blouse.

The programming change would be undetectable from the piloting station, and in fact, except for one tiny, delib-erate anomaly, would come into play just moments before the ship exploded. It would be a clean death for the crew, an instant death. They would feel no pain. That was the way Ganz preferred to work. Efficiency, without needless cruelty.

Retreating quickly the way hir had come, Ganz closed the entryway to the power section and peered down the passageway. The ship was still and silent. Hir walked calmly off the ship and out through the port security gates. Within moments, hir was lost among the crowds of Grissondon City.

An hour later Ganz returned to the port, but to another section, where hir own ship was docked. This ship was quite similar in appearance to the one hir had just left. The ship-board security system was far tighter than the other's; nevertheless, Ganz checked the ship thoroughly for mal-function or sabotage. Then hir waited, chatting occasionally with the shipboard cogitative system. They had a polite disagreement as to whether or not hir should neutralize Ruskin here, where it would be relatively easy. Ganz ac-knowledged hir own bias toward doing so; hir had left the job unfinished before, and that rankled. But the Jeaves-copy in the system urged forbearance: Ruskin might, after all, perform as desired, and without him the best that they could hope for would be so much less.

Ganz was a *hrisi;* hir was not a political person. Hir was aware that hir employer, Stanley Broder, represented a splinter faction of the Tandesko hierarchy and not the main quorum. What hir was doing now might not in fact be pleasing to the main quorum—almost certainly would not be. But that mattered little to hir. Ganz did what was contracted for: no more, no less. And since the Jeaves-copy carried some of Broder's command authority, Ganz agreed to forbear. But hir couldn't quite get that original contract out of hir mind, the one which—to hir shame—hir had failed to complete.

When the Tandesko courier ship *Unity* departed for deep space, Ganz watched on the monitors. An hour and thirty-four minutes later, Ganz received hir own departure clearance. Ganz paid scant attention to the sight of the space city receding astern, but paid close attention indeed to the courier ship ahead. Hir flew a parallel course, observing closely the spectral signature of *Unity*'s exhaust. Hir noted the tiny variation hir was looking for in the exhaust—not enough to affect the ship's performance, and well within operational limits—but enough to verify what hir needed to know.

Ganz watched the characteristic rainbow flash and the momentary distortion in the starfield as the courier made the crossover to K-space and vanished from the Kantano star system. Ganz nodded to hirself and prepared to make the same leap.

The courier's destination was Betelgeuse, a supergiant red sun nearing the end of its natural life. Orbiting the sun was the Starmuse scientific outpost, nominally an interworld research station, but in fact the domain of the Auricle Alliance. Aboard *Unity* were two Tandesko scientific observers, en route by treaty arrangement to monitor the Auricle scientists, who in turn were monitoring the star, preparing to watch stardeath in process.

The courier's passengers would never arrive at their destination. But Ganz would arrive in their place.

* * *

Grissondon City and Kantano's World were well lost
astern by the time Ruskin gave his ship's computer the go-
ahead to make the crossover jump to K-space. He did not
do so casually. First he'd checked the entire system from
top to bottom, and all of the navigational instructions; and
all of his work was double-checked by Ali'Maksam. It wasn't
merely his distrust of an untried cogitative system that troubled him, or their inability to identify the additional software that Farsil had spoken of. It was also the message
carried in the wafer that Farsil had handed him—the message from his home office, from Judith. *"You may be followed by someone masquerading as an Auricle loyalist,
someone who may try to remove you. . . ."* But the system
and the nav-calcs checked out, and he couldn't *not* go just
because of a warning of something he already knew anyway.

"Do it," he said to the console.

"Very good, sir," it answered.

And he and Tamika and Max rested back in their couches
arrayed before the curved viewscreen of the ship's tiny
bridge, while the system counted down. . . .

■

Gravity flicked off.

The viewscreen in front of his eyes stretched like an
elastic sheet as the ship turned inside out and back again
. . . and so did his stomach and his mind. . . .

■

It was as though his head simply opened up, and out of
it came floating thoughts and feelings and memories, like
balloons rising into the ether; he reached out and tried to
capture them, but only a few came within his reach . . .
*two creatures scampering after him, reeling drunkenly
through the trees . . . a fortress floating in orange clouds
. . . a tall figure, looming. . . .*

■

Feelings of wary speculation floated by, feelings of fear
and distrust, feelings of self-consciousness, of astonishment;
feelings that were not at all his own. . . .

■

Time seemed to flow like syrup, clear and thick, stretching slowly into endless strands. . . .

•

Time and space melted, shimmering, and recrystallized with a very strange *ping*. . . .

When his eyes refocused, he searched the viewscreen instinctively for stars, for a familiar frame of reference. He found none. A galaxy full of stars had been transformed into a frieze of slow-moving splinters of color. Like daggers, the bits of color revolved through a kind of translucent ice, faceted and fractured; a glint of color disappeared at one fracture line *here*, and reappeared at another, *there*. This was the look of K-space; this was all the viewscreen could show them of space until they made the crossover back out, at their destination.

Ruskin sat forward abruptly, shaking his head. He turned to his companions. "We all still here?"

Tamika was still gazing at the screen. She seemed not to have heard him.

"Console: screen off," Ruskin ordered.

The viewscreen darkened. Tamika started. She sighed and met his gaze. "Hypnotic," she murmured.

Ruskin nodded and called to Ali'Maksam. The Logothian was motionless. "Max!" he repeated sharply. "Ali'Maksam—are you okay?"

The Logothian's head was tilted at an odd angle. Ruskin released himself from his couch and approached his friend. The Logothian's breath hissed sharply in and out; at the edge of his mind, Ruskin felt Max's fiery discomfort. The Logothian was radiating empathically; he was in distress. Ruskin hesitated. "Ali'Maksam!" He reached out to touch his friend's arm.

"*I am here!*" Max said with a sudden gasp, jerking himself upright. He turned his visored head from side to side. "Off lights, please!" Ruskin quickly complied, plunging the bridge into darkness. There was near-silence for a moment, just Ali'Maksam hissing in pain. Gradually his breathing slowed, and he whispered, "Thank you. I—"

"What *is* it, Max?"

The Logothian's voice rasped in the dark. "I have never done—that—in the presence of Humans—before." His breath whistled in and out. "Your minds open up—so startlingly—in that moment." He was struggling to control his voice. "I—stood in the way of a *torrent* . . . of fears and hopes and pains. Never have I felt so much, so fast." He sighed in a long hiss. "I will be all right in a few moments. But I would like to open my visor. I feel claustrophobic."

"Take your time," Ruskin murmured.

"Thank you." The Logothian's visor creaked open.

They waited in the dark, aware—though they could not feel, see, or hear it—of the ship's mercurial movement through the twisted strands of K-space that its generators created before it. Ruskin tried to remember what he had felt just moments ago, during the crossover; but the memory had fled with the stars on the screen. *(Dax, did you catch any of that?)*

No answer. Had he lost Dax?

He tried to remember: What had he been feeling just before the jump?

That, at least, came back to him. He'd been worried, thinking of the message from Judith: ". . . *someone masquerading as an Alliance loyalist.*"

How would Judith know about such a thing? There had been a faintly apologetic tone to her message, he'd thought—and no reference at all to the software transfer that Farsil had mentioned. Where had it come from, if not from Judith? There was nothing in the system except the functional cogitative software and his own data, loaded from slivers. Unless something else was quite cleverly concealed . . .

"Rus'lem."

He started, sensing a movement in the darkness. It was Tamika; he felt her hand on his shoulder and her voice in his ear. "I'm going to lie down in the cabin." There was something in her voice that tugged at him; she was more than tired, but he couldn't tell what was wrong.

As she groped her way to the exit, he waited in the darkness with Ali'Maksam and thought: *(Dax? Are you there?*) He felt a quiet stirring within. (*Dax, where have you been? What* happened *during crossover?*)

The inner voice answered with uncharacteristic slowness:
((*It hit us hard, Willard. . . . I'm reorganizing. . . . I think we learned some things . . . and maybe lost some things . . . but I'm not yet sure what.*))

Ali'Maksam stirred beside him and finally spoke. "Willard, Tamika suspects the wrong people. I fear this."

Ruskin blinked in the dark. "What do you mean?"

"I sensed . . . images from her. And suspicions."

"About what?"

The Logothian was slow to answer. "About the assassination attempt. She has suspicions—that I differ with. It would be better if you asked her yourself. I should not speak of thoughts I was not intended to share." He paused, and there was a tiny click. "If you wish, you may bring up the lights again. We should probably do a check of the onboard systems."

Ruskin sighed. "Lights up slowly, please." Max was right about checking the systems. But very soon he wanted to talk to Tamika.

They moved in the dark, until gradually their movements stopped and their breathing slowed. Tamika hadn't wanted to talk right away. Eventually, though, as the tension and energy flowed away, lassitude set in—and so too did the concerns that for a few brief minutes had been driven from their minds.

Ruskin wanted to know what Ali'Maksam had sensed in her, but he didn't want to ask straight out. In the end, he didn't have to. Curled spoon-fashion against him in the dark, she whispered. "The noliHuman. That's what I was thinking about when we went over. In case you were wondering."

Ruskin opened his mouth and said nothing. He breathed against her hair, waiting.

She rolled away from him. "That's probably one of the

things that Max sensed. He knows that I know . . ." Her voice faltered.

"If he knows, you might as well tell me."

"All right . . . that it was a noliHuman that tried to kill you. That it was probably connected with the Querayn." Her voice was a sigh, speaking away from him in the dark.

He called for light, blinked as it came up slowly, a dull orange glow gradually brightening. "Why do you say the Querayn?" he asked—even though the same thought had occurred to him. "Because I *thought* I saw a noliHuman looking at me? That's not enough of a reason." When she didn't answer, he said, "Twig, I'm not that sure what I saw. And there are lots of noliHumans who have nothing to do with the Querayn, and vice versa."

"I know that." She rolled back against him, gazing up at the ceiling. "But a lot of times first impressions are right. Think back to Skybase. Remember, when you saw those Querayn, how you almost went into a trance—until Max called you away? Now why was that? I'll bet it was the NAGs." Her eyes shifted toward him, then away. "I'm just telling you what I *feel*. I know it's not proof—but I can't put it out of my mind." She turned and gazed at him. "Ali'Maksam is a friend of the Querayn. Not just a colleague. A friend. I saw that in *his* thoughts when we crossed over. Just the way he probably saw all of this in mine."

"Yes, but—" Ruskin exhaled, understanding now why she had left the bridge so suddenly. "Twig—"

"I'm not saying you should say anything about this to Max," Tamika said. "Probably you shouldn't."

"Do you suspect him?"

Her breath caught. She held it a long time before answering. "I'm not saying that. I'm just saying—"

"*What?*"

"God help me," she whispered, "I don't know. I just know what I feel."

"And that's that you don't trust Max."

She shrugged helplessly. "I *did* trust him. Mostly. But now—" She took a ragged breath. "I don't trust the Querayn, that's all. And he's a friend of theirs."

Ruskin considered that. "He's our friend, too, Twig," he said finally. "He saved me from who knows what kind of violence, when he stopped my blackouts." She shrugged, beside him. "And even the Querayn argue nonviolence. They don't go around assassinating people. And what would they have against me, anyway?"

Tamika gazed at him without speaking. She brushed his face with her fingertips. "I don't know, Rus'lem," she whispered. "I just don't know."

Ruskin sighed, closing his eyes. He wished that he could project all of these questions against his eyelids and shuffle them around and make them fit, one question answering another. He wished he could make the tumblers fit, mesh, spin, click, unlock. Open.

With that thought firmly in mind, he drifted off to sleep.

He dreamed of a dark fortress, adrift in a sea of amber mist, its embrasures glowing like the dying coals of a fire. And surrounding the fortress, floating close by in the amber but unable to reach it, were several tiny figures, darker still. He could not tell who or what they were, but he was afraid of them. If he could only reach the fortress himself, he could protect what was there.

But he had built the fortress, hadn't he?

What, he wondered, or whom, was he trying to keep out . . . or in?

Interlude

✳

Death had not come, nor spoken an answer. But the whispers, the voices of the dreams continued: not all the time, like the tightness and the hurt. But often enough to make Bright

think
 wonder
  sing
was I wrong   ?

Perhaps the voices were neither of dream nor of death, as Bright had thought of dream. Of death.

Perhaps the voices were of life. A new beginning.

Bright was filled, consumed by a new idea, one that could start only with a question, and just the hope of an answer:

Can one sing
 of new life
  from within   ?
Can such a thing come
 from one such as me   ?

The question had never before occurred to it in just this way. In all of its long life, never had Bright seen new life appear—except far away, in the dark and the void. And it was hard to know whether it emerged direct from the old life, or sprang fresh from the hollow valleys of space, from the channels of time.

Bright supposed that it could have asked, long ago, but somehow it never had. It could ask Near, or Small;

but they could give no answer, just a gentle musing song. But what of the distant dark-life that drifted about the great/empty/dark/world in such quietude, that wandered and never cast light of any sort upon the slates of time? What brought that dark to life? From what source did it spring?

Voices
voices within
dream
or life in me
do you know
Have you heard   ?
Have you sung   ?
Can you tell   ?

To the great emptiness, Bright called out its question and its mystery, knowing that it might wait long indeed for an echo of a reply. Indeed, if anyone knew, never had Bright heard it spoken of.

Wasn't it strange that in such a lifetime, a mystery so haunting could be unspoken of? But if the voices were not of dream, nor of messengers of death, then they must come from Bright itself. A wonder great, a wonder indeed.

Speak to me
my children
if you are of me
and I of you
and if you would spring from me
I would have you know my world
my wonder
my song

There was a great silence in answer: only the great ringing rhythms of Bright's own fires burning.

But Bright was unworried, Bright could wait.

Even if the voices should bring not just life to the

new but death to the old, Bright would seek its own understanding, its own rejoicing.

*Life was long
   and for such a mystery and a glory
      what mattered such a thing as waiting   ?*

CHAPTER 23

✳

"Do you remember these two gentlemen, Willard?" Ali'Maksam spoke quietly as he called the next frame in a long series onto the viewscreen. It was a split image of two human males. One was an official of the Auricle Alliance Hall of Congresses, whom Ruskin recognized, though he could not recall the man's name. The other appeared to be a Tandesko diplomat, wearing the distinctive three-pointed starburst of the Triune on his shoulder.

"They look very familiar," Ruskin said.

"They should. I'm glad at least some of these data files are intact." The Logothian pointed to the Auricle official. "That's Alexander McCarth, Explorations Chair for the Science and Technology Congress."

Of course. Now he remembered: he'd seen the man several times in person, and may even have worked with him. McCarth wielded great power in certain areas of Alliance policy. Ruskin thought that he did not like this man, but he couldn't remember why.

"And the other—" Max pointed to the slim, bony-faced Tandesko diplomat—"is Jodec Brandon, special Triune envoy. You might remember the occasion. They were addressing one another rather forcefully on the subject of interstellar exploration rights."

Ruskin nodded. There was that resonance of recognition—the awareness that he'd once been personally involved in these issues. He recalled the feeling, but not the events. The feeling that he recalled was frustration.

Ali'Maksam continued, "At issue was the question of how new territories could be staked out without the two big powers falling into war over it. Some of the smaller powers were present, too, of course; but their voices carried less

219

weight, pragmatically speaking." He paused and reflected. "The unexplored worlds were not represented at this meeting."

Ruskin cocked his head. "Is that supposed to be funny?"

Max's lips curled into an oddly reptilian smile. "Let's just say that they had no chance to voice their own preferences." He inclined his head and brought up a new frame: a geo-political star chart. The regions of Auricle and Tandesko influence were partially intertwined with one another. Both had neighboring frontiers, but a projection of desirable and accessible frontier regions showed a clear overlap of interest. "In any event, the range limitation of exploration ships has kept the dispute from boiling over—a condition that would change radically if something such as, say, your proposed gateway were ever to come to fruition."

Ruskin nodded. He felt a tic in his cheek muscle and stroked it absently.

Max continued, "To get back to the meeting, however, certain forward-thinking groups, like the Solomon Organization, and Tamika's Omega group, became more vocal in their dissent—which, by and large, was ineffectual."

"At least we were trying!" Tamika yelled, her voice echoing from the galley. A moment later she appeared on the bridge, bristling.

Ruskin watched the two through slitted eyes. His head was reeling slightly. *Dissent.* Why did that ring a bell?

"Quite true," Max was saying. "Don't misunderstand me. My own Society of tele'eLogoths adopted a similar position, though to be honest, our outlook was more idealistic than practical."

"And what about the Querayn?" Tamika said sharply. "Where do they stand?"

Max's eyes glittered behind his visor. He spoke softly: "The Querayn, too, believed that the dominant positions were wrong. But their position was even more theoretical than ours; it was scarcely voiced in public, and certainly little noticed."

"But you know their position well, don't you?"

Max stretched calmly. "Yes. I worked with them, as you know—though mostly on other matters. It was partly their theoretical work on the nature of consciousness that led me initially to wonder if Willard's affliction might be the result of nano-agents." He peered at Tamika as though he quite well understood her feelings. "Their work had suggested certain possibilities, some of them rather frightening. My knowledge of that work led me to contact E'rik Daxter when I perceived Willard's difficulty. I knew Daxter to have expertise in that area, also. Though I had no direct connection, I was able to reach him through the good offices of several friends. And no, Daxter is not Querayn, so far as I know, nor did I reach him through the Querayn."

"Is that all?" Tamika demanded, hands on hips.

"Tamika—" Ruskin began weakly.

"If you mean—"

"I mean that the person Willard saw who tried to kill him was a noliHuman," Tamika snapped. "Doesn't that suggest a connection to you?"

"Tamika," Max protested, "I do not believe that the Querayn would attempt murder. Even if the assassin was noliHuman, that does not mean that there was any connection."

"But you don't know that, do you?"

"No, I don't, but—"

"Stop it!" Ruskin shouted. "Just stop it! Both of you! I can't stand it!" He massaged his eyebrows. "For *God's* sake, don't the two of you start feuding."

There was a moment of silence. "Sorry," Tamika murmured. Max sighed almost inaudibly.

"Yeah." He switched the image-frame back to the Alliance and Tandesko representatives and studied their faces, thinking of all the disagreements that those two individuals represented. The quiet arrogance of the one, the unyielding rigidity of the other. Memories were stirring in the back of his mind; he sensed Dax at work, trying to bring them into clearer focus. "Max—Tamika—" he pleaded. "Help me with this. I remember . . . *feelings*, damn it." He pressed his fingertips to his forehead, searching. What he felt was a memory of . . . what? It hit him suddenly. "*Disillusionment.* I remember feeling disillusionment." He looked up. Tamika seemed as puzzled as he. "But about what? Max, you knew me then. Do you know what I was feeling?"

The Logothian settled back in his couch. His diamondlike

eyes sparkled. "Yes, Willard—you felt disillusionment. Do you remember why?"

Ruskin struggled. "It . . . had to do with *that*—" he pointed at the screen—"and it had to do with Breakst—I mean, ah, what the hell?—Starmuse." If he could only piece it together. Disillusionment with Starmuse? But Starmuse was a scientific research program. What was there to be disillusioned about? The long-range goals of opening up the galaxy? He looked at Max, Tamika, Max. "Was it the Starmuse program?"

Tamika answered: "What about our discussions? You did express feelings—"

He shook his head vigorously. "It was before that. Something was wrong." He got up and paced; his pulse was quickening. "Why did I just almost say 'Breakstar'? Every time I think of this project, I think of 'Breakstar.' But it's 'Starmuse.' Not 'Breakstar.'" He looked back and forth between them. "Right?"

(*Damn it to hell, anyway! What did I do to those data files? Why did I wreck them?*)

"I've heard you use the term 'Breakstar,'" Max said. "Mostly in offhand moments, I'd say. But as far as you've told me, the Betelgeuse project is called 'Starmuse.' Poet of the star." He shrugged. "Or observer of the star. It seems reasonable for a group gathering to watch a star die."

Ruskin chewed his lower lip, thinking. His eyes went to Tamika. "Have I talked to you about it, Twig?"

She hesitated. "I've heard the name. Maybe when you were asleep. Or unconscious, at Daxter's laboratory. I don't know what it means."

Something in me does, though, Ruskin thought. Something in me knows.

He sighed and called the next frame onto the viewscreen.

He napped in the pilot's seat after supper, the viewscreen blank in front of him. But though the screen was blank, his mind was not: the images they had called up out of his data files kept swarming before him. In his dreams he walked through an amber-hazed forest, those same images floating above the treetops. He was not alone here; with him in the dream were two creatures, stalking along behind him, just out of sight among the trees.

The name reverberated, sang in the wind among the branches:

> Breakstar . . .
> Breakstar . . .

The two creatures scampered, darted from cover to cover. But farther away, someone else was moving through the woods, as well. Perhaps more than one someone. He remembered suddenly the fortress floating in glowing amber, and he knew that those strangers out there in the woods were the same ones he'd dreamed of before, hovering in the amber, watching the fortress.

The two creatures, though, were different. They didn't care about the fortress.

They were here to study him.

And they looked familiar.

He knew, somehow, that they remembered every move he made, every thought that went through his mind. Like hounds on a scent, they followed a trail through the back-country woodlands of his mind. Or of his brain. It seemed to him that they, if anyone, ought to know what it was he was trying to remember.

> Breakstar . . .
> Breakstar . . .

He stood still as a statue for a time, then beckoned to them.

There was silence, and a quick rustling. One creature hopped into view, then the other. They crept close. For the first time, he could see their appearance. The first had large translucent ears and four enormous eyes set close together; it looked like a kind of fox.

> ((That is why I'm called a 'kindah.'))

Ruskin blinked, startled to hear the thing's voice in his mind. *Kindah?* His gaze shifted abruptly to the other. It looked more like a long, lanky lizard, with a wild cat's face—and a sort of Cheshire cat's grin.

> ((And that is why I am known as a 'sortah,'
> Sir Willard. We are the terrakells at your
> service.))

Looking back and forth between them, he felt as though he had stepped from one dream into another. And then he remembered where he had seen these creatures before, though they had looked different then. They were the creatures in E'rik Daxter's laboratory, the shapechangers that had so unnerved Ali'Maksam. Were they the "additional programming" that Daxter had given him?

> ((Yes, indeed, sir!))
> ((At your service, sir!))

He gazed at the two in astonishment. *(I see. And what have you done for me—what have you found, O Terrakells scampering in my brain?)*

There was a pause of what seemed like minutes or hours before they answered in refrain, their bright eyes boring into his:

> ((We find—))
> ((—lies within lies upon lies—))
> ((You hate the Tandeskoes—))
> ((You love the Tandeskoes—))
> ((—upon lies within lies.))
> ((The Querayn—))
> ((—make you nervous—))
> ((—and fascinate you besides.))
> ((But that is a lie.))
> ((One is—))
> ((—or the other.))
> ((Beware of what you know—))
> ((—or of what you think you know—))

He wrenched his gaze away from theirs and turned around in a helpless daze, wishing he could awaken from this dream. But the terrakells had him trapped here, and they were going to torment him with the one fact he already knew—

—that he could trust nothing that he knew.

But what about the other things? What about, for instance . . .

> Breakstar . . .

To which the terrakells answered:

> ((It's in there. In your memory.))
> ((We can get it for you. If we can just tweak it free . . .))

(Then, for God's sake, do it!)

* * *

He awoke with a start, sweating. "Max!" he barked. "Tamika!" Jesus, his head was spinning. Where was everyone? What had he just been dreaming?

He blinked, and it floated before him, like an image in the viewscreen:

Breakstar.

So simple, really. In concept, if not in execution. They were going to blow up a star. The people at Starmuse: they weren't sitting there waiting for a supernova to happen. They were making their own. They were pushing the star to burnout, they were tripping the switch, they were—

Playing God.

Jesus.

Was this what *he* was working on? Was this . . . Starmuse? "It's all a fucking lie!" he bellowed, suddenly shaking his fist at the viewscreen, slamming it down on the console. "It's all a bloody fucking lie!"

"Willard! What's wrong?" Tamika stumbled in from their cabin.

"The whole God-damned thing!" he shouted, turning but scarcely seeing her. He felt as though he were still dreaming. "The whole—damned—project—is a lie! Where's Max?" He caught Tamika's arm; surprise and fear crossed her face. Startled, he forced his hand to release its grip on her.

"I am here, Willard," Ali'Maksam said, stepping onto the bridge. His suit was slightly askew. He looked as though he had been sleeping. "What is it?"

"The Starmuse project. It's phony from start to finish, isn't it? 'Breakstar' is the real project—the one that's being carried out under cover of Starmuse. They're not there to observe. They're there to *trigger* the supernova." He stared at his friends. "And that means . . ."

Max stood in the far corner of the bridge, watching him. *What is he thinking? What is Tamika thinking? What am I thinking?*

He drew a breath. "That means not just studying how to

make an interstellar gateway—it means *making* one. Not in a hundred or a thousand years, but now! I don't know *how* they're going to do it. But that's what they're doing! Oh, Christ!" His thoughts were scarcely ahead of his words; his own astonishment was still bubbling up inside him. And yet he knew he had not uncovered it all. It was as though he had drawn a cloudburst from an angry thunderhead; but the cloud remained looming, sullen and mysterious.

Max's voice rumbled. "If you believe that true, Willard, then—"

"Then all that stuff we were talking about, who gets what and which faction of worlds will control—it's all going to happen now. Not next century. *Now.* Christ, no wonder." His voice failed him.

"No wonder *what*, Willard?" Tamika whispered.

"The disruption of relations . . . the possibility of war." His throat tightened. "If this is true, it's going to cause a major eruption between the Alliance and the Triune, with everyone else caught in the middle. No wonder people are willing to commit murder. If the gateway really worked, it could open up *thousands* of new worlds to explore, to colonize." He made a gesture to Tamika. "To exploit. To contact new species. Whoever controlled the gateway could control . . . well, there's no telling, really." He raised his eyes to look at her. "But why me?" Tamika's gaze was full of bewilderment and anguish. "Why do they want to kill *me*? What do *I* have to do with it?"

There was silence until Max spoke, his expression inscrutable: "The answer to that is surely in your files. Or in your mind. It must be found. Which is more intact, Willard?"

Ruskin stared at him for a long time without answering. Three days left in starflight. Three days to put the pieces of the puzzle together.

CHAPTER 24

✳

Turning inside out
Floating
Images rising like bubbles in champagne
Starbursts, and space stretching like taffy . . . and against the glow, the tall figure moving closer, closer and now it was almost near enough to see its face just a little closer was it noliHuman or Tandesko or perhaps even Auricle it was raising its hand to kill
and the face came into focus
and the face was his own

•

Time the catalyst that changes all things, turns worlds upside down, inside out
Floating in the mist, the dark fortress metamorphoses becoming the thing that changed and caused change both prison and prisoner
Within its corridors a killer stalking not knowing its quarry not knowing itself . . . and two animals two terrakells but were they following to protect the killer or the victim

•

Time too short
Uncertainties multiplying and remultiplying
Who are the victims
who the killers
who the changelings

•

Coming together the pieces
but how much emptiness remaining

•

Structures emerging in space like ice crystals blossoming into snowflakes; theory and emotions melding like matter and energy

Complex of forces too difficult to map . . . too difficult too little time too many patterns emerging from Willard's memory . . . would he understand them in time to make clear where he stood

if he didn't change again

if Dax didn't fail

if Tamika trusted long enough to let him do what had to be done . . . ?

■

Fear and determination ringing through the mist like dissonant chords, overlaying images of love

Protect him protect him protect him don't make the same mistake twice trusting in the untrustworthy

■

((Losing control
   losing control!))

Gravity pushed him down in his seat. He struggled to focus, to clear his thoughts, and the effort took time. There was so much bewilderment, so many thoughts in his mind that were not his own. Did crossover always do this, did it always lay open the soul? Or was it the presence of Max, or the emotional stress? He blinked repeatedly, and finally his eyes worked. Before him, the splinters of colored light were gone from the viewscreen; in their place was something that nearly blinded him, that made his eyes swim again.

There was a billowing furnace of light out there—a vast, dust-hazed, crimson-tinged sun, viewed at extreme close range. Alpha Orionis: Betelgeuse. As the computer stepped down the light intensity, great dark swimming spots, supergranules, came into view on its surface. And far off to the right, a region of brightness. The sun filled the viewscreen; they had come out close to its surface, within its extended atmosphere of gases and dust. They would be getting a lot closer. *Betelgeuse. A dying giant. We're here to watch it die.*

To make it die.

He remembered, and wondered: What if it went supernova right now? Would they go ahead and do it without waiting for him? Did they need him? He thought that they did. But why? That was one of the things he didn't remember. *Too few pieces fit, even now.*

He massaged his face with a grunt. His skin tingled with a hot flush. His head hurt. He felt an ugly surge of adrenaline, of aggression. He felt an urge to hit, to strike out at something, to kill. He took a deep breath and tried to channel the feeling back into himself. Where it had come from he didn't know, or even want to know. *Control it; bury it; kill it.* As he exhaled slowly, he felt a semblance of inner control reasserting itself; and only then did he turn around to look at his shipmates.

He'd forgotten that only Tamika was on the bridge, and on her face was a dazed expression as she stared at the sun. She shifted to look at him, and her expression turned to horror. "Willard, what's happened?" she whispered, her voice flat with fear.

What's happened?

He looked at his hands: they were too thick, callused. He raised them to his face. Something hadn't felt right, didn't feel right. He started to rise from his couch.

((WILLARD, DON'T MOVE!))

He froze at the sound of Dax's voice in his head. *(Why? What do you know about this?)*

((Something went wrong in crossover. We lost control. We're trying to fix it now.))

Something went wrong? His hands changed? "System!" he murmured huskily. "Can you put a view of the bridge on screen?"

"Mirror or straight image?" the console asked.

"I don't care! Just show it!"

"As you wish, sir."

The viewscreen blinked off and turned into a near-perfect mirror. Ruskin started, and gazed at his visage in dismay. His eyebrows were thick and bristly; his cheekbones were heavy, his skin olive and swarthy and very tough, his eyes dark and deep-set. He looked frighteningly like the man who had attacked Tamika in her apartment. As he lifted his hands again, palms up, he noticed that both index fingers were tipped with throbbing blisters—tiny lasers, charged, itching to fire. His second and third fingers had grown razors for nails; his little fingers ended with steely hooked claws. He was lucky he had not torn his own face open. "What have you done?" he whispered. *"Dax, did you do this?"*

He rose to a crouch and stood before the mirrored viewscreen, waiting for Dax's answer. He glared at his own image, prepared to do battle with it if necessary—as though it could step out of the screen to strike him.

He felt a sudden rush of dizziness and nausea, and feverish heat. He gritted his teeth, blinked his eyelids hard, struggled to remain standing as he determinedly faced what he had become. *I will not give in to it!* Suddenly the heavy, brutish features began to melt away from his face. His skin began to soften; slowly it lost its olive color and turned pale; his eyes lost their dark and desperate glint. His body was aflame with invisible heat. But the throbbing in his hands ceased, the calluses grew smooth, the nails shrank to ordinary size. Within minutes, his features had returned to normal, and the flush of heat began to subside. And through the accompanying roar in his ears, Dax was explaining:

> *((The crossover threw us—and it must have thrown them, too: the unfriendlies, I mean. It must have triggered an unscheduled program and set them haywire. We couldn't quite control it; but at least now we know what could be coming.))*

Ruskin rubbed his face, wincing and stretching his facial muscles. *(Such a damned weird sensation.)* He peered at Tamika's image in the mirror, meeting her eyes as she sat almost rigid with fear; he tried to will reassurance into her gaze. But how could he, the way he felt right now? He cleared his throat; his voice was gravelly. "They . . . got a little out of hand for the ride, Dax tells me. The NAGs, I mean."

Tamika nodded, said nothing.

(Am I okay now?)

((More or less.))

He leaned forward and put his hands on the console. "Screen back to view of the sun," he said. He frowned until the image steadied again on the fiery mass. "Back it off, please." The image shrank, until a limb of darkness appeared at the edge of the screen, then all around the sun. "Keep shrinking it."

Tamika gasped. As the angle widened, the distended shape of the sun became visible, and the cause of the distention and the brightness in one area. So close to Betelgeuse it looked as though it would collide was the close companion star, Alpha Orionis B, nicknamed (he remembered) Honey. It was a giant sun in its own right, though beside Betelgeuse it looked a midget. Surrounded by a thin accretion disk of glowing gases that it had probably captured from Betelgeuse, Honey was the source of the tidal distortion of its primary; and the bright region on Betelgeuse's surface was the effect of the smaller sun's radiance. The viewscreen blinked, and in its upper right corner a black overlay appeared, with a round, reddish star at its center: the other companion, Alpha Orionis C, Lost Love, much farther out, hanging at the edge of dusty night.

"Find me the station," Ruskin requested.

"Starmuse main station?" the console asked.

"What the hell do you think? Yes. Main station."

"As you wish, sir."

"And call them. Make sure they know we're coming. We don't want this star popping off before we get there, do we?"

"Very good, sir. No, sir."

Sighing, he rubbed his temple. He knew, as though he had always known—one more memory-bit emerging from the mists—that the Starmuse station had a complex shielding system to protect it not just from the close-range heat and radiation of the sun, but from the full fury of a supernova. Their little ship did not.

Something sparkled in the air near Max's couch. The Logothian's virtual image appeared, sitting in midair. Max had stayed in his cabin this time, expressing a desire for privacy in crossover. Maybe it had helped and maybe not. Ruskin was sure he'd tapped into at least some of Max's thoughts during those moments thick with dream and madness. He gazed at his friend's virtual image, trying to remember what he'd picked up; but it was all a jumble—each of them with more than enough worries. Only very sane people should engage in starflight, he thought—at least with a tele'eLogoth on board.

"We are there," Max observed, his image gazing at the screen.

Tamika looked at him without speaking.

"So we are," Ruskin murmured with a mixture of anticipation and fear. "So we are."

Coming out of K-space was no treat even for Ganz. But once the disorientation had passed, hir forced hirself back to full consciousness—and worked quickly to establish hir position, and Ruskin's. The red sun and its sibling were enormous, and the research station was located very close to the upper edge of the primary's photosphere, a region in which the tracking of other objects was a tricky business, to say the least. A sweep for Ruskin would require either blind luck or a wider sensor scan than Ganz could make from hir own ship. Not a believer in luck, Ganz fired off three tiny remote probes into diverging orbits far above the sun's surface.

Within an hour, Ganz had hir own position as well as the position of the station. Finding Ruskin's ship took a while longer, but eventually that was accomplished, as well. Ruskin was closer to the sun presently than Ganz, and a little closer to the station. It was now or never, if Ganz was going to take the safe course and remove Ruskin from the picture.

"Well, Jeaves-copy, what do you think?" Ganz asked the shipboard cogitative system.

The system sounded surprised. "I thought we had agreed upon forbearance."

"It was possible that you had reconsidered," Ganz said, almost wistfully. "To destroy him now would be relatively easy. Even a simple fusion charge might suffice. But once he's close to the station, it will become much harder. And once he's arrived at the station—" Ganz sighed. The system didn't answer. It didn't have to. They both knew that Ganz had ample tools for a one-on-one elimination; and this time, knowing in advance Ruskin's little defenses, Ganz wouldn't fail. But there was always that desire to *guarantee* hir wouldn't fail. The stigma of having failed once, even if it wasn't hir fault—hir had hir pride as a *hrisi*.

"Have you been able to reach your brother?" Ganz asked.

"It is too early. We must be patient," the system answered. "Communication in this medium is very difficult. All kinds of interference. Remember, I'm trying to be discreet."

"Well, don't be so discreet you forget to do your job."

The system waited through a moment of dignified silence. "You do your job, and I'll do mine," it said finally.

Ganz did not answer immediately. Hir had other thoughts to mull over. When Ganz spoke again, it was to request a com-link to the research station lost somewhere out there in the blazing mists of the sun. It took time, but finally the system established data-contact—not with the station, however, but with another ship, in a converging orbit. A message scrolled across the bottom of Ganz's viewscreen:

"ALLIANCE WARSHIP TO ARRIVING VESSEL: PLEASE STATE NAME, REGISTRY, ORBIT, AND PURPOSE."

Startled, Ganz said to the Jeaves-copy, "Reply: 'This is *T. S. Unity*, bringing relief Starmuse observer from Triune Science Committee. Request clearance or escort. . . .' "

((Willard, you've remembered a great deal already. You must act in faith: when you need the pieces, they will be there. The wheels are turning, Willard; the wheels are turning.))

He shivered at the image: a trillion little wheels spinning inside his skull—complex chain molecules folding and rotating and linking and separating—altering him and plotting and threatening to take whatever he thought he knew and replace it with something else. But Dax was right; if he didn't act in faith, they might as well leave right now.

"There's an approaching patrol ship asking for identification, sir," the console said.

Ruskin looked up. They would soon be within rendezvous range of the station. "Yes. Thank you. Tell them it's Willard Ruskin from Kantano's World. Uh—Associative Frontiers Institute. Tell them that, too."

"Very good, sir. But they want to know the name and registry of the ship."

Name of the ship? Ruskin realized suddenly that he had never thought to name the ship. He'd merely taken a registration number. How could he have been so forgetful? A ship ought to have a name. He looked around; his friends were watching him quietly, waiting for him to finish the communication.

"Willard, are you all there?" Tamika asked finally.

He took a breath. "Yes. Well, all here or not, we need a name, don't we? System, give our name as *A. S. Enigma.* And store that in permanent registry file. That's your name."

"Very good, sir," the system said. A moment later, it added, "We are cleared and will proceed under escort to the station. Would you like me to handle that part?"

Ruskin blinked, mesmerized by the view of the sun, closer and more massive-looking now than ever before. Glowing the color of lifeblood. Like the blood that pulsed in his own heart and brain, teeming with life of its own. "Yes," he said absently. "Yes, why don't you go ahead and do that?"

The station was a reflecting silver sphere against the glowing plasma of the solar photosphere. It was immersed in the light-emitting layer of the sun, which was actually its coolest part, only thousands of degrees hot; from here, the neutrino-image of the distant core blazed like a welding arc in the midst of a billowing sunset.

As they approached, flanked by two patrol vessels, they discovered that the silver sphere was not itself the station;

it was a great reflective bubble, an n-space forcefield blocking the heat and radiation of the sun. In concert with the
station's n-space generators, they warped *Enigma* through
the bubble with scarcely a tremor—only to find themselves
approaching a second and smaller bubble, floating in the
golden watery glow of the light that had gotten through the
first one. They warped through that second screen as well;
and again through the third and final envelope of n-space.

The station proper floated before them now: an insect
hive, a dark fortress against a hazy amber glow.

Ruskin stared at it, instinctively reached out toward it,
as though he could walk toward it—if only he weren't
trapped in the amber himself. He stared at it for a long
time before whispering to the console, "Take us in to dock,
please."

CHAPTER 25

✳

The ship glided into one of the docking nooks that pockmarked the outside of the station. As it bumped to a stop, the dock structure wrapped itself around the ship, bonding to the hull like a second skin. The hatches opened and security robots glided aboard.

The search was thorough. Ruskin and the others waited on the bridge while the robots scanned and probed, not just the ship's holds, but the control console as well. It was an hour before they were allowed to leave the ship.

Once inside the station, they were met by human security officers, who took Max and Tamika to a separate room. Ruskin was the only one with clearance; his friends would have to wait until he found someone to authorize their presence. Ruskin followed an agent into a small office, where he was fitted with a gold-and-iridescent security bracelet and informed that he would be taken at once to see someone named Dr. Sharaane. "She'll be glad to see you, Dr. Ruskin. They've all been pretty frantic, wondering if you would make it here in time," the officer said.

Ruskin followed him out. The name had set a bell ringing in his mind, but he couldn't place it. *Dr. Sharaane . . .*

If the station on the outside had looked like a malformed hornet's nest, on the inside it was a blown-glass citadel. The corridors were clear-walled and asymmetrical; it was like walking through a hollow latticework of crystal fibers. One could glimpse a variety of offices and labs, but there was a shimmering unreality about them; none of the rooms seemed to be quite *there*, except when they actually passed an open doorway and could glimpse people inside. Ruskin imagined that he was walking through a glass Klein bottle, the topology of which passed through a five- or six-dimensional space-time. He wondered if there was an n-space generator at work somewhere in the station, twisting the architecture out of normal space-time. It wasn't exactly K-space: just a slight displacement out of the continuum, he thought.

It was hardly standard architectural design; the power consumption had to be enormous. Of course there was no shortage of power here, if they could tap even a fraction of the energy flux outside the station's shielding. But why do it?

Dr. Sharaane. His mind fairly vibrated with memories just out of reach. There was something here that would not let him go. He felt as though he were caught by a moving dragline, pulling him underwater into an airless abyss. He drew a breath and hurried to keep up with the officer. *Dr. Sharaane.*

The corridor appeared to dip, and beneath his feet he glimpsed a room filled with scientific holos. Before he could ask about it, his escort led him around a curve and it rippled out of sight. A moment later, they were in a wide, translucent-walled foyer. Until now, they had passed very few people; but here people were moving about, and they mostly looked young, harried, and business-like. A tall, green-eyed man waved and called, "Good to see you, Willard!" Staring, Ruskin watched the man disappear through a doorway. He turned to query his escort, but the officer was already gesturing impatiently for him to hurry.

The doors at the end of the foyer dissolved at their approach. They walked into a room that was practically alive with a wavering, ruddy light. For a moment, he saw no one else in the room; he saw only the wall-screen filled with the face of the sun, convection cells and spots of dark coolness swimming against the great hypnotic glow. The close companion star, Honey, was just visible in the corner of the screen. He stood, mouth half-open; then he heard: "Willard! Thank heaven you made it!"

It was as though a wind had arisen from nowhere, carrying the scent of a distant ocean and a rush of memories of a life long ago, in another world, another reality. In the back of his skull, he felt a chamber opening. He knew that voice.

(Dax! Oh shit—oh for chrissakes, Dax, why didn't you tell me?)

"Over here!"

He turned. Rising from a console cluttered with holos was a tall, impossibly bony-looking woman with curly auburn hair and round eyes with enormous pupils. No. Not enormous pupils: large eyes with deep maroon, almost black irises. They had fooled him the first time he'd seen her eyes; they'd fooled him again now. Her skin was a light, burnished brown. She wore a rust-orange jumpsuit, the color of the sun.

Dr. Sharaane. *Thalia* Sharaane. He blinked at her through a mist, trying to focus on her face, trying not to succumb to the wave of dizziness that was sweeping over him.

"Aren't you going to say hello?" She was smiling, but with a trace of puzzlement on her face. "Where the hell have you been? Did you have a good flight? What's this about some friends coming with you?"

"I—yes—our flight was fine," Ruskin whispered. He cleared his throat and tried to return her smile. "Hello . . . Thalia. It's been a long time." He took a step toward her. *A lifetime. An eternity.*

Their eyes met, and the corners of her mouth dimpled upward. "A very long time, Willard," she said softly. "Can you still give me a hug?" She dismissed the security officer with a wave and walked toward him.

Ruskin stood paralyzed, watching Thalia approach; he felt as if an electrical current were singing in his head. A flood of memories was rising in him like an ocean tide: himself, standing with Thalia Sharaane on the Wall of Thespis on Calaise, watching the changing colors as the Three Suns set over the Thousand Lakes; Thalia grinning at him over an ice cream sundae in Cambridge on the fourth world of the Pleaides Triangle; the heat of her body awkwardly embracing his, loving and welcoming. . . .

His breath escaped him in a frightened rush as she put her arms around him—tentatively at first, then with feeling. Was she trembling as she touched him? The smell of her, lemongrass and musk, filled his head and his thoughts. He didn't want to, but he couldn't help . . . remembering how much he had once desired her.

(Dax, help me!)

> *((These memories run deep, Willard, and powerful. It's hard to know—))*

(If I could only fit it all together! But it's too much, it's too fast. Dax, I loved her, didn't I?)

> *((The memories are confused; but we have to understand it. The terrakells will help. . . .))*

"Willard! Ow!" Thalia broke the embrace abruptly, with a grimace. "I'm glad you're happy to see me, but don't break my back!"

"Sorry," he whispered. Anger flickered through his mind, and then was gone. *Anger?* Had he been hugging her too hard? Maybe . . . with the memories and all. "I—" His voice caught and he found himself breathless. What could he say? *I'm sorry, but until a minute ago I had forgotten that you existed, but now I remember: we were lovers. And why did we stop . . . ?*

"You don't have to say anything. I think I know how you feel." Thalia smiled sheepishly. "It's good to see you—but it's strange, after all this time." She beckoned toward her console. "But come on. No time to dwell on that. Let me bring you up-to-date. Then I'll give you a quick tour."

Wait—hold it! he wanted to cry; he needed to get his emotions sorted out. Instead, he cleared his throat and stammered, "That's terrif—I mean, great. But, Thalia—"

She glanced up quizzically.

"Well—about my friends." He was struggling to put together a coherent thought, coherent words. "They need—"

"Don't worry," she said brusquely. "They'll be given quarters in the visitors' section. Friends of yours are friends of—well, you know." She shrugged. "They'll have to stay in the restricted area, though, unless we can get a fast security check on them. Actually, Willard—" and her tone became almost reproving—"I'm surprised that you brought people along without clearing it first." Her eyebrows twitched.

It was his turn to shrug, his face flushed. "I, ah, wasn't

aware until the last minute that I'd need their help," he said, thinking that even to himself, that sounded lame.

Thalia looked at him, puzzled. "Help? Well, I doubt that will be possible, given the time. But don't worry, security's working on it." She flashed a bright, hard smile, apparently dismissing the subject. She glanced at the console again. "There's very little time to spare, actually. What the devil took you so long? Didn't you get our messages? We're coming up on the end of Stage Two right now, and convergence is happening faster than we'd predicted."

Ruskin nodded, not answering. *Stage Two . . . convergence . . . ?* He was still lightheaded, memories echoing in his mind. He and Thalia, loving and quarreling . . . *(Dax, is it my imagination, or did I just provoke a jealous response from her?)* He rubbed his face, trying not to betray his confused feelings as new memories swept through him: Thalia, angry because he had sought advice from someone in the Science Council whom she thought incompetent; brooding, because he'd left her alone too long at a party; withdrawing, when he couldn't give her exactly the kind of reassurance she needed, when she needed it.

　　((These feelings—))
　　((—are real.))
　　((—are a powerful part—))
　　((—of your memory.))

Dax? No, not Dax. It was the terrakells: a thousand little feet traipsing the pathways of his mind. He might as well ask: *(Are these the things that drove us apart?)*

　　((Not sure—))
　　((Still emerging—))

Still emerging. Thalia was showing him data now on the state of the solar core, its fusion evolution nearly at an end, its instabilities evident only to instruments deep in the star's body. He could follow it, but barely. He took a sharp breath, remembering that Thalia had been supremely competent in her realm of n-space mechanics and astrophysics—so good she had almost driven him away in fear of his own failure. And yet . . . even in the face of her great skill, insecurities had always lurked.

He caught the words, ". . . where you'll be working,"

and Thalia was looking at him for a reaction. She frowned. "You look pale, Willard."

He closed his eyes for a moment and shook his head. "Just tired." And for an instant he wondered: Was it possible that he could confide in her? And the answer came to him an instant later: not if you can't even remember what drove you apart.

"You were supposed to arrive rested," Thalia said impatiently. "Things are happening fast."

He nodded numbly. "I'll be working directly with you?"

"Part of the time. During Stage Four, we'll all be in the control center, well away from prying eyes." In response to his mystified look, she sighed. "I assumed that you knew. We now have observers from Tandesko and Leipzicon and the Querayn Academies here to observe 'Starmuse,' and any or all of them could be suspicious about what we're really up to. We're still under Alliance quarantine, but when that Tandesko ship made it in long enough to measure the anomalous core emissions last year—"

"Huh?"

"Surprised you didn't hear about it. It set off a whole political thing. By some miracle it was kept quiet, but in the end we were forced to bring on board a contingent of foreign observers. All of whom are being given falsified data. If they knew how fast the sun was *really* burning—well, anyway, that's why you're wearing that thing." She indicated his bracelet. "Anyone without one of those physically cannot cross into the areas where Breakstar work is going on. That's one reason this station is designed the way it is. Obviously you're not to mention Breakstar to anyone not wearing a bracelet, and it would be best if you talked about it to no one you don't know personally."

Does that include you? he wondered, even as he murmured, "Right."

"So if a visitor asks, you're just studying the sun. And you're too newly arrived to have much to say. You have no idea when it's going to blow." Her eyes narrowed. "I'm afraid that applies to your friends, as well—at least until we've run security on them. Okay?"

He nodded, frowning.

"Then let's go show you the station." With a gesture to follow, she led him out the way he'd come in.

Walking through a crossover corridor between two sections of the station was like passing through a faceted crystal. "A lot of people find the n-dimensional layout confusing at first," Thalia said.

"I wonder why."

She glanced back with a trace of a smile as he hurried to keep up. That was another thing he remembered now: she always walked fast. Sightseeing with her had always been a pain. As he caught up again, she said, "It's not just for security, though. Partly it's to give us better use of the space we have, while minimizing the volume that has to be shielded. And of course our waste heat is dispersed through radiators that are shifted out of the local continuum."

"Uh-huh."

"But the big reason is to give us an edge when the star actually goes. The only way to adequately protect the station is to get it out of local space before the shock wave hits. Even with radiation shielding, the concussion would obliterate us. So we get a head start—"

"By having half the station already shifted into n-space?"

"Actually, more like seven-tenths of the station. But yes. Mind you, we're not *that* sure how the blast will affect the local n-space, either. But that's our hope." She pointed. "In here." They walked through a glimmering blue trapezoid.

He felt a momentary sensation of twisting, as the air rippled around him. They emerged onto a narrow balcony. It overlooked a large control room filled with people and holographic work stations. At the front of the room a huge display showed a changing selection of images—some of them graphs and data, some satellite telemetry, others images of Betelgeuse itself.

"Control and mapping," Thalia said. She led the way down to floor level.

The work stations were arrayed in tiers, with a number of supervisors walking among them, looking over the shoulders of, or bending to speak to, the operators. Several stations were enclosed in privacy-screens—not for security, Thalia explained, but to minimize distraction. "Anyone in this room is cleared to see any of the information here." Ruskin nodded, walking alongside her; his head was spinning, but with a growing sense of familiarity. He *felt* that he should have come expecting everything he saw right now. His fingers tingled, itching to touch work-station controls. Would he remember in time? Would he recall the knowledge he was supposed to be working with?

"Willard, how are you?" a thin-faced man asked, glancing up at him. Before Ruskin could think of a reply, a woman three stations over had noticed him and waved.

"Hi, Juan," he answered thickly. The name was on his tongue before it was in his mind, but he knew as he spoke that it was correct. "Hi, Sabrina," he said to the woman. Piece by piece, the memories were arranging themselves; he could practically feel them clicking into place. *(Are the rest of the pieces coming?)* he asked Dax.

((God willing.))

He nodded to himself. *(Do you believe in God, Dax?)* There was no answer.

Thalia led him to the front row and a curved console equipped with multiple thinktank holos and operator inputs. "The mapping station. You can control it all from here," Thalia said.

He nodded, swallowing. "When do I start?" he murmured.

"As soon as you've been brought up-to-date on the core condition and the newest projections. Also, we have some changes in string tracking to go over with you. And—as soon as you've brought *us* up-to-date. Willard, your recommendations never reached us! You said you got the changes we transmitted to you?"

Scowling, he shook his head. "No, I—"

"Hell! Well, that explains why you got here so late, too." Thalia's expression darkened with anger. "Well, there's no time to worry about it now. You'll just have to study fast."

"What were the—?"

"When you see all the data, you'll know. But look, we've got to have your recommendations for shaping and mapping—and soon. When we hit Stage Three, you'll be living at this console until it's over. But Snyder needs to lay in the timing before that."

"Right," he murmured, keeping up the pretense even as a rush of guilt swept through him. How long could he continue to hide his ignorance—and who or what would he hurt with it?

((*I'm trying to keep you from hurting anyone.*
If you can make it through the review, we
just might be able to pull it all togeth—))

"Do you want to spend a little time on the system before you brief us?" Thalia asked.

"Yes. Good idea. And Thalia—I really do need the help of my friends. If you can expedite even a partial clearance for them—"

Her eyebrows bristled in puzzlement. "Well—I'll work on it. But first—" Her face relaxed.

"What?"

"I think there's enough time for you to have a *quick* lunch with me."

He cocked his head and smiled. "Okay." And a tiny voice in the center of his mind said,

((*Good. There are some things I need to talk*
to you about. We're finding some interesting
things here in the attic.))

His smile never wavered, even for a moment.

If he carried on an intelligent conversation with Thalia over lunch, he had only Dax's word for it. He viewed the entire affair as if through a shadow-screen, a play of dark and light, and the murmuring voices of actors only distantly related to him. He had plenty else to keep him occupied.

He stood in a spotlight, pinned by three intersecting beams of coruscating light. All else was in darkness, except for the shadow-box play with Thalia off to one side. It took him a while to decide whether or not to remain in the spotlights; eventually he realized that it was a two-way illumination. His lips were moving; but other voices were speaking silently, as well; the spotlights were like holo-beams, carrying images to him, taking his words away.

■

The K-space penetration into the Brant-Higgs-field must be precisely aimed for successful gravitic refraction. . . .

■

The intersection of the projection with the n-dimensional hyperstring will cause barely measurable expansion in the dimensions n_1, n_2, and n_3; however, the introduction of the black hole singularity will significantly alter the equation, as follows . . .

■

Maximum gravitic refraction and core intensification, with Ranlom-field focusing of neutrinos back into the core, will augment core collapse by a factor of . . .

■

Type IV supernova is expected to produce an abrupt neutrino flux on the order of 10^{53} ergs, of which 0.1% will be captured and redirected by Ranlom-fields. . . .

■

The question of disillusionment is important for several reasons, among them the need to identify potential chokepoints in your own thought processes. . . .

■

Five minutes after lunch, Ruskin remembered nothing of his meal conversation with Thalia; he remembered only the maelstrom in his forebrain. Somewhere in the back of his mind, an eddy of thought revealed that Thalia was now ready to meet his friends.

"You are Ali'Maksam Tokandro," Thalia said, frowning slightly as Ruskin introduced both of his friends.

"Tokandro Ali'Maksam," the Logothian corrected her, bowing slightly.

"Forgive me. I have seen some of your work."

"Indeed," whispered Max.

"The consciousness research is most provocative."

"Ah," Max answered. "You are referring then to my society's joint research with the Querayn?"

"Of course, yes. I confess I do not recall all of the individual contributions." Thalia's frown deepened. "And you are here to assist Willard in his evaluation of the star?"

Max opened his hands wide. "I am here to help him in any way I can."

"And are you studying consciousness here, as well?"

"I always endeavor to study consciousness. That is my field," Max said calmly.

"But," Thalia persisted, "some of the Querayn feel that the study of the star is itself a study of consciousness."

Max's voice dropped low. "I must defer to their work on that question."

Ruskin listened to the exchange, aware of Tamika's *Who is this person?* expression. "Max has been my right-hand man with much of the cogitative processing," he said, breaking in. As Thalia turned, he changed the subject hurriedly. "And this is Tamika Jones. Tamika—Thalia Sharaane, the Director of Astrophysics on Starmuse."

"Pleased to meet you," Tamika said, extending a hand.

Thalia's eyes shifted to meet Tamika's. She shook hands—rather coolly, it seemed to Ruskin. "And you are here as—" She waited for Tamika to fill in the blank.

Tamika straightened perceptibly as she heard the implicit challenge. "Companion," she said simply.

Thalia's eyes flicked to Ruskin and back to Tamika. "I see." Her smile did not seem any warmer than her handshake. "Welcome, then."

"Thank you," Tamika murmured.

Thalia shrugged. "Not at all. I'm sure we can find something for you to do." Her gaze narrowed as she turned back to Ruskin. "And now, Willard—suppose we get you started. You have a great deal of catching up to do."

CHAPTER 26

✳

The console in the mapping room surrounded him with
its welcoming arms. In the soft darkness of the privacy-
screened work station, the holo control-nudgers embraced
him, prepared to respond to his touch. He extended his
hands, caressed the nudgers, made ready to immerse himself in the streams of data. *(Dax, I hope you're ready to
capture a lot fast. I may need any or all of it.)*

He squeezed the nudgers and light sprang into the
darkness.

∎

Images and details of the Breakstar project flowed past
like sparkling plankton in an incoming tide. He was aware
of other researchers tapping different streams in the tide:
adding, altering, drawing from it. The tide of data was a
living thing, responding each second to the changing con-
ditions of the star. He barely glanced at the real-time data;
what he needed was the basic knowledge that was already
second nature to the other researchers. Once it had been
second nature to him, too. He drifted, dipping and sampling
from the tide.

Data holos danced and sparkled around his head:

Betelgeuse was nearing the end of its natural life as a
star, anyway; but somehow that end had been drawn much
closer by the Breakstar process. The fusion fuel at its core
was now nearly exhausted: hydrogen and helium all gone,
carbon turned to neon and oxygen, oxygen now burning to
silicon. The silicon would soon begin fusing, in a tremendous conflagration, to iron. With a heart of pure iron, the
star's fusion fires would abruptly die. Even at billions of
degrees and astounding pressures, the iron was incapable
of fusing to produce energy. In fact, only one thing could

happen, and it would happen almost instantly: the iron nuclei would disintegrate, electrons and protons would crush together to produce neutrons and ethereal neutrinos. The core would collapse, in milliseconds, to nuclear density and beyond. Part of the core would rebound explosively; but the rest would be gone forever.

The star that *was* would already be dead. But out of the energy of that final crushing collapse would flash a tremendous burst of neutrinos, and a shock wave that would blast away the sun's outer layers in a cosmic-scale explosion. Out of the blast would come a hail of newborn heavy elements to seed the galaxy—a sacrificial offering from a dying sun to the next stellar generation. For a brief time, Betelgeuse would become its own funeral pyre, outshining the entire galaxy.

And at the very center of the sun's core, where trillions of trillions of tons of neutrons were crushed into nothingness in an instant, a black hole would yawn into being: a singularity, a hole in the fabric of four-space. It was that singularity which would open the entry point for the gateway that was to come.

Yes . . . but how . . . and what else . . . ?

And the other critical component of the process . . . was an enormous loop of cosmic hyperstring, even now stretching out toward Betelgeuse in its ancient oscillation through the complex metrics of galactic n-space.

The hyperstring . . . familiar, but . . .

The data confirmed at least some of his suspicions. While Betelgeuse was nearing its end in cosmic terms, it might have had a thousand years to go in human terms, if it were not for the intervention of Breakstar. He had guessed, or remembered, correctly. Breakstar was accelerating the process, snuffing out the star prematurely—*creating* the black hole at Human bidding, timed with the approach of the hyperstring. In fact, the hyperstring was crucial; it was the fantastic gravitational potential of the string that was being used . . .

Yes? But why do they need me *in the control room?*

He felt a sudden tremendous reluctance to scan further; he felt a wave of dizziness. . . .

■

Data flickered.

((Don't you know?))

A grogginess had come over him; he tried to shake himself free of it. What was happening in his head? He couldn't remember—

((You're purposely avoiding the truth.))

(What? I'm not—I'm trying, I swear, but this fog—)

> *((You don't want to remember. You just reviewed all of that material and repressed it as fast as you could.))*

(Nonsense, Dax! I remember—)

> *((What? Tell me.))*

(Well, I—the structure of a supernova, for one thing.)

> *((You knew that before. Do you remember how you were going to make the supernova?))*

(No, but I didn't see that.) He struggled, focusing his thoughts backward. *(Are you saying that I saw it—and lost it already?)*

> *((Not lost. I've got it all recorded. But you're blocking your own understanding, Willard.))*

(But why would I do that?)

> *((That is the question. Did you notice that the data files here are more complete than your own? They're undamaged.))*

(It's true, then, that I sabotaged my own files?)

There was a long silence before Dax answered:

> *((Let's try something.))*

The view of the data-holos was suddenly stripped away, like a sheet of paper being torn back. In its place came a now-familiar view of a forest. Ruskin was standing at its edge, grasslands and mountains behind him. The forest looked dark, and vaguely ominous. Two small creatures waited for him, flanking an opening into the woods. The terrakells.

"Have something to show you," said the kindah.

"If you dare," said the sortah.

Ruskin was almost overcome by dizziness, by a sudden feeling of nausea. Nevertheless, he stood his ground. Something in him objected terribly to what was being offered here. (And what would happen if someone came into his work station and found him staring blank-faced, like a zombie?)

> *((They'd only find you motionless for a second*
> *or two. In deep thought—))*

whispered one of the trees.

He nodded. "I suppose you want me to follow you," he said to the terrakells. There was a pounding in his heart and it was growing.

The two creatures loped away into the woods. He followed. The path was dim, and it wound among the trees and climbed and descended tortuously. The terrakells glanced back at him with eyes that seemed to be trying to pierce his soul. What were they looking for? Was this another view of his own mind, his own heart? The path looped and came to a small clearing—and a pool, dark and still, banked by smooth stone and spongy moss. A fragment of the sky shone through the treetops.

The terrakells settled at the edge of the pool, and Ruskin came to stand between them. The creatures peered down at the surface of the pool; he let his own gaze drop. At first he saw only a perfect reflection of treetops framing a cloudless sky. Then, and he wasn't sure why—perhaps it was that a breeze stirred the air—he suddenly shivered; and a deep anxiety, not quite a fear, gripped him as he peered into the water. Something was coming into view, rising out of the darkness of the depths, something man-shaped and glistening. He couldn't quite catch his breath; he was trembling.

It was a man, yes, swimming up out of an impossible depth. A man that looked like . . . him. He bent forward, cold with fright, but unable to resist trying to see more clearly.

And the man came into focus, just beneath the surface; and it *was* him. But it was different, too—a Willard Ruskin from another time, another place. He reached out as though to touch the other Willard, but stopped short of disturbing the water's surface. Another figure was rising from the depths, beside the first. It was Thalia. And as the two rolled in the water to face each other, he could feel the tension between them like a pressure front passing through the still forest air. He heard Thalia's voice whisper, as though in his ear, "What makes you so special?"

(No!) he cried, before the other Ruskin could answer. He felt a shroud unraveling from his memory, and behind the shroud was a secret place, a place he remembered now, a place of pain. *(Stop it, Dax!)* he whispered. But no one answered.

And still he couldn't tear his gaze away from the sight of the younger Ruskin and Thalia arguing. The shroud was gone now, exposing the memory: the dispute that had raged between Thalia and him for months, before it destroyed their relationship, before it caused him to leave the Science Council on Ceti Alpha, caused him to leave for Kantano's World.

He strained to hear what Thalia was saying to him, three years ago. In the curl of his own lip, he could see the bitterness and disillusionment. And he heard his words, in memory, an instant before he saw them spoken: "If you side with them, then you're no better than they are!"

And her response, so typical: "Why should *they* look out for your interests if you won't look out for them yourself? You're living in a dreamland, Willard!"

"But look at what they're doing! I can't control it! I never intended for it to happen like this!"

Impatience clouded her face. "You can't hold something like this back, once it's in motion! If you care so much, why don't you stay and fight for the way it ought to be done? But don't cry if you don't win every battle. Grow up, Willard!"

And the pain contorting his face: "How can I fight it if they won't even recognize whose work they *owe* it to?"

"Then it's up to you to show them, isn't it?"

In the darkness of the water, the two figures faced each other angrily; and in the still of the forest, he watched them with a cold tightness in his chest. Just what was it they were talking about? He could almost remember. *Whose work they owe it to . . .*

((Let go of it—))

((Let it float free—))

said the terrakells, from somewhere out of sight. Let it

go from *where*? he thought. But he already knew; and if they found the key to set it free in his mind, he didn't know if he could bear to . . .

■

"Willard, did you hear me? How are you coming with that review?"

Looking up, he saw Thalia peering over the side of the console, just the top half of her lanky body visible through the privacy-screen. "I—*yes*, I'm making progress. I mean—"

"Good. We need your recommendations soon. Are you almost ready?"

He struggled to focus his eyes. "Soon," he murmured. "Thalia!" She had started to draw back from the privacy-screen, but her head reappeared, eyes questioning. "Thalia, I just—"

"*What*, Willard?"

"I . . . why is it so important that *I* be the one to do this?"

She gazed at him in disbelief and shook her head. "You can ask?" Then she pulled out of the screen and was gone.

■

Gone too were the images of his former self and his former lover. And gone were the terrakells. He was not sorry; they only brought him pain and anxiety. (*Dax, are* you *there?*) He didn't disguise his annoyance.

((*Yo.*))

(*Dax—isn't there some other way to do this? Can you just tell me—?*)

((*You have to find the memories yourself, Willard. We're scouts; we're not a memory playback machine.*))

(*Yeah.*) He took a breath. (*Well, look, do you mind if I do some work here for a while and see if I can pull it together that way?*)

((*Hey, it's your life.*))

(*What the hell's that supposed to mean?*)

((*There's only so much I can do until you find the associations. However you want to do it.*))

(*Well, I want to do it this way.*) He sighed. The memory

of that long-ago argument with Thalia still echoed in his mind. Fuck it. Where was he in his study of Breakstar?

The graphs and holos were still there. He squinted and focused. A cosmic hyperstring loop: an enormous flaw in the structure of n-space, a remnant of a phase-change in the early universe, when the seven fundamental forces separated out of the unified primordial force. It was swinging in the direction of Betelgeuse, in the course of an enormous, galaxy-spanning oscillation. Like a cosmic rubber band, the loop was growing longer and narrower as it came this way; its other end was anchored in the supermassive black hole at the center of the galaxy. Clearly the string and the coming supernova were to be linked in the formation of the gateway. But how?

He scanned the files, hoping to find a straightforward explanation somewhere among the exabytes of data. But anyone who used these files already knew what the project was attempting to do. He had no choice; he had to try to assemble the thousands of pieces into a whole.

He scanned faster. At first he wasn't aware of the assistance of Dax and the NAGs; he was like a child on roller skates, unaware of an adult's hand gently supporting and pushing him from behind, until his speed began to build; and eventually he realized that he was processing information far faster than he could have managed on his own:

Changes in the neutrino flux pouring out of the sun . . .

Velocity and position of the approaching hyperstring cusp . . .

Fleet of K-space-generating satellites deployed through the sun . . .

Continuing projections on gateway configuration; among the variables, time of triggering and speed of siphoning . . .

In the back of his mind, something was happening: understanding was starting to occur. It was almost a physical process, an accretion of tiny grains of information, arranging and rearranging themselves deep in his mind. Certain grains triggered his own recall, filling in gaps, or setting off sequences of associations. He began to feel that he *knew* this information; he began to anticipate data before they appeared. He felt the momentum building; the child on roller skates was going faster and faster. . . .

A K-space projection provides the gravitic refraction from the hyperstring, altering the gravitational characteristics of the core . . . Ranlom focusing of neutrinos . . . increasing the compression and rate of fusions . . . drawing the star rapidly . . .

The vision grew clearer in his mind. He could visualize the physical process occurring, physical reactions that no human could view directly. He could sense the equations that described it all, still just out of his grasp. How was it that he felt such a tingling sense of *knowledge;* what was that itching sensation in the center of his forebrain, the feeling that something was about to shiver forth?

The data spiraled in circles in his forebrain, formed a broad accretion disk that filled the sky in his mind's eye. The itch intensified; became a trembling pressure. He kept scanning, drawing information as fast as he could absorb it. Or faster: it was not quite a blur, images emerging from half-understood data, half-perceived relationships. He searched for he knew not what—

It came abruptly as he passed a critical point, some cusp in the data flow: the accretion disk irised open like an enormous eye, a pupil filled with darkly mysterious reflections, welling up out of his memory. If he could just focus on them—

There was a diamond-point flash in the center of the eye, illuminating the images:

The history of Breakstar unfolding before him; his own formative work . . .

■

Dear God, I invented Breakstar—?

■

Ten thousand bits of memory came together and crystallized—

■

—bits he had been struggling to remember, tied to that crucial fact: he was the creator of it all. Without him there was no Breakstar. He could scarcely draw a breath, stunned by the realization.

I created Breakstar.

And why had he left to become a mere consultant, worlds away? What had driven him from his own creation?

Out of the starburst came another center of darkness, and it was the pool in which he'd seen the images of himself. And in the darkness of the pool he saw another image: two people fighting . . .

His stomach knotted as he recognized Thalia and Tamika struggling, wrestling silhouetted against the stars—past and present lover—and he knew that they were locked in a battle not for his heart, but for his mind. *But why?* Didn't he control his own mind, his own thoughts, his own heart?

> ((*No, you don't—but you're beginning to see it.*))

(*What—?*)

> ((*The death struggle.*))

His breath caught. (*Between them?*)

> ((*Between what they represent. What your mind has been unwilling to let you remember.*))

What was Dax talking about? Yes, it was he who had conquered the equations; he who had designed the method by which a star approaching the point of supernova could be coaxed along and timed to go at just the right moment; he who had shown how the hyperstring could be used to speed the collapse, how it would then join itself to the resulting singularity to create a permanent opening in the fabric of space; he who had shown how, by combining two cosmic-scale structures, they could open a gateway that would span half the galaxy.

And having laid the theoretical groundwork . . . he had left the program in disillusionment. But why? Because he'd feared it was being misused? Or because he was being deprived of the credit and control that he believed should have been his?

He wasn't sure.

And yet he hadn't stayed away; he'd come back as a consultant. The memory filled him with a crawling uncertainty. His arguments with Thalia, his discussions with Tamika—(*Dax, what's wrong with me?*)

> ((*We're getting a pretty good idea now, aren't we?*))

(Not good enough!) He had to *know.* Even if he remembered everything he had ever known about the project—even if he could do his job perfectly—what did he Willard Ruskin want to do with that knowledge? It wasn't enough just to do his job. *What if the job was the wrong thing to do?*

•

"Willard, we need you for a while. Can you close up on that?"

•

He had to know . . .

•

"Willard, do you hear me?"

•

What? Startled, he opened his eyes and saw Thalia over the console, leaning through the privacy-screen. "What?" he croaked. He stared at the holodisplays, trying to remember her question. She wanted him to leave. . . .

"Willard!"

He started again—and this time nodded, a wave of awareness flooding him. "Right," he murmured. He turned off the holos. Looking up into Thalia's dark, questioning eyes, he rose from his seat, leaving the console behind.

CHAPTER 27

✳

"The critical thing now," Snyder was saying as Ruskin walked into the satellite control area, "is to frame to within a few seconds the time we want to hit the thing. We can still do some throttling at the end, but—" He paused and glanced up at Ruskin. "Willard! Man, we thought you weren't going to make it! What happened? Have you brought yourself up-to-date yet?"

Ruskin smiled automatically; it was practically a habit now. Snyder, yes—he remembered—part of the group he'd once worked with. Astroengineering type. A builder. Now a gateway builder. "Um—only partially," he answered. Then he added, in an attempt to sound more reassuring, "But I'm covering ground fast."

"Good. Sorry to yank you away from your review. But time is short, short, short." Snyder was a straw-haired man, lanky and pale, with blue eyes. His mouth twisted in thought. "I don't know *why* in hell that data didn't get to you weeks ago. But anyway, the string's approaching faster than we'd predicted, so we had to speed up the core crunch a bit. We're going through the oxy burn pretty fast and—"

"Ah-hah. I need to go over that data, then," Ruskin said, stalling.

"What the hell have you *been* doing? Look, for some of these projections, we might have to juice the Beetle in about forty hours," Snyder said worriedly. "Sure, we want accuracy—why else bring you here to diddle the equations for us? But we've got to have a *number* soon. *Real* soon." He nudged his display controls for a moment, then looked up. "Accuracy won't count for much if we blow the window, right?"

"Righto." Ruskin tried not to let his thoughts show as

257

something new became clear to him. The equations, yes: they were imprecise and difficult to work with. And that had been his special gift: understanding the dynamics of an oscillating hyperstring joined to a black hole. He'd been correlating the probable path of the gateway through various star populations between here and the center of the galaxy. The present path of the hyperstring could be tracked well enough, but how its motion and elasticity would change under an abrupt new stress was a matter of conjecture; and it was a critical question. Even with the most rigorous analytic techniques available, it was a little like tossing dice to chart the course of a new highway across the greatest wilderness in history. Better to have some idea of how the dice were loaded than to shoot blind. And he, Willard Ruskin, was the one who knew the most about how the dice were loaded.

But did he still know?

((I think you do, Willard.))

New images formed in his mind, released from their captivity somewhere in the lost realms where Dax and the terrakells wandered. And there it was: laid out like a chessboard, the equations and the metrical representations of n-space over which he had pored for months. Years, maybe. Before the NAGs, these computations must have been a part of his daily consciousness. How had they gotten buried so deeply? Dax and the terrakells knew.

But did he know the equations well enough to make a statement now?

Memories were sliding into place even as the question hung poised in his mind. "There are several possibilities," he murmured. He pointed at the display. "Are these the tracking figures?" Snyder nodded. Ruskin closed his eyes, calculating mentally—astounded to find that he could do so. Numbers dissolved, coalesced, danced, crystallized. "The earliest would require core-collapse in . . . roughly forty-one hours. That's the earliest, not necessarily the best." His heart pounded. *That soon?* He had indeed nearly missed it then; much later and he would have arrived in the heart of the thing. Did he know what he was talking about? He was breathing quickly now. . . .

Snyder sat back, ran his fingers through his hair. "That's

nice, at least we're in agreement on that. But we've got to get it tighter than that. We've got the last batch of sats ready for deployment, and they'll be controlling all the rest for the final squeeze."

"So—"

"So their programming has to be laid in within—I'd say, twenty hours from now, at the latest."

Thalia stepped over from another console. "What's your outside time, Willard?"

Head thrumming, he closed his eyes. Would the answer come? Numbers danced, gleaming; and images of changing shapes and stresses. "The last window closes in about sixty-four hours, I think. That would be the tail end of the acceptable cusp." He opened his eyes. "Subject to string measurements. That one has a larger margin of uncertainty."

Thalia's dark eyes bored into him. She seemed unsatisfied. "How far along are you in your review?"

He shrugged; the movement made him dizzy.

"It seems to be taking you quite a while," she said.

"I was a bit unsettled—but it's coming together." His throat was constricted; he spoke thickly, urgently. "I could do it faster if I had Ali'Maksam helping. There are differences in the system—"

Thalia frowned, turned away. "I'll see what I can do," she said abruptly. "If it's what you need."

His breath released a little. "It would help. Also, since a lot of my analysis was run on my own thinktank, I'd like to pass these updates through my shipboard system, to check for inconsistencies."

"All right. And . . . your other friend?" Thalia wasn't looking at him. She seemed to be finding something intensely interesting on the console.

"Tamika."

"Right. Tamika." Thalia pressed something on the console. Snyder had pushed back to give her room; he was listening, head cocked. "Does she need to see this material?"

"I guess not."

Thalia nodded. "Okay. Did you want separate accommodations, by the way?" She looked up. Her eyes were unexpressive, but he heard the unspoken inner question.

He drew a soft breath. "Together will be fine. We could stay right on the ship, actually."

Her pupils seemed to contract, but otherwise her face didn't change. "That won't be necessary. We'll give you quarters." Her attention returned, businesslike, to the console. After a few seconds, she added, "You can go finish up your review if you want. Can you find your way back to your work station?"

Ruskin nodded thoughtfully. Yes, he murmured. He could find his way back.

It took him hours longer to complete the review. By the time he was finished, he felt as though he'd been operating on automatic forever: the data flowing in from the station's cogitative system mingled in a kind of chemical synthesis with the aquifers of memory emerging from his mind, and the resultant understandings produced a turbulent flow in his brain, here completing a circuit of comprehension and there enclosing cells of confusion that rose like bubbles in a carbonated stream. It all seemed distant to him; there was a buzz in the back of his head that kept him from quite connecting with the sensations entering his mind, whether from the outside or from his memory. It was a stream of knowledge flowing past, devoid of emotional content.

Concluding, finally, that he had studied as much as was useful, he removed from the console a data-storage sliver which he'd filled for transfer to his shipboard system. He took several deep breaths, then turned off the privacy-screen. Around him in the control room, people were working intently, monitoring sun, satellites, and approaching hyperstring. He left the control room and walked with some uncertainty through the corridors until he found his way back to the docking wing. A security officer told him that Max and Tamika had moved into the visitors' residences. Asking the officer to inform his friends of where he was, Ruskin boarded *Enigma* in its docking pocket and began loading the new data into the shipboard console.

An hour later he was seated on the bridge, flanked by

Ali'Maksam, questioning the console. "First, can you tell me if the analytical systems that I gave you originally are consistent with the ones I've just loaded?" He glanced at Max, who was watching impassively. Max had just been granted a "special observer" clearance that allowed him to witness this. Tamika, on the other hand, had been barred from boarding the ship until the console was again secured.

"Indeed I can, sir," the console said. "They are compatible—at least in part."

"What do you mean, in part?" Ruskin asked.

"Portions of the two systems are identical; but there are gaps in the original files. Without specific knowledge, I would judge that the original files were damaged—that is, that selected parts of them may have been erased."

"Any other differences?"

The console was silent for a moment. "Yes, there are several areas where, I would say, certain inconsistencies suggest that refinements have been made in the analytical technique."

Ruskin was puzzled. "Oh? Which version was refined?"

"The version that you loaded in flight, sir. Shall I show you the comparison?"

"Please do."

As the screen flickered with columns of coding, Max stirred. "The refinements look like your handiwork," he whispered.

Ruskin shot him a glance. "Do you understand all of this?"

"The equations? No. But I do recognize the style of your work, Willard. Your signature is in the form of the changes."

Ruskin watched the screen for a moment longer, before saying, "Please hold there."

"As you wish." The image froze.

Ruskin turned to the Logothian. "Max. Have you been observing me?"

Max's eyes gleamed behind their visor. "In what sense?"

"Empathically. My behavior, my demeanor. The flow of my thought."

"Superficially, of course. But Willard—you know that I would not deep-probe you unless you asked me to." He tilted his head, so that his eyes seemed to slant toward Ruskin.

"Max—I want you to keep a close watch on me from here on out." And as he said it, he wondered, do I really mean that? Do I really want *anyone* to know what's going on inside me? But how else to know? "If you can, would you tell me now—take a look and tell me how I seem to you? Do I seem to be thinking . . . like myself?"

"Very well." Max gestured toward the lights.

Ruskin extinguished the bridge lights and reduced the screen intensity to a bare minimum. Then, as Max opened his visor, he asked the console to continue displaying the information. As he watched, he tried to forget the Logothian motionless in the gloom, and concentrated solely on the analytic structures being displayed. Again he found himself absorbing—and to a surprising degree, understanding—the flow of information. But again he was emotionally disconnected from the understanding that was building in his mind. He could see that he had, in previous months, taken an analytic method used by the Breakstar group and improved upon it. And then, perhaps during his blackouts, he had sabotaged his own work. But even now he had no real sense of why, of how he *felt* about it.

After the thinktank had completed its comparison, he ordered it to construct a new analytic tool, using as many of his refinements as could be combined with the Breakstar group's version. He wanted to perform a new timing analysis to see whether his refinements would produce a meaningfully different solution, a different shape for the gateway.

"As you wish, sir," the system replied.

Ruskin stared at the dark console. Something was puzzling about that voice, something familiar, but he couldn't quite place it. Probably imagining things. He sat in silence until Max spoke, startling him.

"You seem more confident. You seem to have regained a considerable fraction of your memory and intellectual faculties, and also your *sense* of having your memory back. I cannot vouch for the accuracy of all of your recall—however, I am surprised, and joyful for you, Willard." Max regarded him thoughtfully in the dark.

Ruskin blinked back at him. "And do you find that the *person* you sense, that the *personality* that you sense, is the same as the Willard Ruskin you knew before?"

Max hesitated. "Willard, none of us is the same person today as yesterday."

"You know what I mean, damn it."

Max let out a slow, hissing breath. "The answer is yes. And no."

Ruskin tilted his head jerkily. The feeling of uncertainty . . .

"It is difficult to describe. You are calmer, I believe, than you have been. And you are more intact, in the sense that parts of your memory that were missing are back. And yet . . ."

He waited. The pause was unbearable. "*What*, Max?"

"You are still at war with yourself," Max whispered. "You are struggling to gain and hold understanding. But you are on shifting sands. Your certainty appears and slips away. You fight to retain what you recapture—and some part of you struggles to let it go again."

Yes.

"You are trying hard, Willard."

"Am—" he fought for breath—"am I winning?"

Max eased his head back. "I do not know. I can only hope."

Ruskin blinked again, found his eyes welling with tears. *Am I ever going to know who I am?* "Max," he murmured, "I must know this: Can I trust my analytical faculties? Can I do my job here?"

The Logothian did not move. "I am not expert in that area, Willard."

"But you're an expert on *me*. You know my consciousness." His voice was becoming strained. "Do I have the capabilities I had before?"

Max was motionless, except for his breathing. At last, as Ruskin was about to speak again, he said, "I believe so, Willard. I believe I would trust your scientific judgment as much now as ever. Does that help?"

Ruskin gulped a breath; his eyes and lungs were burning. "Yes. Yes, Max. Thank you."

The Logothian gazed at him silently. He snapped his visor closed.

But Ruskin was looking inward, for his other confidant. *(Dax, is he right? Should I believe him? Am I all still here?)*

*((About your scientific abilities? You seem to
have become functional, yes.))*

*(And the rest? My personality? Am I still struggling to
put myself together?)*

((You know the answer.))

(But am I all here, blast you?)

*((Yes, Willard, you're all still here. And so
are we. We're all still here.))*

All. Of course. The NAGS. Still here. Unfriendlies and
all.

"Are they ever going to let me out into the station?"
Tamika had her fists knotted; she was struggling to contain
her frustration.

It seemed as though they had been apart for weeks, rather
than hours. Ruskin touched her cheek, wishing he could
smile. "They're working on your clearance, Twig. But I'm
afraid . . . they don't consider a *companion* as vital as a
scientific collaborator. Pretty stupid, huh?"

"Who's 'they'? That hostile bitch you introduced me to?
What was her name?"

He nodded, turning absently to inspect the tiny quarters
they had given Tamika. They'd assigned him a different
cabin; it seemed the order to put them together hadn't come
down. Still, the room was pleasant enough, if utilitarian.
"Thalia," he murmured. "Her name's Thalia."

"Oh yeah. Thal—" Tamika's voice cut off in the middle
of the name. Astonishment, then bitter understanding,
came over her face. "Thalia Sharaane?"

"Right." Ruskin turned back to her, surprised by her
tone. "Thalia Sharaane. She's the Director of Astrophysics
here."

"Is that Thalia Sharaane, your ex-lover?" Tamika's tone
was modulated, carefully controlled.

Ruskin swallowed. He didn't remember having told Tamika about Thalia. But, of course, there was no reason why
he wouldn't have, back in the still half-forgotten days when
he and Tamika had come to know each other, had grown
close. "That's right," he said huskily, and felt a sudden urge

to laugh. They were such opposites, Thalia and Tamika. For all of her competence, all of her intellectual achievements, Thalia was in many ways a perennially frightened girl, jealous and possessive. Tamika, who had never quite learned to believe in her own worth, carried more warmth in her vulnerability and puzzlement than Thalia ever had. And he? He had fallen for both of them.

"Jesus." Tamika turned half away from him, her mouth twisted in a scowl. "Did she know about me?" Her eyes flashed back to him. "Or is she always like that with other women?"

Conflicting impulses caught him halfway through a shrug, a smile. "I suppose she felt jealous—even after all this time. She has a streak of that in her, I'm afraid."

"I guess she does."

Half nod; he finally managed to swallow. "Hey—Twig?"

Troubled, frightened, angry golden eyes met his, narrow slits that drove from his thoughts whatever it was he had meant to say. Her eyebrows quivered. "My name . . . is *Tamika*," she growled.

His lips trembled. "Twig—you're the one I love now." He said it so softly, he wasn't sure whether or not she'd heard him.

Her pupils widened slowly; she placed her hands on his shoulders, touching lightly. "Yeah?" she whispered. "You say all the right things. But can you prove it?"

He drew her close, felt himself rising. "I think so," he murmured into her hair.

Her arms went around his neck, hugging tentatively. "Do you know my name?"

"Uh-huh. Twig."

"Tamika."

"I *want* you, Twig." And he remembered now, though it seemed so long ago, how much he did love her, had loved her.

Her arms tightened their embrace, her lips whispered, "I want *you*, Rus'lem."

Stumbling to the bunk, they made love with urgency and haste, not knowing who might interrupt them at any moment. He thought he had never felt closer, more desirous of her, more certain that he would be torn from her before the consummation of his desire. He was not; but when he climaxed, moments before she did, his mind was suddenly filled by an image of a great red exploding star seeding the universe, and a premonition, almost an ecstatic vision, of new life being reborn out of cataclysmic death. And in the afterglow, lying together with this woman who now seemed almost nameless to him, not needing a name, his thoughts turned to icy clarity and filled with answers to questions he had ceased asking. The equations of n-space shifted and hardened in his inner vision, and shifted again; and focused in their perfection and framed by their imperfection, he saw clearly the mapping that must be. He saw precisely the moment that the supernova must begin.

As the coverlet rose and fell slowly over Tamika's breast, he gently stroked her hair until he was certain she was asleep. Then he slipped silently out of bed and dressed. He needed to talk to Thalia at once.

Interlude

✳

If only they would answer

There had been that flurry, the breath of new voices;
and yet it could not touch them, could not find them
again

Can you hear   ?
Do you know   ?
Are you me   ?

It had to know. They were different, those voices,
each different. Never had Bright felt so uncertain, so
needy; Bright had to know

Bright's fires rang
Bright's fires echoed
But nowhere came an answer

I will wait
I must wait
Can you speak   ?
answer
please

CHAPTER 28

✳

"Sir Bremen?" said the security robot.

The assassin turned and stared silently at the thing. What was it going to be this time? Hir'd been waiting for many hours now since arrival, and the most helpful thing that anyone had had to say was that hir identification was being processed. Being processed! There was no point in trying to break through security at this point, when hir was totally a stranger to the station. But time was fleeing! And hir had no way of knowing what Ruskin was doing, except from what little the Jeaves-copy was able to ascertain.

"Your clearance has been approved," the security robot said.

"What took so long?" Ganz asked distantly. It took hir a moment to respond to the false-name Bremen. That was a bad sign. *Concentrate!*

"I can only say that the clearance was made as quickly as possible," answered the robot. "Apparently there was confusion because two representatives, not one, were expected to replace the previous Tandesko observers."

"I explained about that. My coworker was taken ill at the last minute, and no other was available."

"Yes. Well, if you will allow me to attach this bracelet to your wrist, you will be permitted to move about at will through the observer areas of the station." The robot was holding up a narrow brown band.

"I see," Ganz said, extending hir left arm. The robot deftly closed the bracelet around hir wrist, explaining that should hir find it uncomfortable or wish to remove it, hir could report to any security station. However, hir must be wearing the bracelet when moving about the station.

"And what," Ganz said, "does this bracelet signify?" Hir

held hir wrist up to examine it. The bracelet appeared to be made of a brown metal mesh.

"Brown," said the robot, "indicates 'foreign observer' status. You are free to move through the unrestricted areas. However, you will be prevented from entering the restricted zone. Only silver and gold wearers may enter the secure areas."

"And how do I distinguish one from the other?"

"Observe the doorway signs. In any case, you will be physically unable to pass through any doorway into a secure area." The robot added, as Ganz was about to turn away, "I will now take you on a brief tour, if you so desire."

Ganz thought for a moment. There was probably no better way to get a feel of the station's layout. And if the robot got to be a pain, well, there were ways of getting rid of pains.

Jeaves knew that it had to decide soon what action to take with regard to Ruskin. It had, fortunately, been able to get a signal through to its counterpart, so at least it had some inkling of what to expect from Ganz.

But from Ruskin? It was as hard for Jeaves to evaluate Ruskin as it was for Ruskin to evaluate himself. Clearly the man was still torn, as his friend Ali'Maksam had indicated, but he seemed much closer now to achieving a condition of stability. The question was, *which* point of stability would he settle on: the control of the NAGs of Broder and Gorminski, or of Jeaves's other employer, or of E'rik Daxter—or his own thoughts and feelings? And at this point, what could Jeaves do about it, even if it knew the answer? It could help Ganz kill Ruskin, or try to prevent it. But that seemed about all.

And Jeaves remembered the violent transformation that had come over Ruskin during his last emergence from K-space. That, more than anything, was the danger signal that Jeaves feared.

It was a final irony, in view of the difference of Jeaves's goals from Ganz's: that Jeaves might have to aid Ganz in destroying Ruskin, if that was the only way to keep him from going violently out of control.

Tamika was depressed, but not surprised, to find Ruskin gone when she awoke. She had little time to reflect on the fact, though; what had awakened her was the door buzzer, and when she opened the door she found herself facing a security robot, who informed her that she'd just been granted "observer" status. If she would please extend her left arm, she would be fitted with a bracelet. . . .

A little later, as she followed the robot-guide into the main observers' room, she found herself studying the bracelet on her wrist. Brown. Restricted to unsecured areas. She wasn't surprised, though she found it a bit irritating. In theory, she was supposed to know nothing about the secret project in the guise of Project Starmuse. In practice, she was going to have to smile and chat with the other observers: Tandesko and Querayn (the thought stirred her to anger: she remembered the noliHuman assassin who'd tried to kill Rus'lem) and probably several others. And she'd have to wait, and hope, that Willard would find her and share in at least a little of what was happening.

Don't be too sure.

She shivered. Where had that thought come from? She had a sudden unpleasant feeling of danger, and no reason she could think of for feeling it. She thought of Rus'lem, thought longingly of last night (or this afternoon, or whenever it had been), and wondered suddenly if he might be in danger. Of course he was in danger—they all knew that— but why this sudden oppressive feeling?

You might have to help him.

Well, of course, but . . .

Where were these thoughts coming from? She had this odd sensation that thoughts were entering her head from the outside, but that was ridiculous, unless someone somewhere was projecting thoughts at her telepathically. But who could be doing that? Max?

No, not Max.

Who, then? She blinked. Wait a minute . . .

((Don't be afraid.))

Don't be afraid? She clenched her hands into fists as the room seemed to blur around her.

((You needn't—you mustn't fear—))

There it was, clear as a bell in her head. Who are you? she wanted to scream, but didn't dare. She exhaled and peered around the room. *Don't be afraid,* said the spider to the fly. Yes. And wasn't that what the angel had said to the Virgin Mary as he scared the living bejesus out of her?

She detected a trace of humor as she heard, in her mind:

((I assure you I am no angel. . . .))

"This way, please, Ms. Jones," the security robot interrupted, blinking patiently at her. Startled, she looked to see what it was gesturing toward: the front center of the room, where several human and humanoid individuals were clustered around a series of consoles. Above the consoles, a large screen showed a wide-angle satellite shot of the sun. "This," said the robot, "is the information area, where you can monitor scientific observations and, if you like, address additional questions to the host cogitative system. You are free to use these consoles at any time."

"Thank you," Tamika murmured. She wanted to listen to the robot, but that voice in her head . . .

((It's okay, I'll still be here. Learn what you must.))

Stunned, she followed the robot as it led her toward a refreshment counter. She listened with only half an ear; it made sense to learn her way around the station, but really, she had no intention of pretending to be a scientific observer.

((Mark well what you can. You never know what may be useful. But never mind the science. It's all phony, anyway.))

She blinked, tensing.

((You may not always be confined in this place. But notice those who are here.))

She didn't know why; but she glanced around. There was something familiar about one of the individuals near the front consoles. A heavyset humanoid, Tandesko. She couldn't remember seeing it before; and yet she felt she had. "Is that what you mean?" she murmured—and caught herself, realizing that she was addressing a voice in her head.

((Perhaps . . .))

What was it the voice had said about not always being confined here? And what *was* this voice talking in her head?

((Soon—please. Would you mind taking a seat in the back just for a moment?))

Numbly, she obeyed, realizing that the security robot had just thanked her and handed her a small plastic square with lighted diagrams flickering through it: a pocket map of the station. The robot was gone. She sank into a chair, taking a deep breath, and closed her eyes, hoping that she would not faint, that it would all somehow make sense. She shivered again, feeling the sense of danger return. *(Now will you tell me who you are and what you want?)*

((Of course. We're already acquainted, in a way. My name is Dax, and I'm here to help—))

(What—?) Her blood ran cold. Dax? But how? Her eyes flickered open; the room seemed to be spinning; she clamped her eyes shut again. *(What are you doing in me?)*

((I migrated from Willard while you were in intimate contact . . .))

(You mean—when we were—you mean in his—) Her heart thumped with indignation. The instant she was aware of it, it steadied.

((I regret the invasion of your privacy, but I perceived an overriding need. You may have to do more here.))

(More of what?) If she had cried it aloud, her voice would have cracked.

((Look at your bracelet.))

She looked—and realized that a band of warmth surrounded her wrist. The brown bracelet that the security robot had placed around her wrist was glimmering, slowly turning iridescent and gold.

((I am altering its molecular structure to resemble that of Willard's. You will soon be able to enter the secure areas.))

She stared dumbly at the bracelet.

((It is possible that Willard may be in dan-

*ger. And you may be the only one who can
help. . . .))*

Ruskin stood with Thalia and Snyder and went over the
numbers with them one more time. "You're sure now?"
Thalia asked. She was dressed in a black-and-gold jumpsuit;
her eye movements and hand movements were quick,
decisive.

"As sure as humanly possible." As Ruskin said it, he felt
a rushing in his ears, as all of his doubts came swarming
back—doubts not about the computations but about what
he was doing. Was he playing into the hands of the unfriendly NAGs? Was he a fool to help the Auricle scientists
whose Breakstar project he had once walked away from?

My Breakstar project, he reminded himself. He had the
opportunity now to exercise some of the control that had
once been denied him. A memory flickered through his
mind: of rage, years ago, when his recommendations had
been run roughshod over. But he had come back; he had
planned to do this work, before his mind had been turned
upside down by the NAGs. Whatever his doubts, it was now
or never. The star was going to be broken and remade in
a new image, regardless of his actions; his hope, if he had
one, was to direct the gateway along the most promising
possible path, to make the star's death as meaningful as
possible.

Death? Was that term relevant to an inanimate thing,
even such a thing of cosmic power as a supergiant star?

"Are you all right, Willard?" Thalia asked, her eyes large
with concern.

"What?" he murmured. "Yes—yes, of course I am."

"You look tired."

He shook his head, and without thinking, found himself
asking, "What was it you told me about the Querayn scientists? About them believing that the sun could be a living,
conscious being?" He felt a touch of dizziness as he asked
it; he didn't even know why it had come to mind.

Her eyebrows went up. "What? Are you feeling guilty?"
She shrugged. "They have no proof, but we can't prove

them wrong, either. Don't tell me you're going to start in with that now!"

He gaped at her. In the instant of an eyeblink, he felt Dax—or perhaps the terrakells—stirring in his brain. An image blazed against the window of his mind: Willard Ruskin asking a gathering of scientists whether they shouldn't be cautious, whether there might not be unforeseen consequences of their actions—never mind that he himself was the chief architect of their plan. He'd had no omniscient visions, and certainly no thought of living stars; but it seemed such a godlike thing to do, blowing up a star. And who knew what effect a stargate might have on other star systems, or even on space-time itself, by stretching across the galaxy?

"Willard, what's wrong?"

"What?" He blinked his eyes wide open again. Thalia was gazing at him worriedly. "Nothing . . . nothing." Scowling, he peered over Snyder's shoulder at the console. "I was just thinking it through one last time." He pointed to a progression of lights on the screen. "Is that the satellite launch sequence?"

Snyder nodded. "Final deployment starts in just over an hour." He looked up at them both, and his tired face crested with a smile. "Thought we'd never make it this far, didn't you?" He lowered his eyes back to his work, his fingers moving on the console. "I know *I* wondered."

Ruskin stepped back and gazed at Thalia. Her face was absorbed in concentration. He felt his fists tightening involuntarily as they both watched Snyder communicating with subordinates in other labs, shepherding the final timing coordinates into the station's cogitative network, for loading into the satellites. Barring an unexpected change, Ruskin realized, the die was being cast.

His eyes wandered over the various displays, and he noted the input from a remote location: Room Zeta. Wondering what it was, he bent to take a closer look at its readings, which seemed to focus on inner core measurements. Thalia noticed what he was doing and remarked, "If you *really* wanted to get the best possible mapping, that would be the place to do it from. Of course, you might be vaporized." In response to his raised eyebrows, she said,

"It's a remote station, deep in the sun. It's the ideal location for mapping the gateway formation—since we don't know what data transmission from the satellites is going to be like at the time of maximum activity. We actually did consider putting someone in there to do real-time fine-tuning at the end. But it's just too dangerous. We aren't sure that our escape system can pull the room out when it blows."

"Why do you call it a *room*?" Ruskin asked in puzzlement.

"It's really just an extension of this station, connected by a K-space peninsula. For practical purposes, though, it's a separate station, since we're prepared to cut it loose when we pull out of four-space." Thalia's eyes narrowed, as though she were a little surprised that she had to explain this.

Ruskin thought about it for a minute. "What if you had a *volunteer*?"

Her eyes were intent, expressionless. "Why? Were you thinking of volunteering?"

He shrugged, gave a little smile. "Not really." The dizziness was returning. He felt flushed. His mind filled with an image of chains of molecules, folding and unfolding, point meeting point, instructions and meanings emerging from an astonishing, bewildering array. Was that Dax, trying to understand what he was thinking, what he was doing?

The image faded. He was aware of his hands knotting into fists again. "Well, actually—I might," he heard himself saying. "After all, what's the point of all this, if we're going to be afraid at the end? So much has been invested—isn't it worth risking, say, *one* life, to make sure that you get the best possible data? Especially if there are controls on the station that would let someone really ride it at the end, fine-tune it down to the wire?" (*Dax, what the hell am I talking about?*)

"And probably be destroyed with it?" Thalia asked.

"Well, so maybe the volunteer will go up—but maybe he wouldn't—and even if he did, there's still the possibility of making a difference at the end—maybe between success and failure. The gateway would be a permanent living memorial." He grinned, and it felt like someone else's grin, not his own at all.

Molecules twisting into place with blinding speed, link-ages ratcheting into place . . .

((Willard—get the hell out of here!))

He stiffened. What—?

((Now!))

Thalia was glaring at him. "Forget it, Willard. I'm vetoing the idea, and we don't have the time now to argue the point."

"But—"

"If you wanted to make a case for it, you could have come on board months ago, like everyone else." Her lips tightened into thin lines, her eyes hardened. "And now, dear friend, would you please get your fanny down to the mapping console and start getting ready to do the rest of your job?"

He opened his mouth to protest, felt a rush of unreason-able fury, heard Dax pleading to him:

((Willard, for God's sake! Move it before I
lose control!))

(What the hell are you talking about?)

((Just go!))

Thalia's expression showed no compromise. "I'll be down there in a few minutes, myself. I have to check in on the com-link center first." She turned away, as though in dis-missal.

With a shrug that belied the unreasoning rage that was building in his chest, he obeyed and left the room.

The rage and dizziness overcame him in the corridor, and he staggered against the wall, fumbling for a doorway. His face was hot, flushed. What was going on? He rubbed hard at his eyes. They felt numb; his vision was shimmering in and out of focus. *(Dax, for God's sake, help me!)*

Dax's answer sounded weak:

((I . . . can't . . .))

(What's wrong, Dax?) He was feverish; he was starting to shake. He pushed his way through a doorway. Where was he? It looked like a lounge. Hard to be sure; his eyes

were going mad; he saw no one else in the room. *Dax,
you've got to tell me what's happening!)*

((I . . . Willard . . . losing it . . .))

"Wait! Dax!" he croaked aloud. "You can't just leave me
like this!"

((. . . hope you can control it . . . !))

Dax was gone, or was lost in a roil of wind in the center
of his brain: molecules blowing away, connections disintegrating, order disappearing into chaos. He felt himself
falling . . . falling into a fire, into the center of the sun . . .
but the sun was closing in upon him, turning to darkness.

And in the heat and darkness, everything blurred. . . .

He sat a long time in a world of mist and darkness.

He sat in a world of rage, of coldly vengeful calculation.

He knew what he had to do.

This world, this project, this station was a thing of evil.
In the hands of the enemy, it was an abomination, a weapon
to establish dominion over not just a tiny fraction of the
galaxy, but all the galaxy, all life, all freedom. An enemy
of freedom, was what it was. An enemy of the true people.

He could destroy it. But far better to take its helm and
turn it to the cause of righteousness. Turn the weapon of
the enemy against its own creator. He focused clearly and
distinctly on that goal and looked within himself to see if
he was ready, if he was coiled. His fingertips gleamed; he
examined the razorlike claws that emerged from the last
three fingers, and the tiny laser that glinted at the tip of
his index finger. He smiled.

(Don't . . . don't . . .) A tiny echo in the back of his mind,
the voice of doubt.

Crush doubt. What must be done will be done.

Who will be first? The one who knows most how to complete this project the way the hated Auricles would have it
completed. The head of astrophysics . . .

The sequence was already started, but it was not too late
to alter the outcome, if the brains of the operation could
be removed. . . .

There was a sound outside in the corridor. He came to full alert. Rising slowly, silently, he crept to the doorway and flattened himself at its edge so that he could peer out into the hallway. Voices—and one of them, female, he recognized:

"Damn it, security, haven't you found *anything* on him? He's been gone for over an hour—and we need him on the console. We need him now."

A faintly metallic, robotic voice answered: a full-station search had been initiated, but Ruskin seemed to have disabled the auto-locator on his bracelet, and it could take time to find him, especially if he did not want to be found.

Ruskin? The originator of this hated enterprise? He would have made an excellent target, if he had not already been destroyed—and remade—into something much, much better.

The female voice spoke again, and sounded terribly distressed, and angry. Good. Anger. How much better that he strike against the enemy angry.

Thalia Sharaane and a security robot came abreast of the doorway and turned to look in. "Security," Sharaane said, speaking through the robot to a central control station, "we're checking the lounge on—"

He reacted instantly, grabbing her arm and jerking her in through the door. The robot spun quickly to defend her, a floodlight blazing from it, illuminating the room and almost blinding him.

Almost. The robot was no match for him. His own eyes adapted to the bright light instantly, and the needlebeam that lanced from his finger destroyed the lamp and pierced the robot's shell and flashed through its neuronal network, stunning if not incapacitating it. His right foot flew straight out and caught the thing in its top section, crushing it at the impact point and sending it flying back out the door. Sharaane struggled to pull away from him. He scarcely noticed. He punched the door control to seal the room, then smashed the control.

"*What the hell are you doing?*" she screamed. "*Who are you?*" She brought her right hand around in a fist and hit his jaw.

He smiled and released her as he swung his right hand

and knocked her across the room. "I am the one sent to kill you," he said, picking her up and pinning her against the wall. She struggled futilely. His smile widened. "I am here to destroy all of the enemies of freedom. And you are the greatest of them, with the possible exception of Ruskin. But you have already done what we needed of you." He placed his fingertip in the middle of her forehead.

And began counting to himself, as her struggling turned to screaming curses, then to gasps, and finally to wracking sobs.

CHAPTER 29

✳

Tamika did not know why she was running down the hallway. But she felt an urgency like an ache behind her breastbone that made the burning in her lungs seem irrelevant. Someone shouted at her; she ignored the shout and kept running. She knew only one thing: she had to get to Willard, before it was too late.

If she could find him.

The public address system had been paging him for the last half hour, with increasing urgency; and the voice of central security, which Dax somehow was tapping and piping into her head, was talking about a stationwide search. What could Willard possibly be doing? Unless he was no longer in his right mind . . .

((He may well not be.))

(You don't sound surprised.)

((I've been expecting a sudden unfolding, a catastrophic change in his inner control. I've been sure that they've been waiting to do something like this.))

(They?) Tamika raced down the hallway and, at the end, breathing heavily, looked both ways. *(Which direction?)*

((Try left. "They" are the unfriendly NAGs.))

(I thought you had them under control!)

((Relatively speaking, yes. I've been able to prevent them from controlling him. That doesn't mean that I was controlling them. There was always the risk of their breaking free, at least until I understood their plan.))

(And now you do?) She ran quickly down the corridor, pausing at each doorway to peer inside. She received a few startled glances, but most of the rooms were empty. Most

of the people were apparently at the central control stations.

*((Certain processes which I was mapping in
Willard before I split away from him suggest
that he was programmed for murder.))*

Her heart nearly stopped. *(Murder—?)*

The thought was interrupted by a voice in her head reporting that a robot in section 7B had declared an intrusion, then had stopped sending.

Willard. She remembered his transformation on the ship, during K-space transition—and much earlier, in her own apartment. Dax read her thought, as he said:

((His attack on you was a flaw in the programming—an aberration. But when he recognized you, he came to his senses. Tamika, you may be the only one who can stop him! Go left to the end and down a level— quickly!))

Ganz quietly left the observers' lounge on hearing Ruskin being paged for the second time. Hir scanned the security channels on the transceiver implanted in hir ear and quickly ascertained that Ruskin had indeed disappeared. Ganz's pulse quickened. *(Jeaves-copy,)* hir murmured, shifting channels on the transceiver.

(Acknowledged,) hir ship replied.

(Have you been monitoring the security channels?)

(Affirmative. Ruskin is missing. He may be undergoing an alteration, as you've been expecting.)

(Or he may have snapped. I must be there to determine his state. He may have to be destroyed so that I can carry out at least the remnant of his mission.)

(You do not know the timing, and I have no guidance to offer,) the Jeaves-copy cautioned.

Ganz moved with surprising speed down the corridor. *(There is no help for that now. Do you have any information on his last known whereabouts?)*

There was a hesitation, irritatingly long. As hir waited for Jeaves-copy to answer, Ganz consulted hir station layout map. Hir assumed that vital information was missing from it, since it was intended for unsecured observers. But it was all hir had, at the moment.

(*Jeaves-copy?*) hir repeated finally.

(*Looking,*) the computer answered, somewhat testily.

Ganz didn't care about the computer's emotional state. Hir paused before a door display that was flashing, NO ADMITTANCE. It was perhaps time, hir thought, to find out whether hir security-breaking utilities would perform as advertised. (*I'm going into the secured area,*) hir said to the Jeaves-copy.

(*That might not be wise,*) Jeaves-copy began.

It didn't matter. Ganz had already begun tuning the nanoprogrammer embedded in hir forearm, testing the field that crossed the doorway to determine whether it could be compensated for by the programmer. A tiny beep, sensed in hir inner ear, advised that the programmer had completed the requested compensation. Ganz stepped forward, hand extended toward the doorway. Hir hand slipped away, repelled by thin air. Ganz scowled, and with a glance each way down the corridor, applied hir shoulder to the invisible barrier. Hir pushed carefully. Hir felt the resistance of the door only for an instant; then hir staggered as the force of hir push was deflected to the side.

Ganz cursed silently. (*Jeaves-copy—*)

(*Acknowledged. Did you succeed?*)

(*No,*) hir snapped. (*Did you?*)

The ship hesitated before answering. (*A security robot has gone offline. That may be his location. And Thalia Sharaane has disappeared in the same sector.*)

It was possible, then, that Ruskin was already performing his mission. But Ganz had to know.

There was a sound in the hallway. Ganz whirled. A young woman raced down the corridor toward hir. She stopped at an intersection just short of Ganz, hesitated a moment, seeming not to see Ganz, then turned to her left and raced away.

Ganz remained motionless only for an instant. Then hir leaped to follow the woman. She was the one hir had seen with Ruskin back in the Kantano system, and just a short time ago in the observers' lounge. If anyone was going to lead hir to Ruskin, it was this woman. Hir ran quickly,

silently. *(Jeaves-copy, can you help with this door-code?)*
(Trying. It's difficult; it's an n-space manipulator.)

Ganz saw the woman disappear to the right out of the corridor. *(Don't give me excuses for failure, robot. I'm following the woman. If I lose her, I could lose everything.)*

The wall on Ganz's right shimmered, and hir came to a halt. Another NO ADMITTANCE message winked at hir. Ganz thrust a hand at the doorway, and it was repelled as before. Coldly, suppressing anger, hir began trying one more time to break the code.

"Sir—may I ask what you are doing?" A young man was approaching from behind hir, looking suspicious. The young man spoke into a small communications device, speaking too softly for Ganz to hear.

Straightening, Ganz smoothed hir blouse, blurred hir appearance by gentle stages, enough to confuse, not enough to draw attention to the process. "Sir, I fear that I have lost my way. I was certain that this was the way I had passed before, but—" Ganz gestured at the half-reflective doorway in exasperation. "As you can see—"

"Yes," the young man said. "It says, No Admittance. You are not permitted to go that way. You are wearing a brown bracelet, sir. You must stay in the observers' areas."

"Yes, yes," Ganz murmured. "I have only just arrived on the station. Perhaps you could direct me—" Hir waved hir hand in apparent befuddlement.

The young man's expression was wary. Ganz judged that hir story was not believed. That was too bad; but perhaps not entirely. The young man was wearing a bracelet of iridescent silver. That could be useful.

"Sir, I think you'd better come with me to the security station," the man said.

"Oh, but is that wholly necessary?" Ganz asked, extending a hand, palm up, toward the man. A tiny puff of vapor jetted toward the man's face from an orifice in Ganz's middle finger.

"I'm afraid—" The man choked in midphrase and fell to the floor, clutching his throat. He trembled for a moment, then was still.

Ganz wasted no time. Bending over the body, hir flicked out a cauterizing molecular knife blade, sliced the man's hand off cleanly at the wrist, and removed the security bracelet. As hir straightened, hir focused mentally for an instant, then directed another puff of vapor at the body and stepped away quickly.

The corpse lasted as such for perhaps four seconds. Consumed as though by the air itself, it collapsed inward and turned to a fine mist. Then the mist became transparent and disappeared, vanishing into the air—and into the floor—as carbon dioxide, water, ammonia, and a thin soup of other elements. Ganz sniffed the faint pungency in the air, noted with satisfaction that no trace of the young man remained, and turned hir attention to the bracelet. Its latching mechanism was not evident. Undoubtedly Ganz could solve its puzzle later, but right now hir had more important things to worry about.

Using the molecular blade, Ganz neatly removed hir own bracelet. Holding the other in hir left hand, hir turned back to the doorway and stepped through.

Counting . . . one hundred thirty-two . . . one hundred thirty-three . . .

The numbers rolled through the mind of the thing that had been Ruskin, as he kept Thalia Sharaane pinned to the wall, laser-finger at her forehead.

"Damn you!" she whispered. "If you're going to kill me, why don't you just do it?"

He scowled. Kill her? Indeed, he would . . . as soon as he had finished counting. *One hundred thirty-four . . . one hundred thirty-five . . .*

Must kill her!

((Must . . . count . . .))

Yes . . . he had to finish counting first . . .

Sharaane struggled futilely. She was weakening; he was pressing her hard to the wall, and she was having trouble breathing. "Bastard!" she gasped. "Who—in hell—are you?"

His mind seemed to stop.

Hell?

Hell was where she and her like belonged. And that was

where he would send her, as soon as the count reached—

His vision darkened, and his head roared with pain.

((Stop . . . it . . .))

Must kill her, must kill—MUST—

((Not . . . until . . .))

. . . *hundred—what—until WHAT?*

((You—MUST—COUNT—))

There was a vise tightening in his throat. Darkness growing in his mind. Vision blurring. Buzzing in his head, louder with each passing second . . . he was aware of the woman kicking, striking at him with her fists, but it was no more than the struggling of an insect.

Insect.

The thought repelled him, almost made him drop her. But his purpose burned through the haze, steadying him again. *This woman is the head of scientific control. Only she can guide the process accurately from here. I must destroy her to take control of the gateway formation. I must . . .*

He placed his razor-sharp nails against her face and felt the urge to slice deep, through flesh and bone. Three beads of blood appeared on her cheek.

Must . . .

His throat constricted sharply, and the thought began to escape him. He struggled to recapture it, but the pain blocked him. His fingernails pulled back a few millimeters. *What . . . was I . . . thinking?*

((You must . . . put her down . . . while you COUNT!))

No! he wanted to scream. *Who are you? Who are you? What are you?*

((I am—))

The voice in his head was choked off; his eyes widened; his head snapped up and back. The woman in his grasp peered at him with almost as much astonishment as fear, dark eyes impossibly large. "Thalia—" his voice said, and it was more a gargle than a vocalization. What was he saying? And what was that sound behind him?

He slammed the woman against the wall, let her go, and whirled. The door was dissolving. That was impossible; he had smashed the controls. But it wasn't opening; it was simply disintegrating in a cloud of smoke and dust. Standing in the doorway, passing her hand around the edge of the door frame, was a slim dark-haired woman, familiar looking, with golden cat eyes. As he stared at her in bewilderment, he was aware of the other woman, Dr. Sharaane, slumping to the floor behind him. This new intruder must be destroyed. He started to move toward her, but was halted by a sharp command: *"Wait!"*

She had stepped forward; it was her voice that had startled him. There was something about her that was terribly familiar—

"Rus'lem!" she snapped.

Again he halted in midstride, his head cocked sharply. He hadn't even been aware that he was moving. *Rus'lem.* A name? It seemed to coil about his head like a wisp of vapor. Whose name? What did it matter? He crouched to spring.

"RUS'LEM, REMEMBER!"

He froze. He . . . could not move. He was infuriated. Bewildered. The words caught at him, enfolded and bound him, like a net of vapor and smoke. He could not move, could not speak.

His face turned to fire.

((You must stop . . .))

Stop—? Who—?

((. . . now. You must stop—NOW!))

He stared dumbly at the woman and thought, this woman is interfering. I must—

What?

"What have you done, Rus'lem?" she cried. "What have you done? *Damn it, come back to me!"*

As he gazed stupidly at her, his vision turned to a darkening swirl, and she blurred before his eyes; and everything blurred . . . he was burning up from the inside out. . . .

Tamika stared in shock at the two figures crumpled on the floor in front of her. The monster that had controlled Willard's body was disappearing; the massive swarthy brow and cheekbones were receding, and Willard's face, the face

she loved, the figure of the man she loved, were returning.
But the other person, the woman he'd been attacking . . .

"Jesus Christ—no!" She hastened past him to examine
the woman. It was Thalia Sharaane, the head of the project,
the woman Rus'lem had introduced her to—his former
lover. Dear God, why had he been trying to kill *her?* What
did the NAGs want? "I've got to get help," she whispered
under her breath.

    ((No, you mustn't—))
  (I've got to. She may die.)
    ((Could you explain this?))
  (No, but—)
    *((Then let me help her. If she's still alive . . .
    stretch her out, quickly. And place your
    hands on her face—over her eyes.))*

Uncomprehendingly, Tamika did as she was told. She
straightened Sharaane out on the floor, then laid her palms
over the woman's eyes. She felt a tingling in her hands. A
flush came to her own face.

    ((I must do this very fast. . . .))

Then she understood. As Dax had produced NAGs on her
palms capable of turning the locked door to dust, so now
it was sending an army of cell-repair machines across her
skin and into Sharaane's body the fastest way possible,
through the tear ducts of her eyes. Tamika's hands were
growing very warm.

The woman gasped. Tamika drew her hands away. Sharaane blinked her eyes open and seemed to focus on her.
"What are you doing?" Sharaane whispered.

"Don't try to talk," Tamika said, rising. She turned to
look at Willard. She would not have believed that it was
him, if she had not seen the transformation before—if this
rough-hewn killer were not now, as she watched, turning
back into the man she loved. She knelt beside him, placing
a hand on his face. He was burning with fever. He groaned
at her touch. "You'll be all right," she said. "Rus'lem, you'll
be all right." Even as she said it, she disbelieved it. How
could he ever be, when at any time he could . . .

    *((Keep your hand there a moment longer,
    please—thank you—yes, that is good.))*
  (What are you doing?)

((Communicating. Yes. Control has been reestablished.))

(Are you sure?) Tamika stroked Ruskin's face gently, feeling that perhaps by touching him, she could reestablish the reality of who he was, what he was. His skin temperature was dropping. His face looked far more like his own now, but was still a bit puffy. Details were being filled in, remade and smoothed over.

Within her, Dax answered with calm certainty:

((Yes. And we know now what else he was programmed to do.))

There seemed to be voices all around him as he awakened. Telling him to remember . . . remember what . . . ? Looking down on him was . . . Tamika. The memory of what had happened came to him like a hot flame. "It was you," he whispered. "How did you do it? How did you know?" And before she could reply, he had the answers in his own mind, from Dax.

((I'm sorry, Willard. It had to be done.))

(You told me that you wouldn't cross over into her; you told me she was safe from the NAGs. . . .) His inner words died away. Dax had lied to him. But under the circumstances, how could he be angry?

"Rus'lem, don't—"

Tamika's words were too late. He was already sitting up. He touched her face, and smiled sadly. The smile fell away as he turned to look at Thalia.

She was lying quietly, breathing slowly. Her eyes were open, but she seemed unaware of his presence.

Tamika stirred. "Dax—" she began. He looked at her questioningly. "Dax crossed from me into her," Tamika said finally. "He may have saved her life. I think . . . I think he's preventing her from recognizing you now."

((Correct. Willard, it's time to move. The project is entering its final phase, and if you hope to do anything about it, you don't dare let security find you here.))

Ruskin took a deep breath. *(I don't even know what it is I want to do.)*

((I can help you with that. But you've got to get away from here. Find Ali'Maksam. Move, Willard.))

Ruskin reached out and touched Thalia's face. She was alive; she was breathing; she did not know that it was he who had tried to kill her. He let out a long breath and rose quickly to his feet. "Stay with her," he said to Tamika.

She looked agonized. "But I can't leave you—"

"Please. You've helped me already. I need you to help me again." He cradled her cheeks gently, peered into her puzzled eyes. "I'll be all right. I love you, Twig." Then he hurried out into the corridor, past the damaged security robot. Voices were approaching from around the corner to the right. He darted silently in the other direction.

CHAPTER 30

✳

Far from the station, the fleet of gensats encircling the sun moved through the searing heat of the photosphere like a flock of birds winging their way into a crimson sunset. This sunset burned at a temperature of thousands of degrees, but the satellites—powerful, intricate, intelligent machines—were undisturbed by the heat, feathered as they were by protective layers of n-space. Several of their cousins, whose shielding had failed, were now vapor, their meager elements added to the fiery plasma of the photosphere. This was the outer layer of the star, where visible light was emitted; the fire and violence here only hinted at the furies deeper within.

The gensats were bringing Alpha Orionis closer each moment to a violent and premature death. In an intricate choreography, they moved through carefully computed changes of position. Like felker birds riding air currents, they sailed in the convection zones of the Betelgeusian photosphere, hovering and maneuvering on the upwelling currents of plasma, their invisible wings of force spread wide to derive lift from the updrafts of ionized gases. Hovering with infinite patience, they spun their webs of spatial distortion, their threads of stardeath.

In the star's core, nothing was happening quite according to normal. A three-pronged assault, most of it utterly invisible in the four-space continuum, was guiding the time of the supernova toward the correct moment for the capture of the hyperstring.

Aboard the K-space sats, powerful generators had already driven their talons deep into the sun. Two years ago, huge conductive magnetic fields had appeared around the "wings" of each of the satellites. Drawing upon the energy flux of hot plasma stirring through the magnetic fields, the wings had channeled power back to the K-space generators. And the generators had come to life as one.

Like the radial spines of a sea urchin, fourteen hairline cracks had appeared in the space-time inhabited by the star; fourteen threads of altered space opened, converging at the star's center. From the center, a single spike of K-space shot out of the star, out into space, stabbing blindly into the infinite night . . . except that approaching from that direction was another wrinkle in space, the narrowing loop of the hyperstring, invisible to mortal eyes in four-space but incredibly massive and fast and, anchored at its far end by an enormous black hole, trillions of times tauter than a piano wire.

When the spike and the hyperstring met, the two spatial defects instantly combined, forming a stressed gravitational link between the n-dimensional heart of the hyperstring and the heart of the star. The hyperstring carried an astounding gravitational potential. Refracted by the K-space distortion into the heart of the star, that potential was joined to the existing gravitational field of the star, increasing the squeeze on the matter in the star's core, drawing it tighter, hotter.

Another web of K-space projections reached out to a much closer target: the core of the companion star, Honey. That connection was wider, an actual channel: a siphon tube through which Honey was being bled from the inside out. Fiery matter from the core of the companion was blasting through that tube onto the core of Betelgeuse—adding mass, stirring the flames hotter still.

The remaining sats generated not K-space but Ranlom-fields, wrapping the sun's core in a vast neutrino-catching web. Most of the star's energy was now being emitted in the form of neutrinos; and a fraction of that energy was being reflected back, focused with great precision into the core, driving the chain reaction still faster.

For two years, the fusions had been burning at an enormously accelerated rate, transmuting elements in an alchemist's nightmare: carbon, neon, nitrogen, magnesium, oxygen, and others, the chain of fusions sliding rapidly toward silicon and iron, drawing the star ever faster toward the inevitable end. The iron core would grow until it reached the Chandrasekhar-Ruskin Limit—when it could no longer support its own weight, and in a single instant, would collapse. The temperature would soar to forty billion degrees; and as the core was crushed out of existence into a black hole, the implosion would release not only the shock wave that would blow the rest of the star apart, but also a stupendous blast of neutrino energy that would momentarily outshine the light of a million galaxies.

A portion of that neutrino burst, caught by the Ranlom-fields, would be channeled back into the K-space connection, shaping space-time at the final instant. If everything happened according to plan, when the hyperstring was nailed into the newly formed singularity, a gateway would ripple open down the length of the hyperstring, all the way to the center of the galaxy.

The gensats and their fields worked quietly, steadily at destroying the star. They could be controlled and throttled to the end; but in the absence of new instructions, they would execute their mission precisely as programmed.

Thalia was just coming to as the security squad arrived. She blinked and focused on the woman's face peering worriedly down at her. It took a moment; then she recognized the face as that of Willard's friend, Tamika Jones. What was she doing here? The woman pulled back, and a male security officer appeared, waving a medical diagnostic scanner over her.

"Get that thing out of my face," Thalia grunted, brushing it aside.

"Are you all right, Dr. Sharaane?" the officer asked.

She levered herself up to a sitting position, wondering what she was doing on the floor in the first place. "Yes. I'm all right," she murmured, though she felt a vague blur in the back of her mind that suggested that she was not all right at all.

"You gave us a hell of a scare." The officer helped her to her feet. "There's a smashed robot out in the hall. And what happened here?" He pointed to a large oval hole in what used to be a door.

Thalia stared at it and felt a sickening sensation in her stomach, a terrible rush of déjà vu. What *had* happened to the door? She felt as though she ought to remember.

She looked at the woman Tamika again. "What *are* you doing here?" she asked, and was startled to realize that she felt grateful for the woman's presence.

"Don't you remember?" Tamika asked.

Thalia closed her eyes. "No."

"You don't remember being attacked?"

Attacked . . . Yes, she'd been attacked. She remembered now. But by what, or whom?

The security officer whirled on Tamika. "What do you know about this?"

"I remember now," Thalia interrupted. "I looked into this room, and—*something*—attacked me. . . ." Her voice trailed off.

"Who was it, Dr. Sharaane? Do you know?"

Thalia shook her head. "No," she whispered, suddenly remembering her fear. "I'd never seen him before."

"Then—" and the officer cast a suspicious glance at Tamika—"we're talking about a Human?"

"I think so. Yes, a male Human, muscular, with harsh features." Thalia blinked, shifted her gaze to Tamika. "Did you see? Does that sound right to you?"

"Yes," Tamika said softly. "That sounds about right."

The officer scowled. "Would you mind telling me who you are, Miss?"

"Tamika Jones. I—"

"Jones? The companion of Dr. Ruskin?"

"Yes, I—"

"Do you have clearance to be in this area, Ms. Jones?" The officer's tone was brusque.

Tamika silently held up her left wrist; on it was a silver-and-iridescent bracelet. The officer looked taken aback and rubbed his nose thoughtfully. "As I was saying, I came in," Tamika said, "and saw what was happening—"

"And stopped it?"

"I wouldn't say that. I—well, I guess I startled him. I

shouted; I remember that." She swallowed, evidently having trouble getting the words out. "And he dropped her, and . . . ran away. I don't know where he went." She shifted her gaze back to Thalia. "I came over to see if—if Dr.—"

"Sharaane," Thalia said.

"Yes. To see if Dr. Sharaane was all right. And that's when you arrived." Tamika looked at Thalia, as though for confirmation. So did the officer.

Thalia gazed silently at the woman, feeling that somehow she hadn't told the entire truth, but not knowing just how. Thalia felt a curious urge to back her up, nevertheless. "That's right. The truth is, I believe that Ms. Jones here saved my life."

The officer scratched a note, scowling. "But your assailant is on the loose at this time—is that right?"

Thalia blinked. "Yes—yes, I suppose he is. Please put out a full alert—and keep searching for Dr. Ruskin." She drew a breath with difficulty. "There may be a connection with his disappearance. I don't know." She squinted, trying to realign her thoughts. Her mind was reacting strangely to all this. She felt oddly calm. Drawing a breath, she smoothed down her torn and rumpled clothes. "And now I must get to the control room."

"I'll send someone with you." The officer snapped a finger at one of his men. "Now, Ms. Jones, would you please—"

"I need her to come with me," Thalia interrupted. She was surprised by her own words.

The security officer looked unhappy. "Dr. Sharaane, Ms. Jones was granted observer status only. I don't even know why she's—"

"She has a bracelet, and she'll be there on my authority," Thalia snapped. She had the feeling that there were things she wanted to ask this woman.

The officer opened his hands, surrendering.

"Thank you," Thalia said. "And now, Ms. Jones, if you please." She gestured toward the door.

As they stepped out into the corridor, flanked by a guard, she glanced to her left—and for an instant thought she saw someone approaching. But when she blinked, there was no one. Just a shadow, perhaps, through one of the crystal-like walls. She shook her head and pointed to the right.

"This way . . . Tamika. You're going to see the control center." And as she said it, she wondered why she had made that particular decision. There was a great deal she didn't know about this woman—including how she had gotten that bracelet, and how she happened to have appeared, just when she was needed. Nevertheless, the woman had saved her life from . . . whatever, whoever, that monster had been. Against all logic, Thalia felt unshaken by what had just happened. She felt unafraid. And she felt, for whatever reason, that she should trust this woman, this Tamika Jones.

Ruskin found Ali'Maksam in one of the observers' lounges, talking to two noliHuman Querayn. He paused just inside the room, watching them from a distance, feeling an odd reluctance to interrupt. What was Max doing with the Querayn? And noliHuman, no less. And why did Max look angry?

The assassin . . . noliHuman, I believe . . .

He drew a slow, unsteady breath, remembering Grissondon City, and the assassin. Had it indeed been a noliHuman? Was it conceivable that Max, after all, was involved?

((Take a look at this, before you start distrusting your best friend.))

Before he could ask Dax what that remark meant, a scene opened up in his mind, an image so vivid that he had to grope for the door frame behind him to keep from reeling.

It was Grissondon City: the concourse on which he'd glimpsed the assassin while walking with Tamika. And there was Tamika, at his side, talking about the supplies they might need; and every detail seemed as clear as if it were happening this instant, the noise and smells of the crowd, the movement of Tamika at his side, and the people passing by on his left, going the other way. At the edges of his vision, there were certain blurred areas, where his eyes had not quite caught everything. But as his head turned— there, framed dead center, was the figure that had caused his heart to falter when their eyes met for a fraction of a second; the figure that had evoked a memory from the forest, where a tall figure had killed him and then killed him again.

He stared at the remembered figure, the image burning into his inner eye. And he saw, yes—a tall, vaguely dark figure whose features were somehow indistinct, but who resembled a noliHuman. *(It was a noliHuman, then.)*

((Maybe. But look carefully.))

(I am—) And the thought died half-formed. The image in his mind seemed to become clearer; it was as though he had somehow blinked something out of his eye that he hadn't even known was there, obscuring his vision. It took a moment to realize that the figure was shorter than he'd thought—and now it didn't look like a noliHuman at all. *(How are you doing that? Dax, this guy is* Tandesko.*)*

((Righto.))

(Why didn't you tell me before?)

((I didn't know. I'd wondered; but it was only after certain other memories had unfolded that I was able to filter this image for extraneous nonvisual elements.))

Ruskin was stunned. He was aware now of several individuals in the room, including Ali'Maksam, turning and noticing him. Max started to walk in his direction, but he held up a hand, signaling the Logothian to wait. *(What do you mean, "filter this image"?)* He blinked. It was hard to concentrate on two realities at once.

((I mean, the image in your mind was not formed entirely from the visual input of your eyes.))

And then he understood. The figure he had seen was a Tandesko illusionist, capable of manipulating visual perceptions at a distance. Then, in fact, he had only been *made* to think that what he had seen was a noliHuman. . . .

((The telepathic component was something I had been unaware of. But now that I know of it, I believe I can assist you in defeating it in the future.))

Ruskin was scarcely aware of Dax's next words, because his gaze had just alighted on someone who had entered on the far side of the room a few moments after he had. He had at first taken the man for another noliHuman. Now, as he focused, his vision went through the same transformation he had experienced a moment ago in his memory; he blinked, and the noliHuman was suddenly ten centimeters shorter, and its face was no longer a noliHuman face. It was a Tandesko face. And it—or *hir*—was quietly and unobtrusively studying him. Their eyes met, and in that contact, Ruskin felt the same electric shock of recognition he had felt back at Grissondon City.

This time the killer did not disappear into the crowd. It turned its body a few degrees toward the front of the room and pretended to watch the scientific displays there.

Almost rigid with fear, Ruskin moved deliberately along the side wall, toward Ali'Maksam. The Tandesko remained still, but its eyes followed his movement. *(Any ideas?)*

((*Stay out of its reach, if you can.*))

(That's helpful. Any other ideas?)

In response, he felt the band of tension in his chest ease; and his breathing slowed and deepened. Ali'Maksam had noticed his approach and was extricating himself from his conversation.

((*If it followed you this far, it is possible that it is planning another attack. On the other hand, it may be here to observe.*))

(Observe what?)

((*The success or failure of the original* NAGS *programming, I would guess.*))

Ruskin steadied himself through a moment of dizziness. *(Dax, do you mean that the Tandeskoes did this to me?)*

((*Yes, I believe so. Tell me, Willard—how would you describe your feelings about the Tandesko Triune?*))

The hatred that rose in him at the thought of the Tandesko worlds almost caused him to lose his balance again. He reached Ali'Maksam's side at that moment, and as Max began awkwardly to introduce him to someone named Querayn Senior Karel, he shook his head, caught Max's arm, and tugged the Logothian away from the startled-looking Querayn academician and toward the doorway. All the while, he raged inwardly at Dax: *(I hate the Tandeskoes! You know that.)*

((Do I? Then look at what I've found in the memory banks.))

(Dax, this isn't the time—) His protest was too late: his mind blazed with a memory of the forest lodge back on Kantano's World—him talking freely with two gentlemen and their robot; and as he talked, he was expressing a willingness to cooperate in a plan to ensure that the Auricle Alliance's new stargate would not lead to a monopolization of the galactic frontier. And the two men, though they disavowed official ties, were from an outpost world connected with . . . the Tandesko Triune. *(Dax—damn your hide! Are you suggesting that I knowingly sided with—)*

He could not complete the thought; he suddenly felt as though he were floating in free fall. This could not be real. "Max," he said breathlessly, "we've got to get out of here. We've got to talk."

"Willard, what is the matter? Security has been paging you."

"That's the least of my problems. Can we find an empty room?" *(Dax, can you change my appearance—enough to keep a security scan from spotting me?)*

Ali'Maksam led him to an observers' study cubicle, just off the main lounge. The Logothian's scaly forehead wrinkled as Ruskin closed the door and locked it. "Willard—your face is changing! Are you in danger of—"

"No," he interrupted, "that's already happened, and I survived it. This is—I've asked Dax to disguise me. Look, I don't have time to explain, but—" He hesitated, suddenly afraid to share too much.

((Don't be an idiot. You need every friend you have.))

He grunted and continued, "I want you to listen to my thoughts, to pick up everything you possibly can. I want you to tell me if I . . . if I can trust anything I'm thinking, Max."

The Logothian nodded soberly, settling into a crouch. "I will try, if you will dim the lights."

Ruskin sighed his gratitude and hit the lights and in the darkness turned his attention inward. *(Now—out with it, Dax! If you're suggesting what I think you're suggest-*

ing . . .) And he felt a thickness in his throat, and he didn't have to hear Dax's words to know what it was saying, because the memories were spilling over his mind like water from a burst dam, and he thought he heard the terrakells chuckling (Are they going to pry loose *everything* in my subconscious?), but it didn't matter, because he knew now that it was true:

He had spoken to two men named Broder and Gorminski, whom he'd met through Tamika's Omega group; and he'd agreed to work with them. Furthermore, he'd agreed to a set of hypnotic implants that would help him to carry out their plan, that would protect him from betraying his own intentions, while he manipulated the gateway formation in a way that would open it to all worlds, not just the Alliance. The memory hitting him now was so vivid, it made him feel that he was turning inside out. "It was all a lie, then," he whispered, scarcely aware that he was speaking aloud. "I never hated the Tandeskoes at all." *(They planted that to keep me from betraying my real intent. But Dax—I insisted that my own autonomy be protected! That robot Jeaves, damn it to hell forever, assured me before it put me under for hypnosis!)*

((That's right.))

(AND I NEVER AGREED TO BEING INFECTED WITH NAGS!)
  ((No—and perhaps it was that inner resolution that made you rebel when they double-crossed you and made the NAGS implant instead.))

As though it had happened yesterday, he remembered the rage that had bubbled up inside him as he'd talked with the men after the supposed hypnosis session. He didn't know what they'd done; he only knew that he was angry, that something was trying to work its will in him, that his mind was coming apart on the inside. And finally he'd threatened them, hardly knowing what he was saying; he'd threatened to expose all of them for traitors and criminals, and he'd stormed out of the lodge.

And they'd—regretfully, no doubt—sent their agent, their Tandesko assassin, to have him destroyed. But thanks to the NAGS, he couldn't be killed.

((Their control through the NAGs was pow-
erful but not foolproof. To them, you were
an experimental animal gone berserk.))

He was scarcely breathing now; he forced himself to take
a deep breath; he was aware of Ali'Maksam's presence at
the edge of his mind as he tried to fit these pieces together.
(So they sent me to kill Thalia? That was their plan?) He
took another breath as Max stiffened in surprise, then relaxed as the memory of Tamika's rescue passed through his
mind. *(And then I was to change back to "Ruskin"—only
their Ruskin—and I was to map the gateway. Not for everyone—but for them! And they sent the killer to destroy me
if I failed . . . because they realized that their NAGs programming was unreliable.)*

((So it would seem.))

*(And by now they must know why I survived, the last
time they tried to kill me, and they will have taken steps to
prepare.)*

((That would be my guess.))

*(Then I must kill the killer—or go where it cannot reach
me.)*

((Yes . . .))

And into his mind came the one place where the killer
could not reach him—where he might still have the power
to do what was right with the gateway, if he could *decide*
what was right. And the thought frightened him half to
death.

"Willard!" whispered Ali'Maksam.

"Yes!" he groaned. "Max, tell me! Am I in my right
mind?"

"There is so much I cannot judge! But I sense much of
it; I sense that you may do something irrevocable. And I
cannot be sure that it is right. Willard, do not rush into
this!"

"The programming is set. There's no time for any other
way!"

"But who is this killer?" the Logothian cried. "I saw no
Tandesko in the lounge!"

Ruskin stared at his friend in astonishment. *(Dax?)*

((Your friend is an empath. Without prior

warning, he may be even more susceptible
than you to the illusionist's arts.))

Ali'Maksam tilted his head to an alarming angle. "An illusionist? I do not know, Willard, I cannot say." His voice was filled with fright, with despair.

Ruskin rose. "Max, I have to go. I have no choice."

The Logothian's visor snicked shut. "Then I shall go with you."

"It will probably cost both of us our lives."

There was no hint of irony in Max's answer. "Haven't we come this far together, Willard?"

Ruskin's heart nearly broke. "Yes. Damn it, then, let's go."

CHAPTER 31

✳

"Where *are* we going?" Ali'Maksam whispered as they hastened down the translucent corridor.

Ruskin didn't answer at once. He was keeping a close watch for his enemy. He thought he'd seen someone behind them as they'd left the observers' area; but it was hard, in this n-space architecture, to tell if a movement was just down the same corridor, or in some parallel branch. "Into the sun, is what I had in mind," he said finally. "*Deep* into the sun."

"That's what I *thought* I sensed. I'd thought perhaps I was wrong." The Logothian kept pace with him. "Still, it should be interesting."

Ruskin nodded and kept up his stride. They were between the docking section and the observers' area, a stretch that seemed to echo with emptiness. Most of the staff would be at their control stations now, with time-zero approaching. Although he and Max had already passed two entry points to the high-security zone, he'd shaken his head at both places. He wasn't quite sure why; he knew that he needed to talk to Thalia, but something kept him from turning that way—perhaps fear of discovery. But that was ridiculous: if security was going to spot him on their monitors, they could do it as well here as anywhere in the station.

((Maybe not so ridiculous, Willard. You need your data files, don't you, for what you're planning?))

He nearly stumbled over his own feet. Of course—but there were only two places where he had access to his data. The control room, and . . . *(I can retrieve the data from the ship, can't I?)* He didn't know if the ship was a safe place to be right now, but if he could put the files he needed into a portable unit . . .

Max had paused at a corridor intersection. "The ship is this way," Ruskin said, pointing left.

"The ship? Are we leaving the station at once, then?"

"No, but—" He cut himself off with an impatient gesture. There was no time to explain. Half a minute later, they were in the corridor outside the docking section, and Ruskin suddenly halted. "I don't know if we'll make it past the security desk. They'll be watching the ship for sure. Even if they don't recognize me, they might stop us because they don't know me." He rubbed his chin, thinking. "They have no reason to stop you, though. Can you go on board and load all of the Breakstar files into a portable unit?"

"I'm not sure that I would know precisely what to load."

"Bring everything. Download the entire system memory. That would be simpler, anyway." Ruskin pointed into a shadowy room off to one side. "I'll wait over in that cargo area. Can you be fast?"

"I'll try," the Logothian promised. "Willard, take care that you are not seen."

"Right. Now go." As Ali'Maksam strode toward the ship, Ruskin ducked into the storage area and crouched behind a stack of empty cargo pallets.

As he waited, he tried to think if there might be some way to get to Room Zeta, the deep-sun station, without first going to Thalia. It seemed unlikely. Even if there were an n-space passageway connecting Zeta with Breakstar station, what were his chances of locating it? It was hard enough to find his way where he was supposed to be. But if he went to Thalia, there would be a thousand questions—and so little time! *(Any suggestions, Dax?)*

((I think you can safely ask Thalia for help.))

(Are you crazy? Do you know what she'll say?) And an instant later, he remembered. Dax was now in Thalia, as well, and could speak to her or influence her thoughts. Ruskin didn't exactly approve, but it did put matters in a different light.

((I might point out that if I hadn't gone into Thalia, she would quite likely be dead now —at your hands.))

He felt a hot rush of guilt.

> ((*I wouldn't have violated her privacy with-
> out good reason.*))

> (*No, of course not!*)

> ((*Willard—oh, never mind. Your feelings, at
> this moment, don't matter.*))

Grunting silently, he hunkered down and sighted past the cargo pallets, watching for Max's appearance. Or the Tandesko's. He felt anxious and vulnerable; he felt like a fugitive. How would he fare in the face of another attack by the Tandesko? (*Dax—can you heal me, if necessary? Better yet, can you help me defend myself? Can you restore my weapons to me?*) He rubbed his index fingertip, where the tiny nub of the laser remained, though he presumed it was disabled.

Dax was slow in answering.

> ((*Willard, it might require my unbinding
> some of the unfriendly NAGs. Do you want to
> risk that?*))

He didn't answer at once, but instead stared grimly out toward the corridor. He saw a shadow move into view, then away; but he couldn't see its owner. A chill came over him, and he at last answered. (*If you have to—yes.*)

The wait stretched longer. If Max was in trouble, how would he know about it? He wondered if he had been foolish to put Max at risk. Perhaps he should go check, and the security desk be damned.

He rose, preparing to step out of cover—and the Logothian's tall, white-suited profile appeared in the entrance to the cargo area. Ruskin hurried to join him. "Did you get it all?" Ali'Maksam nodded and handed him a small gray-cased data-unit. "Good work. Let's go find Thalia."

As they hurried through the corridors, again he had the feeling that someone was moving in silence, just out of sight, behind him. Probably his imagination. He didn't pause to see if his imagination knew something he didn't.

As they neared the control room, he remembered that he was still in disguise, and he asked Dax to restore his facial appearance. He felt the hot crinkling of skin, bones, and muscle altering. Just short of the control room, a squad of two security men and a mech stepped through a wall to cut them off. "Dr. Ruskin, come this way," he was ordered. He didn't argue; but he was relieved when they took him directly to the control center, where he was headed anyway, and to Thalia. She was at the command console, with Tamika. He tried to ignore all the eyes that shifted to stare as he approached.

"Willard!" That was Thalia's hoarse cry; but Tamika got to him first, hugging him ferociously, then stepping back.

Ruskin gazed at them both with fierce affection: Tamika, trim and compact, in a gray tunic and pants, her golden cat eyes flashing with joy; and Thalia, tall and bony and awkward, eyes impossibly dark. Thalia had changed out of her torn clothing into a blazing red jumpsuit. Ruskin felt a rush of gratitude for their safety—and fear for the danger that he brought with him.

As the guards began to withdraw, he snapped a warning: "Stay close! There's a Tandesko spy in the area. An illusionist. He may be passing as a noliHuman, or as something else. Expect him to be armed and dangerous."

A ripple of alarm spread out among the consoles. "Tandesko?" Thalia asked. "In the secure area? Are you sure?"

Ruskin nodded and peered around, wondering if the assassin might not be in this room now. His gaze was drawn to the huge display screen. Betelgeuse blazed: scarlet-orange, enormous, seemingly eternal. That was all about to change. He glanced at the console display. The sun's core was mostly iron now. The squeeze was tightening. Time to Stage Four initiation: fifty-seven minutes. "Thalia," he said, his eyes still scanning, "I've got to get to Room Zeta right away."

"Willard, we've been through all that. . . ." He glanced back at her as her voice faltered. Her eyes closed and reopened. "*Why?*" she whispered.

"Because I am a source of danger here. And because the Tandesko knows what we're doing and intends to sabotage the gateway formation and the mapping." He hesitated for an instant, acknowledging her astonishment. "If you transfer control to Zeta and isolate me there, I can keep the Tandesko from interfering."

"But Willard, that's—" Thalia broke off and pressed her forehead with her fingertips, shuddering, as though in pain.

"How can we know?" she whispered. "We've seen no Tandesko here. We can't just—"

"*Who do you think tried to kill you?*" he erupted, shouting, oblivious to the shocked expressions around him. He saw Tamika's alarm and knew what she was thinking—that it was no Tandesko but Willard Ruskin who had tried to kill Thalia—but there was no time to explain. "Damn it, Thalia! Do you know who tried to kill you? *Do you?*"

"No—I didn't see—"

"Well, I do! The Tandeskoes!" He seized her shoulders, shook her. "Thalia, they used *me* and now they're trying to get rid of *you* because your essential work is done! There's no time to argue! Tell me how to get to Zeta! I can safeguard the project, even if they attack here!"

Thalia swallowed. Her huge, dark, maroon eyes were filled with pain, with uncertainty. "Level four, *A*-twenty-four section," she murmured at last. "The transport's there." She turned to the security leader. "Escort him—on my authority."

"Good," Ruskin said. "I'll need Max with me."

"And me!" Tamika cried.

Ruskin shook his head, feeling a sharp jab of pain. "You can't help with this, Twig. I'm sorry."

"I can—!"

"No!" Thalia snapped. At Tamika's defiant glance, she shrugged. Her eyes were hard now. "That's on my authority, too. They will probably not come back," she added, as though speaking to no one in particular. Her voice was devoid of emotion.

Tamika's eyes narrowed. She edged a fraction of an inch toward Ruskin; her hand reached out, then stopped. Her head barely moved as she nodded her acceptance.

Ruskin's heart ached fiercely, but he could think of nothing to say. He turned—

—and saw someone climbing the steps toward the control center exit. A tall technician, with sloping shoulders.

His vision shimmered and the man's true features became visible as Dax said simply,

((It's him.))

"Stop that man!" Ruskin shouted, pointing.

Bewildered, the guards wouldn't have had a chance if

two men and a security robot hadn't come in through the door at that moment. The new arrivals blocked the technician's path as he reached the top of the steps.

The man—or thing—moved with astonishing speed. It leaped over the railing and away from the guards before even the robot could react. One man fell, clutching his throat. The thing spun as it landed and changed directions, darting toward the back of the room. It seemed almost to become invisible as it moved. Two of the guards fired their weapons—missing the Tandesko, but almost hitting several scientists, who scattered, diving to the floor.

Ruskin froze in a moment of indecision. Should he stay and fight, or try to lead the Tandesko away? Suddenly he was aware of Tamika and Thalia close to him. "Get down!" he snapped, pushing them toward the floor. And as he looked up again, he saw the Tandesko leaping over a row of consoles, flying directly toward him. He aimed his index finger. *(NOW, DAX!)*

((Not enough time . . .))

A sharp pain in his gut doubled him over. He hit the floor and rolled.

((Sorry! I had to get you down!))

He saw the killer leaping over him, and as it changed directions and doubled back, he made his move. From a crouch, he sprang straight up—and caught the Tandesko from beneath, flipping it sideways. He heard firing again, and shouts of pain and fear, and as he turned, two more people fell. He smelled something like almonds, and knew real terror then. A console near him was dissolving in a cloud of smoke.

*((I can handle the cyanide, but he's using
NAGs to disassemble molecules. If we get hit
with that, I don't know . . .))*

Ruskin turned and saw the Tandesko back up near the door. It was pointing at him—or at Thalia, on the floor—with a hand extended stiffly. Ruskin felt a burning pain in his right forefinger—

((Shoot, Willard!))

—and he pointed, and a lance of laser-light flared where it hit the Tandesko, and its hand seemed to explode. The killer froze for an instant, its eyes burning into Ruskin's with some unreadable fury; but before Ruskin could aim again, the creature had spun again and darted—and was out the door and gone.

Ruskin gaped at the aftermath. At least two consoles were smoking, disintegrating even as he watched. Numerous people were on the floor, some hiding, some crawling to help the wounded, some dead. Many dead. *Cyanide*, he remembered dizzily. Probably microbursts of it, manufactured by NAGS on or in the assassin's body. He prayed that the ventilators could clear it quickly. Tamika and Thalia were both rising shakily, and he trembled with gratitude at Dax's presence in their bodies. "Max!" he called, in sudden dread.

For a moment he heard only the shouts of others—and voices of confusion in his own head, but not his friend. His eyes went to the display screen and the glowering sun. Stage Four initiation: thirty-nine minutes.

"I am here, Willard." From beneath a console emerged the white-suited, visored Logothian. "I hid myself; I am sorry," he whispered.

"Bless your heart, Max! Will you still come with me?"

"I wouldn't miss it," Ali'Maksam answered.

Ruskin turned to the two women. He was not as calm as he had thought; his blood was running hot and feverish. What had Dax turned loose to give him the power to fight? "Thalia?"

She was enraged, snapping out orders to her security crew; she turned her head with a glare.

"Get him. Stop him," he whispered. She nodded.

"Twig?" Tamika turned from gazing around in bewilderment. The terror was plain on her face. He could think of no words except her name. "Tamika—"

She swallowed, nodded.

Blinking, he picked up the gray-cased data-unit, turned to Max—and ran for the door, grabbing a security guard to lead the way.

Level four, A-24 section. Lots of flashing red lights in this area. An alarm was sounding monotonously, warning people to clear the area. *"This section may be unstable during breakaway. . . ."* a recorded voice droned.

"Reassuring," Ruskin murmured. The guard shot him a reproachful glance; he did not look happy to be here, especially with an assassin possibly coming this way. He was probably wondering if he would be expected to go to Room Zeta with them. Ruskin impatiently waved him on.

The Zeta transport station was guarded by a robot security system. Their guard had to use an override code to get Ali'Maksam past the security barricade; Max's "special observer" bracelet would not have gotten him through. After a brief drop-lift ride down, they came to one last obstacle, a dull gray, prison-type security screen. The guard passed his own bracelet across a reader, and the screen went down.

"Here you are," he said, waving them into what looked like a small, empty tube-train station with walls of crystal. A metallic portal in one wall irised open, and they peered through into the interior of a small transport car. "The controls are marked," the guard said. "Just press GO. If you change your mind, you can press STOP anytime up until you actually start moving. Then there's no turning back until you get there. Good luck." He looked at them hopefully.

"Thank you," Ruskin said. "As soon as we're off, you can head back." The guard looked relieved. "Max, let's go." Ruskin followed the Logothian into the car, then peered out again. "Be on the lookout for anyone you don't know," he called to the guard.

He hit the GO switch.

Three things happened, almost simultaneously. The guard gasped and dropped to the floor. A blurry shape leaped through the portal into the car. The door irised closed.

"Look out, Max!" Ruskin screamed, diving across the car.

The transporter started moving.

CHAPTER 32

✳

By the time his eyes came back into focus, the Tandesko was practically on top of him, hands outstretched. Ruskin had fallen against a seat and could not roll away, but his fingertip was pointed at the killer, and it was throbbing.

For an instant, their eyes met. Ruskin felt something queer happening inside himself; a long, terrible moment passed as he reflected upon his chances of survival, as he waited for Dax to fire the laser.

A metallic voice startled him: "GANZ—DO NOT! WILLARD—WAIT!"

He didn't move; couldn't move. Space-time itself might have frozen; nothing could happen; nothing could move, except the fast-running stream of his memory sluicing by him with images of the last few moments. Dax was causing some incredible acceleration of his thoughts.

((You recognize that voice?))

And then he knew who—or what—had called out. The gray-cased box. The copy of his shipboard thinktank.

"TRUCE!" said the gray box. "TALK AND REASON."

Ruskin's immediate reaction was incredulity. But the assassin, after a moment, took a step backward. Ruskin noticed that its right hand was damaged from their previous encounter—it did not possess instant healing, then—but the hand also looked functional enough to kill. "I can wait," stated the assassin. It stared at Ruskin for a few seconds before saying, "How did you get there?" Ruskin was puzzled, until he realized that the "you" being addressed was the gray box. The Tandesko, without waiting for an answer from the box, asked Ruskin in a voice that was smooth but with a trace of a lisp, "And you—do you withhold your fire, for the moment?"

Ruskin didn't answer. It was the first time he had gotten such a close look at the assassin: the ridged cheekbones, the deep-set, narrowly slitted eyes, the protruding bone structure where eyebrows would have been on a Human. This Tandesko was of a very special breed—more than an illusionist, a *hrisi* assassin, the best of the killers. It—or *hir*, since it was gendered, but its gender had no correlate in Human terms—wore a loose-fitting jumpsuit, perhaps one-piece, perhaps two, which seemed to hint at all colors while actually displaying none. One of its two eyes remained fixed on Ruskin while the other shifted, scanning the interior of the car.

Ruskin felt a faint vibration, reminding him that they were moving at a speed he could only guess at down a tube of n-space toward Room Zeta.

((He's asking for a truce.))

Dax's words stirred him from his reverie. He rose slowly from his awkward position, and lowered his laser-weaponed right hand. *(Just you keep that laser charged,)* he warned Dax. Without taking his eyes off the Tandesko, he called out, "Ali'Maksam!"

"I'm here," Max said, from behind him. "I'm unhurt."

Nodding, Ruskin spoke to the Tandesko. "Since it is in my interests to live, I will hold my fire—for the moment. Agreed?"

"Agreed," said the Tandesko.

Ruskin drew a breath. "What shall we do, then? Gain a mutual understanding before you try to kill me again?"

The Tandesko turned its head slightly. It might have been grinning; it was hard to tell. "That depends upon you—and upon our friend." It nodded toward the compact data-module lying on the floor.

Ruskin pursed his lips. Making no sudden moves, he crouched and picked up the box and placed it on a nearby seat. Out of the corner of his eye, he glimpsed Max still half hiding behind another seat. And at the end of the car: a forward view, arrowing down a long, glowing tube of light, an ethereal subway that looked as though it could go on forever. He was aware that they were deep in the body of the sun now, and diving deeper. Only the n-space field protected them from instant death.

((Willard, don't be distracted!))

His eyes flashed back to the Tandesko, his heart thumping. But the assassin had not moved, not even its eyes. Ruskin grunted and spoke to the thinktank unit. "I didn't know you were turned on."

"There was no need to speak of it before," the voice said.

(Why is that voice familiar?) Ruskin took a breath, trying to make his thoughts clear. "You seem to know this Tandesko," he said. "What did you call—" and he glanced at the assassin—"hir?"

"Hir name is Ganz," the box replied. "Yes, we are acquainted."

"I see. Then—" and Ruskin hesitated again, not wanting to voice his fears; he had *trusted* his shipboard system. "Then there is more to *you* than I might have guessed."

"A fair statement. You knew me once, by a proper name."

Familiar voice. Ruskin glanced at the box, glanced at Ali'Maksam. *(Dax, when—?)*

And a memory suddenly unfolded:

As they boarded *Enigma*, the Yonupian advised them of a software upload, ostensibly from Ruskin's employer . . . yet neither he nor Ali'Maksam could find a trace of it in the ship's cogitative system as they left Kantano's World light-years behind. . . .

He blinked, as that memory faded and another one opened, this one farther back:

Walking through the lodge, he spoke with a black-and-chrome robot, which they had agreed would perform the hypnotic implanting. . . .

"*Jeaves!*" he whispered.

"At your service, sir," the box answered.

He was so stunned that he almost forgot Ganz as he stared at the box; but he caught a slight movement from Ganz and his eyes flicked back defensively.

The Tandesko *hrisi* had shifted its own stare to the gray box. "So, Jeaves-copy," it said. "You are at Mr. Ruskin's service. Whom, then, do you truly serve?" There was a warning edge to its voice, and Ruskin tensed, thinking of their fragile truce. The truce was at Jeaves's suggestion. If Jeaves discredited itself with Ganz . . .

The robot's voice was unperturbed. "Don't we all work for the same cause?"

Ganz's expression seemed to darken, the eyes drawing inward slightly.

Ruskin glanced back at Ali'Maksam. The Logothian's eyes were faint, motionless diamonds behind his visor; there was no telling what Max thought. Ruskin backed a step or two away from the Tandesko and stole another glimpse forward, to their streaming motion through the n-space tube. He thought he saw something bright in the distance: the end-point, Zeta station, deep in the heart of the star. He was reminded that time was passing. What was Ganz planning? And how long before Stage Four initiation and the beginning of the end?

((I estimate seventeen minutes to Stage Four. . . .))

The hyperstring was fast approaching its closest point to the star, the loop narrowing to a sharp cusp . . . and in seventeen minutes the final sprint to the core collapse would begin, the gensat power increasing at the very end. He needed time to prepare the mapping, to make his fine-tuning changes in the strengths of the fields, in the rates of temperature modulation, in the shape of the collapse and the moment of black hole formation: tiny changes that could affect the way the string was caught, the vibrations that would ring down its length when it was snagged and anchored in the singularity. . . .

He realized that Ganz was again watching him. Trying to decide what to do with him, now that matters were no longer so clear? *What would I do with myself?* Unable to think of an answer, he deliberately turned his back on the Tandesko and watched as the transport car arrowed toward a jewel-like bull's-eye at the end of the tube.

The destination grew with dramatic speed. The car slowed as it approached the station, and with barely a vibration, slipped into its dock. A small sign lighted: *Arrival,*

Room Zeta. Then the viewing section went blank gray, and a portal irised open at the front of the car. An empty room beckoned.

Ruskin glanced uneasily at the Tandesko, who had not moved. He shrugged, picked up the case containing Jeaves, and said to Max, "After you." They stepped out into Room Zeta, Ganz close behind. A short passageway; beyond it was a small, unoccupied control room—a miniature version of central control, with two work stations. The room was brightly lighted but windowless. They might have been deep underground; there was little to suggest that all around them, just angstroms beyond the boundary of the n-space field, were the fierce fires and crushing pressures of a living sun.

Most of the encircling wall was a smooth pearly surface. "Viewscreen?" Max suggested.

Ruskin glanced at the controls with a frown. He moved his hand over the center console. The wall blazed to life with orange light. He fiddled a bit more, toned down the intensity, and broke the display into a variety of perspectives and wavelengths. Everything was coming in from satellite remotes, over n-thread data channels. He spent a few minutes looking over the readings.

"Mind what you do." Ganz enunciated hir words with great care. The assassin had taken up a position near the wall, just behind Ruskin, where it could observe in relative safety.

Ruskin answered with mock cheer: "Feel free, everyone, to say what's on your mind." A light was flashing on the com-circuit; he activated the channel. "Ruskin here. We're at Zeta."

The voice that answered seemed a lifetime away. It was Thalia's. "Willard, is that you?"

He cleared his throat. "That's affirmative."

"You arrived safely? Did you see any sign of the Tandesko?"

Ganz's eyes locked with his and his voice caught in his throat. "No . . . sign. Does this station have control now?" The words, *Keep control there and cut us loose,* formed in his throat and died there. Even now, he wasn't willing to give up the chance for control.

"Fine-control and mapping are yours, and locked in," Thalia answered. "Stage Four activation will start in thirteen minutes. After that, your telemetry will be more reliable than ours. We're commencing shift of this station out of four-space now."

"Good. Cut us loose. Protect the station."

"That'll be our call, not yours. Willard—hold it a moment—"

His hand moved over the console, bringing up readings as he waited.

When her voice returned, it sounded more distant. "Willard, the guard that led you to the transport was found, murdered, in the transport station. No sign of the Tandesko. We're—concerned."

"Understood," Ruskin answered, glaring at Ganz. "Recommend you disable the transport mechanism."

"That's already been done."

"Then I've got to get busy here. I'll check in when I can." He cut the circuit without waiting for a reply. "And now," he announced to the others, "I really must get busy. Jeaves—" He hesitated, wishing he didn't have to trust the robot program; but he had little choice. "I'll be needing my data files. We're now at the main console. Can you upload?"

"If you'll plug me in, Dr. Ruskin, I'll transfer all the data for you," Jeaves answered.

No screwing around with it, either, he started to say, but caught himself. Ganz was still watching, evaluating. "Thank you, Jeaves," he murmured.

"Of course, sir."

He swallowed his anger at the false deference. Jeaves had double-crossed him once already. He handed the gray case to Max, who began looking for the appropriate input connector. While the Logothian dealt with that, Ruskin glanced briefly at the Tandesko and then tried to put the assassin's presence out of his thoughts while he studied the telemetry readings. *(Dax, watch that guy for me. If it makes a move, I want to know before my ears twitch.)*

((I'll do my best.))

(If I only knew what it expects me to do.)

((I imagine hir doesn't want you to know; it's

*watching for your actions to be triggered by
the* NAGS. *Any obviously conscious action
could be interpreted as a failure in the* NAGS
programming.))

*(Then I'm at its mercy, unless you can decipher and sim-
ulate the programming. Or—I could try to kill it.)*

((That might be smart.))

It took him a moment to catch the sarcasm. Even with
Dax on his side, his chances against a trained assassin were
not good. Better that Ganz could be satisfied, or fooled.

Studying the holodisplay, he tried to make sense of what
was happening out there in the star. The K-space gensats
should be readjusting their power as collapse approached.
The hyperstring tracking was coming in, and he saw a small
error that needed to be compensated for. *(Dax, I need all
of the faculties you can give me.)*

((Coming . . .))

There was a blurring and freezing again of his time sense,
a feeling of motionlessness in motion. He was aware of
chains twisting and molecules rotating . . . and somewhere
in a forest, two small creatures were climbing a pair of trees,
reaching toward a dark fortress high above in the amber
mist; and he knew that he was already in that fortress, but
he was a prisoner there, lost in a maze of his own making,
and he needed help in finding his way out. He had thought
that all he needed was the ability to process information,
but he perceived now that there was something even more
vital.

But it was all shifting and blurring. . . .

CHAPTER 33

✳

Data streamed in a whirlwind around his head, grains of
sand carried on a cyclone. Ruskin was a juggler dancing in
the storm, heedless of its fury, keeping a thousand glass
balls airborne over his head. He was barely aware of the
others in the control station with him. Their faces seemed
to peer at him out of the tumbling glass balls: an assassin,
a robot, a Logothian. And all around him, sealed in the
glass balls, the readings and calculations and projections
and estimates. And he, the juggler, was to spot and catch
the correct balls in order, to line them up and toss them;
to find the precise projections, the mapping of the stars and
sky, the changes to call for out of the wind.

The end had begun.

The main station, where all of the others waited, had
drawn away, submerged in the layers of n-dimensional
space, cushioned against the approaching cataclysm. A remote corner of his mind approved, noting that his view of
the whole affair was much clearer than theirs now; he was
the one who could call to the wind for changes—not great
changes, perhaps, but it didn't take great changes to affect
the motion of glass balls on the wind.

But even as he was juggling, the storm was gathering in
fury. And somewhere, high in the storm, a voice of
unearthly power was crying out in astonishment and
dismay:

** My children **
** what   ? **
** how   ? **
** why   ? **

* * *

Never had Bright felt anything like this
            the pain
                  the dizziness
                        the bewilderment

and in the belly of her flame, something
                  terribly terribly wrong
                        hot hard

      what ?
            how ?
                  why ?

And something was answering
            something tiny but powerful
                  something as frightened as she
And so she called out

            Sing to me please
                  Can you sing ?

Ali'Maksam was so focused on Willard, with half an eye
on the Tandesko assassin, that for a time he didn't even
notice the new presence in the field of empathic tension
that enveloped them. And when at last he did, he was
chastened by his slowness to recognize its source. After all,
hadn't he and the Querayn been half expecting it all along?

"*Create a strong enough K-space field in the heart of a
star, and among the consciousnesses that well up out of the
void, you may find not just the thoughts and hopes and
fears of the brave observers, but the mind and soul of the
star itself. . . .*"

With those words, a century before, the Querayn mystic
philosopher Kay'il Kônô had predicted stellar consciousness. And Ali'Maksam, largely in an act of faith, had be-

lieved the assertion more likely true than false. And now here it was:

Pain!
Confusion!

The feelings rang with clarion power. Consciousness indeed: but underlying the power, Ali'Maksam sensed, the sun did not know what was happening to it. Feelings of incomprehension rang out and rang again. Something had invaded the sun, something invisible; and now its life was being squeezed away. Could the sun dream of what was to come? Ali'Maksam hoped not, prayed not.

The Logothian trembled, tried not to tremble. Grief sang in his heart. What a wonderful and tragic opportunity: to commune with a star—but only in its death! If only he could deepen the link·in the minutes remaining? Before they *both* died.

But he had another vow to fulfill and that was to assist Willard if he could. And Willard right now was struggling to understand the cataclysm that had already been set in motion; and in the next moments, under the terrible eye of the assassin, he must make his final judgments.

Must learn who his true masters were.

Must learn what the Querayn and Jeaves had done to him. And Max.

And Ali'Maksam whispered, *Willard, however I have wronged you, I pray that you will now find yourself, even in the heart of the maelstrom!*

Ganz had never felt so helpless. Hir weapons were armed, hir nano-agents ready. Hir could take the control station if hir wanted; hir could kill Ruskin and the serpent-man; hir could choose to obey or ignore the advice of the Jeaves-copy, or even destroy the robot intelligence altogether. Hir could do all or none of those things. Hir could stand like an Auricle pawn or a *horka*, a failed student, and do nothing at all.

Ganz, Tandesko *hrisi* assassin, did not know what to do.

Hir target, Ruskin, was completely absorbed at the control console; though almost motionless, he clearly was tapped deeply into the processes that were even now destroying this sun. But though Ganz could understand some of the readings visible on the console, hir could not begin to follow what Ruskin was doing. Jeaves-copy no longer seemed reliable; and Ganz had no other way of judging whether or not the human was doing what Gorminski had programmed it to do.

Most signs indicated that this human Ruskin had freed itself of the programming. And yet, even if that were true, what could Ganz gain by killing it now? Could Ganz—here, now—make the crucial decisions that would turn Breakstar into a Tandesko triumph? The supernova was inevitable—and any action now might only render the gateway nonexistent or useless, not just to the Alliance but to the Triune, as well.

That was not supposed to be Ganz's mission.

But what *was* hir mission now, if the NAGs had in fact failed?

The assassin's attention was drawn to the viewscreen, drawn by the lurid light of the swollen red sun, its fiery countenance soon to blaze huge and brilliant and white, its neutrino light to outshine, if only for a moment, a sizable fraction of the visible universe. What was the likelihood that any of them in this small room would survive that cataclysm, even isolated across an n-space barrier?

Hir eyes flicked back to Ruskin and hir attention to the question: If hir was to die in the next minutes, did hir want to die with this job unfinished? Ganz had once tried to kill Ruskin and failed. Did hir wish to go quietly into death now with that failure intact?

But a *hrisi* did not kill for personal satisfaction.

Ganz shuddered at a sudden resonance of pain—shuddered carefully, even in the pain, not allowing hir reaction to show. Hir had just felt something strange, something powerfully compelling, something never felt or imagined before. A terrible moaning sound was reverberating through the inside of hir head—a sound like the groan of a ship dying at sea, or of the sea itself.

Or of something else dying, something so great and terrible that Ganz could not imagine anything like it ever being alive at all.

Killing me
    You are killing
        Dream of death come at last
Without dream

The sun was dying.

The K-space field enveloping its core was tightening, the connection to the hyperstring strengthening, the leakage of degenerate matter through that connection turning to a cosmic fire-hose. But the loss of that matter was inconsequential; the core was nearly pure iron now, and it was compressing under the stranglehold of gravity and the vise of the K-space field. The fusion process had almost stopped, and yet the temperature was climbing through the billions of degrees. Soon the iron nuclei would disintegrate and the core would collapse toward finality, toward infinity.

Ruskin could not help thinking of the times that he and Tamika (or Thalia) had watched some world's sun sinking crimson and beautiful into a reflective sea and spoken of a "dying sun." Never had he dreamed of the bewilderment and fear that filled his world now. In some inner landscape he was standing on a hilltop, flanked by two terrakells; and they were watching a sun go down, only this time it was not setting, it was truly dying. And he was the one who had killed it. And something in him wanted desperately to stop it; but that time was past.

He had wondered, but had never actually *believed* that a sun could be living.

** Who are you **
   ** why **
   ** why **
      ** are you killing me   ? **

What was that voice? His own mind's interpretation of haunting wonder? Of the despair that rang through and through his mind?

But he had choices to make, and fast; the numbers and maps and projections of the galaxy filled his head along with the cries, and he saw the alternatives, the possibilities, if only he knew which to choose. By refashioning the K-space compression and the neutrino focusing, he could influence the speed and precise shape of the collapse, the distortion of space that would open the gateway. If he shaped the collapse this way it would shift the ripples of the gateway deeper toward certain regions of stars; if he shaped it that way, the mapping might be clearer, the string vibrations changed, the gateway path subtly altered.

And which would be the most desirable?

And the choices were only the beginning; for without precise mapping of the formation, the choices meant nothing. Without the mapping, the gateway might never be used. That was where all the power lay, in the mapping and in the control.

And behind it all was the question: What would silent, threatening Ganz do when his choices became clear?

Crystallized in his mind was the pattern he had given to Snyder and Thalia, which he could, if he chose now, fine-tune. But shimmering away from him, eluding his every grasp, was his memory of why he had chosen that pattern: Was it the choice of a good Auricle loyalist giving his side the advantage, or that of a dissident, a rebel who would not have his creation used for domination? Or was it the choice of a madman who no longer knew what he wanted or why, a madman whose choices were made in an ecstasy of falsehoods?

Max, help me!

(Dax, help me!)

At the edge of his mind was the presence of his friend, Ali'Maksam, recognizing his anguish, calling out to him:

—*Willard, you must recognize that which is you and abandon all else*—

And deep within his mind was the struggling voice of Dax:

*((Find what is beneath. Too many factors.
Too many enemies.))*

What was Dax talking about? *Too many enemies?
((Willard, I understand now—there are* two
*enemies, not one! My control is slipping; you
must find your own mind and spirit; none of
us can control that. . . .))*

It was all too dizzying. *Max, I need you now. You've got
to tell me who I am. Only you know me well enough to
help.*

He saw the numbers flickering by as the star's core grew
hotter and denser. Many decision points had already passed
and were beyond help now, but even after the extinction
of the star, in the moment of the collapse and the explosion,
he could alter the field that would bind the hyperstring and
the black hole for all eternity, or change the configuration
of the entryway.

He could make decisions that would give God Himself
pause. But did Willard Ruskin want that kind of power?

Or did he just want to drop it all, to speak to this strange
being the sun, to savor *its* last moments, to learn of its life
that was now ending? It might be possible to extend the
end for the star, to stretch out these moments, though
perhaps at the cost of the gateway.

Yes . . . His fingers touched the console, initiating the
changes.

No! His fingers froze.

Ali'Maksam was moving toward him, in the blood-light
of the stellar images, his friend's movements slowed and
distorted by whatever strange processes were affecting his
vision. His thoughts seemed to clear. *Max, are you coming
to help me?* And then he realized: Max needed darkness to
shed his visor and hood, darkness to probe the mind and
soul of his friend, before it was too late.

Ruskin's hand went out to the console, darkening the
room lights, so that only the bloody glow of the sun in the
viewscreen lighted the room. Then he darkened the viewscreen, so that only the pale ghostly forms of the data-holos
were visible, then shaded even those down so that they
were scarcely visible in the ink of darkness. He was aware,
before the darkness swallowed them altogether, of Ganz

the assassin stirring, moving toward them; and he could fairly *feel* the light of the star around them, though he could not see it.

But Max was at his side, opening his visor and hood, and it took only moments for the Logothian's mind to reach across to his and to enfold his thoughts, probing downward through the layers of thought that were not his own:

> —*Willard, rotate*—
>   —*let yourself rotate within and spin free*—
>   —*spin free*—
>   —*spin free*—

Max, I do not want to be controlled!

And whatever Max was doing, it was as though layers of translucency were being stripped away from him; and with each layer, the light that was his own spirit shone a little brighter in the center—

—dancing with the terrakells—

—and Dax, puzzled, saying:

> ((*There are* Querayn NAGs *here? I am astonished!*))

And the corner of his mind that was watching from above heard Dax's words and froze in astonishment and consternation—and finally turned to Ali'Maksam and cried, "*The Querayn! Have they been controlling me as well?*" And his cry was so sudden, and so distressed that he was hardly even aware that he was shouting aloud. But in the empathic enfolding, he knew Ali'Maksam's answer instantly, because there was no way to conceal such a thing, despite the distraction of Dax's exclamation:

> ((*That is why it was so difficult!*))

And over Dax's words, the Logothian whispered aloud, "Yes, the Querayn. And Jeaves. And I myself. We thought to protect you from the enemy. Willard, I was wrong!"

And in that instant, he saw Max talking to the Querayn Senior back in the observers' lounge and knew that those two had met before; and he saw the Querayn's intense and curious glance at him.

"*You,* Max!" His voice almost failed. "You . . . ?"

The Logothian's voice strained to the breaking point. "I

helped them. They wanted only to stop the Tandesko med-
dling. To know the star. To save you."

"To save *me*?"

"I meant only to protect. I'm sorry, Willard—sorry that
they didn't give you—"

There was a sudden movement in the darkness, and the
lights blazed bright. . . .

He couldn't see. His chest was on fire. With each breath,
the hole in his chest burned hotter. He couldn't move,
couldn't think. The fire sang and burned bright. He barely
heard Dax's words reverberating:

((*DONT TRY TO MOVE!*))

His eyes labored toward focus—and he became aware
that something long and thin and steel had pierced his chest,
gone all the way through his chest cavity, pinning him to
the seat back. The pain was inconceivable; the lance must
have gone straight through a lung. When at last the sea of
red came into focus, it was to the blurred vision of the *hrisi*
assassin gazing at him from the distance of half a meter.
Ruskin could not breathe, or even blink.

"Querayn tool." The assassin spoke deliberately, with
contempt.

Ruskin could not answer.

The Tandesko's head turned. "Your friend betrayed you,
it seems." Hir eyes shifted—toward Ali'Maksam.

Something of the pain dropped out of Ruskin's body, a
strand of nerves gone dead. He managed to move his eyes
slightly, following Ganz's look. He could just make out
Ali'Maksam hissing in distress in the corner, face buried in
his hands.

"Your betrayer cannot stand the light," Ganz observed
coldly. "How sad."

Through the haze, Ruskin was aware only of his rage at
Ganz. But Ganz's words brought back the memory of Max's,
and he knew this now—that Ganz spoke the truth. Max had
betrayed him. Max and the Querayn had implanted NAGs.
Not just the Tandeskoes, but the Querayn as well. *Why?
Ali'Maksam, why have you done this to me?*

The fire in his chest did not sear him so deeply as the flame of that knowledge.

Dax's words drifted through, a cooling breeze:

> *((Willard, I am dissolving the needle in your chest.))*

The assassin's eyes focused on him. "Human, would you prefer a chance to live?"

Ruskin forced his eyes to the data displays. The sun was dying like a snuffed candle. In less than a minute, the final collapse would occur, and the supernova. In the back of his skull, a voice was crying out, the voice of the sun, rattling with bewilderment and fear:

** Death O Death O Death **
** Why do you not speak **
** Why do you not sing **

Does it know what's about to happen?

He met Ganz's eyes and rasped a breath past his vocal cords. "Do you think any of us will live through this?"

The assassin's gaze narrowed, hir eyes drew deeper into hir brow. "That will yet be seen. But you could die sooner, or perhaps later. Would you tell me now: How do you intend to guide the gateway formation?"

Ruskin stared at him in silence. "Perhaps I would tell you," he grunted at last. The pain in his chest had gone away, and he realized now that he had freedom of movement. He felt a fevered flush and heard Dax's whisper:

> *((The needle is gone. I am reproducing agents as quickly as possible, in case they're needed.))*

Which sounded to him like a go-ahead.

Because one thing he *knew* was that he had no intention of bowing to this particular deliverer of death. Certain ways in which Dax's agents might help him came into focus.

"And perhaps," he whispered, completing his answer to Ganz, "you will have to guess." He spoke the last words so softly that the assassin had to strain toward him to hear— but even before the words were out, Ruskin had put his body into motion. He dived to the side, shouting, "Jeaves— lights out!" And the room was plunged instantly into darkness, and he was already changing directions as he hit the floor and rolled.

And something in him was changing, responding to the urgency, because he felt a new hardness in his muscles, and his eyesight adapted to the near-total darkness with incredible speed—so much so that he both saw and felt Ganz strike out at him, narrowly missing. Almost without thinking, Ruskin spun and pointed and fired, and the laser beam that shot from his finger caught the Tandesko in the shoulder. But he'd betrayed his location, and Ganz fired a tiny sputtergun, which raked Ruskin's right arm. The pain sent him off balance but didn't stop him. He spun away behind the console and took aim again and fired.

The flashing of the weapons was like a stroboscopic lightning, frozen figures shifting with each flash. Ruskin's time sense skewed out of normal: he felt as though he were walking, drifting through an invisible matrix of time and space where three variations, or perhaps four, or perhaps infinite variations of himself were shifting in and out of focus, taking control of his actions; and only one was the real Ruskin.

He thought he knew now which was the real Ruskin, but they changed almost too fast to follow.

The thought was a deadly distraction, because Ganz was already moving, fast, not toward Ruskin but *past* him; and as hir passed, a puff of vapor hit Ruskin's skin. And his skin began to dissolve, and his left arm.

((*GET OUT OF THAT CLOUD!*))

—Dax screamed in his mind, and he was moving anyway; but it felt as though his arm was literally coming off, turning to a sheet of pain.

But Dax's army of reconstructors was already flying into action, and even as the assassin's NAGS were tearing Ruskin's body apart atom by atom, Dax's NAGS were furiously putting it back together again. His arm was made of fire, but it wasn't crippled yet, and his right finger still had a laser; and as he slid across the front of the room he saw Ganz again and pointed and fired and the assassin's shoulder burst into flame.

And in the light he glimpsed not one but three or perhaps four Logothians, and he couldn't tell which was the real and which the virtuals; but at the edge of his consciousness, he felt Ali'Maksam trying to speak to him. (*What do you want?*) he screamed, refusing to listen to the one who had betrayed him; but the voice at the edge of his mind was insistent:

—*Do not fault me, Willard! You have only seconds left. You must turn to the sun for help! To the sun*—

The thoughts were so peculiar that for an instant he didn't comprehend them at all. Then he understood what Max was saying: Could the *star* control its own death? Was there power behind that moan that had so become a part of the reality here that it was almost lost in the babble?

In the breath of his indecision, Ganz had turned and leaped—not at Ruskin but at the console. The viewscreen blazed back to crimson-orange life, and in the glow of the collapsing star, Ruskin could see the mapping console itself dissolving into smoke. Ganz's cry of maddened triumph filled the room.

In the heart of the star, protons and electrons were being crushed into neutrons, and then out of existence, as in the space of a single moment, the core collapsed upon itself.

The image on the viewscreen showed a brilliant shock wave blasting outward through the sun, and the station itself shook and began to distort.

PART FOUR

✳

TRANSFIGURATION

"I change, but I cannot die. . . ."
    —Percy Bysshe Shelley

CHAPTER 34

✳

Tamika was torn between awe and fear, standing beside Thalia at the command console as they watched the final stages of the star's destruction. The station itself was now fully withdrawn into n-space, with only n-thread links still open to the monitoring satellites. The station was no longer within the sun's space-time at all. The image of that doomed orange ball on the viewscreen was coming to them across multiple shifts in spatial dimension. It seemed no less immediate for all that.

Somewhere deep in that sphere was a small station, protected by n-space shielding, but far closer to the soon-to-be-released forces of the supernova. Somewhere deep in that sphere was Rus'lem and his friend Max and, Tamika feared, the Tandesko assassin. She'd been not at all reassured by Willard's one communication. Why had he not made contact again?

She'd wanted to ask; but Thalia was preoccupied as time-zero approached, even with active control out of her hands. They were attempting to map the gateway from here, in case Ruskin failed at Room Zeta, or didn't survive to bring the information back.

Thalia seemed icily calm about the possibility that Zeta station might simply disappear in a haze of plasma. Perhaps she couldn't bear to contemplate it. Did Thalia still love Willard? Tamika wondered. Did they both stand to lose someone precious when this thing blew?

In fact, the woman seemed altogether, remarkably, cool. She and her people had somehow brought order to the control center after the chaos of the Tandesko attack. The dead and wounded had been carried out, the damaged consoles bypassed as much as possible, and shattered morale cobbled back together. Most everyone here seemed to be operating in a condition of controlled shock; but Thalia controlled, or hid, hers better than most. When Tamika heard her talking to another console about cutoff criteria for Zeta, she could hardly stand to hear the words. Behind the jargon, they were talking about severing the connection to the remote station, and virtually guaranteeing the death of anyone still there; and through it all, Thalia's voice remained hard and punctuated.

And what use am I here? Tamika thought. She'd volunteered to go to the infirmary to help tend the injured; but Thalia had insisted that she stay, insisted that her knowledge of Ruskin might be needed if things got confusing. Well, things were confusing, all right; but there didn't seem much she could do to help.

For the last twenty minutes, Thalia had been trying to raise the station—Willard, Max, anyone—without success. The stationwide search for the assassin had also failed. They all now harbored the same suspicion of where the Tandesko might be. And control had been locked into Zeta.

"Neutrino fluctuation at zero-six-niner," someone announced, causing a general stir. "Fusion has stopped. The squeeze is on."

Tamika was just responding internally to that news—that the core of the star was dead—when someone else screamed, "We've got it, people! We have collapse! We have collapse!"

On Thalia's face there was scant reaction, perhaps a barely perceptible tightening of the jaw muscles.

"Here we go—" another voice said.

None of these changes was visible on the face of the star that showed on the screen; but shock wave measurement and neutrino flux were shooting off the scale.

And hidden in the heart of the star, at the center of the implosion, a black hole was forming.

In a few hours, when the shock-wave reached the surface, this orange sphere would blaze into a beacon that would light the galaxy.

"Rus'lem," Tamika whispered to herself as tears began streaming down her cheeks.

* * *

How to feel
　　to know
　　　　to understand

It was happening in such an eyeblink of time, and it was
not natural. Surely not natural. Was it Bright's own, or
something of another realm:

Of consciousness
　　of will
　　　　of spirit
　　　　　　to be felt
　　　　　　　　not touched

*The music ends
　　the song dies*

Tightening from within, consuming, and no way to reach
to stop to grasp to understand

Time ends

Bright had seen death

　　　　　　　　　　I have seen death

Conflagration seeding cooling darkening fading of rhythm
and being. Bright had seen oldlife seed newlife of spirit hot
from flame. But in the new did anything of the old remain

*oldlife spirit ?
oldlife song ?*

When time ends all ends

Could newlife burn in the belly of its fires, could it blossom in the flame

> *Do you burn*
>> *do you grow*
>>> *do you sing   ?*

There was ponderous dizziness, losing everything, something changing within that hurt that stole power that made it want to twist itself inside out

> *Won't you please*
>> *speak*
>>> *sing*
>>>> *tell who*
>>>>> *are you*
>>>>>> *are you*
>>>>>>> *are you*

And in Ali'Maksam's brain, pain was the blank slate, the tabula rasa upon which all questions were written, all pleas filed, unfulfilled wishes cast upon the heavenly waters.

Cast your wishes to the stars. . . .

And they had done it. Whatever he had been wishing to prevent or protect was gone now, ashes: Willard betrayed, the star destroyed, the gateway created but out of control. How had it gone so wrong? He'd betrayed Willard to the Querayn in order to save him from the Tandeskoes. And the Querayn had betrayed them both: denying Willard his free will, despite their promise to Ali'Maksam. And what had they really wanted: not the gateway, but this contact with the star, even at the cost of its death? So much loss, so much innocence destroyed!

And now? The explosion had begun, but Ganz had ruined the mapping station, so that none of them might see its formation; and Willard, fighting for survival, had virtually disappeared into his own maze of conflicting selves and wishes, until even Ali'Maksam, who knew him best, could scarcely separate the false from the real.

And Ali'Maksam, no fighter, had camouflaged himself with his own virtuals and given his friend the one thing he could think of to say:

Turn to the sun, Willard, to the sun. . . .

Telling Willard to do the thing he himself wished to do. But Ali'Maksam's soul was too seared by the pain of the sun—too immense or too alien; he could not reach it with his own mind, he could only reverberate like a church bell in that outcry.

And echo with his own pain, the betrayal of a friend.

And wonder: Had it had to be so?

Willard, if you are still there, if you can hear . . . Willard, I sensed the danger you chose at that lodge, but you would not be dissuaded. And I knew no other way! I trusted the Querayn to assure you freedom to find yourself. I tried to protect you and I failed. But there was a greater need! Neither of us, none of us, wanted the monopoly of the gateway!

And somehow out of the maelstrom, Willard's thought came back: *You knew, then? You knew of the gateway?*

In your thoughts, Willard—I never meant to spy, but I'd seen it and I knew your despair. . . .

But Willard was gone now, lost from the contact; and Ali'Maksam continued spinning in his own thoughts, so lost in the internal rotation that he was scarcely aware of his virtual presences or of his own position, crouched in the corner of the control room watching the frozen tableau of Ruskin and Ganz. The others were paralyzed by the blaze in the viewscreen and the sudden queer twisting of the station itself. And though his eyes saw the jump in the neutrino readings, and deep in his mind he understood that from the neutrino flux would come an even stronger K-space field, he was nevertheless stunned when the fabric of space and of *consciousness* yawned open around him.

He felt a sense of utter foolishness, then joy; he should have seen it coming.

But how could anyone have anticipated this: a star's mind welling up into one's own?

On the sea of consciousness—on its surface float bewilderment and confusion, hints of deadly danger and rapturous peacefulness, and suggestions of what might lie below:

fortress floating in a sea of amber
and a voice from within
** You speak **
the light is you then
and you know me
** I am Bright **
and within you hide the mysteries of the fortress
** and you **
I am in the fortress
** yes **
I created the fortress
** why **
I am killing you
∎

Time the catalyst turning worlds inside out
∎

In the abyss of consciousness, forces vast and tiny moved
together, touching and pushing, testing and mingling—
—Logothian—
—Human—
—*hrisi*—
—and another, far vaster, reverberating
with power and bewilderment—
∎

Bright, carrying the knowledge of eons, searching the
heavens of all life for understanding of what might lie
beyond—
—beyond all existence.
∎

and astonished—
That you
my children
so small
could do this
to me
∎

((If only—))
((If only—))

((You knew—))
((You knew—))

* * *

((How very small we are—))
((We are—))

■

—And how very sorry—
—sorry—
—sorry—

■

But time was the destroyer, which no one could turn back.

CHAPTER 35

✷

Time was a vast bubble expanding in space, and Ruskin was on its surface, peering in . . .

∎

. . . and what he saw were other faces, one of them blindingly bright, peering into expanding bubbles of time, peering inward at *him*.

∎

Reflections in a hall of mirrors:

The gateway was forming even as his mind slipped through this distorted corridor of time. Matter at the heart of the star had been crushed out of existence, the singularity snatching at the hyperstring and holding it secure. The K-space field had multiplied in strength; and the entrance to the gateway was being sculpted out of twisted space-time by the forces he had put into motion a lifetime ago.

In the very shape of that opening were being determined the secrets that could guide future travelers through the treacherous waters of transit—or send them hurtling to destruction. And nothing he could do now could influence that shape or map its secrets.

Ganz, succumbing to madness, had destroyed the very instruments of control. But did that truly matter? Zeta station itself was being twisted into a realm of half existence, and its occupants with it; and with or without instruments, what could any man do now?

A parade of failed dreams:

The Querayn, he perceived, had wanted the project diverted to a study of the star consciousness itself. That was now impossible, though a moment had come and gone when he had nearly yielded. The Tandeskoes and Auricles had each wanted the gateway for themselves; and that, too, now seemed unlikely.

And what did *he* want? He knew now: that *no* one should own the gateway or its secrets. A star was dying for this gateway, and he would have no one rob it of the meaning of its death. He would have the gateway for all or for no one.

An extraordinary world was opening around him now as the space-time that held him twisted like a Möbius strip, as the control station in which he had stood and fought was wrenched out of its universe.

■

Ali'Maksam's soul had become entwined with his own, and he saw now how the Logothian suffered, knowing that he had sinned against his friend, doing what he thought had to be done—though it was a betrayal, knowing no other way; and a terrakell winked at him as it opened a small window into his own past, showing him how indeed he'd been unwilling to listen to reason, or to Max's intuitions, back when it might have mattered.

■

—Willard, I am sorry—
Max, I understand. I forgive.
Their two voices drifted apart and then together again, like spirit elementals. But in this reality of souls entwining, Ali'Maksam's was not the only one wrapped around and mingled with his. . . .

■

There was also a *hrisi* assassin:
It was a stricken Tandesko soul that touched his. The rigidity of *hrisi* training had been overcome by madness; hir had struck a blow in blind destructiveness, obliterating the mapping console that could have brought some order out of this chaos. A madness of death had overcome hir, in the place of the dignity that hir would have wished at the end.

Hir has failed in disgrace. There can be no excusing, no forgiving, ever. . . .
And Ruskin's soul eyed hir soul, willing itself to speak:
I . . . and found itself unable to complete the thought.

Could he forgive an assassin who had tried to kill him, who had savagely killed so many others?

Could he?

•

The station was contorting around him; and though he felt Dax still alive within him, it was clear that they would die together. *(I'll miss you, Dax.)*

((I would remain a part of you, Willard.))

•

But still Ali'Maksam's words were ringing in his ears, ringing as the sun exploded:

You must turn to the sun. . . .

•

And he turned and reached out into the sunset glow, and called to the sun to recognize him who had killed it, him who regretted but could not undo what was done. Him who cried out to his own victim:

—Bright—

—if it is you—

—if you can help—

—if you will be a part—

And the voice that called back was clearer now but it was like no voice, no soul he had ever known before.

•

There was great confusion in the light and shadow now. At Bright's heart was a thing dark and dreadful, a thing that grabbed, that swallowed brightness itself. Was this the thing that had called, that had spoken: *Killing you, I am killing you*

Bright wasn't sure; Bright was dizzy; but Bright called back:

Are you the one   ?
are you the newlife   ?
in the belly of my flame   ?

And the darkness made no answer, but another called out, sang in desperation and sorrow: *Help me help me if you are a part*

And Bright knew then that if the darkness was death to

oldlife, still a newlife was growing, springing fresh out of the convulsions and ashes:

> *I would*
> > *be a part*
> > *yes*
> > > *to cherish the newlife*
>
> *Yes*

And so mingled the souls in the belly of Bright's flame; and Bright began to see the newlife emerging there, began to understand. All of the souls were being drawn into one, a great whirlpool of life and consciousness.

And Bright, more than any other, had the power to shape and form the newlife

as everything changed

∎

<<< *You see it now* >>>

<<< *And feel it* >>>

<<< *Growing* >>>

<<< *Bright* >>>

<<< *You* >>>

<<< *We* >>>

<<< *I* >>>

∎

Tamika
I love you
Good-bye

∎

There was a gathering of light and fire, and the fury of wind and sea: a tornado, a typhoon, a whirlpool into the abyss of infinity, where space became unspace.

And Bright, recognizing newlife forming out of the old, yielded up what it could no longer hold to itself. And Bright became one with its killers.

And Bright shaped the vortex and together they slipped into its streams forever. . . .

The neutrino flux peaked seven-tenths of a second ahead of the model-predictions. Alarm flashed across Thalia's face at the news.

Tamika wasn't sure why this should worry anyone, and she hardly cared; all she wanted to know was whether anyone on that deep-star station was going to emerge alive.

Rus'lem!

In her heart was a bottomless emptiness, a conviction that she already knew the answer. Hot tears welled; somehow she kept them at bay.

On the consoles, data poured in:

"String capture confirmed; load-doubling at mark minus oh-point-eight-seven."

"Field strength just passed critical-two. We should be feeling the effects soon."

"Thalia, we're slipping farther ahead of mark. Is Ruskin controlling this thing or not?"

The director's answer was a whisper: "I don't know."

Someone else's voice: *"We've gone twenty-gee off the plot. We could be losing it. If we're going to save this thing, we'd better do it now!"*

"There's nothing we can d—"

Thalia's words were cut off by a thunderclap. The floor jumped, jumped again—and Thalia crashed into Tamika as they both went down. The quake reverberated through the floor for what seemed an eternity—Tamika struggling to get out from under Thalia, clutching in terror at the ungrippable base of a console, the metal floor vibrating, hammering at her body. Suddenly, as abruptly as it had struck, the quake died away.

Thalia struggled to her feet, cursing. "Everyone okay?" she shouted. She extended a hand, helped Tamika to her feet. Even before many of the others had gotten back into their seats, she called, "Give me a reading on Zeta—" and froze. Her face went rigid. A light was flashing red on her console.

Tamika felt Thalia's alarm, felt terror welling up in her own heart. "What is it?" she whispered.

The astrophysicist's voice was inhumanly flat, the voice of a nonliving thing: "Zeta is gone."

"*Gone?*"

The deadness did not leave Thalia's voice. "That was the primary shock wave. We had no way of knowing how it would propagate across n-space. Now we have . . . now we know. The stress was—" Her voice died. She drew a breath and spoke to the console. "Did we cut cleanly from Zeta?"

For several seconds, Tamika heard only the thunder of blood in her ears, but finally Thalia's voice filtered through saying, ". . . structural damage?" and she saw Thalia nodding bleakly.

The grief bubbled up so fast Tamika was hardly even aware that she was crying, though the tears streamed hot and wet.

At the front of the room, half the viewscreen had gone blank, remote links lost. On the right-hand side, a deep image of the inner sun remained. Through the blur in her eyes, she saw it blossom, like a time-lapse image of a flower opening, into dazzling full brilliance, consuming itself in fire as the shock wave propagated outward.

Someone cheered weakly, and Tamika wanted to kill him.

And inside her, a voice was saying, over and over:

((*Don't lose hope, Tamika. Don't ever lose hope. . . .*))

And she wanted to kill Dax, as well.

There was a general commotion toward the front of the control room, which at first she ignored, because a sudden wooziness was coming over her, and she felt that there was a choir of voices in her head. Voices strange and familiar. And through them she heard shouts, but she couldn't understand what anyone was saying.

*((The mapping console has gone blank. The
telemetry links are out. Willard thought the
only way to map it was from the inside, and
maybe he was right. Maybe there was no way
to map it.))*

Then everything they'd come here for was lost.

*((Something strange happening, Tamika. I
feel funny, like when we went through K-
space.))*

And that was what the strange voices were: Thalia's
thoughts were in her head, a faint babble of pain. So were
many others. But it was more than that: there were louder
voices, and they were growing in volume like a symphony
in crescendo, but it was a symphony of light more than of
sound; and perhaps she was dreaming, *surely she was
dreaming*, but she thought she heard Ali'Maksam's voice,
and Willard's, and something else altogether strange and
wondrous. . . .

■

Worlds turning inside out
*Light stretching like taffy, fire streaming and pouring in
a cosmic fountain. And in the heart of blazing brightness,
a point of darkness infinitely deep; and in the center of that
darkness there was singing, there was life*

■

and voices
*Ali'Maksam spoke of living suns, of sentience so old and
vast that for them to touch a star's mind was a wonder out
of Heaven; and he spoke of sadness and of hope*

■

overlaid with voices
*Dax, filled with astonishment and wonder at the layers
within layers, that Willard had become an agent of
change to the star, as Dax and the others had been to
Willard*

■

rippling with fear and hope
*Forgiveness asked and given; and the bitterness of failure
turning, changing to something new*

■

and reverberating
Willard speaking of self-knowledge, and of living and dying, his voice echoing like timpani

■

**Tamika
I love you
Good-bye**

■

And exploding all around them was a brightness beyond comprehension, a life with thought and memory beyond imagining, not dying now but changing, and drawing them in with it. . . .

It was a long time before the voices and the images faded; and then someone yelled something about the formative K-space field being gone now; and someone else shouted in a voice so choked with emotion it was impossible to say whether it was despair or joy, that it looked as though a stable formation had occurred, a gateway had been created; and a lot of people were weeping, and one crazy loon was singing.

And tears were streaming down Tamika's face, but something within her had turned inside out, and she was no longer grieving; but her arms were comforting someone else who was shaking with grief, and somehow she wasn't surprised to discover that it was Thalia.

CHAPTER 36

✳

Tamika drained the liqueur in one long, slow swallow. It tasted of blueberry and sparkled of rubies. She felt it rushing to her head and was deeply grateful for the sensation.

Thalia watched her with an intent expression that Tamika had come to interpret as amusement. "Would you like another?" Thalia asked, lifting the crystal decanter to refill her own glass.

Tamika shook her head and smiled faintly. "I still need to be able to think."

The astrophysicist nodded as she walked across her office. Her midnight-blue jumpsuit whispered as she moved. Tamika wondered if the woman's choice of color was an expression of her emotions. Thalia stopped, staring at the viewscreen wall. Three days had altered the scene completely. The star that had been Betelgeuse was now a galactic light-stage. The massive shell of hot gases and newly created elements that had been blasted off in the explosion still glowed fiercely as it expanded into space. From the station and its just-launched fleet of replacement monitor sats, the shell was now on the outside, a dozen astronomical units out, a curtain of blazing light that obscured the rest of the universe. To one side, an ill-defined blob of brightness marked what was left of the companion, Honey, after it had been destroyed in a secondary supernova and blown clear of the primary. Lost Love, in its more distant orbit, had not yet been touched. It was truly alone now, the only star remaining of the original three.

Without n-thread communications, Tamika knew, even the closest interstellar neighbors would not see this explosion for years to come. But in fact, of course, the Habitat of Humanity would know soon what had happened here, if reports hadn't gone out already; the neighbors would have plenty of warning before the spectacle appeared in their skies.

Toying with her empty glass, she came and stood beside Thalia. Her eyes were drawn from the beautifully glowing curtain to the vortex of darkness at its center: the black hole, surrounded by a glowing mass of more slowly expanding stellar debris. It was a highly processed image, she knew; the naked eye would see nothing but blinding light in that direction. Down in that vortex, somewhere, was the entry point to the galactic gateway that had been born three days ago. The black hole was not itself the entry point, but its intense gravitational field was one of the forces that shaped the entrance and held it open.

Neither the opening nor the rest of the gateway was visible. No one had expected them to be, without special instrumentation. The trouble was, even the best instrumentation this station had to offer could not discern their shape. The mapping of the gateway had been a failure.

"Have you thought any more about staying to help us?" Thalia asked, without turning.

Tamika exhaled, closing her eyes. She willed herself to see the gateway with her inner vision, willed Dax to somehow make it clear to her. And yet, even if that were possible, would she really want it? She had believed, ever since hearing of it, that the Auricle Alliance should not be permitted monopolistic use of the gateway. If they succeeded in mapping it clearly enough to use, would the Alliance permit that knowledge, or the gateway itself, to be shared?

News of this event was certain to be political wildfire among the worlds of the Habitat. She wasn't sure she wanted to be involved in the upheaval that would follow. The political explosion could be as great as the supernova.

"You know what my stand is on the gateway," she said finally.

Thalia was staring at her, an amused glint in her huge dark eyes. "I'm not asking you to give that up."

"No? Then what? You want to get into the gateway, don't you?"

"Well—" Thalia's gesture was awkward, but it conveyed a surprising passion. "We don't want this whole effort to be wasted. And I for one don't want Willard's death to be in vain."

Willard's death. Tamika's thoughts drifted abruptly: it was still hard to believe that Rus'lem was gone. Somehow she kept expecting a communique: *They've been found, Room Zeta has been found!* And yet she knew that it was impossible; she'd *felt* Willard's spirit, and Max's, passing out of this world; out of this life. But had they passed into death, whatever that was—or into something else altogether? Her mind and her heart churned with uncertainty.

"Maybe death is the wrong word," Thalia continued. "Since we all felt it—are you listening to me?"

Tamika started. "Sorry. Yes."

"We *all* felt it."

"But we don't know," Tamika said. "We don't know what happened to them." And why am *I* the one denying it? Am I so afraid of hoping—and being wrong?

"We don't know," Thalia agreed. "There's no hard scientific evidence for it. But if you had to make a bet, wouldn't you say that Willard's consciousness survived *in some form* through the formation of the gateway?"

We felt him passing, Tamika thought. But surviving? How can we know? Still, it hadn't *felt* as though he were dying. And there was that other thing, that other consciousness.

((There are many things we can never know,
until we see them, or try them.))

(Shut up, Dax. You tell me: Was that a star's consciousness we felt along with Willard's? A real consciousness?)

((Wouldn't we all like to know?))

"I'm not trying to convince you that he's alive now," Thalia was saying. "I hardly dare hope that myself. But we had contact at the end—and you were closer to him than anyone else who survived him." Her voice caught a little on that last statement. "So at the very least, if we could recover anything he might have communicated to you—"

Tamika sighed. "You want me to relive that!"

"We could use hypnotic regression—"

She snorted, and knew that the impulse had come from Dax. "There's someone inside me who can do a lot more than hypnotic regression."

Thalia nodded in understanding. Of course; Dax was in her, as well. "Certainly."

"But you said you wouldn't ask me to compromise."

Thalia nodded again, but with a grimace. "I can't promise on behalf of the Alliance—obviously. And you wouldn't believe me if I did. But there are foreign-world observers here, who certainly suspect that we did more than just watch the star explode. The Querayn, in particular, have been buzzing. I could ensure that they shared in any knowledge we gained here. And once that was out, it would be hard to enforce a monopoly, even if the Auricle Councils were inclined to try."

Tamika gazed at her. "At what cost to your career?"

Thalia shrugged, hiding a faintly sour expression.

For a moment, neither of them spoke. Then Tamika said gently, "May I ask you something?"

Thalia's eyebrows went up a fraction of an inch. The gaze of her dark eyes was challenging, but not without warmth. Tamika was beginning to understand why Willard had been attracted to this woman. In the last three days, she had come to trust Thalia in a way she wouldn't have dreamed possible four days ago. Nevertheless, Thalia had invested years of work in pursuing this project for the Auricle Alliance. Why would she suddenly drop that commitment? "Why are you willing to accommodate my views?" Tamika asked finally. "You have a lot invested in secrecy here. You could do it without me."

Sighing, Thalia turned back to the viewscreen. "To give meaning to Willard's death."

"Yes, but—"

"No, it's more than that. For one thing: obviously, right now we have little to show for what we've done. Oh, we could send exploratory ships in—and we will—and eventually one will survive the trip and return. Eventually, when enough people have died, we'll learn to use this monster." She gestured at the image. "If it can be used. But I don't think Willard would have wanted a lot of people to die in his footsteps—and I *know* he didn't want it to be used just by the Alliance, and . . ." She paused, struggling.

Tamika waited.

"Well, maybe I understood a little of how he felt, at the end," Thalia concluded, her voice dropping to a hoarse whisper. She glanced at Tamika with sharp eyes and turned away.

Tamika felt a twinge of sympathy. However strange it felt to her, there was a bond between the two of them now. She knew it would not quickly disappear. "I think he would want us to use the gateway," she agreed. "If the 'us' included the entire Habitat. All of the worlds."

Thalia shrugged her big shoulders. "Yes."

"But—" and Tamika's words became halting. "I don't know what I could do. It doesn't seem to me that any of the impressions I got—of their passing, I mean—would help much." *(Dax?)* And as she looked inward, she received no sense from Dax that there was anything hidden that she had forgotten, no subliminal cues from Rus'lem about how the gateway had turned out. She doubted that he had even known it himself in those moments of unworldly contact.

Thalia turned back to her. "I understand. And that's why I want to take a gamble. And I want you to think about joining me." She strode across the room to fill her liqueur glass again. Raising her eyebrows in query, she lifted the decanter in Tamika's direction. After a second's hesitation, Tamika joined her for a refill. She allowed a sip of the bracing liquid to glide down her throat. She looked at Thalia warily.

"Now, this is based on your perceptions, as well as my own," Thalia said. "There's no way I could convince a science panel of this without your support—and I *still* might not be able to convince them."

Tamika sensed what was coming, and she wasn't sure she liked it.

"Let us suppose that Willard's awareness survived in some form. Since the K-space field joined us to his consciousness at the end, it seems reasonable to wonder if another K-space field might renew that contact."

Tamika nodded silently.

Thalia took a breath. "And entry to the gateway would of course be through a K-space field."

Tamika closed her eyes. "Of course." She was beginning

to feel a buzzing between her eyes. She wanted to think that it was the liqueur, but she knew it wasn't. *Don't give me hope that will fail. Please.*

"Tamika?"

She kept her eyes closed; they were beginning to leak tears. She didn't want to answer.

"Tamika—" Thalia repeated, and there was a pain in her voice that forced Tamika to finally blink the tears away. "You know, his *loss*—I won't say *death*—was a blow to me, too. You're not alone in mourning him."

Tamika gazed at her, barely seeing the woman standing in front of her, seeing only an image of a black hole and its glaring cloak that hid not only its own secrets but also the secrets of the invisible gateway—and wondering if Willard *might somehow have survived.* Did she dare to hope? In what form could he have survived? In what form could a star be alive? And what difference could it make to her? Willard was lost to her, to her universe.

((You don't know until you know.))

"I'm sorry," she whispered at last, thinking of Thalia's grief.

Thalia seemed not to hear her. She continued, "It's also possible, I suppose, that the whole station survived; that they're drifting somewhere in an n-space field, somehow beyond the range of all of our monitors."

Tamika shook her head violently. She didn't want to find Willard dead in some torn-up station; if someone else wanted to go looking for him there, that was fine. But she *knew* that the station hadn't survived the cataclysm; she'd felt that with a certainty she couldn't explain.

Thalia nodded. "I don't think so, either. But there is the gateway. And there is his friend, Ali'Maksam. And the sun. If we were right about the sun."

Within Tamika's mind, a recollection crystallized of the stellar consciousness she had sensed—and somewhere in there, Max's as well. She had never really come to terms with Max. Was it possible she still could do so? Or was this all madness?

"One of the Querayn observers came to me yesterday," Thalia said, "telling me that they'd sensed the soul of the sun when it died. I didn't tell them what we'd done, though was sorely tempted. But there was a look in this one's eyes; I think perhaps he knew." She squinted through her glass, squinted at Tamika. "It won't be as soon as I'd like. There will be a lot to do first. And it *could* all be wrong. A completely false hope. Maybe he can't let us know how to do it. We could die in an instant. But I intend to try. And I'd like you to go with me."

"Go?" Tamika whispered, her eyes blurring.

"Through, Tamika," Thalia said. *"Through . . ."*

And the world suddenly seemed a very windy place; there was a rushing in Tamika's ears, and she heard Dax's voice talking to her, confusingly; and it all seemed to be spinning, out of control. She felt as though she were already passing through the gateway, and she imagined that she heard Rus'lem's voice calling out to her, caressing her mind. And almost as though against her will, she felt herself nodding.

CHAPTER 37

✳

. . . love you
Good-bye
■

and all things parted
and all parts were as one
and the song ended
■

```
* * * * * * * * * * * * * * * * * * * * * * * * * * *
* . . . . . . . . . . . . . . . . . . . . . . . . . . . . *
* . . . Willard . . . . . . . . . . . . . . . . . . . . . *
* . . . . . . . . . . . . . . . . . . . Ali'Maksam . . *
* . . . . . . . . . . . . . . . . . . . . . . . . . . . . *
* . . . . . . . . . . . . . . . . * BRIGHT * . . . . . . . *
* . . Dax . . . . . . . . . . . . . . . . . . . . . . . . *
* . . . . . . . . . . . . . . . . . . . . . . . . . . . . *
* . . . . . Ganz . . . . . . . . . . . . . . . . terrakells . . . *
* . . . . . . . . . . . . . . . . . . . . . . . . . . . . *
* . . . . . . . . . . . . . . . Jeaves . . . . . . . . . . *
* . . . . . . . . . . . . . . . . . . . . . . . . . . . . *
* * * * * * * * * * * * * * * * * * * * * * * * * * *
```

■

There was no place now; no song; there was only being,
and at its center was the power and spirit of a star, which
had died; but even in dying it had visualized and shaped
the newlife that it was becoming.

■

Bright/Ruskin/Dax/Max/Ganz rode the vortex into the
darkness, spirits commingled, bound inextricably with the
forces that had destroyed them. The vortex took it/them
through the place where light itself died, where space-time
ended and all things began anew. And though the vortex
was held by the darkness, it was not, could not be ruled
by it.

■

Memories did not rule either, but remained: sparkling
motes drifting on the ether

> *Can you sing   ?*
> *meant no harm*
> *no forgiveness*
> *no one should own*
> *Max I forgive*
> *Fargleam call*
> *Tamika I miss*
> *are you new   ?*
> *would be a part*

with little left of meaning; but change continued, and
structure and form; and the being that was, slowly passed
and became something different, something that rang of
death and life

■

And yet
through the dust and the ether
came the thought
I want to be
I must

■

Awareness blew in like a rain from eternity, emerged
from the darkness like a rainbow. And it was a single awareness, transfigured and made luminous.

It knew only that it was, a candle of life reborn.

There was darkness, there was light: there was neither.
Meanings were sifted, words lost, tongues forgotten.
Thoughts began to come dimly to recollection, but they
were confused. And *feelings* . . .

Time was an invisible blade that divided wind from rain,

light from dark, knowledge from feeling. Time was a blade that healed.

Newlife lived where there had been no life at all, where primordial forces flowed, where until now God alone had peered and breathed. The Newlife peered and it breathed and it waited. Within it there were names dimly remembered: Ruskin . . . Ali'Maksam . . . Ganz . . . Bright. And names within names, life within life: memory-of-Dax/-of-Tamika/-of-Ruskin/-of-*hrisi*kan/-of-Storm/-of-Fargleam . . . beyond number. It was an extraordinary union: killers and victims, foes become One, old become New. It was angels of fire dancing among snowflakes; it was mountains and dust-motes sharing life and breath. Was it created in the image of the Creator? It wasn't sure; it knew only that it *was*.

That it *thought*.

That it *felt*.

•

One thing that it wasn't was lastlife.

Almost before it had taken form, it became aware of otherlife streaming into its realm, life hooting and listening and asking and sharing, and sometimes just passing through. Some of that otherlife was alien and curious; some of it became unlife. Some of it was familiar, for a little while, and welcome and startling in its familiarity

Tamika
Thalia
Sunlife

of memories, and hopes. Memories joined

Will you become a part
Yes I will become a part

and interwove
and joined
and gladdened

And otherlife passed through in numbers until their passage became a whisper, scarcely noticed
where there were stranger things to be noticed.

•

The winds and currents of space were not eternal, though they seemed so. The beginning and the end points, where

reality itself was punctured, wheeled slowly through space
and through time, bridging worlds and otherlife, bridging
knowledge and feeling. Upon the winds came seeds of wisdom; and in time the New began to know itself

    its smallness

      its knowledge

        a dusting of pollen

          on the winds of time.

About the Author

JEFFREY A. CARVER is the author of eight science fiction novels, including the recently published *Rapture Effect*, the first volume in a collaborative series with Roger Zelazny entitled *Roger Zelazny's Alien Speedway: Clypsis*, and the epic novel *The Infinity Link*.

Originally a native of Huron, Ohio, Carver has lived in New England since graduating from Brown University in 1971 with a degree in English. In 1974 he earned a Master of Marine Affairs degree from the University of Rhode Island. He has been a collegiate wrestler, a scuba diving instructor, a quahog diver, a UPS sorter, and a word-processing consultant, among other things. His interests include science, religion, nature and animals, underwater exploration, and flying.

He is married to television producer Allysen Palmer and now lives in Arlington, Massachusetts, where he is a full-time SF writer. He is currently working on his next novel, *Down the Stream of Stars*.